1970

ach . be kept

BY FRANK G. SLAUGHTER

Surgeon, U.S.A.
Constantine
The Purple Quest
A Savage Place
Upon This Rock
Devil's Harvest
Tomorrow's Miracle
David: Warrior and King
The Curse of Jezebel
Epidemic!
Pilgrims in Paradise
The Land and the Promise
Lorena
The Crown and the Cross
The Thorn of Arimathea
Daybreak
The Mapmaker
Sword and Scalpel
The Warrior
The Scarlet Cord
Flight from Natchez

The Healer
Apalachee Gold
The Song of Ruth
Storm Haven
The Galileans
East Side General
Fort Everglades
The Road to Bithynia
The Stubborn Heart
Immortal Magyar
Divine Mistress
Sangaree
Medicine for Moderns
The Golden Isle
The New Science of Surgery
In a Dark Garden
A Touch of Glory
Battle Surgeon
Air Surgeon
Spender Brade, M.D.
That None Should Die

UNDER PENNAME C. V. TERRY

Buccaneer Surgeon
The Deadly Lady of
   Madagascar

Darien Venture
The Golden Ones

Surgeon, U.S.A.

Surgeon, U.S.A.

FRANK G. SLAUGHTER

Doubleday & Company, Inc.
GARDEN CITY, NEW YORK
1966

All of the characters in this book are fictitious, and any resemblance to actual persons, living or dead, is purely coincidental.

CONTENTS

___

Surgeon, U.S.A.

Camp Bruckner

———————

Air-raid sirens were warbling the end of a practice alert when
Bruce came through the train gate at Union Station. An instant before, the vast concourse had seemed remote as a
cavern in mythology, crowded with figures frozen in time.
Now, as the lights rose, people blinked like sleepwalkers and
began to move again.

Two soldiers bound for another gate saluted briskly. Still
unsure of his own part in such ritual—last night he had fallen
asleep over the manual—he considered shifting his Val-Pak
to return the salute, then settled for a nod. The station plaza
was now in clear view through the vaulted arches of the concourse. After a dozen strides in that direction, he turned
abruptly to check his carryall. Tonight, even the summer heat
of Washington seemed preferable, for a little while, to the
enigma of Camp Bruckner.

Outside, buses were loading and unloading at the platforms
reserved for the military. Transport to his own camp was
waiting among those olive-drab argosies: once he stepped
aboard, the act would mark the real beginning of his Army
career. The thought was enough to make him veer a second
time—until he had crossed the streetcar tracks beyond, and
a bar had closed around his troubled spirits.

His first sip of bourbon, he found, made him no more

willing to picture the new life awaiting him. The girl who had just taken the next stool but one, and ordered a gin rickey in a tone suggesting this was not her first visit, was another excuse to pause on the edge of that new life before he ventured deeper.

The bar mirror told him she was not much younger than he. Her slender figure had its points—but her best friend would not have called her thin, intense face pretty. She was hatless, and her chestnut-red hair was clipped in a short bob more practical than becoming; there were inkstains on the fingers that closed round her glass, and her linen suit-dress was rumpled. Leaning forward to hold a lighter to her cigarette, he decided he would never have noticed her in a crowd. Then she looked up—and, meeting her gray-green eyes, he changed his mind.

"When you finish that drink, may I buy you another?"

The girl continued to appraise him, with the same deliberate candor. The inventory was thorough enough to make him wonder if he had misplaced some item of his new estate.

"It depends on what prompted the offer."

"Let's say the need to hear my own voice after a journey."

The girl smiled and he saw that her mouth was generous, her eyes warm.

"Did you come *that* far?"

"I've just left a train from Florida."

"When a soldier surrenders, he gives name, rank and serial number."

"Bruce Graham. Major MC ASN 0-270106. Surgeon, U. S. Army."

"No middle initial. Your ancestry must be as Scotch as your name."

"Not for the last few centuries. I was born and raised in Tampa."

"Are you as new a major as you look?"

"Does it show that plainly?"

"A dollar says you just gave those oak leaves a final polish in your Pullman washroom."

"The oak leaves—*and* the caducei. I put on this uniform two days ago. Any more questions?"

"You can tell me your war aims, Major Graham."

The abruptness of the demand startled him. "Why should my war aims interest you?"

"Will you believe me, if I say I'm collecting quotations for my memory book?"

"In the South, a gentleman always believes a lady. Where shall I begin?"

"Let's see if I can make the beginning easier," said the girl. "In the concourse just now, you started for the plaza, changed your mind, and checked your bag. Outside, after a detour to avoid the bus platforms, you turned in here. Sherlock Holmes would deduce you're on your way to your first station assignment—and decided to break the journey."

"Sherlock Holmes would also deduce that you'd followed me."

"Keep that Scotch dander down. Of course I followed you."

"It's my turn to ask a question. Why?"

"I've given my excuse. So you'd supply a quote for my memory book—on the reason and the cure of war. Not that I can't guess the answer. It glows from within. Like a lamp in a window."

"Are you sure the glow is genuine?"

"I'd call it dedication to something outside yourself," said the girl. "Obviously, you cut short a career to join the Medical Corps. Was it a Tampa practice?"

"Until last month, I taught at the Lakewood Medical School in Baltimore. Between classes, I worked with Dr. Schoenfeld on research in heart surgery."

"I'd say you were a pretty hot property, if Abram Schoenfeld needed you. Weren't you listed as essential by the Procurement and Assignment Service?"

"I was for a while. Early in July, I finished a special series in the lab. The school year had just ended—so I decided to put on this uniform."

"Because the Scots are hardy as well as stubborn?"

"Let's say it seemed a good idea at the time."

"Does it still seem a good idea?"

"Are you implying I have doubts—and came here to fortify myself?"

"If you did, it's an extremely human reaction."

"Since you seem gifted with extrasensory perception, tell me what lies ahead."

"Where will you be stationed?"

"Camp Bruckner."

"That's less than an hour from here."

"Until yesterday, I'd never heard of the place."

"Bruckner's part of the Baltimore POE."

"At least I know that means port of embarkation. Is it on the Chesapeake or the Potomac?"

"I believe there's a distant view of the river," said the girl. "Staging areas like Bruckner are the last roundup—before combat units take to the water. Shipping is handled in Baltimore."

"Making Camp Bruckner a port on dry land?"

"You could call it that. When you've been in the Army awhile, you'll find its labels can be obscure."

"If my camp's part of a POE, I could be going overseas." Bruce had not been disturbed by the lecture in military semantics. He had long since decided that this chestnut-haired girl possessed resources not apparent to the eye.

"I can't believe the Army would make a Lakewood surgeon wait out the invasion in England. My guess is you're down for station complement. Or you may find yourself training with a mobile unit to work behind the lines." Again, the girl's face lighted with the crooked smile that almost added beauty to her features. "Am I giving you battle fatigue with my predictions?"

"Keep right on, please. I'll soon have the courage to board that bus."

"I could be wrong, of course. Even the best wars take awhile to get in gear—and cogs have been known to slip. Doctors are going into the services these days by the thousands. Not all of them are getting the jobs they do best."

"I've been warned of that."

"Whatever happens, don't let it spoil that inner glow I just mentioned."

"Suppose I agree to keep the lamp burning. Will you check me out later—to see how I'm fixed for fuel?"

"Can that be arranged?"

"If I'm stationed in this area, I'm practically on your doorstep. Come to think of it, I'm there right now. May I see you home?"

"A car is meeting me here in three minutes."

"If it's a date, you can break it."

"This date's unbreakable. I'd still like to know what I've missed."

"Shall I be frank? Or claim a nobility you know damned well I don't possess?"

The girl lifted her glass in a silent toast. "You must be a good doctor—you're honest enough to inspire confidence. For that compliment, I demand an answer to my original question. What *are* your war aims?"

"Are you always this curious, when you talk to strange men in bars?"

"Always. In your case, my curiosity goes deeper. In fact, it's possible you're the example I've been seeking to prove a point."

"Nothing peculiar, I trust."

"It's anything but that, Major. I'd say you were the American Everyman—still a little strange in a new uniform. The soldier at thirty, fancy-free and unmarried—"

"Who told you I was unmarried?"

"You did—with that prompt attack on my virtue. You

would never have asked to see me home tonight, if you'd left a wife in Tampa."

"You can hardly blame me for trying."

"I don't. It gives you an extra dimension that was lacking when this conversation began—but I'll need more. Did you volunteer to escape a teaching treadmill? Are you secretly in love with war? Do you expect to see your name on the roll of honor?"

"I volunteered because I thought it was my duty. Sorry if that's a dull motive."

"Do you believe our present crusade is a war to end wars? Regardless of the mistakes we made last time?"

"It's hardly worth fighting otherwise."

"You'd be surprised how many men will enjoy this war for its own sake. Some of them will remember it as the high moment of their lives. Are you a different breed?"

"As a doctor, it's my job to save life. To me, war's the supreme evil. I hope with all my heart that this country will never have another. Is *that* dedicated enough to suit you?" Bruce turned to the door, as a horn beeped outside. The panes of the bar were frosted at eye level, but he could make out the silhouette of a car at the curb.

"That will suit me nicely, Major." The girl had already noticed the sound. "As you see, I wasn't bluffing."

"I haven't bought the drink I promised."

"If you don't mind, we'll have our next drink later."

"You can still ignore your date."

"Not after I tell you who I am."

"Does this mean we'll really meet again?"

"If you'll permit me to use what you've just said. You can be sure I won't misquote you. I possess total recall."

He stared without speaking at the card the girl had just placed on the bar. As a Lakewood intern, he had seen reporters' credentials. The police-card identified its owner as Shane McLendon of the International News Service. It was a by-line he had read in a hundred dailies.

"Well, Major?"

"You *can't* be Shane McLendon. You aren't old enough."

"I'll be twenty-nine next month, and I've been a reporter for eight years. The car outside is a courier for my wire service. It's taking me to a typewriter, so I can file tomorrow's column."

"There's a photo with that column. I'd never have recognized you."

"Look closer next time," said Shane McLendon. "You'll see the resemblance. I don't do my profile justice after a day of copy-chasing."

"Like this one?"

"I've been collecting vignettes of servicemen in Union Station since eight tonight. You were the last. Good, I might add, for two whole paragraphs."

"I can hardly believe I deserve that much space."

"You're newsworthy, Major Graham. Take my word for it."

"Even though I'm only an average American, with average delusions?"

"Haven't you heard that nothing's more unusual than the average man? Especially when he's honest in the bargain?"

She left him swiftly, as the car beeped again.

When he returned to Union Station, Bruce found that ten minutes remained before the departure of the next bus to Camp Bruckner. It was an excuse to linger on the platform for a last breath of the humid evening while he reviewed the encounter in the bar. Shane McLendon, he told himself, had been a vital antidote to the mood he had brought from his Pullman. Despite the casual way she had used him, he could even hope that her promise of another meeting had been more than a sop to his pride.

Though the hour was late, Washington still seemed wide-awake and full of restless murmurs. The sound was distant but compelling. It suggested the monologue of a neurotic determined to drown all other voices, the dialogue of a cock-tail-party sage whose voice is a perpetual shout to impress others.

The concept, of course, was a fanciful one—but he could not dismiss it from his mind. . . . Baltimore's voice had been far different. On a night like this, when he could steal an hour from Lakewood, he had heard it just as clearly. Breathing the damp air from the Chesapeake, and noting the home ports of the rusty tramp steamers at the docks, had been one of his solo relaxations during those apprentice years in the hospital.

At times, before those rambles ended, he had wondered if he was spending his youth to no purpose, if he had let adventures in far places elude him. By daylight, of course, he had ignored such disturbing thoughts. As an intern, a surgical resident—and, later, the disciple of a great specialist—he had found a reason for being denied most mortals. He had realized, all too clearly, that his midnight reveries were part of a siren song Dr. Bruce Graham had built-in ways of ignoring. When Abram Schoenfeld had made his research appointment official, when he had seen that the study of the heart and its delicate valves could be a life in itself, he had locked his thoughts of Tahiti in a back room of his brain and thrown away the key.

By daylight, he had continued to thank God for the skills at his fingertips, for the magic touch that enabled him to repeat an intricate anastomosis that might someday correct the oxygen-lack associated with the cardiac abnormalities of childhood—or to dissect out a cervical sympathetic ganglion ten seconds ahead of the Lakewood record. Eventually, he knew, the onset of true maturity would bring true peace of mind. Wisdom, in the words of the Confucian sage, was the only path to nirvana, to that selfless realm men like Schoenfeld seemed to enter at will.

His rise in his profession had been real enough: there had been no need to look elsewhere, after Schoenfeld had proclaimed him vital to his research. It was true that the combined careers of teaching and experimental surgery had left little time for enduring friendships. At thirty, love in the storybook sense had continued to elude him—but he could never complain of loneliness. During those busy years in Baltimore, there had been poker and sailing companions in plenty. And there had been a gratifying choice of romances among the nurses—who, as he had discovered while still an intern, could make their own fine distinction between death and life.

Why, when existence at Lakewood had been so well-ordered, had he volunteered the day after Pearl Harbor Sunday? Had Shane McLendon exposed his true motives, when she had asked if war was a game to him, as it had been to so many others? Was this uniform another substitute for a knight-errant's armor, a passport to derring-do beyond his ken, before his time for adventure had ended?

Don't be a romantic fool forever, he told himself. *This isn't the first time a girl has allowed a man to offer her a drink so she could pick his brains.* Observing that his bus was on the point of departure, he stepped aboard, sought a place by a window, and took his orders from his pocket.

ON JULY 30 42 YOU WILL PROCEED TO CAMP BRUCKNER COMPTON MARYLAND AND REPORT TO THE COMMANDING OFFICER STATION HOSPITAL

ULIO THE AG

The Army's style in prose, Bruce reflected, suited the occasion perfectly. Like all orders worthy of the name, these cryptic words took compliance for granted. They gave no inkling of what tasks he would perform at Camp Bruckner. There was no hint, however remote, that his special training had been properly appraised by the organization that dispatched such commands, signed with initials whose very definitions eluded him.

Vaguely, he sensed that the AG in this telegraphic shorthand stood for The Adjutant General of the Army. Even more vaguely, he was beginning to realize that he had surrendered an essential part of his independence to this same AG. In his case, it was fortunate that he would be trading one set of disciplines for another. The iron regime of the intern and the hospital resident, the months he had spent as a surgical instructor, would surely condition him for whatever waited at the end of his bus-journey. . . . Or so he reasoned while he rolled down his window—and tried hard not to seem too aloof from the chatter surrounding him now that the bus had begun to take on soldiers in droves.

The threat remained, palpable as the ghost-white government beehives that loomed beyond the station plaza. Remembering Shane McLendon's warning, he did his best to shrug it off. His branch of the United States Army, he told himself, would prove a thing apart. If, from now on, his actions were subject to the will of others, if his own success or failure was to be governed by those wills, the Medical Corps at least would be run intelligently. His talents, honed by years of education and training, would not be wasted.

They had been used effectively in Spain, he reminded himself, in the last bitter months of the Civil War, when he had served with the famous medical unit of Dr. Juan Trueta. That was the year he had really come to know Schoenfeld, the year he had learned to fight death on the edge of a battlefield, as calmly as he had fought it in an operating room at Lakewood. Now the experience was behind him, he had found ways to shut it from his mind. Even tonight—when the girl in the bar had taunted his innocence—he had felt no urge to mention that baptism of blood.

It was still odd that he could find no easy way to compare those months in Spain with the far vaster tests ahead. Perhaps that early training was best forgotten, now the political winds had changed. . . . Feeling the bus pick up speed as the lights along the traffic circle changed to green, he closed his eyes and surrendered to weariness.

He had slept through his journey to Camp Bruckner, to dream of a house in Barcelona that had served as his last medical command post—of the gales that had roared through its bombed-out roof, of the rain that had lashed the door of the makeshift operating room in the cellar. When he wakened, another rain had streaked the bus windows, and that top-heavy conveyance had just entered the main gate of the camp. . . . Now, wakening a second time long after midnight, he realized that the same relentless downpour was rattling the window of his cell-like room in the bachelor officers' quarters.

Until his head cleared, he could not quite believe the United States Army had already possessed him—as efficiently as those gates had sighed shut behind the bus.

Reviewing first impressions in this drowsy moment, he could wonder at his disappointment when he viewed his new habitat firsthand. He had not expected flags or bands—or a lonely sentry at a drawbridge—but he had been unprepared for bleak emptiness, for the high, wire-mesh fence surrounding an area vaster than the abandoned fairgrounds it resembled. He had been shocked by the icy manner of the MP who had asked for his AGO card—and phoned ahead to check his name. The feeling that he was being processed (as casually, and as efficiently, as a heifer at a stock show) had persisted when a brisk admitting officer had checked the card a second time—before summoning an orderly to guide him to the billet where he was lying now.

Accustomed to hundred-bed wards in the civilian world, he could not help gaping at his first glimpse of the station hospital, a file of one-storied buildings sheathed in tar paper blacker than the night. Like barracks in a nightmare, they seemed to march to infinity between their duckboard walks, in a sea of red mud. . . . While his melancholy lasted, it was hard to believe that patients could be cared for behind those inky walls, much less that he could function there as a surgeon.

Thanks to his induction in Tampa, he was no stranger to the aseptic bareness of BOQs, or the tomblike hush that filled them after midnight. Some of his aplomb had returned while he undressed—and sleep had claimed him again, almost before he could slide between the Army sheets. This time he had dreamed of Shane McLendon. Since all things are possible in a realm where the id is king, he had found it easy to meet each of her thrusts with ready-made gems of wit. . . .

Completely awake now, he realized it was not the downpour that had roused him, but a sound in the hall. When the tap on his door was repeated, he sat up in bed to face a lieutenant with the caduceus of a doctor on his collar and an OD brassard on his arm.

"Sorry to waken you, Major Graham—but I need help."

The voice of the officer of the day was as strained as his manner: Bruce knew at once that his need was genuine. He, too, had uttered that same request as an intern, when knotty problems had risen in this nadir between dark and dawn.

"Give me a minute to dress. I'll be with you."

"You don't know me, sir—but I know you," the young doctor said. "I was in the audience last year, when you spoke to the AMA convention in Philadelphia. My name's Roger Snell."

"I'm glad you found me. So far, I've no idea where I am, or why."

"That feeling will pass, Major. I had it too, my first week at Bruckner." Snell touched his brassard with a smile that was half-apology, half-relief at the mildness of his reception. "One of our task force commanders just brought in three men from a car crash. The dispensary's handling two of them —but the third has me bothered."

"Don't you have a regular surgeon on duty?"

"Major O'Reilly asked for the best name on call. We're always short on personnel in the weekends. So I took a chance you wouldn't chew me out."

"Far from it. Please lead the way."

The dispensary that served both as emergency room and admitting office opened direct to the ambulance ramps, a short walk from the bachelor officers' quarters. The brightly lighted room was empty, save for a technician busy at a typewriter—and a solidly built officer who wore infantry insignia and introduced himself as Major O'Reilly.

"Sorry to turn up at this hour, gentlemen. As you'll see, Major Graham, three of my boys were joyriding on the turnpike, and lost a race with the Navy. Sergeant Gaither seems to be in real trouble."

Two of the soldiers, waiting for dismissal in the first examining room, had already been treated for minor abrasions. The third case, a white-faced boy with the chevrons of a staff sergeant, still lay on the table in the second room. The injured man's knees were drawn up. When Bruce touched his lower abdomen, he flinched violently and drew them still higher.

"What hit you, Sergeant?"

"A girl on my lap, sir."

Bruce turned to the OD. "Catheterize him, please. It should tell us what we need to know."

Even without further evidence, the situation was obvious. In the car crash, all the occupants had been thrown forward. Some of the force had been cushioned by bodily contact. In Gaither's case, forward momentum had been checked by the weight of the girl on his lap. The abdominal area had taken the full weight of that blow, bursting the bladder much as a bag of water explodes when dropped to the ground. . . . There was nothing too alarming in the prognosis. Blood pressure had been recorded at 120/80, which meant that shock had not yet set in—and the sergeant was the stuff of which college linebackers are made.

The catheter confirmed the evaluation with a gush of bloody fluid. Meeting Snell's eye, Bruce saw that the younger doctor had turned almost as pale as the patient.

"There's the diagnosis, Lieutenant. Better call your urologist."

"*I'm* on GU call tonight, sir. Major Denby's on his way back from New York."

"This bladder must be repaired at once."

"We don't have a specialist available. Unless *you* would consent to operate."

Bruce led the way to the hall. "Is that allowable under regulations?"

"Your orders assign you to this station hospital, Major. I've had only a first-year residency in urology. It didn't include laparotomies for ruptured bladders."

"In that case, for the record, I'll assist you."

Snell's frown vanished magically. "I'll have Gaither prepped at once."

"Is an operating room ready?"

"Ready and waiting, sir. We keep a stand-by team on call."

O'Reilly had moved toward the sound of voices. "Did I hear an operating room mentioned?"

"Gaither will be on the table in five minutes, Major," said Snell. "The motto of our section is service with a smile."

"Wasn't that a rather quick decision?"

Bruce curbed his impatience. It was reassuring to find an officer with genuine concern for his men. "Immediate surgery is indicated with a ruptured bladder."

Gaither spoke through the open door, as a fresh spasm of pain convulsed him. "*Will I be all right, doctor?*"

"Of course. It's a simple process."

O'Reilly turned to the OD. "I thought your section head was the hospital urologist."

"Major Graham taught surgery at Lakewood, sir. If Major Denby were here, he would accept the diagnosis."

"In that case," said O'Reilly, "it seems I owe someone an apology. Probably Major Graham."

"Forget it," said Bruce. "I'm sure you aren't the first officer to question the competence of Army doctors, or the last."

The surgeon had not expected a replica of Lakewood when he followed Lieutenant Snell through the operating-room doors—but he was reassured by what he saw.

The theater was completely equipped. A scrub nurse, and a technician in sterile gown and gloves, were already checking the instrument and dressing tables—and a Wac stood by to act as circulating nurse. The patient was under spinal anesthesia, administered by a Medical Corps officer who seemed to know his job. Watching Snell drape the abdomen and noting that the OD was fast and accurate, Bruce felt almost at home when the scalpel came into his hand.

"Rigidity's rather marked," he said. "The rupture has probably spilled urine into the abdominal cavity. I'll make a low incision, rather than use the extraperitoneal approach."

The blade had already bitten through the skin just above the pubis, incising the subcutaneous tissue and the fat of the lower abdomen. No muscles were severed in this approach, and there was little bleeding in the mid-line area—since the fibrous layers enclosing the muscles of the abdominal wall blended into a tough median strip extending from the umbilicus to the pubic bone. The slit, when it was completed, exposed the peritoneum for another deep slash of the steel—opening the entire operative field less than ten minutes after the patient had been draped.

The star-shaped tear in the bladder wall was now in clear view, in that part of the organ known as the dome, where impact had been most severe. The surgeon closed the rent with a dozen sutures. After the abdominal cavity had been drained of the fluids that had distended the whole area, Snell flushed it a second time with saline solution to dilute the irritation. The closure required only a few more minutes, including the now-standard sifting of sulfanilamide powder into the wound to keep down infection.

When Bruce pulled off his gloves, he saw by the wall clock that the procedure had required only a little over a half hour. Routine though the surgery had been, he felt a glow of pleasure when he turned to thank his team. Lieutenant Snell was still beaming when they entered the scrub room together.

"That was a fine job, sir."

"It was easy all the way, Lieutenant."

"You made it *look* easy, Major Graham. If I'd been operating, I'd have sweat blood. Since I've been at Bruckner, I haven't had much chance to bone up on my speciality."

"I'd have thought otherwise, in a camp this size."

"Most of these boys are strong as horses, and just as healthy. Here in GU, our main job is treating gonorrhea."

Major O'Reilly was still in the admissions room. He smiled broadly when he read the results on the doctors' faces.

"Your man will be out of bed day after tomorrow," Bruce assured him. "In two weeks, he should be good as new. Try to keep girls off his lap in the meantime."

"If the bar weren't closed, I'd buy you a drink," the task force major said. "Gaither's the best communicator in my battalion. I can't finish combat training without him."

In the corridor of the BOQ, Bruce was glad to learn he could find his cubicle unaided. The pine-board hall seemed no less gaunt—but the strangeness had left it, now he had watched an Army surgical team swing into action, as smoothly as his own service at Lakewood. Perhaps it was a good augury for what lay ahead.

A bugle sounded mess call at seven. Snell was at the next shaving mirror in the washroom: their patient, the surgeon learned, was already asking for his breakfast. . . .

Bound for his own meal, he passed the admissions desk, where an orderly handed him a long official envelope.

"This came by courier, sir."

The envelope bore the seal of the House of Representatives. Bruce smiled as he took out the note. It was like Hal Reardon to track him down in this fashion:

Dear Bruce:

Just a word of greeting before you settle in.

Senator Josselyn, whom all good Floridians honor, is hold-ing an open house Sunday noon. At Five Oaks, his place on the Severn. In due course, you will receive an invitation. I'm sure you will accept when I tell you Janet will be her father's hostess.

What the senator has done for me is a matter of record. Perhaps he can get your own Army career under way a little faster. At the worse, I can promise you a refreshing change of pace.

The note, Bruce observed, had been "dictated but not signed" by Harold Reardon: it was still impressive evidence that the representative from his congressional district was never too busy to oversee the welfare of a constituent—es-pecially when the voter had been a fraternity brother at the University of Florida. It was too much to say that Congress-man Reardon was his friend—but Hal had been his self-ap-pointed mentor since their graduation. Mutual acquaintances, Bruce was sure, had passed on the news of his induction.

On surface, the promise of an invitation to Five Oaks was logical. To every resident of the Tampa Bay counties, Lucius Josselyn was the Grand Old Man of the Senate. In Florida, his house on the Pinellas Peninsula was the last word in baroque grandeur. In Washington, the plantation-manse he had rented on the Severn River near Annapolis was a familiar Mecca for political reporters and society editors alike. Josse-lyn had been the inspiration of Hal Reardon's own career since the brilliant young lawyer had run for his first office. In both Tampa and Washington, it was generally believed he would inherit the senator's seat—after his marriage to the senator's daughter.

Bruce had met Janet Josselyn seven years ago: the occasion had been a Homecoming Ball on the Florida campus. Since that gala evening, he had made no effort to resume contact. Janet had been only a meteor on his horizon, for reasons he understood all too well—and, though he could visualize Sunday's gathering easily enough, he could almost resent Hal's assumption that he would be eager to attend.

Naturally, as a native of Tampa in good standing, he would accept the invitation. Even at Lakewood, he had heard echoes of his classmate's spectacular rise in the world of politics. Janet had become something of a legend in that same world as her father's hostess, a duty she had discharged since her mother's death. After seven years, he could hardly admit that he feared this reunion almost as much as he desired it.

Hal's note had added a new—and much-needed—dimension to his day. His step was light when he entered the officers' mess, though he could detect no note of welcome in the long, steam-filled room. There were few empty tables. He chose the nearest, unwilling to intrude on groups that seemed to be lifelong cronies. Seconds after he had unloaded his tray, he was joined by a crew-cut major, whose hostile look was as truculent as his coiffure.

"Nick Denby's the name," said the newcomer. "Thanks to Roger Snell, I know you, more or less. He mentioned a bladder injury they brought in last midnight."

"We were lucky with that one, Major. I operated less than an hour after the accident."

"Where did you train in urology?"

"I had six months' internship on a GU service." Bruce was careful to show no resentment at the abruptness. It was inevitable that the chief urologist of the station hospital would look askance at a potential intruder in his field.

"Snell told you I'd left New York last midnight," said Denby. "Did it occur to you to wait?"

"I operated because he seemed hesitant about attacking a ruptured bladder. An injury of that sort can make plenty of trouble, if it runs into the retroperitoneal area. Fortunately, this turned out to be an open-and-shut job, a stellate tear in the vault. I sutured it and put in a catheter. There was probably no need to drain, but I left two strips there, just in case. You may want to get them out tomorrow."

"You seem to know a great deal about operating on GU cases."

"Surgery's my business, Major. I served for two years as a resident at Lakewood. I've taught at the medical school there ever since."

Denby's hand was not quite steady when he put down his cup. Bruce could not be sure if the reaction stemmed from astonishment or a residue of anger.

"How long have you been in the Army?"

"Three days—counting indoctrination."

"Were you commissioned direct?"

"Direct. And I'm still not sure what it's all about."

Denby's grin, when it broke through, atoned for his brusqueness. "You've put me in my place, Major Graham. I hope you'll overlook a slight case of spleen. I've been in the Army two years. They gave me *my* majority a month ago."

"You must have come through the Reserve."

"And cursed be the memory of my brain storm—when I signed that dotted line. I should have stayed close to my specialty, and claimed teaching chores as an exemption. Instead, I got patriotic. As a result, I was snatched out of practice, just when I was getting a start in the high-income district of Manhattan. Are you beginning to see why I griped just now?"

"I can't say I blame you."

"This is the best assignment I've had since I entered the service, and I mean to hang on here. Perhaps you don't know the advantages of being War Department Overhead. That's what the star on my shoulder patch stands for."

"Just what does it mean?"

"That I'm under the direct supervision of the Surgeon General's Office, more or less. It isn't tenure in the civilian sense, but the idea adds up. Naturally, I hit the ceiling when

I heard a brand-new major had operated in my field. Any idea why you were sent here?"

"I suppose I'm ticketed for overseas, since I've already had combat experience."

"Surely not in the Pacific."

Bruce hesitated. Major Denby would be a guide worth having in this labyrinth of clashing egos—but he had not planned to mention his work abroad.

"I was in Spain, the last year of the Civil War. With a surgical team—organized at Lakewood to work with Dr. Trueta."

"Did you stay till the end?"

"We stayed almost too long. When Barcelona fell, we found a shortcut back to France, through the Pyrenees."

"Did Schoenfeld lead your unit?"

"That's usually the next question. At the time, Dr. Schoenfeld warned us we'd make headlines for the wrong reasons."

"He was front-page news for a week, when he testified before Jake Sanford in the House. Is it true he sympathized with the Communists?"

"We served the Loyalists as *doctors*. For the same reason you let the Reserve call you up, without filing a protest. None of us had political leanings. Schoenfeld least of all."

"Sanford told the press another story."

"Sanford's a born character assassin." This time, Bruce made no effort to mute his bitterness. "Ever since he went on the Subversive Acts Committee, he's been a headline hunter."

"Sanford's a low form of louse—but he can raise one hell of an itch. Is Spain on your service record?"

"Naturally, Major Denby. It was first-rate medical experience for us all."

"In your place, I'd leave the fact unmentioned, unless Britten brings it up."

"Who is Britten?"

"Colonel Benson Britten, our commanding officer," said

the urologist. "I don't mean to cast gloom on your first day in harness, but it's well to be forewarned. A tight-buttoned lip's the rule here on touchy topics. One more question on Schoenfeld, and I'm done. Did he recommend you to the Army?"

"It was the other way round. When he heard I'd volunteered, he asked for a deferment, until we'd finished a research series in open-heart surgery. Our experiments and the school year ran out at the same time—so I took an appeal."

"*Your* burst of patriotism was rewarded with a majority."

"I doubt if the appeal influenced my rank. Most certified specialists go in as majors now."

"It's too bad those rules weren't in effect when I was called up," said Denby. "If they were, I'd be trading these gold leaves for silver before the new year. Not that a glorified clap-doctor deserves to make lieutenant colonel."

"Is that your unofficial title?"

"I've grown used to it. At least it's given me no time to sit and brood. There isn't a busier man in camp. Dry up the discharge and ship them out. That's the Transportation Corps' motto. At the clinic, we call it sin, suffer and sulfadiazine."

"Your work sounds a touch monotonous."

"Gaither was the first interesting case we've had this month—and it was *your* night to operate." Denby rose from the table. "Don't take anything I say too seriously, please. Speaking of the GU service, it's time I was reading Snell's morning report. After Saturday-night liberty, it's longer than your arm."

"I'd offer to help, if you weren't outside my field."

"Don't be too sure of that. They may decide it's part of your education to join my receiving line. If you're finished, I'd better walk you out. Britten's always at his desk early. He likes to find newcomers on the doorstep."

"I'll go straight to his office, if I can find it."

"Start at Administration. They'll route you from there. It's on my way."

The urologist set a brisk pace in a maze of connecting corridors. After the third turn, Bruce knew he was hopelessly lost again.

"It's going to take me weeks to get my bearings."

"Not when you live down the feeling you're in a plywood prison, with every plank alike. Actually, the picture here is far from black. For the Medical Corps, Bruckner is a soft post. It's close to Washington and the girls, if you aren't married—or your wife stayed home. Plenty of weekend passes, and New York only a hop away. Let me mention one more danger, before I leave you. Whenever we billet a medical unit for shipment overseas, and an officer with your rank and spec number goes on sick call, you can be ordered to take his place at an hour's notice. Any task force doctor who can walk gets a fast ride to England."

"When I volunteered, I hoped to get orders to go abroad."

Denby put a hand on Bruce's shoulder. Casual though the gesture was, the surgeon felt it was evidence of acceptance.

"You're a good soldier, Graham. Just don't overdo. A lot of war's ahead—for us all. Let it come to you."

The offices of the station hospital were part of an impressive but unlovely building at the south end of the cantonment. Here, Bruce reported to the adjutant, an extremely well-fed major of the Medical Administrative Corps. Major Krock directed him in turn to the executive officer—who seemed immersed in a stack of ledgers and a clamoring phone, without giving his full attention to either. Impressed by the greatest show of energy he had witnessed since his arrival, Bruce waited patiently until Lieutenant Colonel Whelton had finished a long, mumbled argument on the wire, closed each ledger carefully, and gave him a nervous handshake.

"Here are some forms. When you've filled them out, I'll take you to the colonel."

The mimeographed sheets Whelton spread on the table were quite familiar. Bruce frowned as he turned over the closely printed pages.

"I was given these same papers when I applied for my commission, sir."

"You're in luck, Major. I filled out five sets before I was pigeonholed."

The forms demanded endless details on his education, training, hobbies and languages. While he wrote, the executive officer tossed him another sheet, containing a long list of organizations labeled *subversive* by the Attorney General's Office—from the German-American Bund to the Pavlovian Neurophysiological Association. Membership, Bruce noted with relief, could be denied simply by signing at the end of the list.

When the paper work was finished, Whelton collected the forms in a practiced swoop and dropped them into a file folder before handing the surgeon a smaller card, with spaces for listing purely professional qualifications. This, Bruce gathered, was intended for his commanding officer's perusal. The suspicion was confirmed when the colonel led the way to a door at the far end of the room.

"The CO will interview you now, Major."

The office of the commandant was spacious, with a view of the Potomac; leather armchairs gave it a vague resemblance to the smoking room of a country club. On the square of carpet before the cluttered desk, Bruce came to attention and snapped off what he hoped was a passable salute. The bulky man in the swivel chair returned the courtesy with two lazy fingers.

Colonel Benson Britten, the surgeon decided, was a far cry from the ramrod he had expected. Without his uniform, he could have passed for a torpid minor executive dozing through an unrewarding forenoon and dreaming of his first luncheon cocktail. Unpressed suntans, which Britten's slack torso filled to bursting, added to the air of contented sloth.

The executive officer had also produced a textbook salute. "Major Graham reporting, sir."

"Glad to see you, Graham." Britten had made no effort to rise—though he managed a limp handshake after the executive officer had placed the summary-card on his blotter and faded from the room. "Have a seat, while I look this over."

Bruce took the flint-hard chair in the precise center of the carpet: the armchairs, he gathered, were reserved for more relaxed visitors. Watching his commanding officer under lowered lids, he felt that Britten was making little effort to absorb the information on the card, though he continued to brood over it minutely. The boredom in the colonel's pale face was evidence enough that his mind was elsewhere.

"Graduated from Lakewood, I see," he said at last. "We don't get too many of your kind here. Usually, the SGO sends its wonder boys elsewhere."

"I'm hardly that, sir."

"You skipped ROTC, I take it?"

"I'm afraid so. While I was interning, I never thought we'd have another war."

"You and a million other people. Now that you've learned better, what would you like to do?"

"Whatever you wish, sir."

"We've a full staff, as of now. I'll assign you to the general pool for the present. It's the best I can do, until we ship out our next detail."

"May I ask what duty that involves?"

"You'll be standby medical help for every service at the station, as emergencies develop. Meanwhile, if you need advice, see the adjutant. It's his job to keep you straight."

Bruce realized that this travesty of an interview had ended. He had expected his Lakewood credits to get some recognition. As a civilian, he would have protested this dismissal and insisted that his skills be weighed in detail. The discipline of his uniform had already forced him to a second, even brisker salute before he marched from the office.

Whelton, busy on a phone when he passed the desk outside, waved him on—with an abstracted look that suggested he had already forgotten the new doctor's name. At the adjutant's wicket, the MAC officer glanced up from his own sea of paper work.

"First post, Major?"

"How did you know?"

"The way you're still at attention," said Major Krock. "You can stop bracing, now it's over."

"Where do I go next?"

"Take out your insurance, and buy yourself a war bond to show you're a true patriot. That should occupy you until drink-time."

"For the *day?*"

Krock winked broadly. "There are traditions about a man's first exposure to Bruckner. Don't make the mistake of jumping into the Army with both feet. I'll send an orderly to get you started through the mill."

After three hours of processing, Bruce realized that the adjutant's advice had been sound. The offices he visited were not too numerous—but all of them seemed located at opposite ends of this vast hospital. His leg muscles were aching long before he had made a pay reservation for insurance, an allotment for war bonds—and received his quota of injections at the dispensary. Finally, his photograph and fingerprints were taken for an identification folder and a standard Geneva pass. This, he was told, was a card that must never leave his person. It established him as a medical officer of the United States Army. As such, it entitled him to the same consideration the enemy granted his counterpart in their own medical service.

It was nearly two when he returned to the mess for lunch.

Denby was leaving with a group of officers—but broke away to follow Bruce's progress down the steam table.

"Can I buy you a drink at five o'clock, Graham?"

"By then, I can use one."

"Don't let indoctrination blues get you down. We've all gone through them and survived. What's your assignment?"

"The colonel said he would put me in the officers' pool."

Denby whistled softly. "Somehow, I didn't think Britten would go quite that far."

"He didn't make it sound like a hardship."

"I was thinking aloud—a procedure that's frowned on here. Forget it."

Watching the crew-cut, still-youthful officer move on to join his group, Bruce knew it would have been futile to question him further. Clearly, there were mysteries at Camp Bruckner he must discover on his own. Denby's remark had been a ray of light in darkness. With the light withdrawn, the menaces surrounding him seemed even more ominous.

He spent what was left of the afternoon exploring. The barracks sprawled over hundreds of rolling acres along the Washington-Baltimore pike. The seas of mud, still liquid after last night's rain, were the only constant factors in that ravaged landscape; the duckboard walks were doubtful havens when a truck roared past. Though he moved unchallenged, Bruce could not escape the feeling that he was a spy in alien country—or that he was being followed by unseen eyes.

Here and there, he came upon a macadam-paved drill field. On the far side of camp, he paused at a safety deadline to watch an infantry platoon go through an obstacle course—climbing ten-foot walls with catlike speed, wading in ditches where each man sank to his waist, or inching down a trench beneath barbed wire, while live bullets whined overhead. The sharpest reality of the afternoon confronted him on the next field—a mahogany-tanned drill sergeant, explaining the elements of bayonet-fighting to a circle of athletes stripped to the waist. The instructor seemed almost awkward while he went through the items in that grisly manual of arms, stating their purpose in harsh detail, and giving each move a number. The awkwardness vanished when he translated numbers into action, in a rush at a sawdust dummy.

The slashing blow, spilling a cascade of sawdust to the drill field, was graceful as a *pas seul* in ballet. Watching the bayonet withdraw, Bruce knew he had met the face of war at last. In the years since Barcelona, he had forgotten what such weapons could do to a human body, with an expert's hands behind them.

The drink he ordered in the bar of the officers' club could hardly be called a reward after a day's labor—but he found he needed it even more. He was considering a second when Denby joined him.

"Tim O'Reilly's going to Baltimore for supplies. If you like, we can join him for shrimps and beer."

"Do I need a pass?"

"Our complement's pretty free to roam after five, if there are standbys on hand. We're only restricted when there's a troop movement alert. Then we're stuck here until the transports sail."

Tonight, O'Reilly had dismissed the driver of his jeep. Leaving the main gate with a wide-open throttle, he turned into the traffic stream to Baltimore. Curtailed as civilian travel was by the rigid gas rationing, they met little resistance to their headlong rush. An Army vehicle in transit, Bruce decided, always moved at top speed, regardless of its errand. He welcomed the tempo, after the snail's pace of his day.

Sergeant Gaither, he learned, was mending smoothly; Denby was sure he could rejoin his outfit in time for shipment overseas. There was no further shoptalk until they had settled in one of the fishhouses on the waterfront. Knowing he had been asked here for enlightenment, the surgeon was careful to offer no leads until O'Reilly had ordered their second round of beer.

"Nick tells me they've put you in the general pool," the task force major said.

"I'm still waiting to be useful."

"Probably you'll draw duty in the salt mines tomorrow."

"Tim means the processing lines," Denby explained. "Lacking other employment, it's a safe bet Britten will have you doing physicals."

"A man just out of medical school could handle that sort of job."

"Most of the pool is made up of Medical Corps lieutenants. What's more, they earn their keep."

"It's one routine that's never-ending at a POE," said O'Reilly. "Each man who checks in here must be checked out before he boards a transport. You'd be surprised how many come this far, only to run out of gas."

"Don't squawk, if you get that duty," said Denby. "You might wind up on latrine inspection. It's even duller."

"Surely a station hospital has better work for a surgeon."

"Did you think every specialist in our service drew his own niche?" the urologist asked. "At Bruckner, we have an embarrassment of medical riches, so to speak. The situation won't change, until a second front is opened in Europe."

"Nick's right," said O'Reilly. "For the present, the Medical Corps must make work for its personnel—and ignore ingrown tension. After all, the Army has a great deal on its mind."

"Assuming the Army has a mind," said Denby. "Some observers think it lives by a book that went out of print fifty years ago. They say it *still* can't spell the big words."

"Spoken like a true civilian," said O'Reilly. "The United States Army isn't perfect, but it's the best one we have. I won't expect civilians in uniform to show it proper respect. The least you can do is adapt to its ways. If that means work in the salt mines for Major Graham, so be it. Unless he has friends in high places, he must take his chances as they come."

Remembering Congressman Hal Reardon, and the party he would soon attend at Five Oaks, Bruce said nothing. It was easy to appreciate the frictions existing between Regular and Reserve. Discussions of this sort, he realized, could serve as safety valves after-hours. For the present, it seemed prudent to remain an attentive listener.

"If you won't use your connections," said the task force major, "you'll find the good jobs have long since been filled at Bruckner. It's a law of nature, when the supply exceeds the demand."

"Tim means that Britten has his own stable," said Denby. "He's content with things as they are, and he's opening no new stalls."

The shrimp was excellent, the beer potent. Letting the lazily cynical voices go on, Bruce took what comfort he could from the casual way these two brother-officers belabored each other—and the even more casual way they had enlightened him. It was too soon to hope he had found new friends—and much too soon to ask outright advice. He could hardly doubt that the motives behind this briefing were sincere.

Back at the BOQ, they paused at the bulletin board, where orders for the next day had just been posted. Denby snorted, and leveled a finger at one of the items.

"You've made the news, Graham—just as we predicted."

Bruce scanned the sheet, with narrowed eyes.

MAJOR BRUCE GRAHAM MC ASN 0-270106 HAVING REPORTED TO THIS STATION IN ACCORDANCE WITH PARAGRAPH 12 SO 20 IS HEREBY ASSIGNED TO THE PHYSICAL EXAMINATION SECTION FOR DUTY AND WILL REPORT TO THE CHIEF OF THAT SECTION AT 0800

.

"Don't look so downcast," said the urologist. "It's easy work, and you can handle most of it seated. Remember my warning about speaking your mind in the wrong company."

It was still early evening—and Bruce felt no impulse to retire to his quarters, despite an overlap of impressions that needed sorting. When the other officers had gone on, he turned into the lounge—virtually empty in these last hours of a cantonment weekend. A copy of the Washington *Star* caught his eye, and he sat down beside a reading lamp to scan the headlines. The item he was searching appeared on the first page of the second section—a column set in special type, along with the familiar cut of the author:

AS I SEE IT
By Shane McLendon

The nine hundred words of crisp prose consisted of two-paragraph interviews with men the author had tracked down in Union Station. Each interview followed the same pattern: a contrast of the subject's past with his new status, his reactions to what lay ahead, and his views on the reasons behind the war. Shane McLendon had talked with a corporal from Utah, an ensign from Maine, an Air Force technician from New York, and a paratrooper from Texas. None of the men was identified—but it was evident that the Medical Corps major she had saved for the end was Bruce Graham.

Weighing this printed playback of his remarks in the bar, Bruce saw he had been quoted fairly. In cold print, his estimate of the niche he would fill in the surgical service, plus his hopes for the outcome of the war, seemed on the idealistic side: it was obvious that the interviewer felt his opinions would soon need revising. Yet, in a way he could not define, she had used each of her examples to assure her readers that the war was in good hands. . . . The fact that he had been used as well—to support a special point of view—should have produced its own irritation. Curiously enough, he was more amused than angry. He would have given a great deal to corner this outspoken girl tonight and resume their argument.

With his hand on a coin-box phone, he glanced again at the column. The *Star* was only a Washington outlet for this widely syndicated reporter: a call to that city room would hardly reveal her whereabouts. Shane McLendon had already half-promised he would see her again. It was better strategy to await her next move, lest he seem too eager.

The need to hear a civilian voice remained. Before he left the phone booth, he rang Hal Reardon's number—intending to thank Hal for the communiqué he had received that morning. On the fourth ring, he obeyed an even stronger impulse, and hung up without learning if his representative from Florida was in Washington. Hal's message, after all, required no acknowledgment. Here, too, it seemed wiser to keep his own counsel.

The square white envelope in his mailbox was a formal invitation from Senator Lucius Josselyn and his hostess-daughter, to an open house this Sunday, at their estate on the Severn. A map was enclosed, showing that Five Oaks was less than an hour's drive from his billet. No transportation was mentioned, but this lack did not keep Bruce from dropping his acceptance in the mail chute. He had already observed that an enterprising car dealer had opened a rental agency across the pike.

The day had been long and wearing—and his inability to make human contact at its end seemed part of the general frustration. In the BOQ, he stood for a long time under a shower, in the hope that the drumming water would take away some of his perplexity. Back in his meagerly furnished cell, he was certain he would pass a sleepless night, once he permitted his thoughts to dwell on the depressing forecasts of Denby and O'Reilly. Instead, he found he was too drowsy to fumble for pajamas.

When sleep claimed him, it was an oblivion without dreams.

The physical examination section that served Camp Bruckner was a vast barn; it was located, for reasons only the Army could explain, a good half mile from the hospital proper. Next morning, Bruce reported promptly at the office of the section chief—only to find the cavernous area deserted, save for a sergeant who took his name.

Just before nine, a captain strode through the barn door, his martial bearing slightly obscured by a tendency to over-weight that seemed endemic here, his brow creased in a ferocious scowl. Bruce's spirits had reached a new low when he was summoned to the office, after a ten-minute wait. The label of salt mine, he concluded, was not to be taken lightly.

The sign on the desk read *Captain Calvin Pritchett*. The captain himself barely glanced up as Bruce approached.

"Administration sent me your card, Major." The words were barked, not spoken. "What do you know about physical standards in the Army?"

"Only what I've read."

Pritchett tossed a dog-eared volume into the surgeon's hands. "You'll find the essentials here. I'd suggest you *re*-read them. You're on team three. The NCO will direct you."

The captain had already dived behind his paper barricade. Wondering if a dismissal of some kind was required, Bruce hesitated before he turned to leave the room—only to be brought up short by Pritchett's voice, which had changed to an outright snarl.

"Not so fast, Major. It's customary to *salute* in the Army when you leave an officer's desk."

Bruce clamped down on his anger. This was the voice of the bully the world over: today he was powerless to answer in kind. He snapped into a perfect salute, resisted the impulse to apply his thumb to his nose, and left the office.

In the anteroom, he forced himself to close the door softly, and leaned against the jamb until his heart had resumed its normal beat. Catching a gleam in the eye of the desk sergeant, he spoke in a whisper.

"Is a major *ever* required to salute a captain?"

The sergeant replied in a voice as devoid of color as a train announcer. "Regulations say an officer making a report salutes on leaving."

"Regardless of rank?"

"He had you there, sir. You were reporting for duty."

"Thanks for the correction, Sergeant. It seems I'm assigned to team three. Where do I find it?"

"It's the last line, sir. On the far side of the shed. Captain Seward's in charge."

Seward, a soft-spoken Midwesterner in his forties, welcomed Bruce with a warm handshake that did much to restore his ruffled temper. So did the deference of Lieutenant Travis, the other member of the team. His interview with Pritchett had marked the beginning of the section's working day. Three lines of draftees had already emerged from a disrobing area at the mouth of the shed, to descend on the waiting groups of doctors. Each man was naked as Adam; most of them seemed resigned to their nakedness.

Seward uttered a sigh that was close to a groan, and hooked a stethoscope around his neck.

"Don't let the spectacle depress you," he said. "Those lines only *seem* never-ending—and they *are* men, not pink hippopotami. Among us, we're supposed to give them the works."

"Haven't they been examined before?"

"In theory, they're fit for combat—but regulations call for a final check-out. This is it. Once we've passed them, they're ready for delivery to Baltimore."

"How are the examinations divided?"

"I'll handle the files, and check on doubtful cases. Travis will do chest and heart. You can take hernia, extremities and short arm."

"Offhand, I'd think disabilities in those areas would have turned up long ago. Why is this go-round necessary?"

Seward sat down at his record table and opened the first folder. "It's a good question. Unfortunately, I haven't an answer ready. Don't bother with patent rings, varicoceles, or fallen arches. Remember, each man in your line has already convinced his unit commander he can walk up a gangplank."

Bruce settled in one of the examining booths, as Pritchett's sergeant ordered the three nude columns to move forward. Seward's remarks, revealing far more than he had stated, gave added poignance to the grotesque reality that followed.

After he had examined fifty men, the surgeon was dismayed by the disparity between his findings, and the files the captain produced at his request. Pressing the point in his interviews, he uncovered two salient facts that were, in themselves, a paradox. Many of these new soldiers, it seemed, had glossed over a disability to join the Army. Now, wearied by combat training and faced with an immediate threat of submarines offshore, they seemed ready to exaggerate the very failings that could have saved them from induction.

The chances of last-minute reprieves, Bruce learned, were slight indeed at Camp Bruckner. Before the morning shift ended, he had been faced with nearly every type of minor deformity or injury: feet slightly twisted from infantile paralysis, jaws that barely opened because of old fractures, limbs shortened from breaks that had healed badly, mild hernias, flat feet—and the myriad signs of venery revealed by the check known, in Army vulgate, as short arm inspection.

When mess call sounded at noon, he had lost track of the occasions when he had halted the line to protest a case to Seward, only to have the record stamped *Passed*—and the soldier move on.

"Let's eat at the PX," said the captain. "It's closer than our mess."

Bruce could see that the older officer sympathized with his confusion—though he was careful to avoid the subject until he had brought fresh coffee to their booth in the crowded post canteen.

"I hear Pritchett jumped you this morning."

"For not saluting when I left his office."

"Like most fifth-rate soldiers, Pritchett's a first-rate book man. Every officer in this section hates his guts."

"He has a pretty important job."

"He didn't get it on ability. Pritchett's related to the CO's wife—and he's being a good nephew for all it's worth. His gold leaves will be coming up any day now. Naturally, he hates you for wearing them already."

"Are you advising me to take it?"

"In your place, I'd look frightened each time he barks. It won't be forever. The minute his commission comes through, Britten will move him up the ladder."

"Why should an incompetent get still more power?"

Seward's eyes were on the chromatic glare of the jukebox. Outwardly, he seemed entranced by the fervid rhythms pouring from its depths. "Your record states you've been four days on active duty. You must have learned something about the chain of command—and how it stays unbroken."

"I'm eager to learn more."

"Let's begin with our present assignment. Obviously, you're unhappy about the cattle you've processed so far."

"Is it necessary to think of draftees as cattle?"

"There are times, Major Graham, when a brutal metaphor is all that saves a doctor his sanity. I imagine you're wondering how some of these men got as far as Bruckner. So did I, when I arrived here."

"In our line alone, I counted over sixty cases a horse doctor could have weeded out."

"In wartime, the weeders aren't always that efficient—or that particular. The local draft board has a quota to fill. If that figure isn't met, it feels delinquent. Assuming a man's still warm when his number's called, he goes in for his examination. If there's no obvious insanity or deformity, he's sent to basic training. Otherwise, the enemy might break through and start killing civilians. Or Washington might raise the age limit, and draft-board inspectors might find themselves in line."

"Is today a fair sample of what gets through induction centers?"

"The quality of the cattle doesn't vary much," said Seward. He touched a new button on the jukebox control, flooding the PX with the soothing nostalgia of "The Missouri Waltz." "Don't let that fact spoil your faith in our recruitment program—or the procedures of the Medical Corps. After all, now they're in uniform, we must support these GIs—through the Veterans' Administration, if they wind up in convalescent billets, or separate them outright, with a CDD."

"I'm told that a certificate of disability discharge is frowned on, all down the line."

"Here at Bruckner, it's something to be avoided. Pritchett will generally find a way."

"Isn't a CDD the only alternative, with most of the cases we passed today?"

"Not in Pritchett's scheme of things. If we risked it, he'd have our scalps."

Lieutenant Travis crossed the PX to bend above the booth. "Can you gentlemen take some unsettling news? I've just heard the officers' pool will be six names shorter before the week's out."

"Because of the next shipment?" Seward asked.

"That's the ticket, Captain. Whenever a spec number matches."

"God grant mine isn't among them."

"Does this mean crossing to England?" Bruce asked.

"We've no other place to go, Major. Don't think I'm unwilling to serve my country. It's just that I draw the line on a ship hospital platoon."

"What's so bad about them?"

"Nothing—in theory. A ship platoon is a self-contained

medical group, serving GIs in transit. Eventually, of course, they plan to convert some of those ships into hospitals to bring back wounded. Today, when a platoon reaches the British Isles, it gets dumped on the beach. Most of its officers are lucky to get one month's work in three."

"Call them the forgotten men of the service," said Travis. "A good many American doctors are sorting mail in England these days to earn their keep."

"All that will change overnight, when Europe's invaded."

"We're a long way from invasion status," said Seward. "Right now, the Baltimore-Washington axis seems like heaven, compared to cabin fever on a Scottish moor." He glanced at the wall clock, then rose from the booth. "We needn't cross *that* gangplank until it's lowered. If enough names are drawn, our situation here could improve. We might even begin functioning as doctors again, instead of medical orderlies. For the present, I'd suggest we get back to the mine."

The afternoon was a repeat of the morning, a shift that stretched to the grave.

Adjusting with each case he cleared, Bruce found it a significant experience to watch the stream of flesh pour past. By now, the bodies seemed no more than an abdomen, genitalia, two potential hernias, legs to be tested for varicose veins, insteps to be probed for evidence of fallen arches. At best, little more than a minute could be spared for each appraisal. Whether they were white, black or yellow, whether they were wasted by poverty, plump from good living, or muscled like some latter-day Hercules, he could not think of these men as personalities. And yet, he found rough sorting inevitable.

The largest grouping was the extroverts—the laughing, jostling youths that have filled the ranks since the first army marched to battle. Few of such men seemed troubled by their nudity, by the sweating proximity of other bodies.

Thinking of little except the next fall-out, the next meal and the next girl, they had taken barracks life in stride. Eventually, they would adapt to trial by fire as easily as to other outdoor trades.

The second obvious classification was the introverts. Smaller than the cheerful yea-sayers (with their mock heroics and their barnyard jokes), this group was still far too numerous. Its markings were significant—the averted glance, the blush of shame that greeted the doctors' probes, the minds that seemed to feed on fear. These were the men whose acceptance of the uniform, at best, had been partial. Preoccupied with self-pity, unable to make rewarding contact with others, they quickly developed those exhausting mental tics lumped under the label of psychoneurosis.

The intelligence quotients of such men was often high. If a groove could be found for them—where their compulsions did not conflict with their duties—these draftees might become good soldiers too. The danger here was a crack-up in the first moments of combat, the disaster they might inflict on others when they tested the eternal truth that no chain is stronger than its weakest link.

The third group included the real misfits; the psychopaths born without conscience or motivation, the mentally retarded, the crafty paranoids who were the prize goldbricks in their platoons. Failures in civilian life, they would be greater failures in the Army—but it was not the duty of an examining doctor to screen them out. The tragedy of all mass military programs, it seemed, was in that processing-line—a living illustration that only a certain type could adapt to the soldier's mold. Those who cherished man's divine right to differ from his fellows would suffer most. It was the crowning injustice that such dissenters must be lumped with the mentally disturbed, the cadgers, the downright unfit.

In the end, as always, the Army's overall purpose would prevail. This was not a time to question its iron respect for norms. There was no room for pity in Pritchett's barn today.

Only a quick probe for suspected hernia, a lightning evaluation of the aftermaths of venereal disease, a dismissal of a not-quite-crippling deformity—and a gesture to summon the next case.

Four times in the course of the afternoon Bruce detached men with Seward's approval, and sent them to Pritchett's office for a revaluation—only to see them emerge with a *Passed* stamp on their record. The hour was late—and the line was reaching its end at last—when an eager voice broke into his lethargy.

"Don't you remember me, Major?"

The surgeon glanced up quickly. The freckle-dusted face that looked down at him, and the cockscomb of sandy hair above it, were like a thousand others. Then, as memory stirred, he was back in a surgical ward at Lakewood—beside a bed fitted with a wire cradle that tented the covers to facilitate his examination of this same patient.

"It's Tommy Thorpe. You treated me in Baltimore, two years ago."

"I remember, Tommy. How are you?"

"Fine, sir. Just fine."

Bruce recalled the case now, as clearly as though the Lakewood records were before him. His eyes dropped to Tommy's legs: the left, despite the boy's boast of good health, was thicker than the right. That same leg had been responsible for his setback after an appendectomy—and for his difficult convalescence. Today, the superficial veins were distended, a sure sign that some blockage still existed in the deep venous circulation.

Bruce had operated on Tommy Thorpe himself—removing a gangrenous, ruptured appendix almost piecemeal, and fighting hard to save the boy's life during the peritonitis that had followed. It had been days before the infection was controlled. Then, just as recovery had begun, he had been confronted with a fresh complication no surgeon can prevent—

the "milk leg" of thrombophlebitis, so called because it often occurred after childbirth.

He had used a new treatment, injecting the nerve ganglia bordering the spine in order to dilate the blood vessels. Immediate results had been dramatic, reducing the patient's hospitalization from weeks to days. Now, two years after Thorpe's discharge, some of the original complications had returned.

"How did you get in the Army?" The question had been automatic—and unnecessary. Captain Seward had provided the answer at lunch.

"Like everybody else, I was drafted."

"Did you pass the physical?"

"Not the first time, sir. When I came up again, new doctors were on the board. They said I was okay, and sent me to basic."

"Stand aside, Tommy. I'd like to examine you again."

The line came to an end five minutes later, and Bruce called his former patient to his booth. This time he went over the legs with the utmost care, measuring the circumference of each calf and finding that the left was three-quarters of an inch larger than the right. This, in itself, was damning evidence of abnormality. A first-year intern knew the left leg should be slightly smaller, since it was not used as much as the right.

"Has this condition troubled you lately?"

"I told you I feel fine, sir. Is anything wrong?"

"I can't say, on the evidence. You've had no discomfort since you came to Bruckner?"

"Only on the hike."

"What hike?"

"My company marched over a three-mile course this week, in full packs. I had some pain when we came back to barracks. It didn't seem serious. Just a little swelling and cramping. Lots of us were worse off."

"Did you report the discomfort?"

"I'm not a goldbrick. I want to sail with my outfit."

"I can't let you go, Tommy. Not until we've checked those veins that bothered you at Lakewood." Bruce turned to Seward—who had come over to seek the reason for the delay. "Will you confirm this diagnosis, Captain?"

While Seward was making his own evaluation, Bruce leafed through the book Pritchett had given him that morning. He had found what he wanted when Seward stepped out of the booth.

"What's your opinion, Major Graham?"

"I'd call it a case of chronic thrombophlebitis."

"It may well be."

Bruce opened the physical qualifications manual. "This man can't go overseas with such a disability. It's right here in the book. He shouldn't even be in the Army."

Seward drew a deep breath, and stared up at the rafters of the barn. "Do you stick to that diagnosis—and that decision?"

"Both are obvious."

"I'll have to take this up with Pritchett, you know."

"If he likes, I'll have the case history sent down from Baltimore."

"Just when did you operate?"

"Two years ago, give or take a month."

"Thorpe's general health seems excellent. Wouldn't he have had time to recover?"

"The veins are dilated, the leg's enlarged, and he has pain on walking. What else do we need?"

"Nothing—if you're trying to convince me. I'm thinking about the chief of the section."

"If he passes this one, we should take it to the CO."

"To Benson Britten? He wouldn't know a varicose vein from a thrombosed hemorrhoid. Even if he did, he'd back Pritchett."

"I'll defend my diagnosis before any board of inquiry."

"There's no need to be that drastic," said Seward. "Give

this man an appointment slip. Let him come back tomorrow, for a hospital checkup. It's the best we can do tonight."

"Shouldn't he go into the hospital right away?"

The older officer shook his head. Bruce knew that exasperation was fighting a losing battle with protocol in his mind. "Pritchett's the only one who can order a man hospitalized from a processing line—and he's already headed for the officers' bar. The record states that Thorpe's a company clerk. He won't suffer a relapse, if we wait until morning."

"I'd feel easier if he were off his feet."

"His outfit's been cleared for combat duty. If we can backstop your diagnosis tomorrow, it's possible Pritchett will let him stay behind. I doubt it."

"Is *nothing* simple in the Army?"

"Not when you measure civilian compassion against the need to win a war. Accept that inverted logic, if you can. It's essential to your survival."

"At least we've saved one soldier's life today by rejecting him."

"He isn't saved yet, Graham. Remember one thing more, while you're about it. If Thorpe escapes active duty, Pritchett will take credit for a master diagnosis in his next report. Can I buy you a drink? Or have you swallowed enough GI medicine for one day?"

Later, with the worst of his foreboding soothed by bourbon, Bruce left the lounge in response to a call from the BOQ veranda. A cream-white convertible had just swung to a stop before the building, with Congressman Harold Reardon at the wheel. The girl beside him—a dark-haired beauty as arresting as the car—wore a Red Cross uniform that was an austere contrast to her charms. Apparently, she was oblivious of the stares.

By the time he joined his visitors, Bruce had recovered his poise. When they had been classmates, Hal Reardon's genius for the unpredictable had been part of his panache.

It was like him to arrive at Camp Bruckner without warning—and to bring Janet Josselyn. . . . Bruce had recognized her promptly. The senator's daughter had been widely photographed since the war began.

"I'm glad we found you," said Hal. "Janet was afraid we'd need a search party."

He circled the car with hand outstretched—a rangy, aggressively handsome man of thirty who could still have passed for the star quarterback at his university. Here, Bruce thought, was an example of the vote-getter's ability to improvise, to extract drama from an unlikely occasion. Most civilians of Hal's age, surrounded by men in uniform, would have been ill at ease. Congressman Reardon could have passed for another officer in mufti for reasons of his own—a secret agent, perhaps, whose incognito must be respected.

"You'll remember Janet, from our last homecoming at Florida," he said. "Oddly enough, she remembers *you*—so I hope your ears are burning."

The girl had already given Bruce her hand. "We mustn't expect a busy doctor to reach back so far," she said. "Seven years are quite a gap—even though he did cut in three times."

Her handclasp had been cool but firm: like the perfume she was wearing, it had quickened memory instantly. "If you like," Bruce said, "I'll name the tunes."

"I dare you."

"The waltz was 'Wienerblut.' The fox trots were 'Lady, Be Good' and 'Stardust.'"

Congressman Reardon threw back his head in a roar of mirth. At the university, Hal had possessed a charming laugh: its timbre had ripened with the years.

"I told you the conquest was permanent, my dear. Hang up another scalp."

"Do you *really* remember, Major Graham?"

"I can even name the orchestra leader." Bruce hoped that his fumble at humor had saved him. There had been more truth than gallantry in his statement. The touch of Janet

Josselyn's hand had brought back a bunting-draped gymnasium brave with fraternity banners, a scoreboard uprooted from Fleming Field to celebrate a one-touchdown victory over Auburn. At that homecoming, the dance tunes had seemed to float down from the clouds—and Hal Reardon's date had burned an all-time image in his brain.

"Prove you mean it," said the girl. "Promise you'll come to Five Oaks this Sunday."

"An acceptance is in the mail, Miss Josselyn."

"The name is Janet. A man with your memory deserves a few shortcuts. Besides, Hal was right. I remember *you*, quite clearly. After your last cut-in, you promised to phone me, and never did. This is your chance to atone."

"I'll do my best to regain lost ground." Listening to Hal's description of the shortest route to Five Oaks, Bruce's thoughts moved on. His silence after the Homecoming Ball had been self-protection. As a student with years of apprentice work before him, Janet Josselyn was—quite obviously—beyond his grasp. Even without her commitment to Hal Reardon, he could hardly have risked falling in love with her. . . . The fact that the happenstance of war had brought her to the threshold of his Army barracks was hardly a cause for rejoicing—still less, a reason to hope that things had changed.

"Until Sunday, then?" said Janet.

"Until Sunday."

"You won't forget?"

Bruce emerged from his brooding, to take her hand a second time. "Of course I won't. Can't I give you two a drink?"

"The senator's expecting us for dinner," said Hal. "We stopped here for just one reason—to pin you down." He shook hands too, with the heartiness peculiar to politicians. "Remember my phone number, if you don't like the way the Army's treating you."

"I love the Army—and my love is returned."

"Hyperbole has its uses," said Hal. "Don't overdo it." He slid under the wheel of the convertible, with a casual wave that was half a salute. The gesture included the knot of envious men on the porch of the officers' club. Bruce was hardly surprised when several of them returned the salute, before the cream-white Jaguar roared toward the camp gate.

In the bar, Nick Denby took the stool next to Bruce. "A man who knows congressmen must have hidden charms," he said. "Why didn't you explain?"

"I didn't expect Hal to appear so soon."

"Having Janet Josselyn that close was more than most of us could bear. If *she's* on your side, I'll be careful to walk circles round you. Lucius Josselyn's an asset in any league."

"I've never met the senator."

"There's no need to be modest, Graham. Incidentally, there was a long-distance call for you while you were outside. I told them you'd call back."

Bruce rang the operator in the phone booth outside the lounge. He performed the act without conscious thought. In his mind's eye, he was still waltzing under the orange-and-blue banners of his university.

"Major Graham?"

"This is he."

"Major *Bruce* Graham? Surgeon U.S.A.? Are you still a man—and not two paragraphs I dreamed up over a gin rickey?"

"I'm quite real, Miss McLendon. Are you?"

"After a day in the Senate press gallery, I'm not at all sure. Did you see my column?"

"I did. In yesterday's *Star*."

"Does your pause indicate awe—or disapproval?"

"I liked it, Shane. May I call you Shane, now I'm one of your public?"

"Of course. I'm about to call you Bruce—now I see you've a sense of humor, as well as a sense of history."

"I'm afraid neither sense is working at the moment."

"Has the Army been that hard to take?"

"I'll answer when I've caught my breath." So far, he had been speaking at random. His encounter with Shane McLendon seemed part of another existence—and he had no true picture of the girl herself. Only the impish thrust of her mind was real. "How soon can we hold a second seminar?"

"How about Sunday afternoon?"

"Sunday's taken, I'm afraid."

"You can't be in the doghouse already. No one at Camp Bruckner works on weekends."

"As it happens, I'm lunching at Senator Josselyn's."

"So am I. Hal Reardon said he'd make sure you turned up."

"Do you know Hal?"

"Every reporter in Washington knows Congressman Reardon. He has perfect rapport with the press."

"May I ask how my name came up?"

"Night before last, Hal dropped into the city room of the *Star* while I was finishing my column. He saw your name in my notes—and decided you should be presented to society."

"Did you concur in that decision?"

"By and large, I trust Congressman Reardon's judgment."

Bruce hesitated, for no valid reason. It was logical that Hal should meet a syndicated reporter in a Washington city room—and even more natural that the reporter should appear at a senator's house on Sunday. Nevertheless, he felt his reply would be a new commitment, whose result he could not see clearly.

"I'll look forward to our second meeting," he said at last. "This time, I'll omit my lecture on the war."

"Say what you like, Bruce. I may have my faults, but I'll never misquote you."

"Is that a firm promise?"

"If you'll promise me something in return. Don't fall in love with the senator's daughter too soon."

"Why should I fall in love with Janet Josselyn?"

"Because it's the thing to do this year," said Shane.

The receiver clicked before he could frame an answer.

It was nearly noon when Bruce received his summons to Pritchett's office. As usual, the perpetually scowling captain was fenced in with paper barricades. This time, his response to the surgeon's salute was made with textbook punctilio. Bruce noted that Tommy's service record was on the blotter.

"This man was tentatively rejected yesterday," Pritchett said. "Can you explain it?"

"My report's in the folder, Captain." Bruce was careful to keep his voice mild. "As you see, I've requested permission to confirm my findings with a checkup."

"Go on, please."

"Two years ago, Private Thorpe had a severe case of peritonitis while he was under my care. It was followed by thrombophlebitis of the left leg. I'm reasonably certain there's still active inflammation in the vein."

"Are you basing this opinion on what you saw on the processing line?"

Futile though it was to repeat facts already in his report, Bruce forced himself to continue. "My diagnosis is based mainly on prior knowledge of the patient's condition."

Pritchett dropped the paper he was studying, and passed both hands over his plump features. His scowl had vanished when he stared up into the surgeon's eyes—but it was evident his patience was only skin-deep.

"Your lack of experience with draftees is vast, Major," he said. "You simply can't depend on what they tell you. This soldier's general health is excellent. He went through basic without reporting sick. Now, out of the blue, he asks to be disqualified."

"It was I who disqualified him."

"Is there a significant difference in the size of his legs?"

"Nearly an inch—and the superficial veins are dilated. Add

that to the swelling after Thorpe's hike. As a surgeon, I'd call the prognosis ominous."

"I'm a surgeon myself—and I disagree completely. This man has invented an excuse to escape combat assignment. I can't permit you to swallow his story."

"I'm sure my opinion will be confirmed by a X-ray venogram."

"If Thorpe is rejected, we'll have to fill his place from station personnel. The man we call up will probably write to his congressman—and we'll get hell from the War Department."

"I'll disqualify Thorpe personally, if that will help."

"Because you remember him from civilian life? That would make the matter worse. I'm going to give you a chance to cancel this rejection." Pritchett tossed a red pencil on the blotter. "Write 'error' through your report, then sign your name. We'll overlook your mistaken kindness."

Bruce felt his temper snap at last. "My rejection stands as written. Thorpe should never have been passed by his draft board. *That's* the only error to be corrected."

"Are you forcing me to report you for insubordination?"

"I don't give a damn what you report. The man's unfit for service. If he goes overseas, you'll send him—not me."

Back on the processing line, Bruce worked grimly for the next half hour. Seward, he knew, had read Pritchett's verdict in his manner. There was no chance to confirm that reading until the luncheon break.

"I could have told you his answer this morning," said the older officer. "I wasn't sure you'd believe me."

"What's my next move?"

"You haven't any. Request for review has been denied by higher authority."

"Pritchett threatened to report me. Do you think he'll do it?"

"It's quite likely. Calvin the Great is sure of his ground now. His promotion's just come through."

"Making that lame-brain a *major?*"

"A major, no less—and chief of our surgical service."

"There must be something I can do."

"We've been over that, Graham. It's a hard lesson, but you'll have to accept it."

That same evening, a look at the next day's orders confirmed Seward's news. Captain Calvin Pritchett, MC, had just been promoted to major, with assignment as chief of the surgical service at the station hospital. Two paragraphs down, Bruce read—with relief—that the new major had been granted a week's leave.

He was still staring blankly at the order sheet when the assistant chief of the medical service joined him at the bulletin board. Captain Leibowitz was a highly-trained internist who had brought his reputation from a famous New York hospital. Bruce had heard that both the work and the personnel in his section were outstanding.

"Don't look so stricken, Major," said the internist. "It nauseates *me*, but I can control my feelings."

"I'm still coming up for air."

"The pathologist's doing a PM in the dispensary. Want to have a look?"

"I'd like to, for a change of pace."

Part of the dispensary had been turned into a makeshift post-mortem room. That evening, it was filled with officers. Because of an impending troop shipment, the post had been restricted—and examinations of this sort were not too frequent at Bruckner. Captain Hartmann, the director of laboratories and the station's acting pathologist, stood at the head of the autopsy table. The body was still under a sheet when Bruce sat down between Seward and Leibowitz. Minutes later, an orderly whisked the covering aside to reveal Tommy Thorpe.

"Something wrong, Major?" the pathologist asked.

"I know that boy. He was a patient of mine at Lakewood. Only yesterday, I examined him in the processing shed."

Hartmann, a white-haired doctor whose precise manner was part of his system of authority, was obviously nettled by this meaningless interruption. He spoke with his eyes on the body. "This is a case of sudden death, gentlemen. It occurred near the end of a special exercise—"

"Was he admitted to the hospital?" Bruce asked.

"No, Major. He was reported DOA at the dispensary. Lieutenant Drane is his battalion surgeon. He'll give us the particulars."

Drane, still in sweat-dark fatigues, rose from a bench across the room. "Thorpe's duties with our outfit were largely clerical. Yesterday we learned he'd never been through the obstacle course. He took it this noon. Part of the exercise involved a hike through a tidal marsh, under full equipment—"

"Did he tell you he wasn't fit?" Bruce asked.

"This soldier never complained, Major." Like the pathologist, the battalion surgeon seemed confused by the interruption. "Toward the end, I noticed he was limping. He dropped in his tracks—and was dead before I could reach him. The incident was reported to the provost marshal, who ordered this post-mortem."

Hartmann had already reached for a short, thick-bladed autopsy knife. "When the young die unexpectedly, it's sometimes hard to determine the cause," he said. "This could be such a case."

Bruce stepped into the cleared space around the table. "I can tell you the cause of his death, Captain."

About to make his first massive incision, the pathologist paused with the scalpel in mid-air. "We're always glad to have an officer's opinion, Major. But—"

"This is a fact, not an opinion. Private Thorpe died of a pulmonary embolism."

Hartmann put down the knife, as a murmur of laughter

spread through the crowded room. "Isn't that going pretty far out?"

"I know this boy's case history. May I have the floor?"

"It seems you have it now."

Bruce faced the assembly. Now that impulse had taken him into the spotlight, he could hesitate no longer.

"Two years ago, Private Thorpe was my patient at Lakewood. Thrombophlebitis developed in his left leg, following the removal of a ruptured appendix. Eventually we dismissed him, hoping the vascular condition was cured. Yesterday, I met him on the processing line. I found there was still marked dilation of superficial veins of the left leg—which was well over a half-inch thicker than the right."

"He never complained," said the battalion surgeon.

"I'm sure he didn't. He wanted to go into combat."

"Is that all, Major?" Hartmann asked.

"Not quite. I was virtually certain Private Thorpe still had a low-grade inflammatory process in the deep veins. I requested admission to the station hospital, and X-ray venograms to confirm my findings. Captain—now Major—Pritchett over-ruled my request. The result is before you."

Silence had long since filled the room. Bruce swept on, before the pathologist could interrupt. "What happened today should be clear. The obstacle hike was more than enough to cause a flare-up. A clot formed in one of the deep veins—if it wasn't there already. Part of it traveled to the lungs as an embolus, causing death."

This time, a hum of voices filled the room as Bruce turned back to his seat. Drane's own voice, rising above the others, nailed him in his tracks.

"None of this appears on Thorpe's record, Major."

The battalion surgeon handed the papers across the table—complete with tally sheet, marked with clearances from each section of the camp that had prepared Tommy's unit for overseas. All qualifications—from quartermaster to ordnance—had been met. Each was described, in the dust-dry prose of the Army. Private Thorpe had been cleared for shipment, save for the obstacle course. The physical examination section, at the top of the first sheet, contained no mention of abnormality.

How—Bruce wondered blankly—had Pritchett managed it? A second look suggested the answer. Since a soldier's physical condition was the first item checked while he was preparing for active duty, a new tally had apparently been filled in at the processing center, where Pritchett's rule was supreme. It would have been a simple matter to discard Bruce's notes. Pritchett himself had probably typed the new sheet—omitting the reasons for Tommy's rejection, along with the request for a transfer to the hospital.

The surgeon turned to Seward—who had been a poker-faced observer throughout the discussion—then faced back to Hartmann with a shrug. Seward was a capable administrator. Now that Pritchett had moved up, he would be next in line as chief of the medical processing section, with inevitable promotion of his own in store. None of this would happen if he were asked to rise in defense of a brand-new officer who had spoken out of turn.

"Don't ask me how this record was cleared, Lieutenant Drane," Bruce said slowly. "I can assure you that I rejected this soldier yesterday. This morning, I told Major Pritchett I would stand or fall on the results of a hospital checkup. Now, since the pathologist's is always the final diagnosis, I'll rest my case on Captain Hartmann's findings."

It was a daring move—but the cul-de-sac he had entered allowed him no other option. Bruce was sure each man in the room understood the risk he was taking—and had decided he was a little mad. . . . Ten minutes later, the autopsy knife had told the story. Like so many revelations in medicine, it was something of an anticlimax, though it supported his remarks fully. The pulmonary artery, leading to the lower lobe of the right lung, had been blocked by a massive clot or embolus, accounting for Private Thorpe's abrupt death. The source of the clot was revealed in a deep vein of the left calf, where inflammation had thickened the vessel down most of its length.

"The case is closed, gentlemen," said the pathologist. "Major Graham is thanked for his statement—but the record stands as written. Is there further comment?"

No one spoke as the autopsy room emptied. When the surgeon turned away from the table, he saw that Seward had been one of the first men through the door, with Nick Denby not far behind.

Bruce knew that Pritchett was disliked in their section; by now, he had learned enough of Army life to expect no bouquets for his stand at the post-mortem. He had hardly expected to be treated like a self-confessed leper in the days that followed. . . . Eventually, he stopped Denby in an empty corner of the cantonment.

"It seems I've become an untouchable," he said. "Is there any hope left for me?"

"You're old enough to answer that one before it's asked, Bruce."

"Don't call me Bruce, if you're part of the wolf pack."

"There's no wolf pack—except in your mind."

"Then why have I been ostracized?"

"The officers in this complement are obeying the law of self-preservation. Your diagnosis was brilliant. All of us loved the way you damned Calvin the Great. But you're still due to get the ax. We see no point in bleeding too."

"Pritchett's won. Why should he hit me again?"

"Because it's the Army way. You went out on a limb. You can't sit there indefinitely. Don't ask me who will saw it off. Just be damned sure it's coming."

That afternoon, when Bruce had finished his stint in the processing shed, Seward called him into the office he occupied as Pritchett's successor.

"I'm sure you blame me for sitting tight at the PM," he

said. "Believe me, I had no way of improving matters. I had a fast look at Drane's file before you sounded off. There was no chance to warn you."

"How did Pritchett swing it?"

"I had a fair notion—but I couldn't be sure until I'd taken over here. The sergeant thought you might be interested in this relic." Seward spread a crumpled paper on the desk—a processing sheet, with the physical-examination section at the top filled in and the rest of the space blank. Bruce's rejection was plainly visible, though the word *canceled* had been scrawled across it in red ink and signed by Pritchett. It was evident that the CO's nephew had decided later to discard the sheet entirely and type a brand-new form.

"Put this in your private file," said Seward. "You may find you can use it later."

Bruce folded the crumpled sheet into his wallet. "When will the next blow fall?"

"It's fallen in today's orders. Your copy's in your mailbox."

Seward tossed the flimsy sheets across the desk. The mimeographed list was lengthy, thanks to preparations for a shipment that would arrive that night from Baltimore. Bruce's name sprang out of the smudged type:

MAJ BRUCE GRAHAM 0-270106 MC IS RELIEVED FROM TDY POE AND IS ASSIGNED TO 922 TSU TC SHIP HOSPITAL PLATOON WP RUAT CO ACCORDINGLY NO TVL INVOLVED
                              EDCMR 3 AUG 42

"As cryptograms go," he said, "this one isn't too enlightening."

"The essentials are on the line," said Seward. "You're booked for an Atlantic cruise."

"How soon?"

"Whenever the next ship platoon shapes up here. It could happen in ten days. Maybe sooner."

"I still can't believe the Army wants me sorting mail in England."

"Britten does, and that's what matters here."

"There *must* be better work available."

"You won't find it at Bruckner. I can guarantee that."

"What would you suggest I do?"

"Think of every friend you have in court, and start bucking for other duty. Meanwhile, you're back in the officers' pool—but you won't be inactive long. Denby's always asking for extra help in his lab. He can use another hand."

Major Nicholas Denby's lair in the BOQ, though it was no more spacious than Bruce's own quarters, had an air of permanence. The armchair and reading lamp, the bookcase that hid a bar, suggested that this nomad's cell was also an island of repose. The urologist received his newest assistant with a firm handshake, and closed the door behind him.

"Relax in the seat of honor," he said. "Now that we're behind locked portals, can I offer you bourbon, Scotch, or gin-and-splash?"

"At this moment, I need information more than alcohol. Where do I really stand?"

"Seward must have explained why your number's up."

"Is there an outside chance I still might get a decent assignment here?"

"Not after what you've done to Calvin Pritchett," said Denby. "The Army takes care of its own."

"It slipped up badly on Tommy Thorpe."

"Thorpe was a victim of the system. His people will be told he died in line of duty—and his next-of-kin will collect ten thousand dollars insurance. Just as though he'd been killed in action."

"Pritchett killed that boy."

"Maybe so, the way it looks to you now. Every day in the year, we admit psychopaths to this hospital—because we can't be sure whether their neurosis is real, or the fast pulse that comes with fright. I spend half my time deciding the fate of deviants, and zombies who can't wait to start bleeding the taxpayer. You can't brand a processing officer as a murderer, just because he's hard *and* stupid."

"Pritchett has no right to call himself a doctor. I tried to save a man's life, and got the shaft for my pains."

"So you did. The classic Army shaft, in the classic spot. What's more, you deserved it—by Army standards."

"For telling the truth?"

"For applying the yardstick of absolute justice to a single case, in a single staging area."

"Then you condone the Pritchetts and their ways?"

"Far from it—but we must still admit they exist. Eventually, our service will do its job. The United States will take care of Germany and Japan, and Pritchett will be slapped down to size. Just as *you'll* find your level, when you get through sorting mail."

"I'd have been far more useful teaching surgery at Lakewood."

"Maybe—but the fact remains you asked for a part in this show. You're in the MC now—signed up for the duration. You'll be a lot more useful to the Army if you'll begin accepting things as they are, not as you'd like them to be."

Bruce settled in the armchair—and grinned wanly, despite the violence of his feelings. "What's my first step toward reality?"

"Your first step's obvious. Start pulling wires to break your present bind."

"Seward gave me the same advice. Where do I begin?"

"At one spot in our service that's run with real logic. The SGO."

"Where was the Surgeon General's Office when Britten put me in the officers' pool? When he assigned me to a ship's platoon?"

"The SGO is doing all it can to find the best jobs for its best doctors. It can't do much to improve politics in this way station. Bastards like the Great Calvin can get appointed chief of surgery—and a Lakewood specialist may be shipped to an Army Post Office in England. Idealists of your build will *always* get the shaft at the Camp Bruckners—until they learn to fight back. No army could function on a different system."

"You'll admit the system's unfair?"

"It's damned unfair—and, in this case, inevitable. We had a fine chief of surgery at the station before you arrived. A man named Bob Anders, a hot-shot organizer. He shipped out with the last convoy, to a special hospital assignment in London. Bob had the right pipelines open, and figured he'd be more useful elsewhere. As things stand today, we're only a clearinghouse for cannon fodder. It will be a different story when the reverse flow starts, and we become a debarkation center for wounded—"

"After a European front is opened?"

"When *that* day dawns over Maryland, our three-thousand-bed station will be humming like a beehive. We'll need a surgical chief who really knows his job. In my opinion, the SGO sent you here to organize for that emergency. In other words, to take Bob Anders' place."

"Then why didn't Britten give me the assignment?"

"Because you arrived in the middle of a conspiracy to get the job for his fair-haired nephew. Like the body in a whodunit, you had to be buried somewhere—so Britten put you in the officers' pool. No one would have noticed you thereafter, if you hadn't spoken out of turn about a disabled Pfc, an act that jeopardized Pritchett's advancement. As a consequence, you're about to be buried even deeper."

"Obviously, I must complain to the SGO direct."

"The complaint will be stronger if it comes through channels. Can you go to your professor at Lakewood?"

"I'm afraid not. He was pretty sore when I appealed my deferment. I was slated to begin a special project in the fall."

Denby frowned at his glass. "Something about heart valves, if I remember the literature."

"Schoenfeld hopes to develop workable surgical procedures for children with congenital deformities. Things like the Tetralogy of Fallot and patent septum. It's his lifework."

"No wonder he needed your help," said Denby. "In any case, it's safer to leave him unmentioned, after the part he played in Spain."

"Abram Schoenfeld's a scientist. He had no political leanings when he took us to Barcelona."

"Right or wrong, Jake Sanford called him a Communist on the front page—so you'll have to skip him. Would anyone else at Lakewood go to bat for you?"

"Actually, there's no one I'd care to ask. Since I got my residency, my real work's been with Schoenfeld."

"What about your family?"

"I'm a literal orphan. The day I entered Lakewood, I cut my ties back home."

"You didn't cut them all," said Denby. "What about Reardon? Or the senator's daughter?"

"Hal and I have been out of touch for years. I hardly know Janet Josselyn."

"Either of them could rescue you with a phone call."

"It doesn't seem fair to ask their help. I talked my way into this jam. It's up to me to fight my way out."

"You'll never swing it alone."

"Perhaps I deserve to suffer for a while, as you suggested. I won't die sorting mail."

The urologist tossed up his hands. "Get down from that pedestal, and stop moaning. It's chore enough, explaining life to an idealist. I refuse to coddle a Christian martyr."

Bruce crossed to the hidden bar and poured from the first bottle. The bite of the bourbon eased the band that had formed round his mind while he had absorbed Denby's lecture.

"Perhaps I can get my orders changed to stay on as your assistant," he said.

"You could do worse, at that. This billet has its points, when you compare it to other Army jobs. I see my wife two weekends out of four—and there's enough elbowroom to let me breathe. I've even had time to prove you aren't the only brain at Bruckner. If the end product fulfills my hopes, I'll get my own pair of silver leaves."

"Is this Nicholas Denby speaking? The cynic and clap-doctor? Or do you change character at sundown, like Mr. Hyde and Dr. Jekyll?"

"It's the same clap-doctor—and the same cut-rate cynic. The fact that I'm an urologist produced this research. Troops waiting to be shipped out are primed for a farewell binge. Early in the game, we learned that each time we turned them loose we could expect a near-epidemic of gonorrhea before the week was out."

"What is your discovery? Chastity belts?"

"The next best thing. Sulfadiazine is a pretty specific antidote for the old *Diplococcus Neisser*. I advised the battalion surgeons to pour a gram into each GI before he went on pass—and another gram when he returned. Not a single case was reported afterwards. Except in a few platoons, when the medics couldn't stand over their men to make sure they swallowed the tablets."

"It sounds like a workable therapy. Like most great ideas, it's simple enough."

"Simple, and effective—but there's one angle I still haven't licked. The randier draftees don't like the idea of medication. They're sure it cuts down on their potency."

"Are the fears justified?"

"Only in their minds. While we're discussing sex, you needn't sign in with me until tomorrow. Take my jeep and find yourself a girl. There's nothing like a hayroll to get your mind off the high cost of integrity."

"With or without sulfadiazine?"

"Skip the pills until morning," said Denby. "When you're low man on a totem pole, you need all your strength."

Bruce did not follow the urologist's advice. Instead, he went to bed and slept until mess call. As Denby had intimated, his duties on the GU service were not too heavy. There was time to spare for his problems before Sunday—but he was no nearer a solution when he drove a rented car toward Annapolis, and Senator Josselyn's open house.

He had taken a longer road than the one Hal had suggested, hoping the lush Maryland countryside would soothe his troubled soul. When the prescription failed, he picked up the first route number that led to his destination. Five Oaks, the estate the senator had rented to escape the summer heat of Washington, was a show place of the Severn Valley: from its sculptured boxwoods to the sprays of Cape jasmine on its tall east portico, it might have been lifted bodily from the Old Confederacy.

Today, Bruce saw that it was a proper setting for the senator's open house. A graveled drive led in from the road, skirting acres of velvet lawn that swept to the river's edge. A marquee had been set up for refreshments. A jazz combo (its name was a household word on radio) supplied the music for a score of couples swaying like contented sardines on a flagstone dance floor above the senator's boat dock—and four hundred other guests were scattered like bright butterflies on the greensward.

Entering the turnaround beside the house, the newcomer found himself surrounded by ranks of parked cars, most of them bearing the stars of general officers or the pennons of the diplomatic corps. When he saw the attendant was busy, Bruce maneuvered his own car until the nose was pointed toward the exit. Needless though it was, the act of securing his retreat was a soothing prelude.

At Camp Bruckner he had looked forward to this change of scene; now that this first glimpse had fulfilled his expectations, he felt a strange reluctance to mingle with the Josselyns' guests. If he could believe Nick Denby, a ready-made deliverance awaited him on that immaculate lawn. A few steps would take him to Hal Reardon's side: he had already spied Hal among the boxwoods, deep in talk with an admiral. Or he could appeal to his host direct: Josselyn, a lion-maned lawgiver whose profile would not have disgraced a Caesar, was receiving guests on the portico, and the daughter who stood beside him was a young man's wish come true.

Was it the very perfection of the gathering that disturbed him, the feeling that each actor was ready to perform his role? Was the moment almost too well-suited to his purpose? Like some latter-day Faust, was he about to ask help of the devil, certain the help would be forthcoming at the risk of his soul?

The questions, Bruce knew, were absurd: it was time to step out of the rented sedan and remember his company manners. Yet he continued to linger on the turnaround—while he reappraised his motives in coming here, along with his reluctance to go farther.

Nick Denby had suggested that his first contact with the Army was also his first moment of truth. He could hardly deny that his life up to now, save for the rigors of medical school, had been a sheltered one. So far, each step of his career had *happened*, with no need for Bruce Graham to assert his rights. Because of his surgeon's gift, and the doors that gift had opened, his march toward his goal had been made without setback. Not once—until this collision with Pritchett—had he been forced to ask favors.

In the Tampa suburb where he had been raised, he had been a normal son of normal parents. His father, a Southern gentleman whose ancestors had come from Virginia to Florida with the first railroad, had taught mathematics in a local high school. His mother had been a Yankee whose common sense had saved him from accepting too many family myths. Halfway through the state university, their passing had made him an early orphan, but sorrow had left no lasting scar.

His sights had already been trained on a surgical career, and he had been among the most single-minded members of his class. Premed at Florida had left little time for undergraduate escapades, though a talent for broken-field running had made him a varsity end, earned him a pin at Sigma Nu, and established friendships with such campus gods as Hal Reardon. . . . At Lakewood, the compulsions of his calling had absorbed him from his first lecture. The endless drudgery of internship had been part of a novitiate, a necessary price he was glad to pay for a degree in medicine from the country's finest school.

The honors he had won with his diploma and his residency, the appointment to work with Schoenfeld, had come just as naturally. The great heart specialist had urged him to serve his country at Lakewood rather than in uniform. Perhaps there had been logic in that argument. Today—as he continued to linger on the Josselyn driveway—he could ask himself if his response to Pearl Harbor Sunday had been his first true blunder.

He could not regret the commitment, even now: his deepest instincts assured him that this urge to break out of a hospital cloister had been sound. Another, no less profound instinct had forced him to challenge Major Calvin Pritchett. Now that he had dared to defy a system of authority that had erased a human life, now that he had failed to save Tommy Thorpe, expiation might well be in order. Was it fate, rather than Colonel Britten's nepotism, that was sending him to this tour of duty with a ship's platoon?

Even now, there was time to slip away before his presence was noticed—to let fate decide where he could serve best. . . . His hand was on the ignition switch when he heard a girl's voice call his name. A moment later, Shane McLendon sank into the seat beside him.

"I *thought* you were about to drive off."

"I was toying with the idea."

"Where would Scotland be today, if Robert the Bruce had obeyed that same impulse at Bannockburn?"

"How did you know I'd arrived?"

"I gave the car-park two dollars to alert me," said Shane. "When I saw you were fiddling with your ignition, I came on the run."

"If I tell you my reason, will you keep it to yourself?"

"I know your reason. Having glimpsed your hostess from afar, you hesitate to venture closer. You're afraid you'll ignite a king-sized torch for her. The same torch you snuffed out after a Homecoming Ball at Florida."

"Were *you* at that homecoming too?"

"Of course I wasn't," said Shane. "This has happened so often, I know the routine by heart. Every time I see a man worth taking trouble over, he falls for Janet. Granted, not all of them are quite as leery as you." She nodded toward the portico, where the senator and his daughter, still in the act of receiving guests, made a striking pair. "Observe the all-American beauty. Rich, powerful—and nice as the girl next door. How can a scrawny redhead like me compete?"

"You don't sound too envious."

"I learned long ago to make do with what I have," said Shane. "Besides, I happen to like Janet. Leery or not, I don't think it's fair of you to leave her party. The problems of unrequited love can always be handled out of court. Right now, your troubles with the Army are more important."

"How did you learn about my troubles?"

"This morning, I remembered you didn't have a car—and phoned to offer you a ride here. You'd already left, but a Major Denby answered. He told me an interesting story."

"Not for publication, I hope."

"Definitely not for publication. American parents have enough to worry about these days. I don't intend to raise doubts in their mind about Army doctors."

"Do you blame me for talking back to Pritchett?"

"In your place, I'd have shot him."

"That would hardly have solved the problem."

"There's an easier solution—standing on the portico of Five Oaks."

"Senator Josselyn?"

"Lucius represents your state. He's supposed to lend a hand when a constituent gets a dirty deal."

"I can hardly ask *him* to get me off the hook."

"You needn't be that direct," said Shane. "In your place, I'd take Janet aside, tell her the whole story—and let her carry on from there. She'd love it."

"Just for my own information, are you throwing our hostess at my head because you want Hal for yourself?"

"What a nasty mind you have, Bruce. Where did you learn to think like a woman?"

"I've had quite a few women patients. And I'm asking no favors of Janet Josselyn. The whole idea strikes me as vaguely immoral."

"I expected that reaction," said Shane. "That's why I spoke to Hal Reardon."

"About *me?*"

"The SGO will get a call tomorrow. If the right man's at this party, your troubles will be over even sooner."

"You might have waited to consult me."

"Only to have you turn noble and say no? Like it or not, these people can do you good. Or would you rather turn mouse again—and run back to your lab?"

Shane left the car on that ultimatum, to move down the driveway as rapidly as she had arrived. Shocked into motion at last, Bruce overtook her on the path that led to the portico.

"Don't get your Irish up, McLendon," he said. "You must know I appreciate your efforts."

"Does that mean you'll let me follow through?"

"If you'll let me thank you for the helping hand. Am I forgiven?"

Shane turned to study him, with the intentness he remembered from their first encounter. The anger died in her gray-green eyes, and her lips relaxed in a smile—the gamine's grin that made her seem almost pretty.

"Let's say you're on probation, Bruce. We Irish don't give in all at once. First, I'll introduce you to the senator—then we'll head for the buffet. I'm hungry."

A press of new arrivals surrounded their host on the portico—but Janet had just moved away, to mingle with the dancers at the river's edge. Bruce was tempted to bypass this ritual meeting and follow her: the fact that their arms were linked kept him at the journalist's side until they joined the group on the steps. . . . At close quarters, the senator was still the elder statesman of legend, more presence than man. There was no resisting his charm when he held out his hand after Shane's presentation.

"I can't meet too many friends of Hal Reardon's, Major. There's no better man in the House today."

"So I've been informed, sir."

"I've watched every step of his career—and guided some of them. Gave him his first job in Washington, as my secretary. Even in those days, I expected him to succeed me." Josselyn's laughter was part of his orator's poise: the conventional aside might have been addressed to a multitude. "As a classmate, I'm sure you've kept in touch."

"Not too closely, I'm afraid. It's good to know Hal has your confidence."

"Don't fail to ask our advice, if you need help."

"You're most kind, sir."

"After all, it's why I'm here. Right, Shane?"

Bruce was careful to remain silent in the exchange between politician and journalist. As a guest at Five Oaks, he could hardly confess that he had voted at least once for Josselyn's Republican rival. He had not expected to chat so long in the impromptu receiving line. Evidently, with a columnist as his sponsor, his host had decided he was worth extra attention.

"I'll trust your instinct, Shane," the senator boomed. "Introduce Major Graham to the proper people."

"The proper people, Lucius? Or the *right* people?"

"You know which are which, my dear." Josselyn put a paternal hand on Bruce's shoulder. "Give me a ring for lunch when you're in Washington. Where are you stationed?"

"At Camp Bruckner, sir."

"In that case, you'll have time for Hal as well. I'm sure you've a great deal to talk about."

Crossing the lawn, pausing to bow to dowagers and shake hands with gold-braided rulers from all the services, Bruce continued to admire Shane's dialogues with these potentates. When they broke free at last, at the edge of the marquee, the scene before them summed up the Josselyns' open house and its purpose. The long tables that held the buffet, the swarm of waiters shuttling between chefs and barmen, were far removed from a battlefield. Only the well-tailored uniforms were a reminder that this, too, was a gathering of warriors—who had won the right to feast here, untroubled by such items as casualty lists or ration points.

"Look between the tomato aspic and the Smithfield ham," said Shane. "You'll have a clear view of Congressman Reardon."

"The *last* time I saw Hal, he was talking with an admiral."

"This time, it's Admiral Munger," said the journalist. "He'll join us—after he's reassured the Navy on appropriations." She led the way to a scattering of tables above the river—and signaled to a bar waiter. "I'm hoping he'll have good news for you. In any case, I'd suggest that you dance with your hostess—the moment you can get near her. What are you drinking? Bourbon, or a martini?"

"A martini. Any other instructions?"

"I think not. You can handle yourself—if you don't let your suspicions show too plainly. They're out of place this Sunday afternoon."

The cocktails, when they came, were ice-cold and bone-dry.

Bruce studied his companion across his glass. Her eyes were everywhere, as she greeted still other guests—yet he knew he was still under surveillance.

"Don't let me keep you, if you have a story to write," he said.

The gray-green eyes returned to his face, full-strength. "Watching the great at play is my way of unwinding," Shane said. "Tomorrow's column's as good as written."

"Do you enjoy this kind of party?"

"Extremely—if I don't get too involved. It seems to have a reverse effect on you."

"I'm beginning to feel acclimatized."

"Were you really a friend of Hal's at college?"

"Not too close, if the truth must be told."

"I suspected as much. You were roommates in your senior year. He told me that much."

"I was one of four—in a suite in Buckman Hall. We were in the same fraternity, and played football together. I can't say we saw eye-to-eye too often. Even then, we were aimed at different targets. I never thought we'd meet like this."

"War makes strange bedfellows," said Shane. "How well do you know his background?"

"Enough to wonder a little, sometimes."

"Go on."

"His grandfathers were among the ten richest men in the South. Hal Reardon Senior was a kingmaker when I was growing up in Tampa. Even then, he was grooming his only son for politics. That's why Hal attended the state university, instead of going Ivy League. It was part of the pattern, to establish local contacts. He balanced it later with a law degree from Harvard."

"Do you object to law degrees from Harvard?"

"Of course I don't—but my point is valid. Hal's yet to make a wrong move on the campaign trail. He was our youngest Democrat to go to Congress. Senator Josselyn's in his camp, of course—he owes *his* career to Reardon money. Eventually, as he told us, Hal will take his seat. If his foot doesn't slip, he'll marry the senator's daughter, and aim ever higher—"

"And you object to this success story?"

"I'm not objecting. I'm stating the facts, as I see them. Since our freshman year, I've watched him switch on the charm, as easily as most people open faucets—"

"Charm's a rare quality in our culture," said Shane. "Don't sell it short."

"Perhaps I'm old-fashioned, but I think statesmen should be born, not made—like poets and philosophers. Too many American politicians seem built on a blueprint. I can't help feeling my fraternity brother's been turned into a vote-getter—just as you'd train a race horse, or a big-league shortstop."

"How can we drive the rascals out—if our best people don't go into politics?"

"Assuming the Reardons *are* the best people—not just the richest."

"Look at Hal's record. No one has done more for his state, or the war."

"He isn't in the Army."

"He holds a commission in the Reserve. He plans to see action later. The President himself asked him to stay in Washington."

"As the next step in the success story?"

"Why not—if he's pulling his weight?" Shane reached for a cigarette: she seemed more exasperated than angry. Offering his lighter, Bruce was surprised to note that his plate was empty: he had no idea what he had eaten. . . . His argument, he knew, had been fought on losing ground. The journalist, not he, had reason on her side.

"Don't think I'm impugning Hal's patriotism," he said carefully. "If what you say is true, he can help far more in Congress."

"His motives are his own—and they're sound ones."

"Are you in love with him?"

Shane's eyes had clouded at the thrust. "Most men ask me that question, when we discuss Hal Reardon."

"Do you know me well enough to answer it?"

"I could be in love with him—strange as it may seem to you."

"It doesn't seem strange at all."

Again, he watched the slow, off-center smile transform her features. "I could also be fighting the impulse."

"Because you half-agree with what I've said? Because you want to stay uncommitted awhile longer?"

"Perhaps I realize that his marriage to Janet is an essential steppingstone in his career. I may even think enough of them both to wish them well."

"Yet you urge *me* to fall in love with her. Is that a fair example of feminine logic?"

"Call it another proof that I play the angles," said Shane. "Here comes Hal now. Shall we see who's the best judge of character?"

Congressman Reardon's progress toward the table had been interrupted by an ambassador Bruce recognized from his photographs—and by a Cabinet member who had made headlines by hinting he would resign his post if a second front in Europe remained unopened by summer's end. Hal's style, on both occasions, had been a blend of complete attention and sunny good humor. It was not the first time Bruce had seen his classmate's empathy in action.

"Janet was afraid you couldn't make it," Hal said. "I told her Shane had you in tow."

The journalist rose briskly. "I've been teaching him the techniques of survival. You may be a better instructor. Besides, it's time I cornered a few prospects, in case I run out of copy."

Hal chuckled as he took the vacant chair. "Say what you like about the fourth estate, Bruce. Shane gets results with a minimum of bother."

"Apparently she put you to work in my behalf—"

"Why didn't you tell me you were in hot water, when we stopped at your BOQ?"

"At the time, the water wasn't boiling."

"Nuisances like Britten and Pritchett should be clobbered before they cause trouble," said Hal. "Obviously, the first order of business is an assignment worthy of your talents. Larry Wilson was here a little earlier. He handles procurement at the Surgeon General's Office. When their planning miscarries, Larry can be a rigorous administrator. He'll take care of your problem, now I've put a bug in his ear."

"Did it occur to you to wait—until I had a chance to discuss the situation?"

"No discussion's needed, Bruce. A routine mistake will be corrected—and another martinet and his nephew will have their ears pinned back."

"Did it also occur to you I might prefer to complain in person?"

"The thought crossed my mind," said Hal. "Larry will move faster, now he's had word from me."

"What happens if I refuse Colonel Wilson's help?"

"It's too late to refuse. You stopped being your own boss when you put on a uniform."

"That doesn't mean I have to take orders from you."

"Apparently you still wear a hair shirt under that handsome blouse." Hal Reardon's mouth had tightened briefly, before his mask fell into place again. "You're a good man in a strange world, Bruce. Like other good men, your naïveté is exceeded only by your ingratitude."

"I didn't mean to sound ungrateful."

"Inchworms like Colonel Britten, and his fathead nephew, abound in all public enterprises. Including the one we're launching now to save the world. It's your duty and mine to smoke them out."

"So I've been rescued—and the war effort's been furthered too. I'm not sure I like the way you do business."

"It's the way things are done here—whether you like it or not." Hal's flash of impatience was less than a memory now: his bounding good humor had returned full force. "As favors go, this was a small one. I don't even expect to be thanked."

"I'd feel better if I could even the score."

"I'll settle for the renewal of a friendship," said Hal. "It's been in the doldrums far too long."

"Are you sure you don't want something in return?" The query, Bruce knew, had been graceless, almost rude. He could not regret it, as he sat back to await Hal's reaction. His classmate shrugged, and turned toward the terrace, which was still packed with dancers. The combo had just muted its horns, to beat out a *pianissimo* chorus of a song that had taken the airwaves by storm. The leader, a slender Negro with an attractive air of bashfulness, was crooning the lyric, in a baritone almost as famous as the President's:

> *Don't sit under the apple tree*
> *With anyone else but me*
> *Till I come marching home!*

"Since you're persistent," said Hal, "I do have a small favor in mind. I'm flying to England tomorrow on a special survey. It would ease my mind greatly if you'd look after Janet."

"That hardly seems a favor."

"It could turn into a six-week assignment. As you know, Janet's by way of being my fiancée. I'd like to be sure she's in safe hands."

"Do you feel I'm safe?"

"Remembering your sterling character, I don't doubt it for a moment."

"Just what would this assignment involve?"

"For one thing, I'd expect you to fight off prowlers. For another, I'd expect you to provide escort service, whenever you have the time. Make her feel she's really important. To herself, and to others."

"Are you speaking of *Janet Josselyn?*"

"Don't be misled by surface glamour," said Hal. "Janet's like the princess in the fable. The one who had more suitors than she could count, and wondered if *she* was real."

"This princess looks real to me."

"Right now, yes—because she's doing her job well. She has the best salon in Washington, the most imposing father, and the great world for a guest list. Running that show can be an exciting career—until a blue Monday comes along, and she begins asking herself if it's worthwhile."

"Does she have these lapses often?"

"Oftener than you'd suspect, to watch her now. When those Mondays hit full strength, she wonders if she's just another parasite, riding the war effort for thrills. That's when she can use your wit and wisdom."

"I still can't believe this of Janet."

"You'll see for yourself—long before the six weeks are over. It's one of the reasons I've encouraged her acting."

"I didn't realize your fiancée was an actress."

"Performer may be a more accurate word," said Hal. "In any case, she's about to make area tours for the USO. They could be her salvation."

"What does she do?"

"With microphones to project her, she can mimic anyone from Mussolini to Garbo. So far, she hasn't performed outside her own parties. When she meets her first audience, she may fall on her face. With a friend in the wings to encourage her— someone she can trust—I think she'll go over big. Will you take the job?"

"I'll be glad to—providing I'm in this part of the world day after tomorrow."

"Assuming you are, you'll be most useful," said Hal. "Janet needs a holiday from the apple-polishers who flock round her father. She hasn't met too many men with your faith in humanity, *and* your prickly conscience. I know she's going to find the change refreshing." He rose from the table with his famous smile in place. Bruce could feel the last residue of his suspicions melt in its warmth. "Do we have a deal?"

"With the exceptions noted."

"Of course." The congressman from Florida took the surgeon's hand in the secret grip of their fraternity. "It's time you danced with your hostess. Shane and I have lectured you enough."

The gesture had been part of Hal's easy manners: it was impossible to question its sincerity after he had left the table. Watching him weave among the guests at the buffet in search of new realms to conquer, Bruce wondered why he could not quite control a lingering resentment.

Then, if only to test his own sincerity, he crossed the lawn to cut in on Janet Josselyn.

Janet greeted him with a cheerful nod while he dodged among the couples, to separate her from an infantry brigadier who bristled like a rampant porcupine at the intrusion.

"I'd have ordered 'Stardust' if I'd known you were on your way," she said. "What detained you?"

"Your fiancé, mostly."

"I don't believe I have one at the moment."

"My congressman seems to be better informed."

"Congressman Reardon is a great juggler of other people's futures," said Janet. "As his classmate, you should know that."

"He still expects you to marry him. Don't tell me he's mistaken."

"Will you mind too much—if I warn you I've been asked that question too often?"

"I won't mind at all," said Bruce. "Now we've changed the subject, I think you'll find it's cooler at the river's edge." He had already danced his hostess from terrace to lawn—and the steps that led down to the boat-landing on the Severn.

"Are you abducting me?"

"Only for your own good. As a doctor, I prescribe rest—after your exertion on the floor."

Janet permitted him to guide her to the landing. So far, he could not tell if she was amused or piqued by his boldness.

"Have I been under observation?"

"Constantly, from the moment I arrived."

"Even when you were talking to Hal?"

"Why not? The subject was you."

"What conclusions did you reach?"

"That you deserve adequate protection while he's in England. May I take his place in your schedule, if not in your affections?"

"For how long?"

"He says he'll be away six weeks."

"That's a real tour of duty," said Janet. "Do you feel you can handle it?"

"I think so—with your cooperation."

"Was this idea yours or Hal's?"

"Shall we call it a joint agreement?"

"*I'd* call it high-handed, on both sides. Whenever possible, I like to choose my own escorts."

"Naturally, the assignment depends on your approval."

Janet moved to the edge of the float to watch the progress of a catboat on the river. Forcing himself to pause at the steps, Bruce did not press his advantage. So far, this easy fencing had been no more than a show of company manners: the senator's daughter could still dismiss him with a word.

"Tell me one thing more, Bruce. Was this joint agreement also a *quid pro quo?*"

"If I recall my Latin, that means a horse trade agreeable to both parties."

"So it does," said Janet. "To put things in the vernacular, I'm not sure I enjoy being the filly who's up for grabs."

"Will it help my cause if I assure you my motives are beyond reproach?"

"It might—if I believed you," said Janet. "What would this six weeks involve?"

"I promised an old classmate to guard you with my life. I could hardly do less, after the favor he's just done me."

Janet's eyes were still on the catboat. "Hal doesn't bestow favors lightly. How did he help you?"

"Thanks to his connections, it seems I've been rescued from the doghouse."

"You don't sound too grateful," said Janet. "Did you resent his help?"

"A little. Just as you resent the way he's taking marriage for granted."

His hostess turned from the river. Expecting their easy fencing to continue, he was astonished to find her smile had vanished.

"Perhaps that makes us two of a kind," she said.

"Perhaps it does. The possibility should be encouraged."

"It's a possibility not even Hal could have foreseen."

"Suppose we dine together next Saturday, to see if you're right."

"Next Saturday, I open with the USO in Baltimore."

"That's even better. You can use me as a one-man claque— on the remote chance you need one. And we can dine afterwards."

"So we can," said Janet. "Will you call for me at six?"

At midmorning, a message had reached Camp Bruckner, detaching Major Bruce Graham from his day's duty and ordering him to report at once to the Surgeon General in Washington. The adjutant had authorized the use of a staff car. Less than an hour later, a sergeant from the reception desk at the SGO had conducted Bruce down an imposing corridor to an office with a view of the mall. . . . Now, sitting bolt upright in the visitor's chair, surveying photographs of medical installations from Governor's Island to Australia, he found it impossible to preserve the optimism his summons had inspired. Colonel Lawrence Wilson, the officer who had signed his order (whose name was repeated on the empty desk) remained an ominous enigma while the minutes ticked by.

It was barely twenty-four hours after Bruce's visit to Five Oaks—but the senator's open house already seemed remote as an Arabian Nights' entertainment. The jaunty promises of Congressman Hal Reardon, the impending date with Janet, were part of that mirage. Only the chill of Colonel Wilson's sanctum had relevance when a side door burst open—and a small, alert officer charged behind the desk, slapped down a file folder on its bare glass top, and gave Bruce an appraising glance before plunging into its contents.

The wintry inspection had destroyed the last remnants of hope. Realizing he should have risen at the entrance of a senior officer, Bruce stared unhappily at the colonel's bobbing Adam's apple and waited for the ax to fall. It was all too clear that something had gone amiss—and even clearer that Colonel Wilson was containing himself with an effort.

"It seems, Major Graham, that some doctors are hard to suit." The colonel had spoken with his glance riveted on the folder.

"I'm afraid I don't understand, sir."

"Yesterday, I was told on high civilian authority that you're dissatisfied with your present job."

"That is quite true, Colonel."

"Ordinarily, we don't assign a top-grade surgeon to a station hospital. However, the Army considers ports of embarkation high-priority areas. Qualified specialists are badly needed there, to make final decisions on a soldier's fitness for duty overseas."

"Of course, sir."

Wilson burrowed deeper in the folder. "Here's a partial list of the men at your station. On the medical service, we have Major Ackerman, a certified internist from Chicago. His assistant, Captain Leibowitz, is a coming man in his field. In urology, we have Major Denby, one of the best men from New York. With such colleagues, I'm curious to learn why you object to being chief of the surgical service at Camp Bruckner."

"Unfortunately, Colonel, that isn't my job."

"What are your present duties?"

"I was put in the officers' pool on arrival. For the first few days, I did routine physicals. Since then, I've worked with Major Denby—pending overseas duty in a ship platoon."

"If *you* aren't surgical chief at Bruckner, who the hell is?"

"Major Calvin Pritchett has just been assigned, sir."

The colonel reached for the intercom and barked a demand for the 201 file on Pritchett. He did not speak until it had been placed before him by a breathless Wac.

"Why didn't you report these facts to me at once?"

"It was my first post, sir. I had no notion what my duties would be."

"It was never our intention to waste your skill and training on scut work. The former chief surgeon at Bruckner, Major Anders, had been in charge there since the camp opened. When he was ordered to London, you were selected as his replacement."

"May I ask if the station hospital knew of your decision?"

Wilson leafed through the folder. "That, it seems, was the vital error of omission. I still find it hard to believe that Colonel Britten failed to realize our purpose. Did you complete a classification questionnaire on arrival?"

"It was made part of my file when I reported for duty."

Wilson uttered a brief but blistering oath, a word that contrasted strangely with his prim countenance. "It's clear there's been a basic confusion in your assignment. Under the circumstances, I can appreciate your discontent."

"I hope you realize, sir, that Congressman Reardon interceded without consulting me."

"I wish you *had* complained in person, Major Graham. Such an act, on your part, would have suggested you had some confidence in the intelligence of the Surgeon General."

Bruce accepted the rebuke mutely. Shane McLendon had

said that a word in the right quarters could change a man's whole future in the Army. Here, it seemed, was evidence that her fast footwork had not been wasted.

"I'm not going to reactivate your original assignment," said Wilson. "We'll soon be organizing auxiliary surgical teams to work at the front. Would such duty interest you?"

"Very much, Colonel."

"Each team will be headed by a specialist like yourself, a man who can handle anything that comes to an operating table. He'll command one or more junior medical officers, an anesthetist, and a team of technicians. For the most part, they'll assist field hospitals in advanced areas."

"I did that sort of operating in Spain, sir."

"So I see, from your record. When we're fully organized, I'll see to it myself that you head one of those units. Meanwhile, they can use skilled help at Scranton General, even though you may have to serve as a ward officer. . . ."

The colonel's voice, despite its deliberate lack of warmth, was almost soothing now. Hearing the detailed description of his new duties, Bruce found he could enjoy this waking dream. Scranton General, as every doctor knew, was a model of its kind—a surgeons' Eden, staffed by experts from the best medical schools and clinics in the country.

"Orders will go through tomorrow for your transfer," said Wilson. "We'll call it temporary duty, pending your first combat assignment. Organization of the units I mentioned will depend on events abroad—but you'll be the first qualified man to head one."

"I can't thank you enough, sir."

"No thanks are needed, Major. These are overdue assignments, nothing more."

Back at Bruckner, on the treadmill of the GU ward, Bruce could have repeated most of Colonel Wilson's ice-cold discourse from memory—but he was careful to share his news with no one. The attitude of the station hospital personnel was still on the wary side: a summons from the SGO could have many meanings, and even Nick Denby was careful to seem busy elsewhere.

Next morning, while he was still at breakfast, Bruce received the expected summons to Britten's office. At this early hour, the CO looked more peevish than usual. The new surgical chief stood at a window, his face a mask of foreboding. Major Krock, the MAC adjutant, sat at a side table, pretending to study a folder. In a corner, a corporal was adjusting the paper roll in a stenotype machine: his presence suggested the meeting was at least semiofficial.

"Sit down, Major." Britten's voice was cold as he pointed to a chair in the geometrical center of the carpet. "There, so I can see you clearly."

Settling in the familiar spot, Bruce noticed that it faced the light. Pritchett had assumed the pose of a jaunty inquisitor—and the attitude of the adjutant was one of respectful waiting. Thanks to his special knowledge, the surgeon could almost enjoy these solemn preliminaries. It was a heady joy to realize the commandant could not know that his escape from Camp Bruckner was assured.

Britten turned to the adjutant. "You may begin, Major Krock."

"*You* called this meeting, Colonel."

"As you wish. Tell me this, Major Graham. What prompted you to complain behind my back to higher authority? Even a civilian in uniform should know better."

"To what complaint do you refer, Colonel?"

"Did you or did you not visit Washington without informing me?"

Krock spoke from the side table. "The SGO telephoned me direct. Naturally, I authorized immediate transportation. There was no time to inform you, sir."

"May I ask the reason for your abrupt summons, Major Graham?"

"Colonel Wilson wished to question me about my duties.

He seemed to be under the impression I was chief of your surgical service."

"Did you explain the post had been filled?"

"I did, Colonel." Bruce faced the porcine figure on the window sill as he spoke, with no attempt to cover his contempt.

"We were never informed of the SGO's intentions."

"Colonel Wilson felt my qualifications should have convinced you I was sent here to fill that position."

"Did you expect the appointment?"

Bruce turned toward the stenotypist and spoke to him direct, ignoring the flushed face across the desk and the even angrier man in the window frame. "When I arrived here, I was completely ignorant of military procedure. Naturally, I hoped to be given work suited to my training."

Krock cut in quietly. "You saw the qualification card, sir. It described Major Graham as a diplomate of the American Board of Surgery—the highest rating of its kind in this country, I believe. As he says, the post was vacant when he arrived. At that time, Major Pritchett was still a captain."

It was Britten's turn to glance at the stenotypist. "Very well, gentlemen. If Major Graham was dissatisfied with his assignment, why didn't he say so at his first interview?"

"When you put me in the officers' pool, sir, I hoped you had a real job in mind for me," said Bruce.

"Confine yourself to the questions, Major. You were dissatisfied, as you say. Instead of complaining through normal channels, you went to the SGO."

Krock spoke again. "For the record, Colonel, Major Graham did not visit the SGO on his own initiative—and he has made no complaint, formal or otherwise. I've just talked to Washington on the phone. The major's assignments were investigated on order."

"If the Surgeon General's procurement system went astray, it's hardly my affair," said Britten. "I'm still asking why this officer didn't protest to me, since he was unhappy here."

Pondering his reply, Bruce saw that the CO was trying hard to withdraw from a sticky situation with some semblance of dignity: the formality of that last question, for all its icy phrasing, had its own appeal. He spoke quickly, before pity could lessen his indignation.

"I'd been told a new officer should do his best to adapt, sir," he said. "Naturally, with my training, I felt I was worth more to the Army than short arm inspection in a processing shed, or lab work in Major Denby's service. What really disturbed me, however, was far more serious."

"And what was that, Major Graham?"

"The fact that no one in this hospital but myself was a qualified specialist in surgery—and no such specialist was called on to fill the post." Bruce stared pointedly at Pritchett as he spoke. He could not quite suppress a smile as the CO's nephew turned brick-red. "Needless to add, Colonel Wilson was even more disturbed than I."

"Are you disputing my judgment, Major?"

"I'm disputing nothing, sir. I'm stating the reasons for my bafflement. The facts will speak for themselves, after the matter is referred to higher authority. By then, I'll be serving elsewhere."

"Is that a hope, Major, or a promise?" Krock asked.

"A firm promise—from Colonel Wilson."

"You're being relieved of your duties at Bruckner?"

"Eventually, I'm to head a surgical combat team. Until then, I will be assigned to Scranton General."

The adjutant, Bruce saw, had drawn a sigh of relief—a sound that was echoed, however faintly, from the CO's desk. The flush had ebbed from Britten's jowls when he leaned forward to speak again. Only Pritchett seemed on the edge of apoplexy.

"May I wish you well in your new duties, Major? Next time, I trust you'll give more thought to regulations."

The gesture was routine—the effort of a commanding officer to spread oil on troubled waters without surrendering the essence of his authority. Bruce had risen for his parting salute when Pritchett rumbled into action from the window sill.

"If the colonel pleases—"

"What is it now, Calvin?"

"There's still a matter of discipline involved, sir. I refer to false statements this man made to a group of officers, regarding the death of Private Thomas Thorpe. Making such charges is an offense under the Articles of War."

The adjutant held up a peremptory hand. At his nod, the stenotypist cut the switch on his machine.

"Do you plan to pursue this matter, Major Pritchett?" he asked.

"It's been my plan since the statements were made at Thorpe's autopsy."

Krock waved the stenotypist from the room, then turned to face Bruce. "It's my duty to state that you are not required to answer any questions at this time. If Major Pritchett brings charges, an official inquiry will be ordered, pending court-martial proceedings."

"I'm quite ready to discuss the situation now," said Bruce. "And I'm sure we'll all be glad the discussion's off the record." He swept on, before Pritchett could interrupt. "In my report, submitted before the autopsy, I stated that Private Thorpe should be rejected for combat duty because of a chronic thrombophlebitis. The rejection was overruled—by Major Pritchett. That same day, Thorpe died on an obstacle march. The autopsy established the march as the immediate cause of death—"

Pritchett was on his feet now, his face twisted in a sneer of triumph. "That happens to be a lie. There's no record of rejection on the processing form."

"Your statement's correct, so far as it goes," said Bruce. "Unfortunately, it isn't the whole story. The file to which you refer was altered—*after* my request for rejection. I have the original in my wallet."

No one stirred while he took out the page Seward's sergeant had donated—and held it to the light so Britten and Krock could see it clearly. Behind him, he heard a muffled growl—and wondered if Pritchett would attack him then and there.

"Where did you get this sheet?" the adjutant asked.

"Does that matter? You can see it's authentic."

"I'm asking for my own information. Names can be omitted."

"It came from an office wastebasket, Major Krock. It speaks for itself."

Pritchett found his voice. "This is an outrage, Colonel—"

"*Shut up, Calvin!*"

Bruce made no objection when Britten took the processing sheet and studied every line with myopic attention. In his corner, the adjutant had just converted a deep-throated chuckle into an even deeper cough.

"May I keep this?" the CO asked.

"If you wish, sir."

"Thank you, Major Graham. There will be no charges—and I can appreciate your desire to leave Bruckner."

Britten had already crumpled the sheet. Now, he dropped it in an ash tray and touched it with his lighter. The quiet was heavy in the office while the evidence that would have damned Pritchett flamed into ash.

"This meeting is adjourned, gentlemen," said the CO. "Majors Graham and Krock are dismissed. You will remain, Major Pritchett."

"In your place, I'd have put that sheet on the record," said Denby. "Why did you weaken?"

"I felt that Britten and Pritchett had been punished enough."

"For my money, they deserved the worst flogging you could give them."

The two doctors were drinking a farewell highball in the

club, in the half hour before Bruce's transfer to Scranton General. The eruption in the commandant's office (and the rumors it had spawned) had shaken the station hospital to its foundations: at the last moment, the urologist had appointed himself a one-man committee to speed the surgeon on his way.

Denby signaled the barman for another order, and took their drinks to a corner of the porch. Below, on the mud-caked macadam, the car that would take Bruce to his new billet was waiting: the driver had just gone into the administration office to clear his gate pass. Denby settled in one of the cane-bottomed rockers and lifted his feet to the rail.

"Call those two monsters any name you like," he said. "They deserve all the black marks in the book."

"I'll buy that verdict for Pritchett. I'm not so sure about the old man."

"Britten's a hog in any league," said Denby. "He should be buried with his worn-out medals. Pritchett should simply be drawn and quartered."

"If memory serves, Nick, you sang another tune the last time we discussed the Army."

"On that occasion, I was rubbing ointment in your saddle sores—hoping you'd make the best of a bad situation. At the time, it seemed you were prepared to take a beating without fighting back. It's another matter, now you've got the CO across a barrel."

"No one is being hurt," said Bruce. "Now that Britten's stopped playing the grand inquisitor, I can see him in a better light. Take away his nepotism, and his habit of postponing hard decisions, and you have an average officer. At least he chewed Pritchett out, once his eyes were opened."

"Don't tell me you think the lecture will stick."

"The Army is Britten's life; we're stopgap soldiers. Let's not bear down on his shortcomings."

Denby took a long swallow from his glass. "It's easy for you to be philosophical—with your ticket to Scranton General. Don't forget he'll be my boss for quite a while."

"He's bearable, as bosses go. And you'll be losing Pritchett, once the wheels start turning at the SGO."

"True enough. Calvin the Great will be banished to the backlands, where he'll be far less dangerous. I'd still like to see him broken. So would every man at the station who dares to speak his mind."

"Breaking Pritchett won't bring back Tommy Thorpe. Nor will it make Pritchett a better citizen. I'm preparing to live and let live, if the Army will let me. I'm even hoping my troubles with the brass are ended."

"Knock wood when you say that, Bruce. They could be just beginning."

"I'm assigned to a hospital where surgeons are really useful. Tomorrow, I'm escorting Janet Josselyn to her first camp show. When the European front is opened, I'll have a chance to make medical history. Aren't you drooling with envy?"

"I'd like a date with Janet Josselyn myself—if I were fifteen years younger. I'm reasonably sure I could handle her, with what I've learned in those fifteen years. You may not be so lucky."

"Is that slur meant for Janet, or for me?"

"No slur was intended," said Denby. "I'm only reminding you that the senator's daughter can be damned dangerous to a serious-minded operator like yourself. She may end up hurting you in ways Pritchett never dreamed of."

"That's hardly a fair comment. You haven't even met her."

"I've observed her from afar," said Denby. "I can fill in what I missed easily enough. Beware of rich girls who've had their way since boarding school. They can break more hearts than any Lilith on the prowl."

"I'll keep your warning in mind," said Bruce. "Here comes my driver. After that burst of misanthropy, will you wish me luck?"

"Of course I'll wish you luck. Custodians of other men's

fiancées need all the luck they can get. To say nothing of crusaders eager for their first whiff of powder."

"I'll try to survive both ordeals."

"Think of me, when the senator's daughter has hooked you and you can't shake off the barb. Think of me again, sitting in the weekend shade with my glass—when you're dodging shrapnel in North Africa."

"I must say that's a cheerful send-off."

Denby shrugged. "I hope I'm one hundred per cent wrong. Perhaps you'll be agreeably surprised by the future. I still think it's wiser to expect the worst."

"You've been a far too accurate prophet, up to now."

"Call me when you're free. We might manage dinner, if your new girl friend gives you time off."

A little later, settled with his baggage in the back seat of the car, Bruce took a last look at the post he was leaving. In the blaze of September sunlight, Camp Bruckner had never seemed more desolate. The lone officer on the porch above him, taking his ease in a cane-bottomed chair, only accented the emptiness—yet Major Nicholas Denby, MC, in the act of accepting another bourbon-and-water from the barman, seemed enclosed in a euphoria of his own creation.

In the weeks that followed, Bruce would remember that impression often—and wonder at Denby's prescience.

Washington

An hour earlier, when he had wakened in his neat bedroom, Bruce had needed a second glance at the uniforms in his closet to convince himself that this was, indeed, a military installation, not his quarters at Lakewood. The suspension between two worlds had lasted—not unpleasantly—while he proceeded to the cafeteria for the light breakfast that would take him to the luncheon break. . . . Now, facing his surgical chief in the scrub room, he felt the present click into focus as sharply as though he had just adjusted the dials of a microscope. Even today, weeks after this new assignment had begun, there were moments when it was hard to believe that Camp Bruckner and Scranton General Hospital were part of the same army.

"Sure you want me to do this one, Terry?"

Colonel Terence Miller, an immensely tall man whose billiard-bald head contrasted oddly with simian forearms, smiled broadly across the white-enameled basin and the alcohol solution in which both doctors were submerged to the elbows. His presence here had contributed to Bruce's strange feeling that past and future might be identical. At Lakewood, Dr. Miller had been a resident during his first intern year, before going on to teach in the South.

"Getting cold feet, because your patient is a general?"

"Isn't this patient rather special?"

"Here at Scranton, he's just another arteriovenous fistula."

"And all mine?"

"While I have Abe Schoenfeld's right bower under orders, he'll take vascular cases. My bailiwick, as you well know, is the abdomen."

"I'll handle the scalpel, then, if you'll handle the reporters."

"That's a fair bargain. I think the patient's ready."

When the two surgeons entered the operating theater, General Porter Gaines was already under anesthesia, and the rest of the team stood ready in the glare of the lights. Above, in the spectators' seats, a score of colleagues, augmented by newly commissioned officers in the process of indoctrination, had gathered to observe the procedure. The news of this patient's arrival at Scranton General had spread through the corridors before the operation had been posted: General Gaines was one of the great names from the Philippines, an authentic symbol to a beleaguered nation still badly in need of extra heroes.

The wound that had brought the general to the table was an old one, inflicted when he had walked into a sniper's telescope at Bataan. The injury, at the time, had seemed prosaic: the bullet had penetrated the upper thigh, a clean puncture that had required only a dressing at the points of entrance and exit. Healing, the record stated, had been rapid— but the leg had begun to swell later, and the veins had become dilated and tortuous. A preliminary survey had revealed other ominous symptoms: a rapid pulse, shortness of breath, an enlargement of the left side of the heart.

Later still, the patient had been transferred to California for extended observation. The original clinical picture had been one of heart failure—but both the history and his own examination had convinced Bruce that the true cause of the trouble was the presumably healed track of the bullet. This was a form of vascular trauma he had studied extensively at

Lakewood. The case awaiting surgery today was not the first such enigma he had solved since reporting for duty at this Army hospital outside Washington.

It had now been established that the sniper's bullet, boring into a thigh, had injured both the deep artery and the matching vein. After that rupture, an abnormal condition known as a fistula had formed between the two vessels. As a result, blood flowing under the high pressure of the arterial system had been shunted through this bypass, to enter the comparatively low-pressure area of the veins.

Two things had happened thereafter—and Bruce reviewed these developments while he waited for the anesthetist's nod to make his first incision.

First, since there was no longer sufficient pressure to maintain an adequate flow in the small arteries, circulation in the whole leg had been badly impaired. Second and even more dangerous (because of that sudden release of pressure from the deep artery), the heart had been forced to work much harder to assure a flow of blood to other parts of the body. This, in turn, had caused an enlargement of the organ itself: an overdevelopment of basic muscles, a dilation of valves—and the threat of complete malfunction.

Rigorous preparation had gone into this procedure. The patient's circulation had been tested by exerting pressure above the fistula—closing the abnormal flow, and demonstrating the condition that would be ensured after the shunt had been removed. Without such a demonstration, it was impossible to decide whether surgery would cure the malfunction—or cause such drastic loss of circulation that gangrene must inevitably follow. As they had hoped, the pulse rate had fallen after the blockage, and the blood pressure had almost returned to normal. At the same time, circulation below the fistula had actually improved, showing that auxiliary channels could handle the needs of foot and leg.

All of these interlocking facts had created the true clinical picture, telling Bruce it was safe to operate. With the fistula removed, there would be no further danger—even though it proved necessary to tie off the artery. Massive surgery was still indicated, since an inevitable by-product of this unnatural juncture of vein and artery was marked dilation of vessels in the surrounding tissue. As the operation proceeded, Bruce knew that he must be constantly alert for such developments. This was no place for a mercifully short incision. A wide exposure was a positive necessity, lest he be hampered in this attack on minor but debilitating hemorrhages.

"Ready, Colonel?"

"When you are, Major."

No further exchange was needed as the scalpel came into his hand. While he went about his drastic task, Miller and the two junior surgeons moved swiftly to anchor a nest of hemostats controlling the myriad small vessels the knife exposed. The initial approach was both tedious and cautious. At this stage, it was impossible to define the exact size of the fistula: a false stroke could wreck the patient's chance of survival.

Nearly an hour passed before the damage was revealed down its length. The abnormality was a formidable one—the thick-walled artery, its inner border ruptured by the bullet, the tremendously dilated, thin-walled vein, and the grotesque tubular connection between them.

"It's a monster," said Colonel Miller.

"We expected that, sir."

"Still want to go after all of it—at this sitting?"

Bruce might have resented the question had either doctor been unsure of the other's competence. Knowing Terry Miller as he did, he realized that his Lakewood colleague was merely being realistic. A prodigious operation of this nature might be approached in stages, if the surgeon in charge so wished. . . . The senior officer's suggestion had been an offer of retreat if retreat seemed indicated, without loss of face.

"How's he bearing up?" Bruce asked the anesthetist.

"He's still comfortable."

"We can close without removing the whole complex. But we'd almost certainly fail to cure him—and it would take nearly as long."

Miller, studying the huge incision from every angle, nodded slowly. "It's all or nothing, then?"

"I'd much prefer that approach."

"In that case, I bow to your judgment."

The actual excision of the fistula, now that the operating field had been precisely defined and put in full view, proved to be almost routine, despite its size. Tying off artery and vein on both sides of the abnormality, Bruce addressed himself to the still longer task of ligating each important vessel in the surrounding tissue. The process, though infinitely complex, had its eventual reward. When the H-shaped section was finally lifted from its bed, there was almost no bleeding in its wake. Even before he could place the closing sutures, Bruce could see that the collateral circulation had taken over. The color of both foot and lower leg had improved markedly. So had the volume of the pulse just in front of the ankle.

"Three hours, on the nose," said Colonel Miller. "I was afraid it would take longer."

"So was I, at first." Bruce stripped off his gloves and dropped them to the floor. "How's his condition now?"

"Still good."

"Barring an embolus, he should live to wear his medals. What's next?"

"The gentlemen of the press, I'm afraid," said the surgical chief.

"You promised to handle them, Colonel."

"I'll keep them off your back, word of honor. But they'll expect something from the man who saved Porter Gaines. After all, he *was* a hero of Bataan."

True to his promise, Colonel Miller had cut the press conference short. Time was still consumed revising the statement

the public relations department had prepared for distribution
to the waiting reporters. Still more time was needed to face
the flashlight bulbs—and Bruce was forced to give yet another
half hour to the always-touchy interview he had discovered he
must handle in his own behalf whenever the status of a patient
made such coverage imperative.

The PRO release, he had noted, omitted no detail in the
dramatic sequence of events that had brought this celebrated
casualty from a battle line in the Philippines to his triumphant
rescue. The fact that the surgery itself, for all its ticklish
nature, had been anything but spectacular, had gone unmentioned. Dr. Abram Schoenfeld, secure in his Lakewood laboratory, would smile at these flourishes over his former pupil—
but Schoenfeld could afford to live above the front page, the
radio broadcast, and the Presidential citation. These, after all,
were items the great American public, hungry for proofs of
success on its war fronts, demanded with each exposure to the
news. . . . Today's report from Scranton General had been
a reasonable blend of fact and romance.

Two more operations remained on the morning schedule:
a varicose vein ligation and a recurrent hernia. Bruce performed them both with the surgical chief's team, while Miller
himself was busy with official correspondence. It was after
lunchtime when he shed his operating suit at last and hurried
to the PX for a snack before starting his rounds in the wards.

As always, the long, bright rooms were filled to the last bed
—and he needed only a quick check with the floor supervisor
to realize that most of his new patients, like his first operation
that morning, were here for reparatory treatment. . . . The
soldiers assigned to his care were not too different from those
he had handled in Spain—with one vital difference. In the
cellar at Barcelona, he had fought to save men fresh from
battle. Here, he was usually expected to correct past errors,
to repair old wounds that had, in some mysterious fashion,
reopened, to snatch back terminal cases from the brink.

The first bed on the afternoon list contained another leg

injury, one that went back to the bombing of Wake Island. The record stated that this lanky corporal, ghost-pale after months in traction, had moved into disputed ground to rescue his platoon leader, and brought back a crippling wound for his pains. Unlike General Gaines, his act of heroism had gone unsung in the press. Today, after emergency treatment in the field, evacuation by air, corrective surgery in Hawaii and months of convalescence in the States, the boy had come to Scranton to wait out a long battle to save a limb whose circulation had been damaged almost beyond repair.

In the second bed was a Regular Army sergeant whose chest cavity had been blasted open after the accidental detonation of a grenade in training maneuvers. Rib, muscle and pleura had been laid bare below a shattered scapula—and the lung beneath had been pitted by steel fragments and bits of bone. In earlier wars, without the dusting of sulfanilamide, and the packing of the almost-exposed lung with broad gauze pads, the sergeant would have perished in the field. Today—now that he had fought off the aftereffects of empyema—he had a chance for survival. Thanks to the regrowth of bone from the rib beds, and the magic scalpels that had moved muscle flaps and skin grafts into place, the collapsed lung might expand eventually into a partially useful organ.

The next bed was a different story. Here, the surgeon paused with drooping spirits to study a soldier whose lips were blue-tinged from oxygen lack, whose swollen ankles and abdomen were additional signs of a failing heart. This disability had not been caused by a wound. A rheumatic infection had attacked the mitral valve while the patient was still on maneuvers in Hawaii.

The surgical chief came into the chart room while Bruce was finishing his notes.

"Do you want to keep this man awhile longer, to see if surgery's indicated? We can transfer him to Medicine before the case runs up our mortality figures."

"I'm afraid he's beyond hope, Terry. We've yet to tackle the mitral valve, even experimentally."

"Think you ever will?"

"It's quite possible. Ten years ago, no one thought a patent *ductus arteriosus* could be tied off successfully—yet it's been done. Schoenfeld claims we'll soon be operating for congenital heart disease in children—and he may be right. For a while last spring, I thought I had the answer myself. That's why he was still burning after I appealed my deferment. He wanted me fighting on *that* front, instead of this."

"I'm damned glad you escaped him, Bruce. We need you here even more. Still anxious to join a combat unit?"

"It's where I belong—if I'm to justify my runout on Schoenfeld."

"Which would you rather do? Save a man like General Gaines, or cut out shrapnel in a field hospital?"

"There must be other civilian consultants who can handle that type of vascular case."

"If there are," said Miller, "I can count them on the fingers of one hand. Next time I go to Mass, I'll pray Larry Wilson's mobile unit's a long time in forming."

The surgical chief's praise, Bruce knew, had come from the heart. It did a great deal to make his afternoon's rounds go faster. So, in their flamboyant way, did the headlines describing the success of the operation he had performed that morning. . . . Much of his good spirits evaporated when he settled in the office, put out a hand to dial Five Oaks—and reminded himself that a six weeks' assignment there had just ended.

Watching a rainy autumn dusk change to night on the lawn outside the windows, he wondered how he would get through his free evenings, now that Congressman Harold Reardon had returned from abroad.

He had fulfilled his promise to the letter—driving Janet Josselyn to the camp shows where she had made instant and spontaneous contact with her audiences, escorting her to bond rallies and to charity dances. On occasions, they had dined together in Annapolis, or in a nearby city where her USO troupe was performing. Now and again, when he had been granted the luxury of a daylong pass, they had spent an afternoon at Five Oaks, riding in the Maryland bridle paths or boating on the Severn.

Inevitably, as days changed to weeks, he had realized he was enjoying Janet's company more and more. He could never be sure his enjoyment was shared in full measure—but he saw she had grown to rely on his presence. When he knew he was in love with her—and dared not hope his love was returned—he had kept an iron rein on his emotions, reminding himself that he was a stand-in, with a definite time limit on his tenure. . . . Now that Hal had returned, now that he had refused a reunion dinner that evening (on a fictitious plea of night duty) he could pinpoint the worst ache in his conscience, the knowledge that he had rushed to meet his fate with wide-open eyes.

From the first, he had tasted these delights in the full awareness that his love, to say nothing of more primitive desires, was as hopeless as most men's dreams of paradise. Yet even now, he knew he would have taken the same path again, if it were offered him.

Logically enough, it was not the image of Janet that troubled him while he lingered at his desk. Instead—for reasons he understood too well—he found himself thinking of his last encounter with Senator Lucius Josselyn, in the library at Five Oaks. In its fashion, that meeting had summed up his dilemma: Josselyn had had ample reason for speaking out.

The meeting had occurred near the end of another afternoon on the river. Janet was due at a camp between Annapolis and Baltimore, to rehearse a new routine. They had come in from the Severn an hour before sunset, to give her time to change. It was no one's fault that she had stumbled in the hall: the act of taking her in his arms had been involuntary.

The long kiss that had followed had been another matter. Remembering it now, and flushing hotly at the memory, he could wonder if she had planned that sudden foot-fault on the stairs. There had been other wordless embraces since Hal's departure for England: all of them had begun like this, without warning. . . .

"That was consolation while I dress," she whispered. "Wipe off the lipstick before you see Dad."

"I can't disturb him now. He's on the phone."

"Wait till he's finished, then go straight in. He wants to see you before we leave."

Watching her run up the stairs, and suppressing an insane compulsion to follow, Bruce lingered in the hall while the senator's voice droned on behind the half-closed door of the library. When he heard the click of a receiver, he drew a deep breath and knocked. Josselyn's permission to enter was on the resonant side: his wave of welcome, like his pontifical presence, was part of the slightly theatrical background of Five Oaks. So were the perfecto he had just lighted, the cut-glass goblet at his elbow, the gesture that invited the visitor to serve himself from the sideboard.

"You arrive at the proper moment, Major. Six o'clock was invented for drinking."

"No thank you, sir. Janet and I have a ten-mile drive ahead."

"What's the occasion tonight?"

"She's doing a new act at Camp Carlisle."

"I'm still not clear why you're always at these camp shows," said Josselyn. "Are you part of the entertainment?"

"I've been her chauffeur since Hal left. And her bodyguard, when too many admirers come backstage."

"Janet's had admirers since she was fourteen." The senator blew a smoke ring and watched it dissolve in the Waterford chandelier above them. "So far, she's handled them alone."

"GIs in basic are a somewhat different problem, sir. I think I've been useful, now her horizon's expanded."

"I'm sure you have—while Hal's been away. Will you take it amiss, if I suggest your usefulness will soon be ending?"

Noting the change in tone, Bruce wondered why he was not angrier.

"Hal asked me to serve as Janet's escort, Senator. Are you suggesting I've exceeded my assignment?"

"There's no need to take umbrage, Major Graham. You're an intelligent man. You grasp my meaning."

"Tell me anyhow, so I'll be sure."

"Janet's a fine girl. She's also as romantic as Snow White before she wandered into the dwarfs' forest. Or should I say the home-front side of the war? Naturally, I'm glad she's making a personal contribution. I don't want her too involved, if I can avoid it."

"Does that mean you have doubts about me?"

"I'm making no personal evaluations. It's still my duty to remind you that Janet's future is signed, sealed—and virtually delivered. I'm ending my last term in the Senate. In two years, Hal Reardon will be taking my seat. By then, if not before, I expect them to be married. It will be an ideal match."

"As your guest, sir, I can hardly question that judgment."

"When I call Hal one of the best men in the House, I express the consensus of my colleagues. Don't you agree?"

"I have nothing to criticize in Hal's career. I'd be less than honest if I didn't admit he puzzles me—" Realizing he was expressing his thought badly, Bruce forced himself to be specific. "His enemies say he coasted into Congress on Reardon money, his charm, and a superb sense of timing. So far, they say, he hasn't really been tested. I'm afraid I agree."

"The Reardons are one of the finest families in the South. Hal is the flower of his race. If the best men don't run this country, who will?"

"Senator, the first time I visited Five Oaks, I had the same argument with Shane McLendon. I asked her what *best* meant

—and I wasn't too happy with her definition. May I have yours?"

"The best are men who were born to rule, Major Graham. Men who get the world's work done—who have trained their sons to wear the mantle. What could be simpler?"

"It depends on how power is used, sir. If Hal leaves this country better than he found it, he'll justify his privileges. As I just said, I'm waiting to be convinced."

"Power begets power," said Josselyn, with another orator's flourish. "By and large, the American establishment has justified its existence. In your place, I'd accept the fact that a Reardon will always be here to give orders."

Absurd though it was, Bruce discovered that he was enjoying the hopeless discussion for its own sake. Aware that candor had its perils, he plunged on regardless.

"If you'll forgive the observation, Senator, you're making Hal sound like a top sergeant at boot camp."

"The comparison's welcome," said Josselyn. "Most men are happier when a top sergeant calls the tune."

"Or an ex-corporal named Hitler?"

"I'm speaking of healthy disciplines, not brainwashings." The senator had taken the riposte with no loss in tempo: his basso profundo was still tranquil. "*Our* rulers have always used their power wisely, with enough division of authority to make a dictator unthinkable. That's why you're bound to find Hal—or his equivalent—in the driver's seat."

"Assuming he's right for the job, when this war is over."

"I can guarantee his fitness, Major. His grandfather was a great American. So was his father. Hal will follow in their footsteps."

"In other words, you expect the power structure to remain unchanged when the shooting stops?"

"Do you object to the way this country was governed before Pearl Harbor?"

"I do, sir. To my mind, our refusal to pull our weight abroad made Pearl Harbor inevitable."

"I'm afraid we part company on that left-wing canard," said Josselyn serenely. "I believe this country did all it could to stop the Axis, short of an outright attack. Furthermore, I believe Hal Reardon has the brains, and the connections, to make sure no such betrayal occurs again. Someday, you'll thank God he was your senator."

"The succession is assured, then?"

"As sure as I'm drawing breath. What's more, the Senate will be only a steppingstone. You may live to visit your Florida classmate in the White House."

"Can you see a Southerner there, sir?"

Again, Josselyn absorbed the thrust, with massive good humor. "Hal happens to be a citizen of the world. How many congressmen have the support of both business and labor? How many call Harvard professors by their nicknames, and play poker with Jake Sanford?"

"Are you including Congressman Sanford in government by the elite?"

"Sanford's a rough customer, I'll grant you. On the Subversive Acts Committee he often goes too far. At times like these, firebrands have their uses."

"It seems we're poles apart, sir—when it comes to politics. Perhaps we should end this discussion now."

"Perhaps we should, Major Graham. Let me repeat, Hal Reardon will be one of the great men in Washington, before he turns forty. I expect Janet to marry him as planned, and rise with him. And I don't want you, or anyone else, confusing her. Is that understood?"

"Perfectly, sir."

"You've been a patient listener," said Josselyn. "Obviously, you consider me a Neanderthal who's had his day. I don't mind in the slightest—if you realize I'm in charge here. Don't let me keep you from your escort duty."

When he recrossed the hall, Bruce saw that Janet had brought her car to the stoop. Her radiant smile, as she shifted to give him the wheel, assured him that nothing could spoil their evening.

"That was rather a long session in the library."

"The senator and I were discussing politics."

"Was politics the only topic?"

"He also reminded me that Hal will soon return to look out for his interests—meaning you. It was hardly a time to confess I'd been counting the days, and wishing there could be more."

"So have I, Bruce." Janet's hand had already dropped to the ignition switch: this, too, was a game she had played before, where the driveway of Five Oaks turned into a tunnel of boxwoods. Before the Jaguar could coast to a halt, her arms were about his neck—and, once again, her kiss was as uncontrolled as the embrace. While their lips clung, he fought hard to contain his desire. . . . He was losing the battle rapidly when she broke free—and he realized her breathing had hardly quickened.

"If you like," said Janet, "I'll repeat his lecture, word for word."

"I hope you weren't eavesdropping."

"There was no need. He's used it before when Hal's been away—and I've gone out with other men."

"I'm not unique, then?"

"Both Hal and my father believe in the divine right of kings. They think of *me* as a pawn. That kiss was the pawn's way of getting even."

A steady drum of rain aroused Bruce from reverie. Returning to the present, he saw that a near-cloudburst had inundated the lawns of Scranton General, and rose to close the office windows. . . . A review of that moment among the boxwoods (before he had driven Janet Josselyn to her camp-show rehearsal) had been long overdue. Now that he could value it in perspective, he saw that it had been, in the truest sense, a portent.

From their first date, he had realized that the senator's daughter resented her bondage: it was no longer possible to believe she resented it too deeply. Janet, in short, had been trained to become the loyal wife of a politician as ruthlessly as Hal Reardon had schooled himself to become her husband. Now, of course, it had become her *raison d'être* again. Who was he to wonder at her submission to the inevitable, when there were no limits to the future she and Hal would share?

That kiss on the Five Oaks driveway, he repeated, had set the seal on an interlude that was now part of history. No one could be blamed but himself, if he continued to hunt on another man's preserve after he had been warned away. And yet, even as he faced that gloomy conviction, he knew the embraces he had shared with the senator's daughter had also been signs of an inward need—that Janet Josselyn had found her own release in his company.

Was it too fantastic to wonder if those stolen hours in a cream-white Jaguar were the only happiness she had ever known? Would Janet have given him far more than schoolgirl kisses, if he had dared to break her father's bondage?

It was a small consolation to take these dark questions to his bedroom at Scranton General—but it did help to salvage his pride.

Sergeant James Lowell, Concord, Mass.
Bruce read the words aloud from the record sheet handed him by the admitting-ward attendant. The name and address, New England to the core, had wakened an echo in his mind —though he could not pin down the source.

"Where is he now?"

"In the first examining room, Major."

It was a fortnight after his renunciation of Janet Josselyn— and he was serving as Officer of the Day on the surgical service. During the day-long shift, it was his duty to examine new arrivals and assign them to the proper ward—or, as in the case of Sergeant Lowell, to cope with problems that had occurred in transit. This patient's admission sheet informed him that Lowell, until recently a patient at Letterman General Hospital in San Francisco, had all but recovered from a leg injury caused by a bomb fragment. New complications had developed while he had traveled eastward, on orders from a higher authority, for a final evaluation at Scranton General.

The procedure in itself was not unusual with officers, since a medical board ruling was required before they could be separated from the service. Almost any hospital could give privates and NCOs a certificate of disability discharge—yet here was a sergeant, seemingly recovered from a wound, who had been sent across a continent for the special processing of Scranton General.

The mystery was solved when Bruce turned to the patient's service record. Sergeant James Lowell had been the first enlisted man to be wounded at Pearl Harbor.

Standing in the doorframe of the examining room, the surgeon was not too impressed by what he saw. There was little about this emaciated boy to distinguish him from other bone-graft cases in the orthopedic wards—and nothing whatever to suggest he was the stuff of which legends were made. Two facts, at least, were obvious. The sergeant's bone graft had healed quite well. But he was still a sick man, for reasons that had no apparent connection with his injury. His temperature stood at a hundred and two degrees, his pulse over a hundred—sure signs that something noxious was astir in his body.

It was obvious that his condition had left him undisturbed, that his confidence in the miracle-working potential of an Army hospital was infinite. His relaxed manner gave Bruce further assurance that he was a model patient. So did the sparkle in his fever-bright eyes, when he answered the first, inevitable question.

"I'm the Lowell you've read about, sir. It's right there on my service record, so I can't deny it."

"Someone had to be the first Japanese target."

"I never thought I'd rate the honor—if you'd call it that."

"I read about the decorations they gave you. Didn't they include the Congressional Medal of Honor?"

"Right again, Major. And I never even smelled powder. Don't tell me I earned all that hardware."

"The Army doesn't hand out medals to everyone." Bruce had begun his preliminary evaluation: a give-and-take exchange of this nature often helped to unwind a patient, though the boy's serenity made such tactics needless. "I see you applied for a return to active duty."

"I won't walk fast enough to suit them—so I'm putting in for limited service as an instructor, at an OCS school in Miami."

"What seems to be the trouble now?"

"Something's going on under the ribs on my right side. I think that is what's making me feverish."

"How did you get your wound?"

"I'm afraid the story's pretty tame, sir. Even though the papers played it up big. The day before the Jap strike, I'd been flown in from the Philippines with a touch of dysentery—"

"How did you contract dysentery?" Bruce's fingers, gently exploring the sick man's upper abdomen below the ribs, had brought a gasp of pain.

"It happened in Manila, after a party with some native friends, in a harbor godown. We'd finished unloading a shipment for Clark Field, and decided to chow up on local food."

"I imagine the godown was off limits?"

"Off limits, Major—in more ways than one. They gave us hell because of it."

"Were you hospitalized in Hawaii when the bombing began?"

"I was an ambulatory case; they were busy at the dispensary, and sent me to another building for a shot of paregoric. I was crossing a road when the bomb fell. I woke up in traction, surrounded by cameras and reporters."

"How did they pick you as the first casualty?"

"I'll never know, sir. I tried to explain it was just an accident—but it was already on the record that I'd beaten the next man to the hospital. Maybe they wanted a GI whose name was easy to spell and sounded like American history."

"According to your record, you've had a hard convalescence."

"It was a compound fracture—and I needed a bone graft to make sure I'd walk again. They were afraid of osteomyelitis for a while. The doctors at Letterman say that danger's behind me now."

A check of the injured leg confirmed Sergeant Lowell's estimate. The maze of zigzag scars had long since healed, and the bone beneath felt solid to the touch.

"We'll take X rays later. It seems your leg's completely well, so this is probably an unrelated illness." Exerting gentle pressure below the right rib cage, Bruce tensed his fingers upward against the muscles of the abdominal wall. Some two inches below the rib cage, he noted the first sign of resistance, a tension that extended to the so-called floating ribs, the bands of cartilage located near the center of the abdomen. Even the light pressure needed to cause muscle spasm produced another wince from the patient, as his body instinctively sought to protect the inflamed organ beneath.

Reversing the technique, the surgeon explored the chest with a series of quick finger-taps, outlining the lower edge of the right lung and marking its limits with a grease pencil. The base of that organ, he decided, was in its appropriate position—indicating that there had been no upward enlargement of the liver, and probably no basal pneumonia. The procedure was an essential one, since irritation of the pleural lining could cause a reflex tenderness in the upper abdomen. Many unwary doctors had operated for gall bladder or other suspected abdominal conditions—when the trouble originated in the lung above.

As a final precaution, Bruce returned to the lower, unaffected portion of the sergeant's torso, using the same tapping technique to make sure each organ gave back the hollow, booming sound of health. By contrast, the position the liver occupied was stone-solid, with its lower edge protruding a full inch and a half beyond its normal position. A deep sigh of pain from Lowell, as he outlined the inflammation with a last, gentle pressure, confirmed a diagnosis that was now far more than tentative.

"Just when did you eat that native food in Manila?"

"Close to a year ago. My dysentery started right afterwards."

"You had treatment in the Philippines—before you flew to Honolulu?"

"They tried hard to cure me, sir. Gave me emetine and carbarsone, and other medicine I can't remember. It seems I picked up a real tough amoeba."

"It seems you did. I'll see you again tomorrow. Meanwhile, we'll run a few tests. And I'll give you something to make sure you rest easy."

The prognosis, Bruce reflected sadly, was now all but certain. It had been an unusual clinical picture—and, despite his satisfaction at recognizing it so promptly, he could only regret his findings. If the laboratory confirmed his views, there was little chance of saving this youth whose name was already part of history.

He had admitted the patient to his own ward, putting him in semi-isolation until he could revalue the activities of the parasite called *Entamoeba histolytica*, which seemed to be Sergeant Lowell's deadly enemy. As he had expected, the boy seemed better the next morning. Temperatures were usually lower at this hour, and the opiate he had prescribed had guaranteed eight hours' slumber.

"What's the verdict, sir? A new flare-up?"

Meeting the intelligent eyes directly, and reading no trace of fear there, Bruce saw no point in withholding part of the truth.

"It looks that way. As you said yesterday, you took on a tough bug in the Philippines. We won't be sure, of course, until the lab reports are in."

"I hope it won't keep me here too long."

"Haven't you had enough Army to suit you? With that leg, you could have had your discharge long ago."

"I know, sir. They offered me a CDD at Letterman."

Bruce took a chair beside the bed. The case had its special irony, and a pathos all its own—but it was not these factors that caused him to break the tempo of his rounds. Rather, it was the note of confidence in this young man's voice, the unyielding air of courage.

"What do they call you at home, Sergeant?"

"Jimmie, sir."

"May I call you that—and ask a few things off the record?"

"I guess you're wondering why I'm still in the service. Two minutes after the first shot was fired in Hawaii, I was out of action. I've been lying in hospital beds ever since, getting over one bone graft and waiting for the next. If I can, I'd like to do more to help win this war."

"I can admire your patriotism, Jimmie. Is that the whole answer?"

"It's only the beginning. I've a nine-year-old brother back in Concord. Right now, he thinks he envies me these sergeant's stripes—and my medals. When he's my age, I hope he'll know enough about war to want it outlawed."

"Do you think war can ever be outlawed?"

"If enough people speak out against it—and make their voices heard."

"Quite a few people spoke up after the last one."

"That was a cockpit fight in Europe, sir—not a real world war. This time, we've got to try a lot harder. We've got to begin where the so-called League of Nations left off."

"What did you do before the Army, Jimmie?"

"I was at Harvard. Halfway through sophomore year, I smelled this one coming, and wanted a front-row seat. As you see, I got what I asked for. Only the performance blacked out early."

"Do you call enlisting the act of a pacifist?"

"I wasn't a pacifist then. I was a kid on the lookout for thrills—and I had a tradition to keep up. My people have been in every war this country's had—starting with the French and Indians, when we were still English. There were Lowells at Valley Forge and Yorktown. We sailed with Perry on Lake Erie—and fought Mexicans at Buena Vista. There were Lowells on Grant's staff when Lee surrendered. And still others in Cuba and France."

"Why didn't you stay on campus, and get a commission?"

"I was in college ROTC when I volunteered. If I'd liked, I could have waited and gone in as a lieutenant. Don't think I'm wrapping myself in the flag. But I feel I've the right to stand and be counted, now I'm headed for the other camp."

"The war to end war?"

"Call it what you like." Sergeant Lowell's voice had not lost its even inflection, but his eyes glowed with purpose. The thin hand on the bed sheet clenched in a fist, then relaxed again. "Things can be different this time, if the *soldiers* get together and turn in their guns."

"What do you have in mind? An expanded American Legion?"

"I thought of that at first, but it wouldn't work. Basically, the Legion's a gladiators' jamboree. It wants to keep things as they are—like any club whose members are getting older."

"Isn't that a universal failing?"

"Of course, sir, more's the pity. That's why we need a brand-new group, with a new approach."

"Just who are we?"

"You and I. Every veteran of the war we're fighting now. Nothing would be easier than merging that group with the Legion. Once we did, we'd find ourselves battling an outfit that's never been an effective influence for peace. We'd have knockdown fights for control at every post, between the old vets and the new."

"I'm sure you would."

"We'll kill ourselves in advance, if we depend on existing pressure groups. In the end, we'd split into factions. Some of us would stay liberal—and be called bitter-enders. Most of us would be sucked into supporting America first—making this country strong enough to take on all comers in World War III. Maybe even starting that war, if our enemies didn't buy our way of life."

"Assuming you're right, you'd still have the problem of organization."

"All the men who fought in this war will have to break with the past, forget such bugaboos as national boundaries and national honor, and work only for peace. It means joining forces, right down the line—including veterans in Germany and Japan."

"Germany and Japan are enemies."

"They could be friends tomorrow."

"It's a tall prescription to swallow today."

"So was democracy, when Jefferson wrote the Declaration of Independence. So was Christianity, in Constantine's Rome."

"Wasn't it Shaw who said Christianity was a magnificent concept that's yet to be tried?"

"Call world peace a dream if you will. It's still a hope that's shared by millions, right here in America. When this war ends, the world will share it."

"Where would your organization start?"

"In military hospitals. Among men who won't leave their beds again—or their wheelchairs. *They* know how war can set back human evolution. Once they're converted, we'd get in touch with GIs everywhere."

"How would you reach them?"

"By using the VA rolls. With those names as a nucleus, we'd call ourselves the Veterans for Peace—and field candidates in the next election. Our movement would snowball, once a European front is opened, and we begin adding families of each new casualty. Later, when we could include men on active duty, we'd run a candidate for President."

"You can't electioneer in uniform, Jimmie."

"Our families could, in V-mail."

"*You'd* get the ax, before this went too far."

"Before I did, I'd put the whole campaign in other hands."

"What would you get from it personally?"

The sergeant flushed. "I want nothing for myself, Major. Only the satisfaction of knowing my brother will never fight a war. I owe him that much—because I *was* the first American wounded on American soil."

"The obstacles are enormous."

"Don't you like my idea?"

"I like every part of it, Jimmie. I'm still trying to see beyond those roadblocks. Take first things first. You can't put your plan in motion from a hospital bed. Not while you're an NCO."

"I might—with the right help."

"You could never be your own spokesman."

"I wouldn't try to be. I haven't the brains, or the words. That's why I need a sponsor."

"Finding one won't be easy."

"I've already found one. Congressman Reardon has just about decided to back me."

Knowing he had blinked hard at the sergeant's bombshell, Bruce forced himself to speak calmly.

"Where did you meet Congressman Reardon?"

"At Letterman General, when he was making a tour of hospitals on the Coast. He's a wonderful man, sir."

"So I've been told," said Bruce drily. "Did you discuss your idea at Letterman?"

"Right from my cot. He sat down and talked, like we're talking now. It seemed a ready-made chance to get someone important behind me."

"This was before you noticed the pain in your side?"

"Weeks before. The flare-up hit me in transit. When I told Congressman Reardon I was down for limited duty, he promised to have me transferred here for my check-out."

The pattern, Bruce reflected, was taking form. Hal was obviously the "higher authority" mentioned in Sergeant Lowell's orders—and the sergeant had come to Scranton General for a definite purpose. What Hal had not expected was the recurrence of a liver ailment Jimmie had picked up in Manila —or that he would become Bruce's patient because of it.

"Did Congressman Reardon have you sent here so he could keep in touch?"

"That's it exactly, sir. The minute he's back in the Capitol —and his desk is clear—we're having a real talk about my Peace Party."

"Does it already have a name?"

"That's the working title. I figure this is the best break I ever had."

"Have you discussed your ideas with anyone else?"

"Only with friends at Letterman. Most of them hooted me down. Or warned me I'd be court-martialed, if I spoke my mind to a doctor or an officer. Congressman Reardon was different. The minute I opened my mouth, I felt he was with me."

"Wouldn't it be better to wait a little longer before committing yourself?"

"I *can't* wait, Major. Not with a big man on my side. Do you suppose I could phone his office tomorrow? In case he's back—and has forgotten?"

"I'll handle your phone call, Jimmie—if you've made up your mind. This time tomorrow, we should know what's wrong with you. I hope you'll be well enough to have a visitor."

"Get me well in a hurry, sir. I'll have a lot to do—now the ball's rolling."

When he had finished his rounds—and found he had a half hour to spare before his next operation—Bruce made fruitless attempts to reach both Hal and Shane McLendon. The congressman, he learned, was en route to Washington. The journalist could not be reached at all.

Bruce hung up on the final attempt with something like relief. He had called Shane on impulse, in the vain hope that she could advise him on his next move: it would have been unfair to toss Sergeant Lowell at her head without warning. . . . He had considered calling Janet, only to discard the idea at once. Since Hal's return, he had refused all invitations to Five Oaks. He could hardly intrude now, with problems Janet could never answer.

The next day, the sergeant's X rays reached his desk, along with a note from his surgical chief, suggesting they confer at once. Colonel Miller had examined the patient, and concurred with the tentative diagnosis. The agreement had somber overtones: Miller had been teaching in New Orleans, and was much more familiar with the behavior of *Entamoeba histolytica* than his younger colleague.

The tests themselves had banished the last doubt. Jimmie Lowell was suffering from an abscess of the liver—a direct if tardy aftermath of the dysentery he had contracted in Manila.

"Is surgery indicated, Terry?"

"I'm afraid so. Of course we'll start by aspirating the abscess cavity, plus anti-amoebic injections. This is a highly resistant bug, so they probably won't have much effect. With his temperature spiking and the white count high, it's a foregone conclusion we're dealing with secondary infection. Do you see it any other way?"

Bruce shook his head. From the first, the prognosis for Sergeant Lowell had been heavily on the minus side—and all that had happened since had confirmed that assumption. Miller, he knew, was approaching the problem in the accepted fashion. The first stage would be a simple procedure—the initiation of an external irritant to seal off the area over the abscess, plus aspiration of the abscess itself and the injection of the anti-amoebic drug. Later, a second, more critical procedure would be followed—an attempt to open the infection and drain it completely, in the hope, admittedly desperate, that the damaged liver would regenerate once the microorganisms attacking it were siphoned out.

"We'll post him, the moment we can fit him into the schedule," Miller said. "In the meantime, we'll beef him up with transfusions. He's lost ground steadily since his arrival."

"Did you explain what you plan to do?"

"He wanted the whole truth, so I told him what he can expect. He's a remarkable young man."

"Shall I notify his family?"

"He didn't want that either—afraid his mother would be worried. We'll ask the Red Cross to get in touch before the second operation."

"Will you permit visitors after the transfusions?"

The surgical chief gave Bruce a level look. "He said you'd ask me that. I've had two requests already—by long-distance phone."

"One of them Congressman Reardon?"

"He's flying in—and plans to stop by in the morning. I've authorized a meeting, if Lowell is well enough to talk. He's extremely anxious to make contact with Reardon."

"Did you know that Hal arranged to have him transferred here from Letterman?"

"Congressman Reardon explained that when he called," said Miller. "He feels the boy has ideas worth discussing."

"So worthy of discussion, Shane McLendon is coming here for an interview?"

"She's the second visitor. How did you guess?"

"Let's say I remember how Hal operates. The author of *As I See It* has a way of turning up when a front-page story's breaking."

"The first man to be hit at Pearl Harbor is certainly news—

when he's fighting to stay alive. Of course I can still say no."

"Don't, Terry. Sick or well, Jimmie's earned the right to see them both—if it's what he wants. I just didn't expect things to happen so fast."

"Things will have to move fast with Sergeant Lowell," said Miller. "I hope I'm wrong, but I'm afraid he hasn't much time left."

Knowing Hal Reardon as he did, Bruce was hardly surprised to learn that he had appeared early the next morning, to spend an hour at Jimmie's bedside. He was even less surprised when he entered his office later—and found his classmate established at his desk, with the contents of an attaché case spread on the blotter.

"Don't tell me, let me guess," he said. "You came here direct from Bolling Field."

Hal bounced to his feet, to offer his hand. Once again, Bruce warned himself to curb a suspicion that was still without a solid base.

"Jimmie Lowell says you had a long talk yesterday—so I needn't explain my presence."

"Was your visit a success?"

"Completely."

"Why are you still here, if you got what you wanted?"

"*That's* hardly a warm welcome."

"I'm sure you've an office of your own at the Capitol."

"Frankly, Bruce, it seemed worthwhile to talk to you—and catch up on my mail while I waited. Both of us have ground to cover."

"I'm operating in twenty minutes."

"Twenty minutes will do, if you'll remove that chip from your shoulder," said Hal. "Let me start by thanking you for taking good care of Janet."

"You didn't wait here to tell me that."

"It was my chief reason, next to my date with Sergeant Lowell. My fiancée is blooming—because of your good offices, and the therapies of the USO. At the moment, I'm not sure who contributed more."

"Are you referring to Janet's camp show? Or the fact she's existed for six weeks without you?"

Hal tossed back his head for his famous laugh. "Thanks to you—if I can believe Janet's own testimony—she found the courage to go onstage for the first time. And thanks to the applause, she's begun to have faith in her ability. Those are important developments, Bruce. Once again, accept my gratitude."

"Janet's the actress, not I."

"You were there to cheer, when cheering counted," said Hal. "The acid test will come tonight. Leo Brodski's catching her new show at Annapolis."

"Who is Brodski?"

"A top director on the Coast. If he likes her, it means a screen test."

"Isn't that moving Janet rather fast?"

"Not with *my* friends behind her," said Hal. "If she tests well, I'll arrange to finance a picture. A comedy for Armed Forces distribution, based on the work she's been doing. With Leo's guiding hand, it can hardly miss."

"Is it always this easy to play God?"

"Only when first-class material is at hand," said Hal. "Do you object to my plan because it seems overoptimistic? I can afford it."

"Why should I object, if it's what Janet wants?"

"Drive out to Annapolis tonight, and see how my conniving has paid off. Shane McLendon's going. She'll give you a lift."

"After she's interviewed my patient?"

"She can manage both—if you'll let her write her story here."

The surgeon turned toward the cabinet. Unable to put his foreboding into words, he did not speak until he had filed the morning reports.

"Your plans for Janet are dazzling, to put things mildly," he said. "I'll be glad to join tonight's applause. Now we've had our round of shadowboxing, will you explain why you've invaded Scranton General?"

"Because of my interest in Jimmie Lowell—what else? He tells me you were a sympathetic listener."

"Are you prepared to help create his Peace Party?"

"So far, we've only explored the idea. I'm immensely attracted by his thinking—"

"What does 'immensely attracted' mean?"

"I'm interested, Bruce—but I'm uncommitted. Sergeant Lowell has latched onto a first-rate idea. Like all great concepts, it needs checking—and seasoning."

"Beginning with a trial run on the front page?"

"Can you suggest a better forum than *As I See It?*"

"I gather Shane welcomed this assignment."

"Jimmie is giving her an exclusive interview, at my request. He's highly honored—and so is Shane."

"What can an interview accomplish at this time?"

"I've told you. By pure chance, I've uncovered a classic American patriot—"

"*I'd* call Jimmie Lowell a citizen of the world."

"Regardless of nationality, this is a vision that could grow wings tomorrow. Granted it's nebulous, so far. Quite possibly, it won't get off the ground. It deserves impartial coverage, the kind Shane can give it. I've thought so, from the day I met Jimmie at Letterman Hospital."

"I wonder who was really in luck, that day at Letterman. You, or Sergeant Lowell?"

"The sergeant, as I just observed, may be just another college boy with a bump of resentment against his century and a need to sound off. On the other hand, his name—and his concept—could be focal points for one of the greatest moral rallies in history."

"With a politician named Reardon as the manager?"

"Assuming Shane's interview is well received, I'll discuss his ideas with key figures in Congress. As of now, I'm prepared to go no further. It would be extremely unwise to launch him politically, at this stage of the war."

"Because a Peace Party can't seek votes until your side begins winning?"

Hal ignored the sarcasm. "Just how serious is Jimmie's illness?"

"We hope to save his life with a two-stage operation. At best, it will be touch and go."

"Is his trouble a result of his wound?"

"The wound is healed. This is a kickback from dormant amoebic dysentery, contracted in Manila."

Hal turned to the window and stared out at the hospital lawn. He gave no sign that he had heard Bruce's remark. Apparently, he was absorbed in a reverie he could not share.

"Will he die if this operation fails?"

"Even with surgery, his chances are poor."

"Does that mean Shane must postpone her interview?"

"Colonel Miller has cleared it. We agree it's good therapy for the patient."

"I'm glad you reached that decision," said Hal. "Obviously, we must move fast, if he's going to die tomorrow."

"You've a valid point there. Dead heroes have their uses. You can hardly promote a dead prophet, unless you create his public beforehand."

Hal swung away from the window. His easy smile had been replaced by an alabaster mask the surgeon remembered almost as well.

"Perhaps you're amused by this goading," he said. "To me, it's in doubtful taste. You *can't* dismiss Sergeant Lowell as another utopian."

"I'm not dismissing anything. I just wonder whether his idea has a prayer."

"It could, with proper timing," said Hal. "Obviously, we

can't let a Peace Party compete with our plans for a United Nations. Eventually, each concept could re-enforce the other."

"Do you think this country's ready to join a new League of Nations?"

"I do, Bruce—once the voters are prepared."

"With powers the old League never had? Like a police force to crack down on aggressors?"

"With a real Peace Party, backed by a union of veterans and their families, *we* might become the first international policeman."

"Only if we can guarantee peace inside America—and make democracy more than a slogan."

"You can't be both a cynic and a one-worlder, Bruce."

"I'm reserving the right to be wary—until I learn what you want from Jimmie Lowell."

"I want nothing, except to give him a hearing. Isn't that better than letting his dream die in a hospital ward?"

"In other words, you may drop him altogether, if Shane's column misfires. Or you may use his credo later—as a political football."

"I've told you I believe in him, heart and soul. Why shouldn't I proclaim that belief later, if the country shares it?"

Bruce glanced at the wall clock, and rose from his chair. The act helped, in some measure, to break the spell Hal's words had cast.

"Call that your round," he said. "You're innocent—until you're proven guilty."

"Fair enough. You'll be at Annapolis tonight?"

"Of course, if Shane will take me. Wish Janet luck."

It was after five when the surgeon returned to his office. Shane McLendon was seated at the table with a portable typewriter before her. A recorder in an open carrying-case was at her side. Its earphones were clamped to her head, and she was typing at top speed.

"The nurse in charge said I could use this space, Bruce. Throw me out if I'm in the way."

"Go on, please. My working day is over."

"One more page, and I'll join you in that happy state."

"You've had your interview with Jimmie Lowell, I gather."

"Hours ago, while you were operating. Your patient was in the groove, so I made the most of it." Shane flicked on the recorder switch, and turned, with complete concentration, to her typewriter. Silence filled the office, save for the machine-gun tattoo of the keys. It was the first time Bruce had watched a high-voltage reporter in action. When Shane cut the switch and pulled the final sheet from her machine, he still felt like an intruder.

"When is that appearing?" he asked.

"In the *Post*, at breakfast time."

"I thought the *Star* was your Washington outlet."

"I shifted last week. Hal felt the extra coverage was worth it."

"Do you take his advice on your stories?"

"Why not, when he gives me so many?"

"Don't forget *I* let you visit the patient. You might give me an advance look."

"Ordinarily, nobody but my syndicate editor previews my copy," said Shane. She picked up the page from the blotter. "You can read this much, if you hurry. A messenger's on his way to collect it."

The page contained several paragraphs, all of them flawlessly typed. Shane McLendon, Bruce gathered, was a journalist who planned a story well before she sat down at a keyboard:

> Pragmatists (and their number is legion) will call this a nebulous vision. They will dismiss Sergeant Lowell's dream as another attempt by the young to oppose the infinite wisdom—and cruelty—of their elders, another echo of a yearning in all men's hearts that can never be translated into action.

The pragmatists, as always, will have the final say. But no reader who believes in the future of mankind can close his ears to these words of Sergeant Lowell's:

"Before this war ends," he told me, "at least twenty-eight million Americans, including those in uniform and their families, will have been touched, in some fashion, by the hand of Mars. Most of those twenty-eight million will be the worse for such contact. If they gird themselves to maintain the peace, nothing can stop them—and such united action is bound to trigger identical movements among our friends, even among our enemies."

I have just left the surgical ward at Scranton General, where our first American casualty faces still another operation in a long battle to survive his wounds. Every instinct I possess tells me that his hopes for a lasting peace are doomed. (I, too, alas, am a pragmatist!) But my heart, if not my mind, has been profoundly moved by this young man's convictions, and his courage.

Will the voiceless, faceless millions he counts on be moved in turn?

When the tide has shifted our way in the current struggle for survival, will those same millions rise up and demand that tomorrow's heroes be wagers of peace, and not of war?

Will our children, and our children's children, learn to rid themselves, once and for all, of the dirty thumbprint of Mars?

Will an unborn generation open their dictionaries to find that *war* has become an obsolete word, a term used to describe an atavism humanity has outgrown, along with the dodo bird and the dinosaur?

The pragmatists, of course, will answer each of these questions with a ringing "No." They will repeat the old, dim truisms men live by. War, they will tell us, like the poor, will be with us always.

Perhaps the time has come for men of good will, the world over, to shout down the doom-sayers—to rise, as a neglected poet named Tennyson would have it, on the stepping-stones of their dead selves, to higher things.

A knock had sounded on the door while Bruce read the last paragraph. Shane took the sheet from his hand, folded it into an envelope, and gave it to the messenger.

"I told you to wait until morning," she said. "There's nothing hungrier than a printing press."

"I'm glad you approve of Jimmie's ideas."

"Would you call that page an endorsement?"

"I'd call it an act of faith," said Bruce. "What's more, I think you're sold."

"Of course I'm sold. Peace is immune to criticism. It's like God and motherhood and the Washington Senators. The baseball team, not those Gray Ladies on Capitol Hill."

"You meant what you said on that page. Don't pretend you didn't back this idea all through your column."

"You've seen the only comment I made. The rest was direct quotes—and Sergeant Lowell, like all young men who believe in their ideals, was heartbreakingly quotable." The journalist closed the case of her recorder and zipped up the cowhide cover. "By now, you must have heard most of it firsthand. I won't bore you with a playback."

"Why should I be bored?"

"Virtue is like true beauty, Bruce—or unselfish love. In its pure form, it's something the average human brain can't grasp."

"I'm afraid that sophistry is beyond me."

"Don't pretend to be dense. Jimmie's dream is a thing of beauty. Keep it so, and it's a joy forever—to paraphrase another poet. The idea of a Peace Party to reform us all belongs with the teachings of Buddha and Socrates—and the Sermon on the Mount. Unfortunately, it has no relation to our century. Or to any century in the sad history of man."

"Isn't man capable of self-improvement?"

"We stick together when our way of life is threatened," said Shane. "Jimmie Lowell will find a million fellow-idealists in Washington alone. Day after tomorrow, those same idealists will need another slogan to hold their attention. One that's closer to home and the dollar sign."

"If you feel this way, why did you interview him?"

"I happen to be a reporter. Your patient's big news again, now he's dying."

"Who told you he was going to die?"

"Nobody, in so many words. I was a volunteer nurse before I turned to journalism. I can spot a raging fever. And I'm not above sneaking a look at a hospital chart."

"We haven't abandoned hope."

"Perhaps he'll live. I know you'll do your best to save him. Frankly, he's worth more to his Peace Party dead than alive."

"Particularly if Hal Reardon takes over?"

"Someone must take over great ideas—and reduce them to human terms."

"You just said Jimmie's ideal was unworkable."

"The *ideal*. Not the idea. It can't succeed all the way, that's obvious. In Hal's hands, it could become a political philosophy. A force for good, even if it only strengthens a peacetime United Nations."

"I doubt if even Hal can pass that miracle. Right now, his main concern is how to advance his own career."

"Why not—if he brings the boy's ideas down to earth? Give him a chance, before you condemn him."

"Strangely enough, that's just what I intend doing."

"You've made a good choice, Bruce. After all, we can't stop Hal now. It's only turnabout to give him his head—and see what happens next. Both of us have already found him useful."

"Both of us?"

"Didn't he put you here in Scranton General? Hasn't he just given me the most touching newsbeat of the war?"

"I can hardly deny either count."

"Let's stop arguing, then. The die is cast for Sergeant Lowell. In your operating room tomorrow. And in the Washington *Post*."

"I still won't admit you're completely right."

"No girl would expect that of a man. Will you buy me dinner if I drive you to Annapolis?"

They had gone direct to Crabtown-on-the-Bay, in the vintage Singer Le Mans roadster Shane used to cover out-of-town assignments. They had dined at a terrace-restaurant on the Chesapeake, with a fine view of the Academy. A bottle of beaujolais and a superb terrapin casserole had done their part to establish an armistice after the battle at Scranton General. . . . Before the dessert, Bruce had shed enough of the day's resentments to enjoy the evening for its own sake. Over coffee and Strega, he had admitted it was far less wearing to dwell on the specifics of his own future than the imponderables of world brotherhood.

It had been even simpler to listen to the story of Shane McLendon—to wonder if her autobiographical mood might be a sign that their armistice was permanent.

Shane—he had learned, to his amazement—had been born in a West Virginia coal pocket, a near-classic trap whose chief features were poverty and despair. The youngest of five, and the only girl, she had endured the wailings of a hopelessly overworked mother—who had deserted her brood when the daughter was ten. Shane had done her best to keep house for her father—he had died two years later, in a blow back at the mine. After her brothers had scattered, she had reached her own turning point, when a teacher had helped her to a scholarship at Oberlin. She had won a second scholarship to the Columbia School of Journalism. Graduation there, at the top of her class, had brought a third award—a year of travel abroad. A police card on a New York paper had followed in due course. At twenty-one, she had joined one of the wire services. Four years later, she had begun a syndicated column. . . . Today, *As I See It* had more than three hundred outlets.

"How did you stay alive while you got your degrees?"

"I took what jobs I could find, Bruce. By then, moonlighting after school had become a habit. Hospital work was one of the fill-ins. I've waited on table at country clubs. I've been a hostess on a Montana dude ranch. For two years, I tutored delinquent brats on Long Island. As you see, I survived. What do you think of my story?"

"I'd call it a testament to courage."

"And I'd call you an incurable romantic," said Shane. "No one deserves a medal for existing. Eventually, a knack for words lit the fuse to my rocket. You might say my trajectory was plotted in advance, just like yours."

"There's a vast difference between us, I'm afraid. I've had solid backing all the way. You've fought from the start."

"I haven't fought that hard," said Shane. "And I wasn't boasting when I showed you that up-from-poverty road map. I only wanted you to accept me as I am—if it isn't too great an effort."

"I'm proud to be your friend. This *is* an offer of friendship, I take it?"

"You weren't exactly seeking friendship when we met in the Station Bar."

"You'll recall I pleaded guilty at the time."

"So you did—to give yourself a chance to retreat in good order. Naturally, you were shocked to find a devious reporter in the cloak of Jezebel. Now you've recovered, do you think you can survive the fact I'm behind Hal? Even if he decides to take over Jimmie Lowell?"

"As I told you this afternoon, I'll try hard."

"Including the knowledge *we've* been friends, for quite a while?"

"Again, that would depend on the degree of friendship."

"Suppose I confessed that I prayed you'd capture Janet while Hal was in England—so I could move in later?"

"Do you mind if we sidetrack such unworthy ideas—rather than spoil our evening?"

"Our evening's almost over, Bruce. It's been fun—now that we've stopped beating each others' brains. You're sure you've no more questions? I'm in a confessional mood."

"I'll ask just one, since we've let down our hair. Where does all this leave us—now it's obvious I've failed with Janet?"

Shane rose from the table. "If I knew that answer, I wouldn't be here tonight. Nor would you. Let's catch the lucky lady's show, while we can still get seats."

Tonight's performance by the USO unit, they were told at the Academy gates, had been staged in a special football arena near the midshipmen's barracks, a many-tiered structure that held almost three thousand spectators, with the acting platform in the center of the field.

The show was under way when Shane drove into the parking lot. At first glance, every place seemed filled with men in blue—but the journalist's press pass brought them to a pair of seats in a lower tier, close enough for a real view of the stage. A row of show girls and a master of ceremonies were stomping out a medley of Navy songs, climaxing with the inevitable "Anchors Aweigh." When three thousand young male voices joined in the refrain, the effect seemed earth-shattering.

"Hal's at ringside, as usual," said Shane. "With the wonder boy from the West. If you ask me, Janet's contract's as good as signed."

"Is *that* the great Leo Brodski?"

"Complete with scowl and camel's-hair coat."

Congressman Reardon and the director were in earnest conference while the chorus streamed down the runway. With the floodlights directly above them, Bruce could not make out their features clearly. Brodski seemed enormous in the bulky topcoat. Its collar was turned up despite the warm evening: the shoulders beneath it suggested a football coach whose bearing was as uncouth as his attire.

"How did Hal snare him?"

"His studio has just put a new war epic in the can," said Shane. "They'll get it in the grind-houses faster if they have Army clearance."

"Don't tell me Janet's entree in pictures is being bought."

"Not entirely, of course. As you've seen for yourself, she has a bag of tricks all her own. I'd call it a good two-way deal. She's ready-made for the camp-show comedy Brodski has in mind."

The opening chorus was followed by a nationally known jazz pianist, whose renditions of "Rhapsody in Blue" and a potpourri of tunes from World War I were brilliantly suited to the audience. He was followed by an equally famous comic, whose routines were received with the same uncritical joy. During these turns, Brodski continued to talk with Hal, ignoring the stage entirely.

"Are his manners always this bad?" Bruce asked.

"Don't hold his lack of attention against him. Leo's only himself when he's in the director's chair. He'll come alive after Janet is announced."

"The program says her act is next." The surgeon felt a familiar lump in his throat as he spoke. Knowing in advance what he would see—and its effect on this audience—he could still keep the illusion he was watching Janet Josselyn for the first time.

Her accompanist was onstage now—making his cross to the keyboard, where he struck the first chords of "Cherokee Rose," the tune that had become her signature music in camps throughout the East. As the message reached the arena, to bring a thunder of applause, the master of ceremonies circled the stage, holding aloft a placard that bore the single word *Impersonations*. . . . The business brought a second reaction, a deep silence that was broken only when Janet appeared on the runway, moved to the curve of the grand piano, and picked up the straw boater that would serve as her first prop.

Tonight, she was wearing the same wine-red evening gown Bruce remembered so well. Her dark hair was piled high—and the kiss she tossed over the footlights assured her audience she was friends with all the world. As always, she needed only a pirouette to step into her first character. The boater was already tilted on her nose. With hands extended palm out, and her sleek legs in a music-hall stance, she was Chevalier to the life, long before her accompanist swept into the patter prelude to "Valentina."

The song, with its flashing *double-entendres*, was received with howls of rapture. Janet followed it with sketches of two other stars: a cinema temptress from abroad, and an all-American Lothario who had just rocked his public by enlisting as a man before the mast. The act was climaxed with a series of ballads, done from the piano top in a style made famous by a generation of torch singers. This time, Janet dared to perform in a style all her own. Her sweet-pitched contralto belonged to a drawing room rather than a stage, yet it was entirely suited to this setting, thanks to the clustered microphones. Aided by that electronic magic, she might have been singing individually to each spectator in the arena—and these lonely young men, divorced from the past, and fearful of the future, were responding with all their hearts.

Janet's formal program ended with the song group—but the Navy refused to surrender her. After a half-dozen encores —when the master of ceremonies had offered his homage for the last time, and she had finally dashed down the runway— Bruce realized he had risen with the others, to cheer as loudly as any sailor in the crowd. The crowning discovery of the evening came when he leaned forward to check on the visitor from Hollywood—and saw that Brodski, too, had joined in the surf of applause.

"That does it, I gather," he said—and cursed the husky note he could not quite control.

"That does it," said Shane. "Take another look at Brodski. How can she lose—with *two* geniuses behind her?"

Feeling his voice choke in his throat, the surgeon did not risk a reply. He was saved when the arena lights went on to signal an intermission—and he heard his name boom over the loudspeakers, with the request that he call the Academy switchboard.

"Would that be Scranton General?" Shane asked.

"I'm afraid so. Terry Miller's cancelled an overnight pass before, when he's known how to reach me."

The guess was verified after they had fought through the crowd to a phone booth. At the hospital, an operating room was being readied for the kind of salvage only a vascular surgeon could handle. Colonel Miller, alert to the perquisites of his station, had secured transport at Annapolis. An ambulance was waiting now, at the main gate.

Shane, who had stood at the phone-booth door, studied Bruce anxiously when he emerged.

"Is it as serious as you look?"

"It's a femoral artery—completely severed, after a brawl in a bar."

"That sounds bad enough."

"We've a good chance to save the patient. Actually, it's only a routine end-to-end suture. The sort of repair job I worked out last year at Lakewood."

"I'll drive you in."

"The ambulance siren will take me there faster. Can you get back to Washington all right?"

"I'll make a caravan, with Hal and Janet. Perhaps I can persuade Brodski to give *me* a screen test too."

"Send him to me, if you need a recommendation. And will you tell Janet I'll congratulate her tomorrow?"

"If you like, I'll tell her she's damned stupid to prefer Hal Reardon to you—even if he can kick down a studio gate. Good luck with your femoral artery."

"Good luck with your next column."

He would never be sure if Shane had offered her cheek

for his kiss—or if it was he who moved forward to put an arm around her thin shoulders, before he hastened toward the blinking red eye of the ambulance. It was only when he was speeding toward Washington that he realized the caress had been both an act of homage and a consolation.

The emergency, as he had expected, turned out to be a standard procedure. Despite the unsolved doubts in his mind, he slept deeply after it was over. When his alarm clock roused him, an hour remained before he would assist Terry Miller, in the first stage of the surgery posted for Sergeant James Lowell. Ten minutes before he scrubbed, he picked up his office phone and dialed Five Oaks.

When he heard Janet Josselyn's voice on the wire, he had steadied his racing thoughts. Last night had proved that she was about to receive a just reward for her abilities. He had no right to spoil her first rapture, as she stood on the brink of an adventure any member of her sex would envy.

"Forgive me if I'm late with my applause."

"Shane told us you'd been called back to the hospital. I *did* want you to meet Brodski."

"I hear he's come East with a gift of stardust."

"It's true, Bruce. He offered me a contract last night, and I accepted. Who told you?"

"Hal mentioned a screen test when I saw him yesterday. After that performance at Annapolis, it was bound to happen."

"They say the tests will be only a formality. Hal's lawyers are drawing up agreements for a one-picture deal. He's putting up most of the money—but he's sure he'll recover it."

"So am I. How does the senator feel?"

"Dad's been a little old-fashioned—but Hal's convinced him I deserve the experience. I still can't believe he's arranged it. Can you?"

"When Hal Reardon goes into action, I can believe anything. What kind of show has Brodski picked for you?"

He listened patiently while Janet described the feather-light screenplay with music in which she would be featured —a boy-and-girl romance in a training camp, with the title of *Pierrette*. The scenario, it seemed, had already been written and scored. Two well-known leading men would be her foils. The director insisted the role had been created for her alone.

"It's rank flattery, but I love it. Do you think I'll disappoint Brodski too badly?"

"You're just what he needs to put his picture over."

"Maybe fun and games *are* what the public wants in wartime. We'll soon know."

"When do you go into production?"

"I'm flying out day after tomorrow for the first tests. Class One priority from Bolling Field—since this is an Armed Forces project."

"Can we meet before then?"

"I don't see how, Bruce. I'm about to leave for a Red Cross bazaar in Philadelphia—and I'll be singing at camps in the area."

"In that case, I'll be part of your entourage at the airport."

"There'll be no entourage, I'm afraid."

"What about your father—and your fiancé?"

"The congressman and the senator will both be in committee. Please try to appear, or I'll feel completely deserted."

"If Terry Miller won't give me a pass, I'll go AWOL."

"Is that a promise?"

"A solemn promise. Someone must cheer you on your way to glory."

Before the first part of the two-stage operation that would determine Sergeant Lowell's chances for survival, a preliminary aspiration had confirmed the diagnosis of abscess—but neither Bruce nor Colonel Miller had expected the anti-amoebic drug they had injected to stem the disease. During the next hour, the colonel's scalpel followed the pattern a desperate situation dictated—exposing the lower ribs on the right side, so he could free a section of the rib cage over the dome-shaped space where the liver lay. The technique was a simple one, excising the bony cage itself but leaving the periosteum in each bed, so the ribs could regenerate later, if the patient survived.

Some three inches of several ribs were removed, along with the softer floating ribs, to permit free access to the damaged organ. Because the pleural cavity sometimes extended well down into this region, such an approach was also designed to create artificial inflammation on the borders of the operative field. This would seal the two layers of the membrane—forestalling an accidental opening of the chest cavity when the area was explored later in an attempt to drain the abscess. To assure this result, Miller packed the space with a strip of gauze soaked in iodoform, then drew the skin together with loose sutures. In the next two days, this mild antiseptic would produce enough adhesions to seal off the field. The surgeon could then enter the liver at will, with no threat to the abdomen beneath it, or to the pleura above.

A light injection with the new drug called sodium pentothal had kept the sergeant quiet during this preliminary procedure. Bruce had left the *Post* on his bedside table and had intended to stop by that afternoon—but an influx of cases from a nearby training camp, where the explosion of an ammunition dump had produced a chain-reaction of injuries, kept him hard at work until midnight.

When he returned the next morning to the room where Sergeant Lowell was still in semi-isolation, there had been no improvement. The temperature was spiking, with a notation of a chill during the night—another indication that the infection was still rampant. The patient himself, sitting upright in the hospital bed with yesterday's *Post* spread open on his knees, was a marked contrast to these danger signs.

Though the red flags at each cheek told of a steadily mounting fever, he had never seemed more carefree.

"Thanks for leaving the paper, sir. I'm still reading—even though I could recite most of it."

"How does it feel to be famous again?"

"Miss McLendon did a wonderful job. I've already written notes to thank her—and Congressman Reardon. Why isn't his name in the story?"

"He wanted you to have your say alone. He'll enter the picture later, if there's a real response to that column."

"People are already responding. The public relations officer says over a hundred calls came in yesterday."

"I hope you won't try to answer them."

"Colonel Miller took care of that. I did ask the PRO to get names and addresses. Is my second operation down for tomorrow?"

"You're posted for nine o'clock."

"I've been a little lightheaded since I read that column—but I never felt finer in my life. It's a wonderful thing, knowing my idea's in the open."

Bruce hesitated before he spoke again. It was impossible to deal Jimmie Lowell's hopes a mortal blow, when the boy himself was clinging to life by a thread.

"I'm sure you realize a Peace Party can't be launched tomorrow," he said at last.

"Of course. Congressman Reardon says we can't even think of looking for votes until America's on top in this war."

"Are you trusting him with your revolution, then?"

"That's what I decided, after our second talk. All revolutions need a general manager. Peace isn't as simple as a sophomore's dream. Even an ex-sophomore can see that."

"Your Peace Party is still a great idea, Jimmie."

"I think it is, sir—and I think Congressman Reardon's the man to sell it to the world. My mother already has a letter telling her to accept his decisions after I'm gone."

"Don't write yourself off, please. We've every hope of curing you tomorrow."

"I'm sure you have, Major Graham. But I read up on amoebic dysentery while I was at Letterman, so I know what my chances are."

"We may have a few tricks you never heard of."

"I hope so—but I doubt it. That's why I'm glad Congressman Reardon's ready to take charge of my dream. Even if it fails, it's been put into words—and I've shared it. That's something none of my enemies can take away. Even an enemy named *Entamoeba histolytica*."

Hal Reardon's office on Capitol Hill was anything but private, as Bruce had discovered in the past hour. Divided down its middle by a fence with a swinging gate, it opened through wide-open double doors to the bustling hall outside. Since the surgeon's arrival, it had been thronged with visitors, most of whom had been herded at the barrier by a male secretary who seemed to combine the functions of an informal host and a barroom bouncer. Hal himself, busy with phones at his desk beneath the windows, had still found time to greet each drop-in while he handled his day's appointments—an impressive stream of lawyers, lobbyists and fellow legislators. A third wave of callers Bruce found impossible to classify—intent, gray-faced men who slipped into the visitor's slot, whispered their messages or took their instructions, and departed as quietly as they had come.

Seated in an armchair in a corner, pretending to leaf through a copy of the *Congressional Record*, Bruce continued to measure the tempo of Hal's day in silent wonder. A politician, he told himself, must function at many levels. Like a banker or a minister, it was essential that he offer maximum exposure to the public—and hypocrisy was an unwanted ghost in his sanctum. It was impossible to believe that Hal's shouts of welcome, his warm handclasps and the laughter shared over private jokes, were less than sincere.

It was just as hard to believe the real Hal Reardon would emerge, now the hall door was bolted at last and the well-muscled secretary had departed.

Hal's last visitor, a hatchet-thin, faultlessly attired man in his thirties, had just left by the side door—an exit, Bruce gathered, reserved for really important callers. Belatedly, he realized this was Hilary Manning, the trial lawyer from Chicago who had given up a fortune in fees to serve as personal counsel for Congressman Jake Sanford of the House Subversive Acts Committee, known derisively to newsmen on the Hill as HOSAC. It seemed appropriate that Manning should end Hal's official day. A scourge in his own right, he was now almost as important to HOSAC as Sanford himself. His handsome profile, as cruel and withdrawn as the carving on a mummy case, had appeared in a hundred press photographs beside his employer, to celebrate another *coup de grâce*.

Hal rose from his desk to stretch his legs.

"You might have warned me you were dropping in, Bruce. I could have made time for you."

"The afternoon was instructive, just as it was. What did Manning want?"

"Sorry, our talk was classified. Incidentally, I'm due on the House floor at six. Jake's speaking for his river-reclamation bill. I must be there in time to vote."

"Backing his annual pork barrel?"

"A lot of my own projects are in that bill. Mutual back-scratching gets the work of Congress done. Don't judge us too harshly."

"I didn't come here as a judge, Hal."

"What other reason could you have?"

"Oddly enough, I'm still hoping to understand you. It hasn't been easy, over the years."

"I've always tried to be the soul of candor."

"Perhaps I'll have better luck today—if you mean that."

"Fire away, Bruce. After all, you're a constituent."

The surgeon hesitated on the best way to launch his attack. "I have two questions to ask you. They may seem unrelated, but they're part of the same pattern. Give me straight answers, and I'll leave you in peace."

Hal settled in his swivel chair and lifted an immaculately-shod foot to his desk top. "I've been fielding hot grounders all afternoon. Why should two more matter?"

"Question one is easy—I hope. Can you make Janet happy?"

"Isn't that being rather abrupt, even for an old classmate?"

"Perhaps it is—but I won't apologize. Do you care to answer?"

"I'll be abrupt myself, since you insist," said Hal. "Can *you* make her happier?"

"I won't deny I've entertained such thoughts of late. You have the inside track, of course. The senator wants you for a son-in-law. Obviously, you can do a great deal for her. The question is—can you do enough?"

"I think so, Bruce. I really do. I won't even say you're impertinent to ask."

"We'll go on to question two, then. I hope you'll answer it just as frankly. What's to become of Jimmie Lowell?"

"I'd say that was your concern at the moment."

"You know what I mean. Are you going to play this tune by ear, and hope America joins the chorus?"

"At the moment, I can't say. As of now—to vary your metaphor—I'm measuring the ground swell, to see if Sergeant Lowell's Peace Party can float there. So far, the measurements are promising. Shane's column caused a sensation, as we expected. Jimmie's idea is a novel one. The electorate's badly in need of novelty, until the news from abroad improves—"

"Never mind the electorate, Hal—you aren't addressing them now. What's your own feeling about a political party dedicated to peace?"

"Can anyone be against it?"

"The hospital's been swamped with calls. Have you taken samples in Congress?"

"Most of my friends hope it will tie in with White House planning. We prefer to wait and see. The idea's planted in the public mind. We'll let it grow there for a while. At least, until we start winning the war."

"Then you *are* playing the tune by ear?"

"For the time being, yes. Meanwhile, Jimmie has made me his heir apparent. He's written his mother, asking her to turn over his letters and diaries—"

"Do you realize you're talking as though he were already dead? What happens to this delayed-action approach, if—by some miracle—he stays alive?"

"In that event, he's letting Shane's column stand as his credo—and buttoning up. Because of his family, I've advised him to serve out his time in uniform. If he lives, and gets his discharge, he can run for Congress later, on his peace platform."

"Would you support him?"

"Of course. Jimmie Lowell may not realize it, but he's a great man from this day forward. If you save his life, I'll spare no effort to make him a world figure. If you lose him, I'll make the Peace Party his monument."

"How?"

"By using publicity where it really counts. You saw what a single column could do—with the right by-line. I have similar outlets, all over the country, in both press and radio. If we decide to roll, we'll have no trouble launching our offensive."

"Will it be a crusade for peace, Hal? Or a modern grand opera, with you as Machiavelli?"

"You can't challenge my motives, or the results I have in mind. The right publicity's essential. No product sells itself."

"And if you still fail as a salesman?"

Congressman Reardon got to his feet. Though his sunny

manner was unchanged, it was apparent he meant to end the conversation.

"Failure's a word I don't use, Bruce."

"You'll find you must use it eventually."

"Not while I have the right friends—and remain on the side of the angels. Sergeant Lowell will die fulfilled, because of me. If my career's advanced as a consequence, I deserve the advancement."

"Perhaps you do, by your code. I'm not sure I could live by that book of rules."

"I've tried hard to be honest. Who can do more for Jimmie Lowell? Or for Janet?"

"How did we get to Janet?"

"Like Sergeant Lowell, Janet is still unfinished business. You said she was one reason you're here."

"That's true enough."

"Since you're concerned about her future—for reasons I'm too good a friend to question—you should be pleased to learn I have the influence, and the hard cash, to put her in a Brodski production."

"Suppose she can't deliver as an actress?"

"Leo will bring out her best in this musical. He's a genius —and it's tailor-made for her style. I haven't looked beyond."

"Meaning this could be the beginning and the end of her screen career?"

"If that's the case, so be it. She'll enjoy this adventure, while it lasts."

"You're backing this one picture, then—and expecting her to do no more?"

"Naturally, I don't want Janet to *stay* in Hollywood," said Hal. "A flair for impersonation doesn't mean she'll turn into a great actress tomorrow. At the worst, she'll keep busy while I finish my stint in uniform. If Brodski doesn't offer her a second picture, she can do camp shows again— until I run for her father's seat. It won't hurt a senator's wife to be recognized as a one-picture star. Not if her name was Josselyn."

"Are you sure she'll follow this routine to the letter?"

"She's behaved so far, Bruce."

"Are you sure it will make her happy?"

"Would she be better off as the wife of a surgeon-teacher at Lakewood?"

"It's a question I haven't asked her. If what you say is true, I never will." Bruce paused, with a hand on the gate that protected the inner office. "At least, it's good to know you've found us worth using. Sergeant Lowell, Janet, Shane. Even me."

"If I've used you, Bruce, you've had full value in return. All of you . . ."

Hal was still speaking, in the same bland orator's tone, when the surgeon marched into the hall.

The bar of the officers' club at Scranton General was a mere nook, opening to a half-moon of tables on a terrace above the hospital drive. That evening, both bar and terrace were deserted, save for two men at a far table. Pausing for his own drink, Bruce recognized the shaven skull of Nick Denby—and guessed that the tall figure beside him was Colonel Otis Kirkland, the chief of surgery at Camp Bruckner who had succeeded the unlamented Major Pritchett.

Both men had come to the hospital for the weekly conference on clinical pathology, a meeting that drew doctors, in uniform and out, from the Washington-Baltimore area. Bruce recalled that he had asked them to join him in the bar before their return to camp, and crossed the terrace to explain his late appearance.

"If the bourbon's free, you're forgiven in advance," said Denby. "It's been too long since the last one, Bruce."

"Eight weeks too long, to be precise."

"How's my score as a prophet holding up?"

"I've no complaints at the moment."

"Sure of that? You look a bit harried."

"At the moment, I couldn't be more relaxed." A quick drink at the bar, Bruce admitted, had given some validity to the statement. The second he had ordered was helping still more. He forced himself to sip more slowly, while he surveyed the urologist's superior officer.

Colonel Kirkland was a striking figure—clean-cut, deep-tanned and silver-gray, an athlete of fifty-odd years in superb harmony with his uniform. There was an outdoor air about him—and a sharpness of diction accented a rather pompous bearing. His manner, when they had shaken hands, had been heavily formal, and he had refused to smile at Denby's flashes of humor. Already it was evident to Bruce that the man had placed him on probation—if not on trial. The reasons were logical when he recalled the cloud of gossip surrounding his exit from Bruckner.

"How did you find the conference, sir?"

"Well worth the journey, Major. Terry Miller is a born teacher."

The discussion that followed, centering on the pathology of the abdominal lymphoma Colonel Miller had presented that afternoon, brought a semblance of animation to Kirkland's wooden visage. His comments, though they were delivered in didactic tones, were to the point. Whatever his personal bias, there was no mistaking a genuine regard for his profession.

"I read about the Lowell case, Major Graham," he said. "What's the prognosis, if I'm not asking out of turn?"

"Bad, at the moment. A liver abscess, complicated by a secondary infection. We're going to try draining it tomorrow, but we may lose him."

"I don't want to sound heartless, but that boy's death could be a blessing in disguise. For himself, and for his country."

"Why do you say that, sir?" asked Denby.

"Lowell's an obvious Section Eight. The PRO at Scranton should never have let that story get in print."

The urologist shrugged—and threw a warning glance at Bruce. "It was an expression of one GI's views, Colonel. He wasn't broadcasting a call for insurrection."

"Sergeants should keep their opinions to themselves. This sergeant, at least, is well out of it, assuming your friend is right about his condition. If he dies tomorrow, he won't have to face a court-martial later."

Bruce had finished his second drink, with no clear memory of imbibing. Ignoring Denby's signals, he met Kirkland's ice-blue eyes—and kept his own voice mild.

"Sergeant Lowell has asked for peace when the shooting's over," he said. "Is that a court-martial offense?"

"Don't forget *how* he asked, Major. An NCO has no right to urge other men in uniform to vote against the war."

"They wouldn't be in uniform when they voted," said Denby.

"That's a quibble, Nick. This war has barely started. It could last five years, or ten. How can we close ranks, if the common foot-soldier starts dreaming now about an armistice?"

"We can't censor a soldier's right to dream, sir."

"We can and will—when the dream belongs in cloud-cuckoo land." Obviously nettled by Denby's attempt to soft-pedal an argument, Kirkland swung back to Bruce. "Do you think your sergeant makes a grain of sense?"

"He isn't *my* sergeant."

"He's your patient, damn it! Couldn't you keep him off the front page?"

"Other enlisted men have been interviewed in syndicated columns."

"Would *you* vote for peace in the next election?"

"As of now, a Peace Party's on the visionary side. At best, it's something to hope for tomorrow."

"I call it utter madness. In the first place, your sergeant

assumes that eight million men in this country dislike military service—"

"I can't call that opinion farfetched."

"*I* happen to like the Army, Graham. So do a great many officers of my acquaintance. We, at least, feel it's a privilege to serve our country. Do you feel otherwise?"

"Of course not, Colonel. Are you about to challenge me to a duel on principle—with Nick as your second?"

Kirkland ignored the offer of amnesty—and banged down his highball. "Do you deny that victory's our first objective? That dissenters must be silenced for the duration?"

"I approve of the objective, or I wouldn't be in uniform. But you can't stop me from hoping for a better world afterwards. I've admitted that an American Peace Party is a farfetched hope. It's still worth exploring."

"How long have you been in the Medical Corps?"

"About two months."

"I volunteered for active duty two years ago. What's more, I gave up a good practice in Little Rock to sign my freedom of choice away. I think that gives me the right to lecture you —for your own good."

Bruce listened with half a mind while the gray-haired officer went on, as glibly as though each stock phrase was new-minted wisdom. Something in the man's tone crystallized his own anger, giving the frustrations of his day a target. Across the table, Denby continued to signal frantically—but he felt a strange release as he ignored the gestures.

"Did you say you're from Little Rock, Colonel? Isn't that Jake Sanford's district?"

"It is indeed. Congressman Sanford's one of my oldest friends."

"Do you feel *he's* helping to win the war?"

"Jake Sanford's contribution has been invaluable, in and out of Washington. He's a great American."

"I'd call him a sick man who needs a psychiatrist."

Denby cut into the stony silence a second too late. "How in God's name did we start on Sanford?"

"Major Graham brought up his name," said Kirkland icily. "I find his comment beyond the pale."

Bruce held up both hands. "My apologies, sir—if I've insulted a friend. After all, you've spoken rather freely about one of mine. Shall we drop name-calling, and go back to abdominal lymphoma?"

Again, the older officer refused the olive branch. "It seems we live in different circles, Major. Until today, I've yet to hear an officer slander Jake Sanford—or the help he's given the Army."

"How has he helped? By looking under beds for enemy agents?"

"Can you name a more vital service?"

"Surely the FBI—and our own Intelligence—can hunt down spies without help from Congress."

"When you've seen combat, Major, you'll know better."

"Have you been in combat, sir?"

Kirkland turned red beneath his tan. "Not yet, alas! Nor, I take it, have you."

"I've been through six months of all-out war. With a volunteer medical unit in Spain."

"On which side?"

"We were doctors, Colonel. Our patients didn't wear tags."

"That means, of course, that you were with the so-called Loyalists. May I ask how you got to Spain?"

"My unit was sent there from Lakewood. It was headed by Dr. Abram Schoenfeld."

"The Russian-born doctor who was branded as a Communist sympathizer?"

"Only by Jake Sanford. Later, he was cleared completely."

"So he was, more's the pity. It seems he had smart lawyers."

"Dr. Schoenfeld's a citizen, in good standing. His loyalty to this country is beyond reproach."

"If that's the case, why isn't he in the Army?"

"He's over sixty now."

"I'm fifty-six, and the Army agrees with me. It agrees with most patriots, who prefer these United States to the Soviet Union."

Denby cut in swiftly: the glance he threw at Bruce was imploring. "We're all in this war to win it, Colonel. That doesn't mean we must *like* it, too."

Kirkland scowled briefly at the urologist, before he faced back to Bruce. "I'll tell you something more, Graham. Pearl Harbor came just in time to save the average American from strangling in his own fat. The disciplines of our training camps are beginning to catch hold. In another year, they'll change millions of self-pitying young hoodlums into men."

"Today's young can't be quite that hopeless, sir," said Bruce.

"I never said they were. All they need is a good drill-instructor to see they keep in step—plus a strong dose of reality."

"They'll get that soon enough."

"So they will. It's something Sergeant Lowell missed entirely."

"He was a long time in uniform, sir."

"Before Pearl Harbor, not after. He was the first soldier in this war to draw a sick-tag—and the first to capitalize on his disability. Up to now, he's dreamed in a hospital bed, at government expense. *He'll* never learn a country must lead from strength, or take second-best. It's the first lesson the Army teaches."

Denby cut in once more, in a last effort to mute Kirkland's roaring. "Correction, Colonel. The Army's first lesson is to keep the mouth shut, the bowels open—and never to volunteer."

"This is no time for jokes, Nick. Once we end this war, we're going to give Germany and Japan a hard time. So hard a time, they'll never trouble our sleep again. That goes double for our other enemies."

"Do we have other enemies at the moment?" Denby asked.

"Stalin won't be on our side, once we've bailed him out. Either we crack down *now*—or we'll end by bombing him, before he bombs us."

"How would we crack down?" Bruce asked. "With a world police force?"

"We'll be the policeman, Graham. An old-fashioned frontier marshal with a gun in each fist. Russia will behave, once we convince them we'll shoot first and argue later."

"Don't tell me you believe the Kremlin will take ultimatums lying down."

"They'll have to, if we're first on the draw."

"First on what draw, Colonel Kirkland? I'm told the United Nations is being organized to discourage itching fingers."

Kirkland sucked in his breath and held it, like a bellows on the point of bursting. It was clear he had advanced beyond anger, that he was making a great effort to deal with a madman in rational terms.

"Do you favor that starry-eyed absurdity?"

"How else can we head off World War III?"

"You'd approve of a United Nations, supported by your sergeant's Peace Party?"

"Why not, when it's our last real hope?"

"If this is your political philosophy, Major, it's apparent you were thoroughly misled in Spain. It's my duty to warn you that you're talking revolutionary hogwash."

"Is it revolutionary to hope for world brotherhood?"

"I'll say this one more time, with Major Denby as our witness. *World peace won't work*. Without a gun at his head, the average foreigner will never mend his ways. When we've destroyed the Axis, we must be prepared to cut down uprisings no matter where they occur."

"Even if that means keeping the Army on a war footing?"

"Deterrence is only a starter. We must gut every factory in the Third Reich. Turn the Germans into farmers."

"The Caesars tried that solution almost two thousand years ago. It was a dismal failure."

"We're discussing the future of America. Not ancient history."

"History has a way of repeating old patterns, Colonel." Bruce turned to Denby, who was staring at his empty glass with the air of a man torn between tears and laughter. "I imagine you were exposed to Gibbon, Nick—even if the colonel doesn't seem to have heard of him."

The urologist spoke with lowered eyes. "Bruce refers to an experiment with the Teutonic tribes, sir. Diocletian dispersed them among conquered populations south of the Rhine—but worse barbarians sprang up in their place. Eventually, they sacked Rome."

"This time, we'll chain them to their plows." Kirkland was really shouting now. "We'll herd the Japs on their islands, with a super-Navy to keep them there. We'll make China a buffer, and let Russia rot on its steppes—"

"What becomes of Europe?" Bruce asked.

"Europe will be a group of third-rate nations, dependent on us for survival."

"And England?"

"We'll use the British Isles as an outpost. If they behave, we'll make them our forty-ninth state."

"What you're proposing, then, is American domination of the world—under American guns."

"Is another nation on earth fit to be the master race?"

"An Austrian spellbinder convinced Germany they were the master race. Don't let him give you lessons in statesmanship."

"Graham, what you've just said is close to treason."

"If it's treason to differ with your opinions, then I'm guilty, Colonel. I thought this was a free-wheeling debate, with a dash of irony permitted. Can't you see you've painted yourself into a corner?"

"I'll tell you what I *can* see," Kirkland roared. "You're a disgrace to the uniform you're wearing."

"That, too, is a matter of opinion. If you weren't my guest, I'd return the compliment."

Kirkland got to his feet with blazing eyes. At his nod, Denby sprang up in turn—giving Bruce a lopsided grin as he did so.

"It's time we were leaving, Nick."

"Perhaps it is, sir."

"Before I go, Graham, I'll offer you a bit of wisdom from the Bible. *He who is not with me is against me.*"

"And I'll trade that for another, sir," said Bruce. "It's from Schiller—a poet much admired by the Austrian spell-binder we were discussing. *Against stupidity, even the Gods battle in vain.*"

Since the patient's condition was critical, the second operation on Jimmie Lowell had been scheduled for early morning.

All the weapons in the armamentarium of the surgeon had been enlisted. Blood donors had been matched to stand by if direct transfusions were needed. Colonel Miller had requisitioned a supply of penicillin: an emergency order had been wired to Boston, since the new miracle drug was still being produced in small amounts, and rigid control over its distribution had been established. At Bruce's request, a prothrombin test had been run, as a handy index of liver function: the figure was ominous, a sure sign that the organ was failing.

When the two surgeons approached the operating table, the pupils of the patient's eyes were yellow with jaundice, and he was muttering in a semi-delirium. Yet he managed to give Bruce his familiar, innocent smile while the younger doctor stood by to watch the pentothal go in.

"Easy does it, Jimmie. We're hoping this will turn the trick."

"I know the score by now, sir. Thanks for trying."

"Start the count, please," said the anesthetist.

Sergeant Lowell lifted his eyes to the ceiling, as the needle was inserted in a superficial vein of his left arm. At the count of nine, his voice slurred off and ceased.

"Ready when you are, Colonel," said the anesthetist.

With the operative incision reopened, it was a simple matter to remove the iodoform packing inserted two days ago. Colonel Miller was waiting, with a long-needled syringe. The point probed deep, through the layer of muscle forming the lower part of the chest wall, and the window created by the removal of the ribs. A dark, purulent fluid filled the barrel when he drew back the plunger.

"We'll want smears of this, at once."

A waiting technician stepped forward with the slides he had just prepared. While he worked, the circulating nurse took extra samples of the discharge to a rack of culture tubes, where the bacteria would be further identified. Bruce studied the surgical chief across the table before he ventured a comment.

"This is more than a simple abscess."

"It's the definite pattern for a secondary infection. We might as well open it. Cautery, please."

The instrument that came into the colonel's hand was a metal loop attached to an insulated handle—and connected to an electric circuit which turned the blade deep red when a nurse flipped the switch of the rheostat. Probing with care, the older surgeon began using the blade to seal off blood spaces of the outer liver surface above the main abscess—an essential precaution, since there was no other way to prevent hemorrhage in an organ that could not be sutured.

It was grisly work. Bruce had sympathized with the shudder that passed through the nurse before she could step back from the table and the odor of burning flesh that hung above it. He had felt the same revulsion when he had first used the cautery. Like the rigors of an amputation, the enucleation of a hopelessly damaged eye, or the massive techniques used to remove a malignancy, it was part of the .price a doctor paid for healing.

In this case, it was soon evident that the price would be, at best, prohibitive. Watching the blade sear through the wall of inflamed tissue lining the lethal crater, Bruce stood by with suction tip and basin until he could siphon off the last of the dark fluid that filled the abscess. His heart had sunk, even before an assistant could measure the contents of the basin. The laboratory had already sent back its report on the smear. It confirmed their first estimate, a secondary infection caused by one of the most virulent of the streptococci.

The surgical chief put down the cautery. "We might as well search the whole area, while we have him on the table."

Blood still oozed thinly from the liver as Bruce packed the cavity gently to control the bleeding by pressure, until the body's normal clotting action could take over, stimulated by the transfusion that had just been started. Taking up another long-needled syringe, Colonel Miller explored the rest of the organ for additional foci of infection—since abscesses of this nature tended to be multiple. Two smaller cavities were identified and drained before he stepped back from the table.

By now, it was apparent that Jimmie Lowell's chances would depend on his youth, whatever immunity he had built up during his year of exposure to the infection—and the surgeon's own faint hope that the drainage he had just carried through would swing the balance. Further probing was overruled by the patient's condition. The anesthetist had given warning of a rising pulse rate—and a second transfusion was already flowing in.

Miller's shoulders were drooping when he stripped off his

gloves. "We'll double the penicillin injection and hope for the best," he said. "It's the only trick we have left."

"I'll stand by till it's done."

"There's no need of that, Bruce. Haven't you a date at Bolling Field?"

"I'll cancel it, if you wish."

"Keep it, by all means," said the older surgeon. "We've done all we can for this patient. I'm afraid it's far less than enough."

Bruce had not believed a senator's daughter could fly to the Coast with only a personal maid in attendance and not a single friend to see her off. The evidence was before him when he walked through the hangar—and Janet Josselyn, in the act of counting her bags, ran up to embrace him in the shadow of the DC-3.

"I was afraid you weren't coming."

"An operation kept me longer than we expected. How soon do you take off?"

"In five minutes."

He held her at arm's length, admiring her with eyes that could not quite conceal his hunger. Her kiss, opening old wounds, had warned him to step carefully round unspoken taboos.

"Who's inside the plane? I'm sure I hear singing."

"I'm sharing this flight with a wing group reporting to San Pedro." Janet ignored the beckoning of a fresh-faced officer who had appeared in the plane door, with a guitar in his hands. "If I can follow Lieutenant Adams, it seems I'll sing for my passage."

"Is your deal with Brodski still firm?"

"Unless I flunk my screen test."

"Give me your mirror and I'll show you that's impossible."

"Thanks, Bruce. Now you're here, I'm confident again."

"Confident, and no longer forlorn?"

"Did I seem forlorn when you came up just now?"

"A little. It's hard to see why—with twenty eager escorts inside that plane, and the best director on the Coast waiting to make you famous. Is there an outside chance we'll meet again?"

"I'm afraid not, if you're pinned to Scranton General."

"Won't you return East before the new year? My unit's sure to be activated then, for service in Africa."

"I'll be at least sixteen weeks on the lot."

"Then this is really good-bye."

He had spoken the words steadily, knowing his armor was intact. Expecting a dutiful echo from Janet, he was shaken when she took an uncertain step toward the plane, then turned back to him with tear-wet eyes.

"Are you hating this too, Bruce?"

"You know I am."

"This is no place to say good-bye. Under the wing of an Army transport plane—with those young savages inside, each with his own plan for seducing me."

"I'm counting on you to thwart those plans."

"Can't you *really* go AWOL and come along?"

"The prospect's tempting—but I've only a two-hour pass."

"Something's kept pushing us apart, ever since we met. Either it's called Hal Reardon—or Leo Brodski."

"Hal's your fiancé-once-removed. He's made this trip possible. And Brodski's a self-confessed magician, who's about to launch you on a great career. You should be thankful for both."

"I am, of course. It doesn't make this good-bye any easier."

The DC-3 was revving its engines for the take-off as Lieutenant Adams appeared in the plane door a second time. Janet shrugged him off—and clung to Bruce's arms.

"We probably won't meet again for the duration," she said. "May I tell you something fairly important?"

"If you're sure I should hear it."

"It's taken all my self-control, but I've managed to stay out of love with you. Hussy that I am, I've a suspicion you'd like to fall in love with me—"

"Will it brighten your journey if I admit your suspicion is justified?"

"Promise you'll fall *out* of love, Bruce. It's better for us both."

"That's asking a lot."

"But not too much—of you." She kissed him quickly before he could speak again, and ran up the steps to the plane door. Making no move to detain her, he stood by while a copilot pulled it shut.

He had planned to wait in the hangar until Janet was airborne. Instead, he turned at once to the jeep that had brought him from the visitors' parking lot. The departure of the DC-3 was only another roar from one of several busy airstrips. He could not even bring himself to look up when its shadow passed above him.

Sanity of a sort had returned when he sought out the lane where he had left his car—but his voice was not quite his own when he thanked an attendant for his guidance and fumbled through his blouse for the key. . . . Janet, he told himself, had given him the best consolation prize she could offer. She had been kind enough to retreat in haste thereafter, leaving him with a safe escape route of his own. It was time to remember he was a romantic boy no longer, that Hal Reardon had won a contest whose outcome had never been in doubt.

He had unlocked the car door when he heard his name called from the next lane. The voice had come from a Cadillac sedan parked two slots away. It was not until the man who had been beneath the wheel stepped into the space between that Bruce realized he was facing Hilary Manning, the special adviser of Congressman Jake Sanford.

The lawyer, Bruce observed, was hatless, though a dark cap of hair clung to his skull like lacquer. Today he had discarded his lounge suit in favor of slacks and a Norfolk jacket. The country clothes did nothing to detract from his sinister charm. Seen at close quarters, his eyes suggested a cruising barracuda.

"I don't believe introductions are needed, Major. We saw each other recently in Congressman Reardon's office."

"What are you doing here?" Bruce regretted his brusqueness at once. Try as he might, he knew he could never match Manning's assurance.

"I asked for you at the hospital—and they said you'd gone to Bolling Field. It seemed logical to follow you. After all, an empty parking lot is an ideal spot for a conference. Or should I say, a discussion of your immediate future?"

"Why should my future concern you, Mr. Manning?"

"It concerns my client, Congressman Jacob Sanford. He asked me to arrange a meeting."

"I have no desire to meet Jake Sanford."

"I can appreciate your reluctance, considering the committee he sparkplugs in Congress. But I wouldn't advise you to refuse."

"Are you about to issue a subpoena?" Bruce asked. "If that's why you've followed me, I'll accept the service."

Again, the lawyer ignored the brusqueness. "As of now, Mr. Sanford hopes you'll answer his inquiries in private."

"What sort of inquiries?"

"He's deeply troubled, Major—by your leftist leanings. He feels you should clarify your position."

"How does Jake Sanford define *leftist*?"

"Can you deny you have marked sympathies for the Communist cause?"

"I'm not a Communist. Nor have I had the slightest contact with the Party."

"Not even in Spain?"

"I went to Spain as a surgeon, to save lives. That was my only reason."

"We have been informed otherwise. When you accepted your commission, the FBI ran down certain facts of that visit."

"Facts—or assumptions?"

Manning shrugged off the distinction. "Since we received that report, it has been substantiated by two separate accusers."

"Who are they?"

"I am not at liberty to reveal names."

"Doesn't the Constitution guarantee a citizen the right to know his enemies—and face them?"

"No one is questioning your rights, Major Graham. As I just said, my client would much prefer to have your voluntary deposition."

"Suppose I say no? Does that mean a subpoena—and flash-bulb publicity?"

Manning's eyes—Bruce would never be sure if they were green or yellow—continued to study his victim, as impersonally as a headsman who has not yet reached for the ax. "Wouldn't it be wiser to meet us halfway?"

"Why should I say anything, until I've seen a lawyer of my own?"

"Lawyer's aren't much help in this situation."

"Unless they're on Sanford's side?"

"The point's well taken," said Manning. "Before you decide, it's only fair to state that we have enough evidence to separate you from the service—if we decide to use it."

"Do *you* think I'm a Communist?"

"What I think is unimportant. Will it help convince you if I name your accusers?"

"I won't know until you've tried," said Bruce. "So far, you've behaved like a jackal who's afraid of his prey. Naturally, you've made me curious."

He had offered the insult deliberately, expecting Manning to ignore it. When the lawyer turned back to his car to extract an attaché case, he warned himself to avoid all show of feeling. The fact that Manning was about to name his detractors was a strong hint that bargaining was possible.

"Your first accuser," said the lawyer, "was a colleague at Camp Bruckner."

"Major Pritchett?"

"The bill of particulars includes conduct unbecoming an officer, and radical opinions incompatible with your rank in the Army. He's prepared to appear as a witness, if we so desire."

"Pritchett's been demoted to a training camp in the West. The demotion resulted from a run-in with me, over his lack of competence. This smear is motivated by resentment, nothing more."

Manning smiled for the first time—if the thin-lipped twitch that distorted his face could be called a smile.

"We realize his credibility might be at issue. The fact remains that your service in Spain—on the wrong side—should have barred you from a commission."

"In whose opinion—Jake Sanford's?"

"Be that as it may, we felt that additional proof of your leftist sympathies would prove valuable. Only yesterday, we obtained that proof—from another witness."

"Colonel Otis Kirkland?"

The lawyer took a second paper from his case. "Colonel Kirkland has stated that you expressed these sympathies in his hearing. You can hardly question *his* integrity."

"Kirkland and I had an argument, which he lost. He's a fool, as I told him to his face."

"Colonel Kirkland is one of the most prominent surgeons in Little Rock. You'll have trouble making your estimate of him stick."

"Does this mean Sanford's planning to convict me—before I appear?"

"It could happen, as we both know."

"Do your worst, then, if you mean to use these trumped-up charges. What's left to discuss?"

"Your case is not quite closed," said Manning. "There's a way out—if you'll listen to reason."

"How can your client let me live—feeling as he does?"

Again the lawyer shrugged off the jibe. Sarcasm, like insults, seemed to pass through his mind without impact.

"He'll expect you to mend your ways, of course. Including your habit of insulting superior officers. Suppose we agree to leave you alone—subject to good behavior. Will you help us convict Abram Schoenfeld?"

The offer had been dropped from the blue; this, too, was part of Sanford's approach. Abram Schoenfeld's appearance before the House Subversive Acts Committee had ended in one of the few defeats the Sanford-Manning team had suffered. The congressman had whipped himself into a frenzy to nail down a conviction. There had been hints of sinister revelations in the headlines, where most of his victims had been tried in advance. Minor witnesses had been hounded; wild accusations had been stated as facts—but the heart specialist, at the time a naturalized citizen of brief standing, had stood firm during his ordeal as a witness. In the end, thanks to the unanimous backing of colleagues at Lakewood, and the outraged cries of both press and public, he had left the hearing with the slate wiped clean.

"Your boss is a poor loser, Manning," Bruce said at last. "Somehow, I didn't think he'd stoop this low."

"Our investigation of Schoenfeld failed because of incomplete evidence. We not only believe he's maintained contact with Moscow—but that he is ready to serve as a spy when the war's over. The fact that he isn't in the Army is a black mark against him. So are the pacifist interviews he gave before Pearl Harbor, his refusal to speak at bond rallies, and his book, *The Immorality of War—*"

"Dr. Schoenfeld happens to be much too old for active duty. His opinions are his own—and the research he's doing at Lakewood is irreplaceable. You haven't a chance of smearing him."

"On the contrary, our chances are excellent. Scratch the average American brain, and you'll find a distrust of Russia.

Bring me evidence that your teacher's kept up friendships in his native land, and we'll have his head."

Bruce hesitated, while he controlled the need to smash a fist against the lawyer's jaw. He had just thought of a way to outwit Sanford. Risky though that way might be, it seemed well worth exploring.

"Exactly what do you want from me?" he asked.

"You were with Schoenfeld in Barcelona. While he was there, we're certain he made contact with political commissars who served on the Loyalist staff. Some of these men went back to important jobs in Russia. Give me at least one of their names. We'll do the rest."

"Suppose I follow through? What's in it for me?"

"I've already told you. We'll overlook your own lapses, and trust you to mend your ways."

"And if I refuse?"

"You'll be called before the full committee. Once these lapses are in the open, you'll almost certainly be dismissed from the Army."

"Because I once served in Spain—and dared to speak up to Kirkland? You'll never swing it."

"Don't put us to the test, Major. Even if we can't break you, we can put pressure on the Surgeon General. We can have your current appointment revoked. We'll have you assigned to a medical dustbin that will make you wish you were still interning. I think you'll find the choice worth pondering."

"How long may I ponder?"

"Congressman Sanford will see you day after tomorrow—in his office at the Capitol. Will eleven suit you?"

"Eleven will do." Bruce saw that Manning was puzzled by his quick acceptance. It was time to leave this beast of prey, before his suspicions were really aroused. "Will our talk be informal?"

"Informal—and off the record."

"I've just one condition. Unless it's met, I won't appear.

Hal Reardon must be there too. I want him to hear all that's said."

Manning considered briefly. "Congressman Reardon and my client have had their differences. By and large, they have identical views on the conduct of the war. He'll be welcome—if he can spare the time."

"I'll make sure he spares the time," said Bruce. "Tell Sanford I'm eager to see him in the flesh. Does he breathe out air or brimstone?"

"A mixture of both, depending on the occasion," said Manning, with another of those fleeting smiles. "I'll convey your message, Major Graham. Meanwhile, may I wish you good luck with your conscience?"

The staff car Bruce had borrowed had a powerful motor. Once he was clear of Washington, he cruised at seventy miles an hour, to reach the city limits of Baltimore in midafternoon.

At a gas station a few blocks from the Lakewood Medical School, he made two phone calls. The first was to Hal's secretary, to make sure of the appointment he had cleared with Manning. The second was to Colonel Miller, asking for a few hours' extension of his pass—now that imperative personal business had brought him to Baltimore.

In the great rotunda at Lakewood Hospital, the usual procession of nurses in starched bibs and capes of varying colors had just begun as the shifts changed in the wards. Bruce paused on the threshold to breathe the familiar air that was like none other in the world, to look up again at the towering statue of Christ in the well of the circular stairway. It was hard to believe that only a few months had passed since he had trod those same stairs as a research assistant in surgery. It seemed entirely natural to take a short-cut to the annex. He was not too shocked when the receptionist at the lobby desk asked his business.

"I have an appointment with Dr. Schoenfeld."

"The name, sir?"

"Major Bruce Graham."

"Of course, Major. I should have recognized you. I'm sure you know the way."

The surgical annex was one of the newer buildings at Lakewood, a towering rectangle of steel and glass. Schoenfeld occupied a private office on the top floor; the laboratory where he often worked round the clock was on the floor below. There was a private lift between, and a small bedroom adjoining, permitting him to rest at odd hours while one of his experiments was in the balance. The door stood open as Bruce hurried down the hall, a sure sign that the doctor's secretary had gone for the day.

The doctor himself was pacing his office, puffing on one of the endless cigars that seemed almost an extension of his bearded face. With the clothes he wore, and with his ham-like hands, he seemed more suited to a plow handle than a scalpel. His shout of welcome, and the huge embrace he gave his former student, did not disguise the worry in his eyes.

"You have brought trouble, Bruce," he said. "I heard it in your voice when you phoned. Now, I am sure."

"It was good of you to give me an hour. I know how busy you are."

"I am never too busy to hear a former student's troubles, doctor."

The formality, Bruce realized, was the tone Schoenfeld reserved for crises. Searching for a proper beginning, he moved to the office window, with its glimpse of the hospital mall, white with interns' coats in this between-shift hour, and thick with memories.

"*You* may be the one who's in trouble, sir. I won't be sure, until I learn just what Jake Sanford has in mind."

"Has that viper emerged from his bog again?"

The heart specialist did not interrupt while Bruce described his collision with Kirkland, the colonel's denunciation, and the half hour he had spent with Manning.

"Surely you guessed this would happen?"

"I couldn't believe it was treason to discuss postwar politics with another officer—especially when the talk was conducted over drinks. I know better now."

"Let me make sure I grasp your dilemma. Sanford's lawyer has offered to drop his persecution, if you'll supply certain information about me. Did you tell him you had none to give?"

"Not quite. I pretended to keep his proposition open, until I could talk to you." Bruce broke off as Schoenfeld turned away. The massive head, clean-cut as a Roman coin, had bent abruptly; the ash from the cigar had fallen unheeded on the half-buttoned vest. It was enough to convince the visitor that a scene from those months in Spain, conjured up by Manning's bribe, demanded explanation.

"What reward did they have in mind?"

"I'm scheduled for assignment to one of the first mobile surgical groups. If I play ball, Manning will let the appointment go through. If I don't, they say they can drive me from the Army."

"That is something Lakewood will not permit."

"Perhaps not, sir. But at least, I'd wind up doing latrine duty at the rear end of nowhere. It's already happened to me once."

"What if they banish you—to this rear end of nowhere? Would you resign your commission, and return to Lakewood?"

"I'd rather fight back."

"You are badly needed downstairs, Bruce. Within the next year, if all goes well, we hope to understand some of the simpler abnormalities of the heart. Perhaps even to proceed with a cure. The Tetralogy of Fallot, for example."

"That would be a true miracle, sir."

"Miracles have occurred before, after many experimental failures. Think what it would mean in our pediatric wards—if we could correct cyanosis in small children by improving the pulmonary circulation. If we could cure such inflammations as bacterial endocarditis. With your help, we might reach those goals. If not in my lifetime, then in yours."

"I can't let Sanford call me a quitter."

Schoenfeld sighed deeply, and put out his cigar. "What I just said was *my* effort at temptation—knowing in advance it would fail. Meanwhile, this demented congressman is perched on your shoulders, like Sinbad's Old Man of the Sea. Since I'm largely responsible for putting him there, I am prepared to remove him."

"You aren't to blame, sir. After all, I volunteered to join the team you took to Spain."

"Your service in Spain was proof of your idealism—which brings us to a bitter fact. You would be far easier in your mind this afternoon, if I could tell you I had no contact with the Russians."

"I won't deny that."

"How can I—when I'm sure you watched me make one such contact?"

Bruce turned again to the window, to hide the tears that filled his eyes. He had not expected this calm avowal from the man who had been his model since his first day at Lakewood.

"The place was the Fonda Roja," said Schoenfeld. "The time, a month before we left Spain. The man was Ivan Susov."

The calm statement brought the scene alive again—the smoky cellar bar on Barcelona's Ramblas, the rumble of a war outside, the crowd of soldiers who had sought refuge from that encroaching doom. . . . Like the others, Bruce had stolen a half hour to drink a glass of wine. Schoenfeld had sat at a corner table that night, deep in argument with a man who wore the Loyalist uniform—though the occasional word that reached Bruce's ears was Russian.

"When I took hospital teams to Spain," said Schoenfeld, "my motives were not completely altruistic. I planned to meet Susov there—or his counterpart. How much did you know of him at the time?"

"Only that he was more ambitious than most of the commissars."

"Today, Susov is a member of the Supreme Soviet. Back in Barcelona, I hoped to use him as my go-between."

"Surely you were never one of them, sir."

"I opposed the revolution from its beginning," said Schoenfeld. "As you know, I escaped from my native land to practice medicine in America—where I was lucky enough to become a citizen. My brother was not so fortunate. Family business kept him in Kiev until the purge trials began. At that time, I learned he was about to be denounced. The meeting at the Fonda Roja had been arranged to transfer a receipt for fifty thousand dollars in a Swiss bank. In return for that receipt, Susov was to arrange for my brother's escape."

"Why didn't you tell this story to Sanford's committee?"

"I had other relatives in Kiev. If I'd told the truth, it would have appeared in American newspapers, along with Susov's name. As a high-ranking Party member, he'd have been forced to destroy them—if only to convince his comrades he was a victim of a Jewish plot."

"Are your relatives alive today?"

"They were wiped out when Hitler invaded Russia. No one but I will suffer now—for a gamble I took in Barcelona."

"You wouldn't suffer either—if the whole story was brought into the open."

"Things are not quite that simple, Bruce. If I told this story now, years after the event, Susov would still deny it. He would produce witnesses to show I was—what Sanford thinks I am. A former Russian agent, who has since defected."

"What's our next move, then?"

The heart specialist sat at his desk to write a few words on a memo sheet. When he handed it to Bruce, he saw that it was the name and address of the cafe in Barcelona, the name of the commissar, and the date of their meeting.

"Here is your clearance, doctor. Use it, with my good wishes."

"Do you think I'd give this to Manning?"

"What harm can it do me?"

"You'll be called a Communist. The kind who took cover when the Nazis moved in."

"I'll survive the slur—and keep my present post at Lakewood. Science is above ideologies. I'm much too valuable in my field."

"Your reputation is valuable, too." Bruce tore the memo sheet to bits, and dropped the shreds in a wastebasket. "I won't let Manning smear you—even by innuendo."

"Manning may not even use the smear," said Schoenfeld. "This could be a trick to improve his own fortunes, through blackmail. He's used it before."

"Even Sanford wouldn't take that risk."

"Not directly, perhaps. I am told *his* graft comes from sources nearer home. Manning is a Chicago lawyer. I have highly placed friends there. Men whose children I've operated on, who feel grateful. It's quite possible they would give business to Manning's law firm, to protect me."

"You're making Chicago sound like de' Medici Florence."

"Chicago is no worse than other cities. Or clever young attorneys, who use a world upheaval to advance their careers. Don't downgrade your country, Bruce—because you've uncovered termites in its foundations. Thousands of Army doctors are doing the work they're best fitted for—and doing it well. You should be one of them. These war years will usher in one of our most productive periods in medical history. I want to see your name among the pioneers."

"I can't put it there by betraying you."

"Even if Manning calls you to the stand?"

"Spain will suddenly grow hazy in my memory. I'll find I can't remember names or dates—or people I met there."

"That could mean contempt of Congress. They might send you to prison."

"I still prefer to fight back. Thanks again, sir—for trying to bail me out. I'll see you again when the smoke has settled."

"Your place will be waiting." Schoenfeld's voice was not quite steady as he enveloped Bruce's hand in his huge paw. "May I ask your battle plan?"

"It isn't perfected, so far. But I can assure you it will be what the French called *guerre à outrance.*"

It was after dark before Bruce reached Scranton General, and he needed two full hours to catch up on routine work in his ward. The chart on Jimmie Lowell was a confirmation of what he had feared. Even with the operation, the patient had grown steadily worse.

Before midnight, the sergeant had lapsed into coma—part of the strange depression of all vital functions ambiguously called "liver death." Bruce put in additional hours at his bedside, in a last, futile effort to reverse the trend—following the extra transfusions Colonel Miller had ordered with blood plasma, and injecting adrenal cortex hormone. Toward dawn, he made a last injection of penicillin, to no avail; the patient was *in extremis.* His last act was to give what consolation he could to the mother, a small, cameo-fine woman in her sixties who had flown in yesterday from Boston.

Both of them stood at the bedside when Jimmie Lowell slipped from life to death. Weary though he was, the surgeon went to his office to call the Washington *Post*—making the announcement of the sergeant's death, and advising the night city editor that Mrs. Lowell would consent to an interview with Shane McLendon, before she returned to Concord with her son's body.

When Bruce wakened, the afternoon papers had already run their stories on Sergeant Lowell, stressing the wound at Pearl Harbor. Most of them omitted mention of his Peace Party—the news point that had created an overnight sensation in Shane's column. This, he realized, was only another illustration of the mounting pressures of the war. Today's front pages were crowded with dispatches from the newly opened front in North Africa. There was no room left for hope that war might some day be obsolete.

Shane had called while he slept, thanking him for the interview he had arranged with Mrs. Lowell: she had left the number of her Washington apartment and asked that he phone her at six—but he folded the slip in his wallet without using it. Shane, he told himself, had worked overtime as his confidante: the adventure on which he would embark tomorrow was a solo effort, with Hal as an unknowing accomplice. He would accept its consequences alone.

In the cafeteria at dinner, Colonel Miller brought his tray to Bruce's table.

"We did our best for the boy," he said.

"The case was probably hopeless from the start. I still hated to lose him."

"Sergeant Lowell had ideas for a better world," said Miller. "I, for one, respected them. Perhaps he's luckier than he knows—leaving us like this, with his hopes intact."

"Have *you* ruled out a better world when this war is over?"

"Take a hard look at our country, Bruce. Try to see it through his eyes—if he'd started preaching his credo as a civilian. He'd have broken his heart to no purpose."

"Are civilians that bad?"

"I've talked with a hundred Jimmie Lowells since we entered the war. A soldier is wounded, maybe decorated—at least, with a Purple Heart. First, he goes home to be a hero for a day. A little later, he finds that heroes can be boring to their relatives, and to themselves. Pretty soon he's had his fill of the bitching—about defense-plant hours, rationing, taxes and war-bond salesmen. If he's a philosopher, he shrugs off that dust storm. He tells himself it's enough to be with his girl or his wife again—or just to be alive. Later still, when his philosophy's beginning to wear thin, he starts to wonder if life on the home front is worth living."

"I can't believe that Jimmie would have turned pessimist."

"Basically, it's a matter of contrasts," said Miller. "Your average GI has risked his life for what his bombproof friends would call chicken feed. When he goes on the town with those friends, they spend more on black-market steak than he earns in a month. Suppose he comes home with a prosthesis for a hand. Or a tantalum plate in his skull—and spinning headaches that won't go away. Why should *he* give up part of his body, when factory workers and desk men are giving nothing? By then, it's only a step to wondering if he should go back at all."

"Most of them go back regardless."

"So they do, Bruce—for a final check-up at Scranton General or elsewhere. The damage has been done, even if we clear them. I can show you cases in the files. Men we pronounced cured, and ordered to their units—only to have them bounce back, in worse shape than before."

"Assuming we'd saved Jimmie Lowell. Can you see him in a psycho file?"

"Probably not. In any case, the question's academic. Day after tomorrow, they'll bury him in the family plot at Concord—the member of his generation who behaved like his forebears. Do you know what his mother said to me today—before she claimed the body? *Thank God my boy did all he could for his country.*"

"Was she right?"

"I think so, Bruce. In his place, I'd rather be a dead hero."

"I can't subscribe to your gloomy views."

"Perhaps I'll withdraw them, after the returns are in. You can't deny the situation's acute—with the war barely under way. I don't mean Section Eights. I'm speaking of decent American boys who survive combat, only to find their spirit broken by their first real contact with home."

"The Veterans hospitals have more than their quota now," said Bruce. "I know those figures too."

"We give them atabrine for malaria. We stop yellow fever and cholera with new vaccines—and we mend bodies with a recovery percentage undreamed-of in World War I. We've yet to find a tonic that restores the human spirit when it collides with human greed." Colonel Miller rose from the table, with his dinner half-touched. "You're off duty this weekend. In your place, I'd get roaring drunk."

Shane's second column on Sergeant Lowell, as Bruce had expected, appeared in the Sunday *Post*.

It was a moving tribute. Once again, the author endorsed his plan for world peace. This time, however, there was a note of straight reportage lacking in the earlier column— which had been, in its way, a call for moral awakening. Shane spoke in glowing terms of Mrs. James Lowell Senior, and her proud acceptance of her loss. The column listed the Lowell family record in each American war; it quoted the inscription Jimmie's mother had chosen for his grave. . . . Like those chiseled sentiments, Shane's prose seemed an extended epitaph. The fact that it was placed among the editorials summed up its diminished news value, when measured by the tempo of events abroad.

Bruce read the column in the taxi that delivered him to Capitol Hill—where he had arranged to meet Hal before their appointment with Jake Sanford. A vital asset to that meeting was on the seat beside him, wrapped in his Army raincoat. He had purchased it in Baltimore, at the optician's shop where he had bought his first microscope. Now that his preparations were made, he felt strangely calm. The fact that Sunday had turned rainy, he told himself, was a good omen. At least it would make the slicker seem natural when he entered the enemy's lair.

Hal was pacing his empty anteroom when the surgeon rapped on the glass-paneled doors. He stepped into the hall with a quick, detaining gesture.

"We're cutting this a bit fine," he said. "Jake's furious if you're one minute late to an appointment."

"This morning, it won't hurt him to stew a little."

"I was hoping you'd get here sooner. You're going to need a few pointers."

"When I made this date," said Bruce, "I told you that I wanted a witness and nothing more. Sanford's methods are familiar to me. He has no idea of *my* approach, so I'm starting with an advantage."

"If you're planning to slug this thing out, forget it."

"Oddly enough, that's precisely what I plan to do."

"Jake has the power to subpoena. Don't learn the hard way." Hal had already hurried Bruce down the corridor, to step into a waiting lift. "Is it true you talked with Manning?"

"The head jackal and I had an extended skirmish."

"That means you've been called in for a deal. If you're willing to give a little, you may survive."

"I'll see them both in hell before I give an inch."

"Stick to that attitude, and you'll be in hell yourself," said Hal. "Give me some idea of what you have in mind. I'll try to smooth Jake down."

"For once, I'll do the talking. You needn't even take sides."

Hal tossed up both hands in a gesture of resignation, as the elevator door clanged open. "We who are about to die salute you?"

"You needn't die with me. Just remember my last words. They may interest you."

They had paused before an imposing door on the top floor of the House Office Building. Across its panel, tall golden letters identified the headquarters of Congressman Jacob Sanford. The portal was a fitting prelude to the room within, an antechamber stripped to the battleship linoleum that floored it. A small metal desk stood beside an inner door—where the receptionist who had shouted permission to enter regarded them dourly. Bruce had not expected the dragon's den to be guarded. He stopped dead when the man rose to take his raincoat.

"I'll keep this with me."

"The major will neither gouge nor bite, Clint," said Hal. "I'll guarantee he has no concealed weapons. Why don't you give yourself a coffee break?"

The guard, a slipshod hulk who might have stepped bodily from one of Sanford's rural courthouses, acknowledged the pleasantry with an even blacker scowl before he departed. Hal made sure the outer door had closed behind him, then addressed Bruce in a whisper.

"Clint would never leave if this weren't really private. You may be in luck after all."

The inner office was high-vaulted like the anteroom. The lighting focused on the baronial desk where Sanford sat, deep in notes and seemingly unaware of his visitors. As a tourist in Washington, Bruce had watched him perform in the House. At a distance, he had seemed a remote, homespun lampoon of the back-country politician, a thing of stentorian bellows and windmill gestures. Here, with a backdrop of lawbooks, with silver-framed spectacles riding the bridge of a nose that quivered slightly as he read, he seemed far smaller than his photographs: the skull, with its sprinkling of ginger-red hair at the fringes, was strangely frail in that light. When he spoke, it was hard to connect this pint-size rustic with the committee room downstairs—where his paranoid whims could take on the color of justice, with no chance of appeal.

"Find a seat, Major. You too, Hal. It was good of you to come."

Warning himself to move slowly, Bruce took the visitor's chair before the desk, and bundled his folded raincoat in his lap. Hal chose a sofa against the wall. There was no sound in the room, save for the scratch of Sanford's pen. When he spoke again, his voice was still gentle.

"Well, Major Graham? My lawyer tells me you're here to confess your sins."

"Of what sins am I accused?"

"I'm sure Manning briefed you. Why waste your time or mine? Or Congressman Reardon's?"

"If this is the start of an interrogation, shouldn't we begin by saying the meeting is bugged?"

"Of course it's bugged. I've got a wire recorder in this desk drawer, and I'm about to switch it on. Give me the right answers, Major. You'll save us both a trip to the Capitol."

"Are you asking me to damn myself?"

"I suggest you save your hide, while you have time. Congressman Reardon will explain what I mean."

Hal spoke wearily from the sofa. "I've already asked him to compromise, Jake."

"You'll never get better advice," said Sanford. "Tell me what I want to know, and your troubles are over. Otherwise, your trial has already begun."

"How can I be on trial, when I haven't been notified of my arrest?"

"You served the Communists in the Spanish Civil War. We have testimony to show you're still a subversive. Will you admit these charges involve not only you—but the man who led you into Spain?"

"I assume you mean Dr. Abram Schoenfeld?"

"I've already shown that Schoenfeld's an agent of the Kremlin."

"*Asserted*, Mr. Sanford—not shown."

"My accusation's on the record."

"Where it died—from total lack of evidence."

"You can supply that evidence. When you do, I'm prepared to dismiss you, as a dupe of men far wiser—and far more evil—than yourself."

"Where does your indictment of Dr. Schoenfeld begin?"

"In Spain, where he took his orders from Russian commissars. Do you deny you carried out his propaganda at that time?"

"On the contrary. I'm proud of the propaganda I spread there. If you like, I'll give you examples."

Hal had half-risen from the sofa. Even Sanford seemed taken aback, though he recovered his poise in a flash.

"You may speak, Major."

It was the opening Bruce had awaited. Observing Sanford narrowly, he moved to the space between desk and sofa, where he could face the recorder.

"I gather you'd prefer events in chronological order."

"If you please."

"We'll start with the arrival of the Lakewood surgical unit in Barcelona." Beginning the attack he had rehearsed so carefully, Bruce spaced each word. "Our first bivouac was in a suburb. Since I'd been born in Tampa, I spoke fluent Spanish. On Dr. Schoenfeld's orders, I spent most of that first day and night among the people, spreading a propaganda campaign that was close to his heart."

"Be more specific."

"The city mains were contaminated. My job was to persuade the inhabitants to boil their water, or die of typhoid—"

Sanford's hand had darted toward his recorder switch—but Bruce had already barred his path.

"Stay where you are—and let me finish!"

The shout, and the glare that accompanied it, caught Sanford off balance. Recoiling from Bruce's fury, he put his wheeled armchair in reverse—so violently, it collided with the bookcase behind him, inundating him in a cascade of legal tomes. While the shock lasted, he did not stir. Fixing him with the same level look, Bruce just escaped a shout of laughter. At that moment, the firebrand of the House Subversive Acts Committee could have passed for a cornered ferret.

"My second campaign was similar to the first, Mr. Sanford. Barcelona was also facing a threat of typhus. Following Dr. Schoenfeld's orders, I spread the news that the disease was caused by body ticks and lice. Thanks to *that* propaganda,

thousands of unwashed citizens used the insecticides we had
brought from America. As a result, an epidemic was nipped
in the bud—"

Sanford made a feeble attempt to rise—then subsided, as
Bruce took another quick step between desk and chair.

"What I've said so far concerns the off-hour duties of our
team. Most of our work was done in cellars, where we set up
field hospitals as Franco moved toward the city. We also did
our best to help keep the civilian population alive. The greatest
problem, naturally, was an adequate diet. Our luck was bad in
that field. A single surgical team could do little more than
share its own rations. Hitler's bombs—and Mussolini's—had
destroyed most of the available food—"

"That's enough, Bruce!"

Hal, it seemed, had found his voice at last. Bruce ignored
the interruption as he closed in on Sanford. The ancient legis-
lator still cowered in his chair. His head had retreated between
his shoulder blades.

"You asked what our team did in Spain," Bruce said. "I
won't describe the evacuation of those field hospitals, when
Barcelona fell. Or how we took wounded men to France,
to save them from being murdered. I *will* remind you that our
techniques for treatment we gave under fire have been followed by every medical unit in the Army. Which is more important, Mr. Sanford? Knowledge that saves lives? Or enemies
that never existed, outside your addled brain?"

Sanford spoke after a fashion: his voice was only a croak.
"What does this lunatic want, Hal?"

Bruce spoke quickly, before Hal could answer. "I want the
truth, for the record. Your colleague's here to listen. That's
his only function."

Sanford had put the desk between them. He was trembling
violently as he seized the phone—but some of his vitality returned with the act. There was even a trace of his old bravado
when he spoke again. "I can put you under arrest, Graham."

"You won't arrest me. Not with this statement on the record."

"What do you expect, after your outburst?"

"All I expect from you is common sense." Bruce could afford to speak quietly now: when Sanford's hands slipped from the phone, he stepped back. "You know you've got no case against me. You've known it from the start. Call off Manning, and leave me in peace. Give me your word you'll stop hounding Dr. Schoenfeld—"

"Is *that* all?"

"If you refuse, I'll quote every word of this meeting to the press. I'll add a sworn affidavit that you offered me a bribe to give false evidence before your committee. And I'll ask Congressman Reardon to be my witness."

The challenge had given Sanford time to recover his composure, though his hands still trembled when he took the reel from his hidden recorder, and dropped it in his coat pocket. Then, assuming a painful dignity, he inched crabwise toward the door.

"For your sake, Hal," he said, "I won't call Clint. As you see, I'm ignoring your friend's theatrics. Manning will subpoena him tomorrow. We can establish his treason before the full committee—"

Hal spoke at last. His face was stern, but Bruce could see the gleam of amusement beneath.

"Jake, it's no go."

"What are you saying?"

"As a member of the Ethics Committee, I'll be obliged to veto such action."

Sanford had reached the door. He paused there, with his hand on the knob. "For what reason?"

"Major Graham is right. You have no case."

"We'll let my own committee be the judge."

"Even your yes-men will balk, if you try to force this through. In your place, I'd cut my losses. Don't force me to withdraw my support where it will really hurt."

"Does Major Graham mean that much to you?"

"Call it quits—or call my hand."

"Suppose I withhold my subpoena. Will you guarantee he leaves Washington?"

"The major is already on his way."

"Do I have your word on that?"

"He'll be out of town day after tomorrow at the latest. Your face will be saved, along with our friendship. Leave things there."

"Very well, Hal. I'll do no more—if your friend is properly disciplined *and* transferred." The congressman stalked from the office, drawing the tatters of his pride about him like a toga.

Bruce moved behind the desk, to right the chair and restore the books to their shelves. The act gave him time to ponder that last weird exchange between the two lawgivers.

"Well, my idealistic friend?" said Hal.

"Why did you tell Sanford I'd be leaving Washington?"

"Before I answer, tell me what you hoped to accomplish here."

"You saw what I accomplished. Sanford's methods are now a matter of record."

"He's taken the record with him. In the next hour, he and Manning will play that spool, curse you awhile—then destroy it."

"Are you asking me to destroy mine?"

"*Yours?*"

Bruce lifted his raincoat, to reveal his secret weapon. It was a duplicate of the portable recorder Shane had used in her interview with Jimmie Lowell. The wire was still unwinding when he moved to the cutoff switch. It had picked up the interview from the start—including Sanford's tacit admission of a bribe, and his compromise with Hal.

"As you'll observe, two can play this game."

"Not with the cards stacked against you," said Hal. "Our

meeting occurred in the House Office Building. Sanford's entitled to congressional immunity."

"Suppose I take this reel to a city editor?"

"The SGO won't let you, Bruce. Not when you're leaving for a camp in West Florida."

"Was *that* what you meant just now?"

Hal spread both hands, palm downward—the dismissal of a question only a born innocent would dream of asking.

"It's fortunate you've a guardian angel in your corner," he said. "When I heard Jake and Manning were after you, I moved fast. There was just time to contact Colonel Wilson, and make sure you'd be transferred."

"How will my transfer make a difference?"

"You saw how I handled it," Hal said patiently. "Jake knew I meant business, when I threatened to cut off my support. He still needed an exit, to save face. Therefore, I promised you'd be leaving Washington."

"Am I supposed to thank you for your diplomacy?"

"I think you will someday," said. Hal. "For the present, I'd suggest you turn in that recorder. In your hands, it's a dangerous invention."

Bruce picked up the metal box, with its tiny, ultra-sensitive microphone. A moment before, it had seemed a potent time-bomb, triggered to blast hypocrisy and bring back justice. Now, with a sinking heart, he realized it was only a useless toy.

"Keep it with my compliments," he said slowly. "I owe you something for your services."

"Only if you insist, Bruce. I'll give it back the day the war ends."

"Don't bother, please. I'm sure you'll have more use for it than I."

He left the office in haste, before Hal could speak again. Once more, he knew that his departure had been an outright retreat.

MAJOR BRUCE GRAHAM MC 0-270106 RELD FR
TDY 9205 TSU TC SCRANTON GENERAL HOSPITAL
ASGD TO 241ST HOSP SHIP COMP CAMP JEFFER-
SON DAVIS GULFVIEW FLA FOR DUTY TDN TPA

Bruce spread the new orders on the bar, to reread them for
the tenth time—and to marvel at an alphabet-soup jargon that
managed to be both terse and redundant.

His second highball had just been set before him, and he
drank it slowly. In a sense, he was not too sorry to leave
Washington, though he would miss the solid sense of achievement at Scranton General. In another, deeper sense he could
not shake off the hopeless rage he felt—the conviction that
he had allowed an apparent victory to change into surrender,
though the memory of Jake Sanford cowering among his lawbooks would be something to cherish always.

The primitive drives of the fighter were still active: even
now, he yearned to march into a newspaper office with the
recording, to demand a front-page exposure of a conniving
bigot. The yearning, he warned himself again, was futile. As
Hal had said, a deck had been stacked: he had accepted a
crooked deal—and it was too late to demand that the game be
replayed. . . . He had been lucky to escape with this assignment to a ship complement. Such units, a study of Medical
Department bulletins had informed him, were select in their
own right, complete hospitals with a floating base that could
take him into action anywhere in the world.

The orders had arrived the next day. In the twenty-four
hours that followed, he had completed his last rounds in the
wards, said good-bye to Colonel Terence Miller, and taken
his bags to Washington to confirm his transportation. At
Union Station he had learned that the Pelican Express, departing at seven the following morning, would drop him at
Pensacola, where he would board a local train for Gulfview and Camp Jefferson Davis.

From the station, he had taxied to the Surgeon General's
Office, just as the nine-to-five personnel was departing. Yield-

ing to the impulse that had brought him here, he had taken
the elevator to Colonel Wilson's floor to request an after-
hours interview.

The procurement officer had not quite exploded when Bruce
asked his first question.

"Major Graham, a good officer does not question his orders.
He executes them."

"I'm prepared for Gulfview now, sir. I still can't help wondering how all this happened."

"Perhaps it will help your future in the Army if you go on
wondering."

"I'm ready to confess I've made trouble in high places—
and to ask your pardon."

"If you must take up my time, come to the point."

"In my place, sir, I think you'd have done the same. So
far, the two best things I've encountered since indoctrination
have been Colonel Miller's department at Scranton and the
attitude of this office. Since my newest orders came from here,
I'm naturally surprised to learn I've been transferred without
warning. I can't help but feel I've been kicked around again."

"Allow me to correct that impression, Major Graham. You
have *not* been kicked around by this office. We've assigned you
for training in a hospital ship complement. When your unit is
fully organized, you'll be chief of its surgical service and
deputy commanding officer. The post calls for a certified
specialist with the rank of lieutenant colonel—which you'll
probably earn in time."

"May I ask the reason behind these new orders?"

"Day before yesterday Sanford's lawyer called here, to hint
that you might be served with a subpoena. Obviously, he expected me to agree that you should be separated from the
Army. I have no intention of sacrificing a competent officer.
Therefore, you are being transferred to West Florida, where
these witch-hunters can't get at you quite so easily."

"I'm sorry I intruded, Colonel Wilson."

"I've been willing to enlighten you—since our meeting's

off the record. You have been extremely useful at Scranton. You should find this new assignment even more rewarding. Just try to keep out of political meat grinders in future."

"One more question, please. Do I owe this escape to Congressman Reardon?"

"You are going to Jeff Davis for reasons noted. Reardon had no part in my decision."

"He'd heard of my orders, even before I received them."

"Only because he happens to be an active committeeman in the House. Since he holds the purse strings, so to speak, he has access to our files. He used that privilege recently, when he asked my permission to inform Sanford that you'd be sent out of the Washington area. It seemed a shortcut in a difficult situation."

"Thank you again, sir. This visit has been most informative."

"Under the circumstances, we can hardly prolong it. Besides, I have another appointment."

"Come to think of it, Colonel, so do I."

At a phone booth on Constitution Avenue, he had called Hal's office, to learn that Congressman Reardon had departed on unspecified business in the West. In a booth at the Station Bar, he had dialed Shane's unlisted number—and hung up on the first ring. Until his resentment had cooled, he knew it was wise to postpone contact. It had seemed wiser still to order his first drink before he rang the journalist's number a second time. . . .

Now, after another highball, he re-entered the phone booth. When he heard Shane's voice on the line, husky and faintly mocking as always, he felt his lassitude vanish. In the same breath, he lost the worst of his anger at Hal—and Hal's incurable urge to pose as a latter-day *deus ex machina*.

"It's nice to be remembered at last," said Shane. "I don't give this number to everyone."

"I'm afraid I've been rather rushed—since you called the hospital."

"Haven't you, though? Where are you now?"

"Brooding—at our bar across from Union Station."

"Brooding's a destructive pastime when it's done alone," said Shane. "It's bearable if it's done in company."

"All I have is this number."

"I'm at 1129, S Street. The Singer Le Mans is at the curb. Would you like me to collect you?"

"A taxi's quicker. Stay where you are."

Shane's apartment was on the top floor of a block of renovated walk-ups that had once been tenements. She answered his ring promptly—and leaned down from the banister to observe his progress.

"My garret must be heaven, since you've climbed so high," she said. "Don't break a leg, now I've lured you here at last."

Her quarters, he discovered, were on the raffish side. Most of the apartment consisted of a studio living room, complete with skylight. Matching Utrillos, a pair of surrealist nudes, and bullfight scenes by Juan Gris gave the room an air of improvised Bohemia.

"No one's keeping me," said Shane. "I sublet this rookery from my syndicate editor, when the Navy grabbed him. Shed your jacket, if you like. If I spent more time here, I'd put in air conditioning."

It seemed entirely natural to drop his Army blouse on the bed in an adjoining alcove, while his hostess moved to a shelf of bottles behind the drawing board that served as her worktable. It was even pleasanter to enjoy the blend of release and excitement he felt in this strange girl's presence. Already, this skylight room seemed as familiar as his own half-forgotten home—and, in the same double vision, a threshold to adventure. Three drinks in an hour, he cautioned himself, might be more than he could handle.

"What's your pleasure, Bruce?"

"I'll skip this round, if I may. When I've recovered from

your staircase, I'll have a bourbon." Still in the bed alcove, he studied himself carefully in Shane's mirror—and found his basic features unchanged. Only his thoughts seemed to blur at the edges.

"You still sound gloomy," said Shane. "Have you had a hard time lately?"

"The road's been medium rough. I haven't stopped to count the bruises."

When he emerged, she was perched on the window seat with a highball in her hand. His own drink waited on the drawing board. He downed half of it before he realized she had ignored his refusal.

"This is hail and farewell," he said. "Or did you already know?"

"Hal phoned this afternoon, before he took off. He mentioned your new orders."

"And took credit for them?"

"Naturally. Doesn't he—for everything?"

"It seems you appreciate my classmate almost as well as I."

"Chances are I appreciate him even better," said Shane. "Would you care to hear more?"

"Why did he kite out of Washington tonight?"

"Janet has her test this weekend. He feels he must applaud from the side lines when Brodski rolls his cameras. Hal's fiancée is a rather emotional girl. Or hadn't you noticed?"

"Did he mention the screen test?"

"Among other matters. It was his way of suggesting I forget him, as gracefully as I can."

"I'm sure you'll manage."

"I managed quite well—at first," said Shane. "When he called, I was still at the *Post*, fighting a column. So long as I kept my mind on my story, it wasn't too hard to absorb what he'd told me. Eventually, of course, I found myself alone here, staring at those damned bullfighters. That's when I willed my phone to ring—and you answered the prayer."

"I'm glad I could be useful. Brooding alone *is* sheer waste—as I just discovered."

"I can name other men who might have called this evening," said Shane. "Does that sound like boasting?"

"On the contrary."

"If I say you were first on the list, will you misunderstand me?"

"Have I misunderstood you, ever?"

"Not so far—and I've tested you severely."

Bruce put down his empty glass and resisted the desire for another. Floating on the euphoria of alcohol, he knew that all things were possible, all philosophies valid. Including the fact that he had brought comfort to Shane McLendon, and received it.

"Tell me this," he said. "Did you really have hopes for Hal?"

"A girl can always hope. Even a girl who writes for the daily press, and should know better. Did *you* have hopes for Janet?"

"Not many, I suppose. At this moment, she seems remote as Hollywood itself."

"If you can say that, your chances for survival are excellent. Shall we put love on the back burner? I'd much rather hear about your run-in with Sanford."

"Hal must have covered that when he phoned."

"I'd like your version too."

Shane did not stir while he described the encounter on Capitol Hill. When he had finished, she continued to withhold comment until he had refilled both their glasses.

"I wish I could have been inside that recorder, Bruce."

"Unfortunately, the backwoods Torquemada got off scot-free—with help from Hal. Isn't there some other way I can destroy him?"

"Give Jake time," said Shane. "He'll be nailed to the barn door, and skinned alive, by men who know their jobs."

"Are you suggesting that amateurs like myself should keep clear?"

"Hal told you the facts of political life, when he confiscated your recorder," said Shane. "You had no place to go with your story."

"I was half-hoping you'd have use for it."

"Not with the laws of libel. It wouldn't get past a copydesk in America."

"You ran the story on Jimmie Lowell."

"He was a genuine hero—and even a hero's pipe dreams are news. Jake would dive behind congressional immunity. He'd say *you* were the crackpot. And the country at large would believe him."

"Colonel Wilson was right, then—to warn me off?"

"It was wonderful advice," said Shane. "And wonderful strategy, shipping you to West Florida. Will you forgive and forget?"

"I'll do my best."

"Can you forgive Janet too, now you're leaving Washington? After all, she's only a poor little rich girl, who'd like to have her cake and eat it."

"Can you forgive Hal? *He's* just a congressman who pretended to love you, when he wanted space in your column."

"That isn't quite true," said Shane. "He's used me, I'll grant—but I've used him too. We've had some good times together. Maybe we will again. He hasn't quite married the senator's daughter."

"And she hasn't married him."

"Let's live on that hope tomorrow—and ignore them tonight."

"Can we?"

"We can try," said Shane. "Isn't that why you're here?"

She had risen as she spoke, to take a quick step toward him. His drink crashed to the floor as their lips met, in a kiss that seared his last scruple away.

He wakened in a dark autumn dawn, to find Shane deep in sleep beside him. It was easy enough to slip from her bed without wakening her—and quite another matter to track down his uniform. The oak leaves of his rank eluded him. He was fully dressed before he found them—on the lapels of her housecoat, where he had pinned them in midnight homage.

When he was ready to depart, he sat at the drawing board to compose a farewell note. The first try was hardest.

> I'll write from camp. Thanks for the bourbon—and the philosophy. I needed both. All my love.

Before the ink could dry, he ripped the sheet to bits. Shane would see through such flourishes instantly. This morning, his only emotion was profound gratitude. He had no right to use a stronger word.

> Did it help you to forget for a while? It helped me.

Again, he destroyed a feeble attempt to communicate. This, too, was facile pseudo despair. Shane would weep for Hal again—and he would yearn for Janet. She would plan ways to lure Hal back—just as he would build bridges to a picture set in California.

> I won't ask you to forgive me. I'll just go on hoping this was your idea too, and thank you for it, with all my heart.

He signed his name to the final note in full—with rank and serial number—before he placed it precisely on the drawing board, with his oak-leaf pins to weight it down. It was a bleakly inadequate expression of his feelings, but there was no way to improve it.

When he tiptoed down the walk-up stairs, his watch stood at six-thirty. There would be just time to catch the Pelican Express.

Gulfview

The spider-legged dock led to a path through palmetto scrub. The path climbed, via steep stairs, to a cleft in the dunes, before it snaked down to the beach where tonight's cookout would be held.

Captain Eric Badger, Bruce's roommate at the BOQ of the 241st Hospital Ship Complement, had just gone ahead to make sure the coast was clear for a somewhat irregular outing. Bruce himself had followed at a slower pace from the improvised landing stage. Standing aside to permit the boat crew to transport the charcoal bags and portable grills from bay to beach, he looked down again at the clearing in the jungle of cabbage palm and water oak. On both sides, the shoreline of Bonita Island was untouched by the hand of man, save for this one scar.

Since his arrival at Camp Jefferson Davis four full months ago, Bruce had felt a comforting kinship with his surroundings: the feeling had compensated for a sense of suspended animation that had followed him from Washington. This country, after all, was not too different from the Florida of his boyhood; he had only to close his mind to the present to imagine he was back on Tampa Bay again. Even the thunderhead dissolving in heat haze to the west was part of memory:

he had watched those black rain-bags approach before, only to pass into the wide reaches of the Gulf of Mexico.

A mile of open bay lay between landing stage and camp. Here, the rectangles of barracks (varied by tents that marked the presence of basic training units) were remote intruders. Bruce's own outfit was billeted on a point thrust deep in the bay. He could just make out the work road, winding through an oleander screen to the blocks that housed the 275th Infantry, a unit training for service in Europe when an Italian front was opened. The hospital ship complement had messed with the 275th since its arrival. So did the men of the 75th Airborne, an elite regiment that had found temporary quarters here, pending its final course of training at nearby Eglin Field.

The town of Gulfview nested in a narrow bay, behind the next point to the east. The copper-plated roof of the Gulfview Inn, now a training center for nurses and an overnight haven for visiting VIPs, was all but hidden in its windbreaks of Australian pines. The ruler-straight road to Pensacola was muffled in a screen of cypress hammocks, like the approaches to the town itself. Once such intrusion had been accepted, this segment of Escambia County looked empty as the day De Soto's caravels had traced the first sea-lane to the Mississippi.

At this hour, with a blue mirage of bay between, it was impossible to believe that those barracks were real, that thousands of men had been herded here to sharpen their skills for destruction.

That afternoon, Bruce had crossed to Bonita Island on a whim—postponing his study of the hospital-ship model Colonel Stokes had just installed in the lounge of the BOQ. As breathers went, it was not too different from other interludes he had stolen since his arrival last fall at Jeff Davis. . . .

His commanding officer, who had served the Medical Corps for twenty years in odd corners of the globe, had been delighted to welcome a new specialist. The complement, he explained, was not at full strength; the nurses who would form an essential part of Bruce's team had yet to reach the Inn, and the only other surgeon in the 241st at that moment, besides Stokes himself, was Captain Eric Badger. For the present, the CO added, training would, of necessity, be on the tentative side. Eventually, they would board their ship at the Charleston Port of Embarkation.

The hospital ship complements now preparing to serve on all fronts, Colonel Stokes had continued, would be self-contained units. Like their counterparts on land, they would function under the Geneva Convention. The vessels themselves would be mostly converted liners: the 241st's own transport would be a once-famous cruise ship, the *President Washington*. Still up-to-date, with its air-conditioners, its spacious lounges, its streamlined kitchens, it could handle over a thousand wounded, and would be suited to either the Mediterranean or the Pacific theaters.

Each ship would be staffed by the Merchant Marine, under contract to the Army Transportation Corps. As always, the actual safety of those aboard would depend on the captain, whose rule from the bridge would be absolute. As commander of the complement, Stokes would be the senior transport officer; as next in rank, and chief of the surgical service, the new arrival would be his deputy.

Last fall, during the first weeks after his arrival at Gulfview, Bruce had realized that such matters could be left to later rulings of the SGO. For the present, the officers of the 241st had been employed as pinch hitters at the station hospital and the various area dispensaries. Stokes's own staff were soon resigned to the cultivation of winter tans, weekend forays in Pensacola, and preliminary exploration of Bonita Island with nurses already in residence.

Bruce had adjusted to the tempo of Jeff Davis as easily as he had accepted the fact that his complement should be training in West Florida, an overnight journey from its point of embarkation. In the same spirit, he had worked long hours at the station surgery, volunteering for wards other than his own when new acquaintances wished extra leave. As a result, his popularity at BOQ had been instantaneous. If he remained an enigma to brother officers, he had only his reticence to blame. A man in his peculiar dilemma, he had told himself, would do well to stand aside until his thoughts had settled. . . .

Early in the new year, with the appearance of their quota of Medical Department troops and junior officers, a shakedown program had been launched, with Bruce in charge of plans and training. Some of his new personnel, though classified as technicians, had turned out to be less than proficient. His rapport with the station hospital had solved that problem. Since the wards were always short of help, enlisted men of the 241st were assigned there for training duty until noon, when they returned to the point for special disciplines of the complement.

In Spain, the surgeon had learned that a blend of speed and precision were of the essence, if instant aid was to be provided for the wounded combat soldier. Following those hard-won techniques, and inventing others as training proceeded, he convinced Stokes that their ship could perform the combined duties of a field and evacuation hospital—once each nurse and technician was letter-perfect in these overlapping tasks.

Using the standard operating procedures of the Army as outlined in its Military Medical Manual, he had worked out a system of drills—covering, as accurately as conditions at Jeff Davis permitted, each phase in the handling of patients in a combat zone. With the cooperation of the Engineer Battalion, all-purpose conveyances known as DUKWs were borrowed when available. These ungainly vessels served as ferries to a mock-up of a ship's deck, constructed on the deep-water side of the point where the 241st was quartered. Called "ducks" by both Army and Navy, the DUKWs could climb to land on caterpillar treads—and swim with unlooked-for speed. Here, loaded to the gunwales with pretended patients, they proved invaluable in Bruce's rehearsals.

Mornings were still devoted to the essentials of ward training at the station hospital. Afternoons found Stokes's entire personnel on its improvised ship. With legs in Thomas splints, arms in traction at angles that would make the hoist aboard difficult, these bogus casualties were shifted from landing craft to pier again and again—until each emergency was anticipated, each awkwardness overcome.

Once the wounded were aboard, Captain Badger and his triage team read the emergency medical tags and checked splints and bandages. So-called serious cases were rushed to a mock-up operating room, for a quick transfer from stretcher to table; less urgent casualties flowed into a tent that served as a ward, for a second evaluation by the nurses and junior officers in charge.

The surgical chief had feared these simulations of combat crises would grow tiresome: he had underestimated the pride of a hospital outfit beginning to find itself useful after a halting start. A final lift in morale had come with the arrival of the nurses—an event that rounded the complement to its full strength. Since most of these girls had undergone rigorous training of their own, it was a simple matter to add them to routines. Their presence had stressed the importance of the task each man was learning, and the need to spread burdens. And, though fraternization of enlisted personnel and the newcomers was frowned on, since each nurse was an officer, their example stirred in every male the urge to do his best.

Thinking of those women in white—and the psychic jolt of their arrival—Bruce found the appearance of Captain Eric Badger on the dune top entirely natural. His roommate, a small-town surgeon from Wisconsin, had adjusted perfectly to his new milieu. He had been a moving spirit in the planning of this recreation area on Bonita Island—and no member of the 241st had been warmer in his welcome of the efficient, and sometimes comely, girls at the Gulfview Inn.

In theory, if not in practice, the Inn was off limits for the camp, save in the early evening hours. Tonight, a sextet of nurses had been included, *sub rosa*, in the weekly cookout, for which lots were drawn at the BOQ, under Badger's supervision. This week, the man from Wisconsin and three lieutenants in the medical service had won the draw. Two captains from the 275th Infantry had bribed their way into the party, with a case of champagne won in a poker game at Fort Barrancas.

When one of the captains had gone on leave, Badger had insisted that Bruce serve as his replacement, rather than hold a special lottery: considering the fill-in assignments the surgical chief had taken for each man in the complement, it was agreed that such largesse had been earned. . . . Bruce had agreed to cross to the island to check the preparations for the cookout—though he had already decided to beg off. Turning to face Badger, he saw that he must phrase his refusal carefully. In this all-male existence, the needs of the flesh were high-priority topics. Withdrawal of any sort was automatically suspect.

"Are the girls here, Eric?"

"They're due to arrive at 1800," said Badger. "A safe hour before curfew. We'll greet them with sixteen pounds of prime sirloin, broiled with my best barbecue sauce, Pol Roger on ice—and Scotch for serious drinkers. What occurs thereafter is no one's business but our own."

"Do you mind if I invite myself out?"

"I mind very much."

"Take my word, I'm too weary to add to the party."

"That's a flimsy excuse. It's time you abandoned this nightly contemplation of your navel."

"Tonight, I'm contemplating a ship's manual. Tomorrow, we're running an evacuation drill. Those, too, are worthy projects."

"Not half so worthy as the easing of your libido."

"Believe me, this is work I can't pospone."

"You've seen Alice Stacey in action—on the good ship Mock-up. Don't pretend you haven't noticed what's under that seersucker uniform."

"I thought Lieutenant Stacey was your girl."

"I'll resign all claims tonight, if you'll leave your hermit's cell."

"Sorry, Eric. Tonight belongs to letters I can't put off—and to a book called *Ship Handling*."

"You're forcing me to speak my mind," said Badger. "This lack of interest in the other sex has caused talk. Half the complement thinks you're secretly married—and unnecessarily faithful. Others say you're a *homme fatal*, nursing a secret sorrow. A few outright realists insist you're queer. What's your real reason?"

"The reason's simple. I'm in love."

"In love—*and* engaged?"

"Far from it. It's a girl I'll never marry."

"Then what's the harm of a stroll among these dunes—with a partner like Alice? Or Cindy Jordan, if you prefer long-stemmed brunettes?"

"No harm whatever—but I'm in no mood to do the situation justice. Lieutenant Stacey deserves better. So does Lieutenant Jordan."

"The Army has trained me well," said Badger. "I'm prepared for negative attitudes in working hours. It's a different matter when a friend poses as a eunuch. The boat leaves in five minutes. You'd better be aboard, unless you enjoy swimming."

"I've confessed I'm in love with someone I can't marry. Won't that satisfy you?"

"Where is this paragon—and why?"

"Right now, she's finishing her first picture on the Coast."

"Are you telling me you're in love with a movie star?"

"She could be one, day after tomorrow."

"And she's turning you down, because her producer can do more for her?"

Bruce produced a grin. "Oddly enough, you've summed up the situation."

"Do you expect me to sell *that* story tonight—when Alice asks me why you chickened out?"

"It happens to be true, Eric. Naturally, I don't expect you to believe it."

The Gulfview Fishing Lodge, now the bachelor officers' quarters of the 241st Hospital Ship Complement, seemed an imposing structure from the bay, with its broad veranda, clapboard siding and hurricane-tested roof. Its presence among the wind-tossed cedars on the point suggested that it was the abode of millionaire Nimrods, whose skills matched their gear. Closer inspection revealed the clapboards were peeling—and it was painfully evident that the roof had lost its quota of shingles in last winter's gales. The lodge still had its comforts—and the room Major Graham shared with Captain Badger was only a shade less spacious than their CO's own quarters.

Remembering that Stokes had gone to Eglin Field that afternoon, Bruce passed both doors on his way to the lounge, a glass-walled porch featuring broken-back armchairs, a pool table, and a rack of tattered magazines. The table had been used to display the new model of their ship, an eight-foot miniature of the *President Washington* constructed to scale, with the port side cut away to reveal its facilities from bridge to bilges.

Bruce spent an instructive half hour exploring the arrangement of the thousand-berth wards, the central supply rooms and the laboratory. The operating theaters, he saw, were located amidships, where they would be the least affected by rough seas. The recreation room and the nurses' quarters were far more spacious than he had realized: a special label assured him he would enjoy a cabin of his own, opening to what had been the liner's promenade deck. . . . Four extra wards for ambulatory cases on the lower deck completed the display. Since the *President Washington* would be a vessel of mercy, it was appropriate that the ship would be rechristened the *Helen S Peters*, honoring a nurse who had given her life at Corregidor.

Bruce's mood had not lightened when he returned to his quarters. The room had been part of a suite at the lodge: its windows opened to Bonita Bay, the maple furniture was covered with sun-faded chintz, and desks stood between the windows for the officers' inevitable paper work. Tuesday, he reminded himself, was mail night: that part of his story on the island had been accurate enough. Letters from both Janet and Shane were in a locked drawer, and he read them carefully before reaching for his pen.

In six closely written pages, Janet Josselyn told a vivid story of the trials and rewards of picture-making. There was praise for her director—who in Janet's view, was shaping a sure-fire entertainment. There were faintly malicious sketches of her fellow performers—and amusing asides on life in wartime Hollywood, where she had leased a house on a mountainside, with an aunt as chaperone.

The senator, Janet added, had been too busy to visit her. Hal had looked in twice at the studio, during war-bond rallies on the Coast. Life in California, Bruce gathered, had its own special boredoms when the senator's daughter was not on the set. Parties had been few, even on weekends. . . . But there was no mistaking Janet's fascination with her work, or her wholehearted enthusiasm for the script of her first picture.

Shane, too, had been a faithful correspondent. He read her last letter slowly, to savor the blend of common sense and wit that cast its own light into his somewhat drab surroundings. It had been mailed from North Africa, where she was ending a series of columns on the success of the landings, complete with vignettes of warriors at work and play in Algiers, Oran and Casablanca. . . . Once again, she had made no reference to the night they had passed in each others' arms.

Faintly troubled by the omission, Bruce took up his pen and printed the address of Shane's syndicate on a sheet of air-mail flimsy, knowing in advance that his mind would go blank before it could shape an opening sentence. There was an easy evasion of that mental block. Yielding to it at once, and censuring himself for the escape, he picked up his desk phone and asked the camp switchboard to put through a call to Washington.

The suspense of waiting while operators in Atlanta, Greensboro and Richmond picked up the call was almost as frustrating as the impasse he had just avoided. Ten minutes later, Congressman Harold Reardon's secretary-bodyguard informed him that Hal was on the floor of the House and could not be disturbed. Bruce had received similar replies to his last three calls: the secretary's assurance that Hal would soon be in touch was part of the man's technique of dismissal.

When he had hung up, he could shrug off the fact that he had failed to make contact with his classmate. Hal, he knew, would hardly appreciate his continuing resentment at the game he had played in Washington—the pretense that he, and not the SGO, had been responsible for Bruce's present billet. Like politicians the world over, Hal had assumed that he had called long-distance to ask another favor, and had used time-honored means to hold him off. . . . He took up his pen a second time, to compose an opening paragraph to Shane, a not-too-humorous description of tonight's cookout, and the mixed motives that had prompted his withdrawal. Admitting that it was impossible to define those motives accurately, he was in the act of destroying the sheet when he realized a visitor was waiting in the doorway—Major Walter Pierce, pathologist and chief of the laboratory service at the station hospital.

"Sorry to intrude on your correspondence, Bruce. But Eric asked me to cover your complement dispensary tonight."

"What's up, Walt?"

"The same trouble, I'm afraid. Your OD wants me to check one of your technicians who reported sick—with headache and a stiff neck."

Bruce got up quickly. There was no need for Major Pierce to dwell on the import of the symptoms he had just reported.

Like other camps processing troops from all parts of the nation, Jeff Davis had suffered its share of contagious disease epidemics. Most of the flare-ups had been such prosaic infections as measles, chicken pox and mumps. During the past week, a more ominous threat had appeared in the barracks—a rising incidence of cerebrospinal meningitis. Here, possibly, was the most dangerous germ known to epidemiologists, since the danger was compounded by the ability of uninvolved carriers to infect others with no immunity.

One case, unfortunately, had made its appearance in Gulfview, when a soldier had collapsed on Main Street. The story had spread consternation through the county—and the post commander had already received numerous requests to close the camp gates and proclaim a full quarantine. Similar epidemics during the First World War had left their mark on the civilian mind. Even with all personnel restricted, the average citizen of Gulfview was half-convinced that the diplococci could reach town on the next breeze from the west.

"Let's look at him together, Walt."

"That was my idea, too. This is the first suspicious case from your group. Your OD wanted you or the colonel to have the facts."

The complement dispensary was a board-floor tent, pitched on the cleared ground that separated the barracks of the 241st from administrative headquarters. Sick calls were held here each morning—and at the close of maneuvers. Five soldiers were seated on the grass outside the flap to await their turn. Inside the tent, the technician on duty was sponging the face of a sixth man, who lay on a stretcher. Behind the dispensary, an ambulance from the station hospital waited with its motor running.

Even before he could descend from Pierce's jeep, Bruce saw that the GIs in line were jumpy: he knew they would bolt without reporting their own ailments, if the dread word *meningitis* was pronounced in their hearing. At Jeff Davis these past days, rumors of an epidemic in the making had flown even faster than in Gulfview.

The technician reported that his patient had complained of a headache on the practice range and had come to the dispensary for aspirin. Alerted to be on the lookout for the specific symptom of neck stiffness, he had sent for expert help at once. Pierce made a brief examination, before he stood aside to permit Bruce to do the same. Even without the thermometer reading, the flush in the man's cheeks would have advertised the fever burning in his body. His gasp of pain, when the surgeon rocked his head gently, plus the marked rigidity of neck and shoulder muscles, made the diagnosis practically certain.

"*Do I have it, sir?*"

"You're going to be all right." Bruce spoke in a low voice, so the line outside would not hear. "All you need is treatment—and the ambulance is waiting." He glanced inquiringly at Pierce. Once the patient left for the hospital, he was no longer under the jurisdiction of the 241st.

"We'll follow in my jeep," said the pathologist. "I'll have him sent directly to Medical C-5."

"Shall I complete his tag, sir?" asked the technician.

"It's complete now," said Pierce. "Don't read it aloud." He had already written four words on the patient's record: *Cerebrospinal meningitis: acute meningococcemia.* "Say something to the men outside, Major. They need it."

Bruce spoke through the open tent flap. "You've all guessed what we have here. It's the first case in our complement—so there's no cause for panic. Remember, a patient has an excellent chance to recover, if he goes on sick call early. Pass the word that *anyone* with a headache is to report at once to this dispensary, night or day. Don't try to cure yourself with aspirin, unless it's prescribed by a medical officer."

On the way to the hospital, the pathologist gave Bruce a rundown on the problem they were facing. As a surgeon, the information was largely outside his range—save for the few details he recalled from medical school.

Like every doctor, he knew the meningococcus entered the body through the nasal passages, where it could grow in a fashion that did no harm to its host—yet posed a deadly threat to anyone upon whom he might breathe, sneeze or cough. This condition—known as the carrier state—was in sharp contrast to the behavior of the germ once it crossed the mucous membrane barrier of the nasal passages and entered the bloodstream.

Here, for reasons science had not yet explained, it attacked the meninges—the lining membranes of both brain and spinal cord—as well as the body in general, through the bloodstream. This was the infection called meningococcemia. Fever, toxicity, stiffness of the neck due to the inflamed membranes, coma as the disease drove into the brain itself, convulsions— all these symptoms marked the inexorable progress of the affliction. The result was a high mortality rate in cases that were not diagnosed promptly. Extensive damage to the nervous system was to be expected, even when death did not occur.

Far less was known of actual methods of transmission, nor could doctors explain how the elusive diplococcus selected those it would attack and left others inviolate. Transmitted as easily as the common cold, it followed a sporadic pattern— spreading like prairie fire through one training camp, skipping an adjacent camp entirely. Until recently, serum had been the only protection against its inroads, with results that were often far from successful. Now, with the widespread use of sulfathiazole—and, more recently, sulfadiazine—additional safeguards were available. Even these specifics were powerless to stop a full-fledged epidemic, unless each case was diagnosed almost at inception.

When they reached the hospital, the man from the 241st was already on a wheeled stretcher, bound for an isolation ward. Bruce had time for only a few words of encouragement before he followed the pathologist to the lab. Here, within twenty minutes, they were joined by Colonel Alford, the chief of the medical service, bearing a small test tube. This, Bruce realized, contained a spinal tap from the patient. A glance told him that the fluid was cloudy when it should have been water-clear.

"You'll find plenty of evidence in this one, Walt," said Alford. "In the circumstances, Major Graham, I'd advise you not to shake hands with me."

Bruce stood aside while the older officer washed both hands carefully and rinsed them with alcohol. At the microscope table, Pierce was busy making his first smear from the tube.

"Did you get the impression he was close to convulsion, Colonel?"

"The diagnosis was so certain I've already started sulfadiazine, without waiting for your report. In the old days, we wouldn't have gotten him until his spinal fluid was purulent. If I'd waited for that, half the men in our isolation wards would be dead by now."

"*Wards*, sir?"

"We opened our third this afternoon. Until Wednesday, our average incidence was only a case a day. Since then, it's been doubling. I've just warned General Ludwig that we're on the threshold of a real nightmare. He's restricting the whole post, as of midnight. With thirty-five thousand men here, the order will only increase the hysteria. By tomorrow, we'll have five hundred GIs with headaches from being scared. And, God save the mark, we'll have fifty more—with enough symptoms to indicate a spinal puncture."

"How many of those would be positive?" Bruce asked.

"Not more than half, if we're lucky," said Alford. "You surgeons get the best of everything. You only need worry over one patient at a time. *I'll* be sweating out a hundred potential cases before this weekend's behind us."

Pierce looked up from his microscope. "You called the shot, Colonel. This slide is loaded with intracellular diplococci."

"I'm on my way to double that dose of sulfa," said Alford. "Good night, Major. You should sleep easier than most of us. After all, your outfit's the most isolated barracks in the cantonment."

Pierce lifted his eyes from the microscope. "Want to take a look, Bruce—now you've come this far?"

"Perhaps I should, at that. I haven't seen a meningococcus since my last class in pathology."

"They don't change."

At the binoculars, the surgeon twirled the fine adjustment until the cells in the smear, caught in the Gram stain, exploded into view. At least half of them contained the invader— a double, biscuit-shaped germ, clear-cut in the pale blue stain as stars in an evening sky.

"How's the view?" the pathologist asked.

"Perfect. But if you'd handed me this slide without identifying it, I'd have guessed it was acute gonorrhea."

"Barring any condition but a meningitis epidemic, you'd have been right, in most cases. The gonococcus and the meningococcus are identical, except in behavior. Here at Jeff Davis, we have a rule of thumb. If the discharge originates in the draftee's urethra, he goes to the GU ward. If it's from his spinal column, it's meningitis."

Bruce continued to study the slide. A thought was taking shape in his mind—but a single elusive factor refused to come into focus.

"It's odd that one of these bugs should attack the urethra —while the other moves into the brain and spinal cord."

Pierce sighed—and turned back to the tray of slides he was

classifying. "I can remember when *I* had time for such specu-
lations. In an Army lab, you're lucky to get your routine work
done. Can I drive you back to your quarters?"

"I'll use the car pool. Get yourself some sleep, Walt. I'll
cover for Eric."

In the entrance lobby, about to take the door that led to
the motor pool, Bruce changed his mind and followed the
corridor to the hospital library. There, after he had phoned
the complement OD to give his whereabouts, he spent an intent half hour with a reference work on bacteriology. When
he closed the book, he had learned nothing new about the
twin microorganisms known as the meningococcus and the
gonococcus—but the thought that had hovered beyond his
grasp was in clear view.

There was no need to ponder further while he crossed the
compound to the PX, where a bank of telephones served
long-distance callers. Silver was available at the cashier's desk,
though the clerk looked faintly outraged at the amount he
asked for. Night had not quite closed in outside when he put
through his call to Camp Bruckner; Gulfview was inside the
Central time zone, but he still had hopes of catching Major
Nick Denby before the urologist left his office.

A fifteen-minute briefing from Nick left Bruce five dollars
poorer—and gave him the exact information he needed. At the
motor pool, after he had requisitioned a car for the short drive
to the point, he found himself humming for the first time
since his arrival at Jeff Davis. Hal Reardon, he told himself,
would have scolded him without mercy for the risk he was
about to run. With the lives of over thirty-five thousand men
at stake, he felt justified in damning the torpedoes.

Even before he could reach the lodge, he was oppressed by
the silence in the company street. No guitar chords floated
from barracks porches tonight; there was no show of light in
the officers' lounge. At the BOQ pier, he saw that the boat
Eric had commandeered was in its mooring. When he turned

into his quarters, he found his roommate in bed with a paper-back mystery.

"Was your party rained out?"

"The girls didn't show. Word got round that the post would be restricted at midnight. Where the hell have you been?"

"At the hospital. One of our T-3s is down with you-know-what."

The man from Wisconsin was instantly serious. "Did he report to the dispensary? Pierce was covering for me there."

"Walt did his job. So did everyone concerned. He called me in because it was our first case."

"Is it severe?"

"Alford didn't wait for a cell count before starting intra-venous sulfadiazine."

"That could mean the bug is building up in virulence."

"Alford didn't say—but I gather it's why he persuaded General Ludwig to clamp on the lid."

"I hear there are a hundred and fifty cases in isolation now."

Bruce shook his head. He had expected gossip to darken the cloud that hung above Jeff Davis.

"Alford told me fifty. And no deaths, so far."

"Thank God for that. How long do you think we'll be restricted?"

"If the epidemic follows its usual course, it should crest in another week, then taper off."

Badger was listening with deep attention now. "Since when did you become an epidemiologist?"

"Since seven-thirty tonight—courtesy of the hospital library. What's really ominous is the bloodstream phase of the disease."

"Meningococci always go through the blood to get to the brain. I know that, without visiting the library."

"True—but in a red-hot epidemic something happens occasionally that's analagous to the pneumonic form of the Black Death. Victims get the bug through the air—quite literally, in the form of droplet infection. They can die, hours after the fever starts, *before* typical meningeal symptoms appear. Even a lumbar puncture might not identify the germ."

"Does Alford think we're approaching that stage?"

"My guess is he doesn't—yet. The next few days will show the trend. A new division moved in on Monday. If *they* start getting stiff necks, we can look for the worst."

"There'd still be no way to spot them—until the germ breaks the mucous membrane barrier."

"We could take nasal cultures, if we had to. By the time they grew out—say two days—even the negatives could have picked up the germ and died."

"You seem wonderfully calm about this," said Badger. "Did the books show you a way to reverse the trend?"

"All the books did was bring the problem down to earth. A phone call to Maryland may have solved it. When does the colonel get back from Eglin?"

"I saw him in the shower just now. He heard the bad news, too."

"In that case, let's beard him now."

"Want to share your brainstorm, so I can share the blame?"

"I'm an expert at extending my neck for the ax; you'll be smarter if you keep clear. This time tomorrow, you may be telling everyone you'd guessed I was a damned fool."

Colonel Gerald Stokes, in clogs and shorts, was pacing his quarters: his well-seasoned brier flashed sparks when he turned to face his visitors. The commander of the 241st, a nut-brown fifty, still kept the athlete's tread that had earned him tennis cups at Army posts all over the world. Normally, he was a man of infinite poise. Tonight, the greeting he gave his juniors just escaped a bark, as he took the chair behind his worktable.

"I was about to send for you both," he said. "The driver who met me at the airstrip knew about our T-3, so I stopped at the hospital. The boy's better already, thanks to the way they moved in on the bug. But they've had ten admissions today—half of them from the new division."

"I didn't know that, Colonel."

"The whole camp's in an uproar. I saw what meningitis can do to morale when I was stationed in Honolulu. Not just to the Army, but to the country at large. General Ludwig's already had calls from Washington. Most of them from Congress, demanding someone's head."

"What other action will be taken, sir—besides the quarantine?"

"The Public Health Service is flying in a team. Unfortunately, they can't get here before Saturday. Some of them were in North Africa."

"Won't that raise an even bigger uproar?"

"The commandant can't deny rumors forever. In another twenty-four hours at the latest, we'll have to admit an epidemic state exists."

"May I suggest a procedure before Public Health is called in?"

"As a *surgeon?*"

"No, Colonel. As a medical student who's done his homework—after a flash of inspiration in the lab."

The CO leaped from his chair to fill his pipe. Bruce felt the temperature in the room had lowered by ten degrees.

"Which should I hear first, Bruce? The inspiration, or the cure?"

"I'm sure you know the bacteria causing meningitis and gonorrhea are almost identical twins."

"If I did, I've long since forgotten."

"So had I—until I worked in the GU ward at Camp Bruckner. Given either organism, a bacteriologist can't tell them apart without using a special culture medium. More important, the twins are alike in another way. Both of them respond quickly to sulfadiazine."

"Go on, please."

"One of the worst headaches at a staging area—as you no

doubt realize—is gonorrhea at the gangplank. Major Denby, the head urologist at Bruckner, had a special solution for that problem. He asked unit commanders to prescribe sulfadiazine for every soldier on an overnight pass. One dose when the men left camp. A second when they returned. Not a single case of gonorrhea was reported from such units."

"How does that interesting fact relate to the problem here?"

"I think there's a definite relation, sir. We already know the meningococcus is even more sensitive to sulfadiazine than the gonococcus. Wouldn't the same medication lick this epidemic—if every man at Jeff Davis was given the same dosage, *before* he was exposed to infection?"

The match Stokes held to his pipe had burned down while he listened. "Was this your idea—or Major Denby's?"

"Nick Denby cooked up a prophylaxis for gonorrhea. The possibility of using his procedure here was my idea alone."

"Did you discuss it with your friend?"

"I did not, sir. If the same treatment is used at Jeff Davis—and fails—I'd prefer not to have his name involved."

The CO turned to Badger. "You're our medical supply officer at the moment, Eric. Could the whole camp be dosed?"

"It would depend on the amount, sir. What dosage did you have in mind, Bruce?"

"Two grams to start. Two more, at the end of a twelve-hour wait."

"The post has enough sulfadiazine for the initial dose. The second could be flown down from Atlanta." Badger turned back to the colonel. "May I make one fast suggestion, sir?"

"That's what you're here for."

"There are nearly fifty thousand men in camp tonight, including that new division. Before we go all out on medication, shouldn't we use our own complement for guinea pigs?"

"What do you say, Bruce?"

"I don't think we can afford to wait, sir. Not even an extra day. The way this thing is cresting, we could have fifty new cases tomorrow, maybe more. With the germ increasing in virulence, some of them are bound to be terminal."

Stokes nodded slowly. "If Alford and his staff weren't on the ball, a lot of his patients would have died already."

"I've another question, Bruce," said Eric. "Has this procedure been tried before?"

"According to the library, there were trial runs at small posts in New Mexico and Alaska. Results were encouraging, but the number of cases was too small for statistical conclusions."

"Then we'd be taking the risk on our own," said Stokes.

"It amounts to that, Colonel. The point is, can we afford not to?"

The CO reached for his phone. "That, fortunately, is a decision for higher authority."

"May I ask how high?"

"We'll start with Jim Alford, and ask him to go to the general. He'll probably kick it up to Corps—or direct to Washington."

"You know what that would mean, sir. Somewhere along the line, higher authority will back away. And Colonel Alford will open another meningitis ward tomorrow."

Stokes put down the phone. "What would you suggest?"

"I think our post commander should be told there's a real emergency here. In Colonel Alford's place, I'd ask him to act at once. On his own authority—starting with reveille. At that time, I'd give each man in this camp two grams of sulfadiazine. And I'd repeat the dosage twelve hours later."

"That would put Alford on the carpet. With the hospital CO away, he's acting post surgeon too."

"I still think the prophylaxis should begin at reveille, sir. I'll be the prize goat, if that will help."

Stokes frowned at the phone, before he settled at his desk. When he looked up, the scowl had begun to change into a grin.

"Thanks for the suggestion, Bruce," he said. "It's quite

likely I'll act on it. And I'm beginning to understand your
reputation as a stormy petrel."

"The official term, sir, is 'controversial figure.' Either way,
I'll be the first to get the ax."

During the next twenty-four hours, Bruce discovered how
well the Army could function, when a genuine crisis brought
out its best.

Colonel Alford, as acting post surgeon, had swung into
action minutes after General Ludwig had approved the drastic but simple prophylaxis. Medical stores had been stripped
of the last tablet of sulfadiazine. A call to Corps Area Headquarters in Atlanta had brought a firm promise of aid. By
midmorning, a plane had left for Eglin Field, with ample
reserve stocks aboard.

Within the locked gates at Jeff Davis, all units and all station personnel were ordered at reveille to proceed to their
battalion aid stations—or to the dispensaries serving their
medical needs. Working through the night, the supply depot
had brought each station its quota of labeled bottles. Before
the lines could form at the tent flaps, a technician was waiting to stand over each arrival, regardless of rank, until he
had swallowed four half-gram tablets of sulfadiazine.

Only routine tasks were performed during the day. Most
troops were confined to quarters, all special training exercises
were discontinued—and each man received strict instructions
to report to his medical section in late afternoon just before
retreat was sounded. The initial procedure was followed without a hitch.

Nurses from the Gulfview Inn, and Wac personnel quartered nearby, received the same medication—and the same
warning to make no contact whatever with civilians. All
through the daylight hours, and well into the first night, medical officers were on immediate call from the hospital switchboard, to handle queries from Gulfview and other towns that
had heard the same dread rumors from Jeff Davis.

Until noon, such queries threatened to swamp the operators. As the day waned, and the world outside the cantonment gates realized the quarantine would be ironclad, the volume of calls dwindled. By nightfall, when no doctor in the surrounding area had reported a case of meningitis, the hospital staff drew its first real breath of relief.

Inevitably, the new medication and the long, hot waits at the aid stations had produced the usual grousing. Bruce had stayed at the hospital all through the day, alternating his shifts with Pierce and Badger. Between them, the surgeons of the 241st had visited each aid station to make their own check. As Colonel Alford had expected, there were a few cases of drug rash in patients with special allergies. One man with an asthmatic history had needed an injection of adrenalin before he could resume normal breathing. Otherwise, it was evident by evening that Jeff Davis had taken the new regime in stride.

On the second morning when almost fifty thousand men had tumbled from their beds to answer the bugle—including the newly arrived division, which occupied a special tent city apart from the camp proper—alert-eyed officers in each platoon could report that the fears of yesterday were lifting. The threat remained: a mysterious nemesis, hovering at each man's elbow, was still real. But the fact that most of these bewildered civilians in uniform remained in rugged health was a massive counterweight to terror. With each passing hour, the residue of terror grew smaller.

Sick calls throughout the camp had produced ten new cases the first morning, making a total of over eighty admissions to the isolation wards. There had been two fatalities—cases that had gone too long unreported because of the patients' ignorance of their symptoms. On the second morning, admissions had dwindled to four. Another case was brought in at dusk—but the second night passed without a single diagnosis of meningitis. For the next twenty-four hours, the admission book was blank.

By now, each man in the isolation wards was responding to the regular doses of sulfadiazine—as dramatically as the thousands outside had responded to the far smaller prophylactic dosage schedule. There had been no more deaths—and the evidence was now clear that Nick Denby's improvised salvation for young men afflicted with venery was applicable to a deadlier menace.

On the third night of the crash program, Bruce turned in early, with a prayer that the night would pass without incident.

Rousing in a misty dawn, a half hour before reveille—and admitting that sleep would elude him—he slipped into a bathrobe and followed the main corridor to the officers' lounge, where he brewed the first coffee of the day. He was watching a hot spring sun burn the last of the fog from Bonita Bay when he heard a step on the porch, and recognized the familiar silhouette of Colonel Alford.

"I couldn't sleep either, Bruce," said the deputy post surgeon. "Besides, it seemed only proper to bring the news myself."

"Is it still good?"

"I'll have the first answer this time tomorrow. As of today, I'd say we were home free."

"No new cases?"

"I've just contacted the last aid station. For the past thirty-six hours, we haven't had us a single psychosomatic fever—or a stiff neck. You've stopped the epidemic."

"Not I, sir. It was your sulfadiazine tablets—and first-rate planning, at all levels."

"Planning was SOP. It was your idea that saved the camp."

"The prophylaxis was first prescribed at Camp Bruckner, sir."

"But *you* dared to suggest that it be applied to meningitis. That kind of risk-taking is so rare in the Army, it puts you in a class by yourself."

"The diplococci may have only run for cover."

"I won't buy that," said Alford. "Nor will Walt Pierce. Not with fifty thousand human hosts to prove otherwise. Not with a clean bill of health for all diseases. D'you realize general sickness has dropped to nearly nothing these past two days?"

"Surely you don't ascribe that to sulfadiazine."

"Perhaps not entirely. If I were a psychiatrist, I'd call it a proof of man's will to endure. Or is that too hard to take before breakfast?"

"Nothing's hard to accept, sir—after this news. May I congratulate you on a victory more important than most battles?"

Colonel Alford flushed with pleasure. "You're the one to be congratulated, Bruce. This time tomorrow, General Ludwig will release the story to the press, giving you full credit."

"Major Denby should share in that."

"He'll be named as the originator of the method. But the man who takes the risk deserves the reward. In your case, I'm sure it means front-page stories all over America."

Eric was shaving when Bruce returned to his quarters. The incandescent grin that shone through the lather was evidence he had overheard the talk on the veranda.

"How does it feel to be famous, sir?"

"Why the formality?"

"Now your VIP status is assured, Major, I feel I should keep my distance."

"All I did was look into a binocular microscope and make an obvious comparison."

"Was Leeuwenhoek so modest when he invented that microscope? Or Semmelweis, when he discovered the cause of childbed fever? Didn't Ehrlich take full credit for his magic bullet? You're the hero of Jeff Davis, my friend—and every mother in this land is taking you to her bosom, now you've made training camps safe for her son. Next Tuesday, you'll probably marry that picture siren you've been mooning about. In your place, I'd be turning handsprings."

Two days later, after the public relations officers at Jeff Davis had released the full story of the epidemic, Bruce realized that his roommate's forecast had been on the modest side.

Compared with other press releases he had read, the account of the prophylaxis seemed modest enough—but the facts had their own drama. The story received wide coverage—on the country's front pages, on the radio networks, in Sunday supplement follow-ups. Photographic teams from two national magazines descended on Gulfview with typewriter and camera. Offers were received from lecture bureaus, together with pleas from editors that Bruce describe the conquest of the epidemic in his own words.

Fortunately for his peace of mind, the 241st had already been scheduled for a series of hikes—on the sound theory that a group about to staff a floating hospital would benefit from standard infantry conditioning. Thanks to his new status at camp, he could have stayed behind to bask in the limelight. Instead, he had volunteered for the whole series of exercises, knowing that a bivouac in the pine barrens would put him beyond the reach of press and radio.

The final accolade came on his return, after he had hung up the hospital phone on a long and cheerful talk with Nick Denby, still preening in a limelight of his own at Camp Bruckner. Before he could leave the office, the phone rang again—and Alford's secretary appeared in the doorway to detain him.

"Another call for you, sir."

"Whoever it is, I'm on a field trip."

"It's Congressman Reardon—from Washington."

Recalling his efforts to reach Hal long-distance, Bruce sighed—and reached for the phone. Hal's tone was both friendly and casual. Despite its easy timbre, it seemed to fill the pine-board room, disposing of time and distance.

"It's good to hear your voice, Bruce."

"It's a surprise to hear yours."

"Sorry to be tardy with my cheers. You've been an elusive character lately."

"No cheers are needed."

"The Surgeon General's Office thinks differently," said Hal. "Your reward will be forthcoming shortly—if my informants are on the ball."

"Knowing we're out of danger here is reward enough. Any lab technician could have done as much."

"There's no need to be modest all your life," said Hal. "From what I see in the papers, you took a real gamble. If you'd guessed wrong at that microscope, you'd be a dead duck today, instead of a live celebrity."

"Omit the lecture, please. If you're as omnipotent as you sound—which I doubt—you can answer just one question. Have you any idea when we go overseas?"

"I'm told your outfit will start moving before the month is out."

"Won't your friend Sanford object if I'm included?"

"You should read the news more often," said Hal. "Jake's up for income-tax fraud, in the grand manner. The Committee on Ethics has asked for his resignation from the House."

"I'm finally in the clear, then? Clear enough, at least, so it's safe to call me long-distance?"

"It's always a privilege to hear your voice," said Hal. "I'd have made this call—even if we weren't both Sigma Nus."

"You can omit the college yells, along with the lecture. What was the reward you mentioned just now?"

"Sorry, Bruce—but it's much too special to discuss. Shane will have the details, when she calls on you tomorrow."

"Is Shane McLendon on her way here?"

"By invitation of the brass," said Hal. "Confirmation will reach you at any time. You can't back out of *this* interview by going on a hike." His voice was suspended in a ghostly chuckle as the receiver clicked in Washington.

The call came at dusk the next afternoon, while Bruce

was checking Colonel Alford's report—a detailed account of the outbreak at Jeff Davis, and the now-established controls that would serve as a guide for other posts. He recognized the voice of Captain Rodney, the camp's senior PRO officer.

"Miss McLendon just arrived at the Inn, Major. She tells me you've been alerted."

"The SGO told me to expect her. Last night, by wire."

"She's catching the midnight to New Orleans, so she won't visit us here. Can you dine with her?"

"The Surgeon General has put me at Miss McLendon's disposal. Doesn't she want to see the camp?"

"The epidemic's cold news by now. She tells me she's doing what's known in the trade as a color story."

"Not about me, I hope."

"You'll be the centerpiece, sir. The life and times of a hospital-ship surgeon, on the eve of his great adventure." Rodney paused to laugh at his own exuberance. "After all, it's an open secret the 241st will soon be moving out."

The drive to the Inn was a short one for officers permitted to use the Gulfview bypass. Disturbed though he was by the prospect of meeting Shane again—with the memory of a night on S Street still vivid—Bruce was calm enough when he parked his borrowed jeep behind the once-famous hotel, and paused in the waning light to scan a second telegram, which had only just arrived from Washington. Like the wire announcing the journalist's arrival, the new message had done a great deal to put current events in perspective.

When he came up the steps, Shane was seated in a corner of the veranda sipping a gin rickey and chatting with several of the nurses he had worked with that day—all of them dressed in the shorts and pullovers that were standard wear for a Bonita Island cookout. At his approach, they scattered to join their escorts in the bar. Shane herself had already given him a smile that put him at his ease.

"You've heard the news," she said. "I can read it on your face."

"Hal's timing is as accurate as usual." Bruce took a seat on the wicker divan beside her, and accepted a cocktail from a waiter. "My outfit goes to the Charleston POE on Monday. Next week, we board the *Helen S Peters* for our shakedown cruise."

"Those orders were overdue."

"The complement's been expecting an order of movement for weeks. What I *didn't* know was that I'd be flown to Los Angeles tomorrow to make a war-bond trailer directed by the great Leo Brodski. With a congressman to do most of the talking, and the star of *Pierrette* to introduce us. What magician accomplished that?"

Shane looked down at her drink, with the familiar teasing smile that was part of her. "Even in the Army, things have been known to happen fast. It's getting them started that seems to take forever."

"Did Hal arrange this—or did you?"

"Neither of us, to tell the truth. Right now, you happen to be the SGO's synonym for happiness—and they mean to exploit you while they can. Hence the flight to Los Angeles. Hal's going along for the ride—mostly because there's no better bond salesman on the sawdust trail. Janet's included for local color."

"Where did the idea originate?"

"In the brain of some Madison Avenue operator, who is also serving his country."

"You're sure Hal had no part in it?"

"He was invited only yesterday. We discussed the matter over cocktails—after I'd set up this interview."

"Apparently he wasn't your only informant in Washington."

"Before I saw Hal, I had a talk with Colonel Wilson. Larry and I are old friends. He violated regulations and showed me an advance copy of your orders. By and large, I think the SGO has done well by you."

"They've let me languish here since November."

"Only because of Jake Sanford. You can come into your own, now that he's resigning from the House. Besides, I would hardly say you've languished in Gulfview."

"Captain Rodney said you'd skip the meningococcus."

"I intend to. My column will concentrate on Major Graham, the man—a colorful illustration of Shakespeare's remark on the sweetness of adversity."

"Because I looked into a microscope—and shared a wild guess with my CO?"

"Last fall, you were being tossed about like a hot potato. Now you've drawn one of the best assignments in the Medical Corps, with a side trip to Hollywood thrown in. The spotlight won't be on you for long. While it is, I'd make the most of it."

"I'm sure I'll dry up at the sight of a camera."

"Not with Leo Brodski to direct you."

"Why is the great man doing a war-bond trailer?"

"Every director makes his quota," said Shane. "According to the press agents, it's *noblesse oblige*. Actually, it's a studio's way of putting the Armed Forces in their debt—so they can use their battle clips when the war's over."

"It's good to know Brodski won't be directing us for unselfish motives."

"I've another bit of news," said Shane. "According to the gossips, Janet's finding picture-making more attractive than the prospect of matrimony. She's in no hurry to announce her engagement to Hal. When I asked him about those rumors yesterday, he admitted they were accurate."

The metropolitan press seldom reached Gulfview—but Bruce had seen more than one mention of Janet in New York columns. The stories had suggested a postponement of wedding bells, due to pressures at her studio: there had been hints that her prospective fiancé opposed an extension of her acting career. . . . He spoke quickly, to cover a rising sense of elation.

"When Hal phoned, he knew we were California-bound. He might have mentioned it."

"Give your classmate his due," said Shane. "That information was classified, until you got your orders. Besides, it's part of his mystique to keep things to himself while he shepherds your Army career."

"Last August, he spoke to Colonel Wilson in my behalf. It hardly makes him my mentor."

"As he sees it, that was your turning point. He feels it's rank ingratitude on your part—if you fail to accept his advice."

"I fought back, when he moved in on Jimmie Lowell. I fought him again, when he insisted on protecting Sanford. Why should I take his advice now—or later?"

"Look back on your career," said Shane. "Try to see it through Hal's eyes. Months of brilliant surgery at Scranton General. Headlines as the doctor who did his best to save a national idol named Sergeant Lowell. Off the record fame as the St. George who bearded a dragon named Sanford. More headlines at Jeff Davis, when you stopped an epidemic. A date with the screen's newest darling, who has proclaimed her independence of the past. Finally, a job any medical man would envy—on a hospital ship, stocked with buxom nurses and strawberry ice-cream sodas. Obviously, a divinity *somewhere* is shaping your ends. Can you blame Congressman Reardon for sharing the credit?"

"Why not just say I've been shot with luck—including the happy chance that brought you here tonight?"

"Is this Deep South sweet-talk? Or was the compliment sincere?"

"It's a statement of fact. Shall we finish this interview at dinner?"

"My interview's finished now," said Shane. "Just to make sure I'm the envy of every woman in America, I'm calling it *My Date with Major Graham*. Dinner's taken care of too. We're invited to the cookout."

"The 241st is honored. So is your escort. Lead on, *mon general*. Tonight, I'm under your command."

On Bonita Island, a deep-red sunset had been overtaken by the moon. The coals in the grills had long since turned to ashes; steaks and hush-puppies had disappeared along with the drinks—and Alice Stacey's guitar had backstopped the last chorus, as eight nurses from the complement, and eight of its officers, had paired off to stroll hand in hand among the dunes.

The two guests had strolled with the others. They had joined the hearty voices—muted a little, now that the evening was well advanced—in a reprise of "The Streets of Laredo," a cowboy ballad filled with standard frontier heartbreak. . . . Now, while the distance between couples lengthened, they found themselves far down a white ribbon of sand—hand in hand like the others, and only mildly surprised to discover they were alone.

The evening, so far, had been incredibly free of tension: Shane had belonged with the group from the start, and this pairing had been part of her effortless adjustment. Tightening his grip of her hand as they descended to another half-moon of beach, Bruce wondered how long this relaxation would last. . . . Would she expect him to take her in his arms, now they were really alone? Had she been hurt, now that the move had been delayed?

When he weighed the news he had just received from California, and the plans he was making for that journey, his need to embrace Shane McLendon—and the fact that the compulsion was actual as hunger—seemed on the monstrous side. The attempt to collect his errant thoughts was sharply broken when she left him abruptly, to disappear in a clump of palmettoes. Guessing her intention, he was careful to wait at the water's edge. The breath caught in his throat when she emerged, naked as Eve and quite as unconcerned. While he stood rooted to the spot, she plunged through the first lazy wave, to emerge in shoulder-deep water beyond.

"Shall I fight off the sharks alone—or will you join me?"

He left his clothes on the sand, and ran into the shallows in a flat racing dive. Shane had already moved into the path of the moonlight. A sturdy swimmer since his Tampa boyhood, he needed all his skill to overtake her two hundred yards offshore.

"Where did you learn to do this so well?"

"Swimming was the first thing I learned, when I could afford the lessons."

Restraint of a sort returned while she circled him in a graceful crawl, using a feather kick to balance the rhythmic flailing of her arms. In the far distance, voices were raised again in song. It was a reminder that Bonita Island was a communal Eden, thanks to the enterprise of Captain Eric Badger—a lotus land where tomorrow was a threat without meaning, and present joys endured.

"You're positive there are no sharks, Bruce?"

"Sharks usually keep clear of a white-sand bottom when the moon is shining."

"What does *usually* mean tonight?"

"Sharks also tend to avoid a swimmer, if he keeps moving."

"In that case, let's move right on."

They swam for a while in silence, to put still more of the Gulf of Mexico between them and the land. Now that he had adjusted to her nearness, he could keep his distance. It was only when her slender body lifted into view on the ground swell—in its bath of phosphorescence—that he lost control of his pulses.

"What's on your mind?" Shane asked. "Answer without thinking, please—even if it does you no credit."

"Will you call me sentimental, if I say tonight's brought back my youth?"

"Why should I? It's brought back mine. Including the sort of fun I thought I'd never have."

"What's on *your* mind—since we're playing truth and consequences?"

"I'm back in a pool—at the Imperial Hotel in Vienna. When I was covering the *Anschluss*. It was my first lesson in *Schwimmen*. The instructor had no English, but we got along."

"I'm back at another cookout—my junior year at high school."

"Including a skinny-dip like this?" Shane asked.

"It was my first offense. Since we're being frank, it was also the first time I made love."

"Who was the girl?"

"Inez de Vega. Or so she said. She was a pickup, from Ybor City. Older than I—and far wiser. You might say I learned from the experience."

"Apparently you're fortunate in your pickups—if I do say that as shouldn't."

"*You* were never a pickup, Shane. You were only pretending."

"You wished I were, that night at the Union Station bar. It made wanting me a lot simpler."

"I want you now—since we're telling all. And I'm going to ask Janet to marry me, when I go out to California. What does that make me? A seagoing satyr?"

"It merely shows you're human," said Shane. "A touch of lechery's nothing—after months of resistance to temptations like Lieutenant Alice Stacey."

"How do you know I've resisted Alice?"

"I could tell—by the way she spoke of you tonight."

"Do you blame me for leading a hermit's life, after S Street?"

"Not at all," said Shane. "In fact, I'm flattered to learn that your memories are stronger than your instincts."

"Memory's only a part of it. If I say you saved me from going slightly mad that night, will you understand?"

"I'll always understand you, Bruce. Especially at moments like this, when you don't understand yourself too well. Will it ease your overactive mind—if I confess I needed you that night, far more than you needed me?"

"I guessed right, then—when I left my note?"

"Your note summed up the situation. Obviously, no such need exists now—with the latchstring out for you in Hollywood, and Hal Reardon in circulation. Shall we go back to the beach?"

"Perhaps we should. We have barely an hour to make your train."

Shane had been swimming another lazy circle, with Bruce as its center. Now, with a chuckle, she moved in to brush his cheek in the swiftest of caresses, before she headed shoreward in an eight-beat crawl. The tingle of that brief contact remained long after he had turned to follow her—careful, even now, to keep a safe ten feet of moonlit sea between them.

It was a longer swim than he had thought. He was thoroughly winded when the ground swell changed to gentle surf again—and he saw that Shane had coasted into the trough between two waves until he could overtake her.

"Give me three minutes to dress," she said. "This time, you'd better look the other way. I've suddenly become modest."

He was careful to keep his eyes on the moon while she moved from surf to shallows; he did not risk so much as a glance ashore until he heard her call. She was standing fully clothed at the water's edge, in the act of fishing a cigarette from his pocket.

"Dressing room's available. I'll wait—at a decent distance."

Donning his uniform while Shane retired to the next dune,

Bruce felt that he had emerged from the evening with honor. Somehow, the thought rang hollow—like the echo of a too-dry sermon whose morality was beyond dispute. He was still resenting that echo when he climbed the steep pitch of the sand hill.

"My watch says we've got five minutes to reach the landing," he told her. "If we don't overdo, we can counterfeit a lovers' stroll."

"Let's counterfeit, by all means," said Shane. "Captain Badger will expect it."

Bruce had feared the return to the mainland would produce problems of its own. Actually, the crossing to the Gulfview Inn was tranquil, and all too short. Shane's hand was still in his—and his conscience, and his truant pulse rate, were in harmony again—when they stepped from his car to the cinder platform that served the junction. They had arrived with seconds to spare. The headlight of the midnight train to New Orleans had just winked through a cypress hammock to the east.

"Thanks again, Bruce—for everything."

"I hope your column passes the censor."

"It will pass with flying colors," said Shane. "Put that down to the good manners of my escort."

"We're still friends, then?"

"Of course. Haven't we just risen above our youthful dreams to prove it?"

The air brakes hissed as the train came to a reluctant stop at the junction: a porter dropped from the steps of the lone Pullman to pick up Shane's bags. For another instant, she paused in the shadows of a baggage truck.

"Give Leo Brodski your all, when you go before his cameras," she said. "He's a cynic from away back—but you'll get along."

"When will I see you again?"

"Shall we leave that to fate—now we've demonstrated we can handle any situation that arises?"

No one else awaited the train at the junction: a conductor's voice from the head car was calling an urgent order to come aboard when Bruce found Shane was in his arms. The tail-light of the Pullman had vanished on the overpass before he realized it was she who had begun that blindly passionate embrace—and that he had returned it, with equal fervor.

He was not in love with Shane McLendon. Their kiss, he assured himself, had been the parting homage of one comrade to another—clearing his mind for a reunion with Janet Josselyn, for the offer of a marriage he desired with every cell of his being. Unwilling even now to return to Jeff Davis and his last night at the lodge, he reached into his tunic for a cigarette, to discover that his date at the cookout had left a memento there—the twin insignia of his rank he had pinned to her housecoat in S Street.

The golden oak leaves were wrapped in the telegram from the Surgeon General's Office, containing his orders to proceed to Eglin Field for transport to Los Angeles. Scanning it with the aid of his lighter, he saw that Shane had written a note on the other side.

> Have fun with your movie star, Bruce. You deserve a whirl, after the beating you've taken from the Army.

Bruce's mental picture of the world's film capital had been on the garish side, a photomontage of date palms and swimming pools and sloe-eyed beauties, a potpourri of song and epic, a land where illusion was king and every wish hovered on the brink of fulfillment. Common sense had assured him that the making of films was a business, not an art. It was not until he had seen Leo Brodski in action that he realized how little this dream factory owed to his layman's ideas of make-believe—or how matter-of-fact the manufacture of illusion could seem, once the tourist had ventured on his first sound stage.

He had departed from Eglin Field in a plane that made a single stop at Denver. Hal had joined him at this point, accompanied by a group of senior officers. They had given the lone major aboard a polite reception—and ignored him until the plane touched down at Los Angeles.

During the flight, Bruce had found no chance for a personal exchange with Hal. There had been none in the hectic weekend that had followed. Congressman Reardon, he gathered, was in constant demand as a speaker. Congressman Reardon had gone straight to his suite at the Los Angeles Biltmore—appearing just long enough at the studio to speak his lines in the three-minute short Brodski had contributed to the Armed Forces.

Janet had met their plane in a fanfare of publicity that included two press agents from the studio to supplement the Army PRO. She had kissed both Hal and Bruce—but the pressure of her hand in his had hinted to the surgeon that greater intimacies might lie ahead, when she could make the time. He had been careful to speak only of indifferent topics in the brief moment the press agents allowed her. And, like Hal, he had made only a short appearance before the cameras.

Bruce had somehow expected the actual filming to be the stuff of which drama is made, performed on a set that combined a South Pacific atoll and a pasha's harem. Actually, the trailer had been shot on a bare stage, with a neutral backdrop in lieu of scenery. In retrospect, the hour-long ordeal seemed a waking nightmare, done in a mask of pancake makeup, in a sweat-drenched uniform, paced by the click of shutters recording each take for the cutting room.

Brodski's assistants had handled all details—including a preliminary rehearsal, and the placement of blackboards off-camera scrawled with the dialogue. The great man himself had appeared to direct the takes with an easy, soft-voiced air of command—from a seat on a camera boom for the long shots, from a canvas chair beneath another all-embracing lens when he was filming close-ups of the principals.

After he had ordered the last shot to be printed, Brodski had swept from the stage, pausing just long enough to suggest that Bruce stop at a projection room the following after-noon to view the finished product. Janet had already been whisked to another sound stage to resume work on her own starring vehicle, now on its closing day of production. Hal, who had been even more preoccupied than usual, had rushed to fill yet another war-bond chore in San Diego.

Bruce's own calendar had been crowded on this next-to-last day in Los Angeles. Utilizing his publicity value to the limit, the Army had scheduled addresses on meningitis con-trol at nearby cantonments; he had been guest of honor at a fund-raising dinner in Glendale, where he had spoken on the techniques of field surgery perfected in the Spanish Civil War.

It had been far too late to phone Janet when the dinner ended—even if he had possessed the unlisted number of the house in the Sierra Madre. Realizing that she must make the next move, he had been glad to accept transport to another cot in another BOQ in San Pedro. . . . It seemed a muted anticlimax to the endless bustle of the day—but he was far too tired to resent it when he tumbled into exhausted slumber.

Awakening refreshed at noon—with a studio pass in his wallet and a two o'clock appointment with Brodski in Pro-jection Room Three—he drove to Hollywood in another hired car. One of the director's staff was waiting at the main gate. Their progress down the streets of the lot, through replicas of a mud-walled fort in Africa, the Tower of London, and a destroyer deck stripped for action, convinced him that the Hollywood of his fancies existed after all, now he was on the point of leaving it.

Projection Room Three was a picture theater in miniature, plus divan-like seats in the front row, equipped with desks and dictaphones to serve the gods of this strange realm. Brodski's entourage sat at a respectful distance. The director was huddled on one of the leather thrones, with a script open before him. In the half-light, his silhouette resembled an untidy behemoth. The growls he uttered—while he blue-penciled a page—seemed a bad augury.

The visitor's fears proved ill-founded: to his amazement, the three-minute short in which he had performed so painfully seemed a small gem of wit. Janet, he thought, had never been lovelier. Hal's ringing affirmation of the virtues of democracy had never been more convincing. His own remarks had blended easily with Brodski's artful showmanship. Even to his doubtful eyes, he seemed a truly dedicated doctor, glad to forsake fame and Lakewood to do his part for victory. . . .

Now, as the lights went on—and Brodski lolled back in his divan-seat to light a cigar—Bruce found it was a shock to return to the everyday. Already, he perceived that he had not been asked here to express his views on the cinema. The fact that the cameraman had hastened from his booth, and the entourage had melted away without orders, was evidence that the rendezvous had another purpose.

"When do you rejoin the Army, Major?"

"I'm flying east at nine tomorrow."

"Is your ship ready?"

"We're scheduled to leave Charleston next week on a shake-down cruise. When we're cleared for duty, we'll get final orders."

"Your reunion with Miss Josselyn will be brief."

"Even this was more than I hoped for."

"So she tells me," said the director. "In recent weeks, she had convinced herself that circumstances would bring you together. It's part of her belief her star is rising—that you are a symbol of her good fortune."

"Will she be disappointed later?"

Brodski leaned forward to study his visitor through heavy-lidded eyes. "Do you refer to her work at the studio or to your personal stake in her welfare?"

"Are you assuming we're in love?"

"It's hardly an assumption. You have been in my camera's

eye. Like all amateur actors, you wore your heart on your sleeve."

"I'm prepared to make her happy, if she'll let me."

"Then I'll speak the truth, as I see it. The picture we have completed is a diversion for men-in-arms—as charming, and as unforced, as Janet's camp shows. It will succeed wherever those men-in-arms have a free evening. What comes next is another matter. Janet has given all she has. To the studio, and to me."

"Have you told her?"

"Until I've put her next picture in work, I'm keeping my dark news to myself."

"You've confided in me."

"Because *you* will keep my secret. In some ways, as I'm sure you'll agree, Janet Josselyn is an exceptional person. She'll never become a great actress—but there's no mistaking her zest for life. If she can find the proper object, I think she's capable of complete devotion. Today, of course, it's her work. Tomorrow, it could be the happiness of a husband."

"Suppose you're mistaken about her talent?"

"Janet has an aptitude, not a talent. A gift for mimicry, a pleasant parlor contralto, an engaging presence. Combined with the farce I have confected as her vehicle, a first-rate supporting cast, and a bright score, she will pass muster. The formula can hardly be repeated."

"Assuming your fears are realized—"

"Don't call them fears. They are certainties."

"Are you asking me to console her, if you cancel her contract?"

"Unless you find the task too heavy."

"In my book, loving means sharing both good and bad. I'd marry her tomorrow, if she'd have me—but I'm not sure she's ready."

Brodski's eyes were on the dead screen, as though he were seeking a portent there. "Janet Josselyn is the daughter of a rich and powerful man. From childhood, she has had the best the world could offer—including the success I've directed. She expects to make other box-office smashes, and to marry the man of her choice. As I see it, you arrived at the ideal moment to capture her—loaded with honors of your own, about to depart on a romantic combat mission, and brimming with plans for her welfare."

"You're making her life—and mine—sound like one of your scripts."

"Believe me, Major, life would be endurable if it imitated art more often."

"I won't argue the point, Mr. Brodski. After all, you're a demonstration in its favor."

The director accepted the compliment with a smile. "To-day, with my camera magic to sustain her, Janet is living fully. She will face her first real test when her next picture fails—and she is forced to find another *raison d'être*. If you can supply it, well and good."

"You seem to forget that she's engaged to Hal Reardon."

"Congressman Reardon is practical, like myself. He already realized that Janet intends to prolong her stay here, despite his opposition. If she turns to you, I'm sure he will stand aside."

"Then you're advising me to steal another man's fiancée—at a moment when she's vulnerable?"

"To coin a phrase, Major Graham, all's fair in love and war. If you desire this girl, pursue her. If she desires you in return, she'll benefit from that pursuit, whatever the result."

"I'll think over your advice. I know it's been offered in good faith."

"You can't think too long, if your plane leaves tomorrow. At six o'clock I am giving a party on the set, to celebrate the close of production. It's in Janet's honor, so I'll expect you to join us."

"Hal wants me to meet him at five. At the Biltmore."

"You can come together, if you like." Again, the director

leaned forward to give Bruce a cool appraisal. "Not that it matters—but how did a man like yourself, and this prince of wheeler dealers, come in contact?"

"I could ask the same of you."

Brodski got to his feet, and marched Bruce toward the door. Despite his hulking shoulders and his lumbering gait, his manner was oddly gentle.

"I happen to be one of the stockholders in this dream factory. We have found Congressman Reardon useful on occasion, and vice versa. Occasionally—your bond trailer is an example—we manufacture illusion to order, as a favor to Washington. Favors are done us in return."

They had walked into the main street of the studio. The incandescent light of a California afternoon, throwing exterior sets into bold relief, made the scene before them even more garish—including the half-hundred extras dressed as cavalrymen and Sioux, sipping Coca-Cola at the gate of Fort Laramie before resuming their battle stations.

"I've answered your question, Major," said Brodski. "Will you answer mine?"

"Hal and I were fraternity brothers at college. Back on the campus, he usually managed to have the last word—as the big man of his class. When I put on this uniform, he insisted on supervising my Army career. It's part of his compulsion to pose as a prophet, with thunderbolts on order."

"Do you object violently to that compulsion?"

"At times, I've found it rather trying."

"I can forgive your impatience," said the director. "After all, it's a trait I share with Reardon. We are both merchants of make-believe, each in his own fashion. The commodity's a potent one, Major Graham: don't reject it too quickly, please. Today, with his survival at stake, man is eager to find a climate where his deepest hopes will bear fruit. So long as my pictures create that climate, *I* will earn my keep. So will the politician who promises us victories and a perfect peace."

"You feel Hal serves a purpose, then?"

"He is well equipped for his role. In the end, he may turn out to be one of this country's leaders. More than once, I've seen a great part turn an actor into a great man." Brodski moved his hands in a wide arc, to embrace the studio and the flawless sky above it. "Peace and happiness are enduring dreams. Does it matter if they are unattainable, so long as they are pursued? In my scenarios, right usually triumphs over wrong. In Congressman Reardon's projection of tomorrow, you will find the same promise. Even if he fails to deliver, he deserves his chance."

"I'd be easier in my mind if he were helping *you*—instead of planning a better world."

"For the world's sake, let's hope your concern is unfounded," said Brodski. "Don't forget you're expected at our party. Now I'll make your fortune in this part of the world, and walk you to the gate."

In the Biltmore lobby, Bruce put through a call to the Reardon suite, half-hoping there would be no response. Hal's voice answered at once.

"You're right on time. How did the trailer look?"

"Smooth as cream. You should have seen it."

"I trusted Leo with Janet. Why shouldn't I trust him with my public profile? After all, he's the best in the business."

"I can endorse that estimate, now I've seen his product."

"Come straight up. They know I'm expecting you."

The upstairs floor was all the surgeon had expected, including deep-piled carpets in the corridors, files of heavy oaken doors, and a receptionist who studied him closely when he gave his name. Hal's suite was part of the overall luxury, a vast living room studded with Empire furniture. A sweeping panorama of the flatlands of Los Angeles was framed in tall windows.

Surprised to find the portal ajar, Bruce walked in without knocking. There was no sign of Hal—and the stranger who came forward seemed part of the decor. Slender as a whippet and as nervously alert, he could have passed for a courtier of the Sun King himself—or a leader of the revolution that had made Versailles a memory.

"I'm Mike Derwent, Major," he said. "Can I mix you a drink?"

"Thank you, no." The recoil had been instinctive. Michael Derwent—a tireless lobbyist in Washington—was president of one of the most active publicity firms in New York. Mistrusting him on sight, Bruce kept his own mask in place. Hal, he reminded himself, had summoned him with a purpose. Derwent's presence had suggested that purpose dimly.

"Your congressman's been opening a box from Brooks Brothers," said the publicist. "Believe me, he's a recruiting poster come alive."

Bruce turned toward the heel click in the door that had just opened at the end of the salon. Hal Reardon—in the uniform of a lieutenant colonel, with the braid of a staff officer twined at one shoulder—stood at rigid attention in the frame. The pose dissolved in a shout of laughter as he crossed the room.

"Don't report me for showboating, Bruce," he said. "This is a dry run."

"When do you begin active duty?"

"A week from Tuesday. Interestingly enough, I've been ordered to Jeff Davis to join the 75th Airborne. Once I'm checked out on parachutes, I go on General Leonard's staff in Algiers." Hal moved to the bar, where he poured and raised a glass to absent heroes. "Now the African war's in gear, I may reach the Med before you."

Derwent chuckled—and settled on one of the love seats that flanked the fireplace. "Notice how well he speaks the argot, Major?"

"I resent that deeply," said Hal. "After all, I *am* in the Reserve."

"Reserve or Regular, I'd advise you to turn civilian again," said Derwent. "All that braid is making your visitor nervous."

"Entertain Bruce while I change, then."

"I'll do my poor best."

"Give him the pitch, while you're about it," said Hal. "I'll listen in." Carrying his glass, he moved into the bedroom. Watching Derwent rise to make a fresh highball, Bruce was sure that the entrance and exit—like the banter—had been well rehearsed.

"We were both asked to Hal's suite for a reason, Major Graham," said the publicist. "Naturally, you resent that fact a little."

"Not until you give me cause."

"After all, you came here to air a personal grievance—"

"Why do you assume that?"

"One usually does, with Hal—it's what public servants are for. Instead, you find I'm about to launch my own line. I don't think resentment's too strong a term."

"I can hardly deny I'm puzzled."

"Shall I begin my pitch—to use our host's term?"

"Please do."

"I'm going to use you as a kangaroo court. Let's hope you'll be impartial." The press agent opened a briefcase and produced a sheet of stationery. "Call this my first exhibit, if you like. It explains much."

Bruce studied the beautifully printed letterhead. Even before its import sank home, the reason for Derwent's presence in Los Angeles had come into full view:

THE JAMES LOWELL SOCIETY
247 Park Avenue, New York

The left-hand margin of the page was thick with names, listed in alphabetical order and dignified with the one-word label *Sponsors*. It was an imposing roll call, a cross section of the nation's leaders in business and the professions. The letter itself, a faultless mimeograph, was five paragraphs long:

Dear Friend:

The first man to be wounded at Pearl Harbor, Sergeant James Lowell has become a symbol for us all, in life and in death. His admirers have joined with me to form a philanthropic, nonprofit foundation bearing his name—whose purpose is to perpetuate the principles and the hopes for which he gave his life.

Had Sergeant Lowell lived, it was his intention to organize all Americans engaged in the present struggle for freedom—and, through them, to help insure world peace when that struggle ended. We can think of no better tribute to his memory than to work together to make that hope come true.

The names on this letterhead are only a small fraction of the men and women who are proud to be known as the first subscribers to the James Lowell Society—a name that will someday have universal meaning wherever men join forces to make a better world.

The undersigned has been commissioned by these founding members to invite you to enlist in our common cause. Membership, at this time, involves no obligation beyond your devotion to the principles stated above. Contributions are—and will be—voluntary.

As our plans mature, you will be informed of their nature. Meanwhile, we need your support. We solicit your advice on the maintenance of world peace. And we ask your prayers for our success.

> Yours sincerely,
> MICHAEL DERWENT

Bruce read the letter twice before he returned it to the press agent. He had tried hard to concentrate on the syrup-smooth words that promised so much and said so little—but he could not prevent his eyes from straying to that list of names on the margin.

"May I ask where this originated?"

"The name and address are before you. We've just incorporated, under the laws of New York."

"The address, I imagine, is also your office."

"For the time being. I'm the recording secretary."

"Did you compose this letter, Mr. Derwent?"

"It was composed by my copy writers—at the request of my client."

"I take it you solicited the sponsors as well."

"Soliciting is one of my chief activities," said the press agent. "In this case, sponsors weren't hard to find."

Hal spoke through the open bedroom door: his tone had an edge of malice. "Tell Mike it's a skin game if you like, Bruce. You can't hurt his feelings."

"Major Graham would never be that rude," said Derwent.

"Major Graham has a reputation for speaking his mind."

Derwent dismissed the interruption with a swift, backhand motion—like a director correcting an actor for jumping a cue.

"I can hardly believe you'll condemn us out-of-hand, Major. The founders of the Lowell Society, as you've seen, are a cross section of the country's finest. We're asking for converts, not for contributions—"

"One moment, please." Hearing his voice cut into the well-modulated recital, Bruce knew there was no way to disguise his anger. What disturbed him most was the knowledge that it still lacked a target. "Are you rehearsing a sales promotion? Or do you want my reaction to this letter, as it stands?"

"Give me your unvarnished opinion, please."

"I don't like a word of it. To my mind, it's slippery with fine phrases—and meaningless."

"Would you care to hear what response it's had in hard cash alone?"

"I'm sure you've collected plenty. Who are you planning to exploit? The American public? Sergeant Lowell's memory? Or both?"

"No one is being exploited. The aims of the James Lowell Society are above reproach. So are its sponsors, and its financing."

"Have you accepted donations from veterans—or their families?"

"Of course. The returns from that source alone have been amazing."

"What happens to such donations—while you're still in the talking stage?"

"Every cent has been audited and put in escrow. Eventually, the lump sum will be used to build a rehabilitation center at Concord—the birthplace of Jimmie Lowell."

"Who pays your expenses?"

"Our charter members, whose names you saw on the letterhead. Most of them are millionaires several times over. They are also dedicated Americans, eager to do their bit for world peace—"

Hal's voice drifted in from the bedroom. The tone was more remote now—and faintly amused. "We can prove that boast, Bruce. There's money to burn in the kitty. All of it voluntary—and deductible."

"Are *you* a contributor?"

"I'm out of this completely. Please hear Mike out. He won't mislead you."

Again, the press agent waved Hal into silence. "A man about to join an airborne regiment could hardly put his name on this letterhead. Let's call Colonel Reardon a sympathetic observer, and nothing more."

"You've already admitted he's your client."

"Hal has been my client since he entered Congress. So was his father before him. I helped organize the James Lowell Society at his request. The connection ends there."

Choked by the tide of Derwent's prose, Bruce hesitated on his reply. So far, he had reacted to instinct, to a contempt he could not control. It was another matter to put his distrust on the line, to brand Derwent as a bird of prey, with his own nest to feather.

"Why not let Sergeant Lowell's ideas develop naturally?"

"I'll answer that question with another, Major. What's more vital, in our day and age? The hero himself—or the hero's image?"

"I prefer substance to shadow."

"Who doesn't? The fact remains that products must be presold before the public will buy—whether it's a new toothpaste, a new car, or a new code of ethics."

"To my mind, a good cause should sell itself."

"You may change your viewpoint, when *our* cause is fairly launched."

"Then you have a launching date in mind?"

"Naturally, we must be guided by the success of our arms abroad. Until then, we can afford to mark time, with those names on our letterhead. Wouldn't you agree that's only common prudence?"

"How can we agree on anything—when I'm not even sure what you're selling?"

"Forgive me for contradicting you—but my selling points couldn't be clearer. In my opinion, it's you who are the victim of fuzzy thinking."

Hal's voice drifted in once more from the bedroom. "You've said your piece, Mike. Catch your train, while you still have time."

The press agent put down his glass. "Good luck with those uniforms, Hal. I'm sure you'll wear them with distinction. I appreciate your reservations, Major Graham, and I'm sure you'll outgrow them. In the meantime, I hope we part with no hard feelings."

"So far, I'm more confused than angry."

"Don't judge me too harshly, please—until the Lowell Society is fairly under way. I know it's hard to believe, but I *do* serve a purpose in our social order. You'll cheer my latest product—when Jimmie Lowell's as much a part of the American home as Dutch Cleanser."

Pacing the wall-to-wall carpet of Hal's salon, Bruce fought off the worst of the nausea Derwent had inspired. The man's presentation, he told himself, had been straightforward: he had pulled no punches in his statement of intent. Sergeant

James Lowell, and the sergeant's dream, were about to be merchandised—as ruthlessly and as brilliantly as a new bond issue. . . . His own reaction, he knew, had been based on simple visceral foreboding: the fact remained that Sergeant Lowell's beliefs would need revision before they could be offered to the public. Who was he to question the names on that letterhead? To insist that the sergeant's credo, and his memory, were about to be fatally tarnished?

When Hal emerged from the bedroom, in well-cut civilian garb, Bruce turned toward him with relief. Compared to Derwent's brass, Hal seemed a manageable antagonist—and a familiar one.

"You took long enough to change."

"I was giving you time to recover from your surprise. It's always a shock, having a *modus operandi* dumped in your lap without warning."

"How else did you expect me to react?"

"Knowing you as I do," said Hal, "I was prepared for the inevitable. I still felt you should be exposed to Mike before you went aboard your ship. After all, Jimmie was your protégé almost before he was mine."

"It's good of you to admit I knew Jimmie once. I thought you'd forgotten."

"Give Mike his due," said Hal. "No one else could have created this foundation so quickly. If we don't lose our timing, the sky's the limit—once the war is over. Isn't that what Jimmie wanted?"

"I'm not sure he'd have recognized his ideas, when Derwent's soft sell is over."

"Isn't it fair to wait and see? The Society's barely launched. If world events take a wrong direction, it could turn into another morning glory overnight. In that event, we've lost nothing by standing pat. If I'm right—and Mike *can* sell the idea—we move in on the ground floor. We can't miss either way."

"In other words, you intend to support the Lowell Society

if it has ten million postwar members. And drop it if its
sponsors run out of gas?"

"That's my privilege, as a free agent. Particularly, when
I'm paying Mike a tidy fee for this tryout."

"Along with thirty other cautious millionaires in search of
a new tax deduction?"

"Now who's being bitter?" There was a rasp beneath Hal's
voice. "Suppose I offered *you* an important part in the Lowell
Society?"

"I'd decline the offer, without thanks."

"Don't be a mule-headed idealist forever, Bruce. We deserve what we can get from this war. When it's over, we'll
probably both be heroes, with yards of service ribbons and
constellations of battle stars. Who could represent tomorrow's
veterans better than a paratroop colonel? And a surgeon
whose name is already known to millions of Americans?"

"What part did you have in mind for me?"

"How would you like to be our first postwar vice-president?
And the director of the rehabilitation center we'll build in
Concord?"

"There are few things I'd like less."

"Because you can't shake off the belief I'm promoting my
own interests?"

"I refuse to trust that huckster you've hired as your mouth-
piece. Don't tell me that *he* can sell Jimmie's credo without
distorting it."

"Will you keep that opinion to yourself, until Mike shows
how wrong you are?"

"I'll promise nothing now. First, I'll have to decide if
you're really behind world peace. Convince me of that, and
I'll join your Society without bribes. I won't even complain
of the way you've groomed me as a stalking horse."

"What gave you such uncharitable ideas?" Hal asked.

"This meeting with Derwent helped. The way you gave
him the floor—and the way you both tried to suck me in.

Now we're on the subject, I suppose this trailer we made for Brodski is part of the promotion."

"Do you object to sharing your glory with a classmate—and a friend?"

"Not at all—if it helps to sell bonds. Just don't assume I've joined your camp."

"Perhaps this isn't the time to mention it," said Hal. "But I think you should make the effort—in fairness to me."

"Because you saved me from sorting mail in England?"

"Don't forget the way I rescued you from Jake Sanford."

"It was the Surgeon General who performed that salvage job, not you. The SGO sent me to Brodski's studio, and put me on a hospital ship. It's true you saved my life at Camp Bruckner, and I've thanked you for it. Your service ended there. As of now, I owe you nothing—so stop breathing down my neck."

Hal shrugged. "I still predict you'll join us, when the Lowell Society becomes part of American life. You belong there."

"How can I join you in anything—when I'm about to ask Janet to marry me?"

Hal turned to the French windows and the vast city below them—starred with the glow of burning gas wells, now that the dusk had begun to obscure its harsh contours.

"All of us are too civilized to lose sleep over a postponed engagement," he said. "Janet's told me she wants to give pictures a whirl before she thinks of marriage. If she chooses to test you as her newest suitor, I can hardly object."

"Not even a politician can be quite so tolerant."

"Do I hear a note of sarcasm even now?" Hal asked. "Are you determined to mistrust me to the end?"

"There's no need to part on that note. Why not simply declare an armistice, until I'm sure of your intentions?"

"Very well, Bruce. Since you won't give me more, I'll accept a flag of truce."

When Hal held out his hand, the surgeon observed that his

smile had not lost an iota of its candlepower. The vigor of
the handshake, too, was undiminished. His fingers ached from
the pressure.

"Friendly enemies, until further notice," said Hal. "If you
plan to attend Brodski's studio party, you should be heading
for Hollywood and Vine."

"Aren't you coming too?"

"I'm speaking in San Francisco tonight. They're flying me
up in an hour. I'm afraid this is good-bye—until we meet in
Africa."

"What makes you think we will?"

"Our paths were meant to cross, Bruce—and I'll make sure
they do. If you're still troubled about our progress toward
the millenium, keep in touch with Shane McLendon. With
that green tab on her uniform, she can go anywhere."

"Is Shane your press agent too? *That* I refuse to believe."

"Shane's mind is her own," said Hal. "Sometimes, when
I'm lucky, she serves as my conscience. Don't tell me it needs
help at the moment, please. You've wounded me enough
today."

Bruce had expected the studio party to be a full-fledged
bacchanalia. Instead, it was an echo from memory lane—
more exotic, in its way, than the Josselyn open house at Five
Oaks, but oddly similar.

Brodski had provided the buffet and the bar, on one of the
half-struck sets of *Pierrette*. There was the same inevitable
showing of guests in uniform, the same laughter rising in
waves against the beat of an orchestra. The name band featured in the film was playing its music now, enlivened by the
director's champagne. The actors were the only bizarre note.
Most of them had arrived in costume and makeup. All of
them seemed gay, as though the party were a coda to the
performances they had just given. The gayest actor of all,
Bruce observed, was the picture's star.

Janet had been leading a conga line when he entered the

sound stage: the file of dancers had just weaved through the set to salute the director, who sat godlike in his personal chair, beneath a hooded bank of cameras. While Bruce watched, the orchestra slipped into the picture's theme song, and Janet whirled to the dance floor of the set—a replica of the Moulin Rouge. . . . Here, she began a buoyant parody of a cancan with Peter Vernon, the song-and-dance man whose name was a synonym for royalty on theater marquees at home and abroad.

Vernon, who played a guest spot in the just-completed film, was responding in kind, as his world-famous grin flashed under the lights. Their dance, Bruce gathered, had been one of the high points of *Pierrette*. The white tailcoat Vernon wore, and Janet's brick-red gown, with its daring décolletage and froufrou petticoats, suited the moment perfectly. The set was still rocking with applause when she launched into the chorus of the song, in pidgin French.

The reprise was brief. When the chorus ended, the band glided into the thumping rhythm of "Tuxedo Junction," and the floor filled with dancers. Vernon had moved on to the leading woman. Janet had allowed herself to be captured by the character juvenile—and even Brodski rose, on a wave of cheers, to lead the soubrette to the floor. . . . The spectacle, Bruce reflected, was worth crossing a continent to witness. Why did it continue to remind him of that Sunday at Five Oaks? Why was he fighting the same urge to depart that had possessed him that afternoon on the Severn?

His diffidence vanished when Janet saw him at last and waved a greeting over her partner's shoulder. With that gesture of welcome, the girl he had loved in Washington became herself again: the tinsel surrounding her seemed no more important than a Halloween masquerade. Insisting that his memory-image was a true one, he moved through the portals of the Moulin Rouge and took the star of *Pierrette* in his arms.

"You're late, Bruce."

"Actually, I've been watching for quite a while."

Janet settled her cheek against his, letting him spin her at will. "Why didn't you cut in sooner?"

"If you must know, I felt like an intruder."

"Never feel that way again, please."

"Now I've captured you, where do I take the prize?"

"Across the floor, to those marble-top tables."

Piloting her among the dancers, Bruce felt his fears subside. This, too, was an echo of Five Oaks—a quick exit from a dance floor, with rewards of a special sort in prospect. Lest the mood be spoiled, he risked no further comment until they reached the bar, and took glasses to one of the tables surrounding the floor. Two bit players—a *poule ordinaire* and a gorilla-muscled apache—sprang up to make way for their star. . . . The show of protocol belonged to the moment.

Settling in a chair with a vast flounce of petticoats, Janet pressed his hand beneath the table. Her smile, like the instant communion between them, had never been warmer.

"What detained you this time? Hal?"

"How did you guess?"

"He phoned just now to say good-bye," said Janet. "Was he too difficult?"

"Not really."

"I'm sure he still feels we're pawns on his private chessboard. Do you mind too much?"

"Not if you don't. After all, he'll think that with his last breath."

Janet listened with complete attention while Bruce repeated the high points of his encounter at the Biltmore. Her fingers were still laced with his. Her eyes, despite the whirl of synthetic gaiety surrounding them, were for him alone.

"Hal has needed a lecture for quite a while," she said. "Thanks for hitting him so hard."

"It was like hitting a pillow—and I'm sure he'll be back for more. He's already planning to track me down in Africa."

"We'll face the threat when it comes," said Janet. "At least he's left us in peace for the present."

"It seems too good to be true."

"I'll tell you a secret, Bruce. I asked him to stay clear of this party. For once, I wanted to enjoy your company properly."

"Then you've really broken your engagement?"

"I'll be honest, and say it's been deferred."

"Even that much information gives me hope. Why the compromise?"

"I had to compromise, to appease my stern parent. *He's* been moaning ever since he heard I'd be making a second picture. If I told him I was jilting Hal too, he'd have disowned me."

"When will the jilting be official?"

"I haven't quite decided."

"Can I help speed your decision?"

"Are you, by any chance, asking me to marry you?"

"Here and now—on a movie set, with your director watching. Naturally, I'd have preferred another setting. I had no choice, now we're about to part again."

Janet had withdrawn her hand while he spoke, to rest her chin on her locked fingers. The air of reverie seemed proper for a girl faced with a proposal. Only the glow in her eyes assured him that this was not part of her play-acting.

"I'm honored by your suggestion," she said at last.

"Is that the best answer you can give me?"

"It's the best I have today. I can't say more, until I know myself a little better."

"Will you be offended if I throw light on your confusion?"

"You couldn't offend me if you tried, Bruce. It's one of the comforting things about you."

"What's happening is simple enough. When you escaped to California, you left your past behind. You haven't yet found a pattern for your future. Meanwhile, you've made a successful picture, with another on the way. Why shouldn't you go on learning to be yourself?"

"Is this a blank check to do as I like?"

"Until your future jells. Why not?"

Janet considered the pronouncement, as her eyes turned to the dance floor—where Brodski was dancing a surprisingly graceful waltz with the soubrette, in a circle of actors who applauded each turn.

"Leo's helped, of course," she said. "He gives this dream-world rules of his own. So far, it seems, I've lived up to them."

"And felt alive, while you did?"

"Completely alive—for the first time."

"Being alive—and knowing it—is a privilege few of us enjoy. In your case, it means freedom from your father—and from Hal. On Brodski's set, you're a queen in your own right. Not just a pawn on a Washington chessboard. Don't lose that feeling, ever. If I can, I'll help you keep it."

"Will you, Bruce?"

"I'll promise not to rush you till you're sure of me. Freedom can be a heady gift, if it's used unwisely."

"A moment ago you told me to enjoy life all the way. Now you're advising me to watch my step."

"That was my Scotch conscience speaking, not Major Graham. *He's* on the warpath tonight—and praying you'll send him into battle a happy man."

"By daring to love him?"

"You took the words from my mouth."

"How soon do you sail?"

"Our shakedown cruise begins next week."

"And you must fly east tomorrow?"

"Direct to Charleston."

"Then this is a real good-bye."

"It looks that way. Now you've heard me out—and put me on probation—I'll take my leave. I mustn't keep you from your guests."

"These people aren't guests, Bruce. They're actors—performing at a party, to improve their stock with a director. So, for that matter, am I. Give me another hour. I'll join you where you like."

"I can hardly invite you to a BOQ in San Pedro."

"Why not go to Puerta del Sol and wait for me?"

"What's Puerta del Sol?"

"The estate I rented when I came West. I'll give you the keys."

"Won't your aunt wait up for you?"

"Aunt Hester's gone up to San Francisco to hear Hal speak. I've given the servants a night off. We'll have our Sun Gate to ourselves until morning." The star of *Pierrette* reached into her bodice, to lift out two keys on a golden chain. "The big one's for the gate," she said. "It cuts the electric eye that protects me from burglars."

"And the second?"

"The second's for my front door. There's champagne in the bar. You won't have time to get lonesome."

Gela

Weekly inspection, a canonical rite in the Army, had been a feature of life aboard the *Helen S Peters* since the 241st Hospital Ship Complement had put to sea. Admitting its absolute necessity both as a doctor and an officer, Major Bruce Graham had discovered it was the fact of military life he disliked most.

The first reason, of course, was purely physical, a feeling of claustrophobia, accented by a faint queasiness, that grew with each descent to a lower deck. Here, the ventilation system of a prewar cruise ship could not conquer the petroleum-tinged effluvia that rose from engine room and bilges; here, while the inspectors moved from ward to ward, not even hospital odors could disguise the fact that this was a vessel bound for a combat zone. Once he had descended into what—for want of a more aesthetic term—could only be called the bowels of his ship, Bruce had no way to avoid that reminder. These same decks, for all their steel bulkheads and dogged-down ports, could be awash with salt water if luck ran against them tomorrow.

The second reason cut deeper. Few of the men and women who snapped to attention on inspection morning had been tested in battle. Until they had survived such tests, he was forced to class them as green troops, for all their training. Those rigorous months—in the mock-ups at Jeff Davis, in

Charleston, on the Atlantic crossing—had been only pale previews of the agony they would meet head-on when the first litter cases awaited their turn in the companionways. Rehearsals for that moment had been thorough—but there was no substitute for the rush of blood in a lacerated throat, the tortured aspiration of a punctured lung, the feces dripping from a torn bowel.

Unbidden, the words of a prayer rose to his lips before the orderly opened the door to the first surgical ward. He had yet to speak the words above a whisper. The training of the 241st had left nothing to be desired: when men on the beach would be giving their lives tomorrow, it was unfair to solicit divine protection for a hospital offshore, or to ask that his staff perform miracles.

Somehow, he felt that these nurses and technicians and university-trained surgeons would live through their first battle with honor. Somehow, he knew they would be ready with the morphine that eased unbearable pain, the suction tube that saved a throat wound from drowning in its own blood, the sharp eye that detected intracranial pressure in a head injury, the telltale sign of hemorrhage inside a plaster cast.

The orderly barked a demand for attention. Bruce matched it with a second ritual order to stand at ease.

Followed by his entourage (Captain Eric Badger, and Chief Nurse Alice Stacey, whose brand-new captain's bars gleamed at the collar of her uniform) he entered the first surgical ward, to face the two nurses and six enlisted technicians who made up the personnel. A glance assured him that each shoe had a dazzling sheen, that each button was closed and every hair in place. Each doorknob was a brass mirror. His white-gloved finger could not find a speck of dust on the tops of the cabinets in the ward office—and the racked charts on the wall were precise as an unsolved problem in geometry.

Since the ward opened to the operating rooms amidships,

and was intended for severe cases, the pipe berths were only two deep, with ample space for the attendants to perform their function. Each bed was made with sharply cornered sheets, the top edges covering just four inches of blanket. Bestowing the expected commendation, and receiving a dazzling smile from the nurse in charge, Bruce wondered if her face would be as radiant tomorrow, after she had ministered to a hundred desperately wounded patients in this same room. He hoped the smile would endure. It could be better medicine for a dying man than the drugs in those well-stocked cabinets.

The inspection proceeded to similar areas on this level, including the three main operating theaters and the smaller emergency rooms that adjoined them. It moved from A-Deck to B, from B-Deck to C—to the general supply-rooms, the pharmacies, and the endless files of triple-tiered beds reserved for less critically wounded on D-Deck. It continued to the deck below, where Lieutenant Slade, the Sanitary Corps officer, waited with his own staff in the hospital kitchen, flanked by his walk-in freezers, his immaculate carving tables and scoured dishwashers, his files of copper pans that made a geometry of their own.

In the commissary, as always, Bruce felt his nameless fear increasing: the sense of queasiness, a butterfly-flutter on A-Deck, was now as definite as *mal de mer*. There was something about these tons of food, and the file of white-aproned processors, that numbed his senses. This gleaming kitchen—scented ever so faintly with onion fragrance—was a forcible reminder that multitudes of wounded would soon depend on the sanitation chief for survival, as definitely as they depended on the healing knife. . . . He wondered if Lieutenant Slade felt the same malaise when he looked through the doors of an operating room.

On the deck below, the inspection moved quickly on the steel grilles above the bilges, where the throb of the ship's diesels was tangible evidence that the *Helen S Peters* was moving steadily toward its goal. At this level, the gush of air from the ventilators was heavy with the odor of fuel oil. . . . There was no need to linger in the engine room. Ship handling was outside the surgical chief's concern, once he had checked the pumps that supplied his wards and the dynamos that served the decks above.

The ritual march had uncovered nothing new: Bruce had expected no sign of neglect at any level. The tour ended with an inspection of the quarters of officers and nurses—and traversed the living space assigned to technicians, medical department GIs, and military police. He was pleased to find the same meticulous attention to detail he had noted below. This, too, was the sign of a taut ship.

The officers' lounge—where the group disbanded—still wore the streamers of last night's dance, though the tables had been stacked and the miniature piano covered. Last night, this long room amidships of the boat deck had jumped with jazz: he had heard the music clearly as he lay reading in his bunk on the promenade deck below. Both members of his inspecting team had been among the revelers. . . . About to mention the festivities, he forced himself to dismiss Captain Badger and Chief Nurse Stacey—with the same salute he had given the attending orderly.

The tests awaiting the hospital complement had been all but visible that morning—as actual, in their way, as the throb of the ship's diesels, or his own heartbeat. Like the prayer he had left in the surgical ward, it seemed wiser to ignore them on this eve of battle.

The paper work that is the bane of medical officers afloat or ashore kept him busy until the midwatch ended. Knowing there would be no other chance to clear his desk in the near future, he stayed with the avalanche of folders until the last report was signed. The afternoon was waning before he stepped out to the promenade deck for his first breath of salt air since the inspection.

The huge white-painted ship was still cleaving an empty sea. The crosswind had subsided, and the Mediterranean was dead calm in a bath of July sunlight. Only yesterday, the boat deck and every available hatchway had been thick with sunbathers, intent on burnishing tans acquired on the Atlantic crossing. At this hour, most of the heliophiles had gone below. Sailors were stripping the tarpaulins from the flood-lights that would illumine the ship from anchor flukes to fantail when darkness fell. Special lamps were mounted on the boat deck to outline the red crosses on stack and super-structure, and the broad green strip that circled the hull—identifying the *Helen S Peters* as a mercy ship for dive bomber and U-boat, and the barges that would bring wounded from the shore.

The fact that the skipper was following a solo course did not surprise Bruce. Even when serving an invasion flotilla, hospital ships steamed toward their rendezvous points alone. The approach was part of the pattern, setting them apart from combat units and identifying them day and night. The exact whereabouts of the present invasion fleet, like its objective, were secrets known only to the captain on the bridge. But the fact that the ship had outfitted at Algiers, and the matching fact that its present course was roughly north by northeast, were enough to define its mission.

Like the others aboard, Bruce had felt the first, inevitable kickback of visceral tension when that mission had been spelled out, in letters even a nonsailor could read. Like the others, he had found compensation in the not-too-doubtful assurance, relayed like psychic adrenalin from his brain, that the rules of the Geneva Convention would prevail in the coming action, that the tasks he would perform below decks would proceed as smoothly as an emergency alert at Lake-wood. Unlike the others, he had found it necessary to drive special knowledge from his mind—including months in Barcelona, when the enemy had used the red crosses of another hospital as targets of reference, and his medical unit had been forced to smear them with camouflage to survive. . . .

At the starboard rail, staring into the heat haze that obscured the meeting of sea and sky, he could still wish for some escort on this voyage. Though it was lost in the blue immensity, Italy was not too far down the eastern horizon. He did not need the dividers in the captain's chartroom to plot the course they were following—or to estimate that they would sight the coast of Sicily before dawn tomorrow. The betting pools had long since closed: the consensus, from ward to forecastle, had settled on that island as their destination.

Only the site of the projected assault was open to conjecture. Most of the bettors favored a beachhead on the Gulf of Gela, with the port of Syracuse a second choice.

Sicily, placed like a misshapen football at the toe of the Italian boot, had the weight of logistics on its side since the retreat of the German army from North Africa. Once in Allied hands, it could become a *pointe d'appui,* from which pressure could be applied to the mainland itself—first by air strikes, then by direct invasion across the Strait of Messina. Bruce had seen enough of the task force in Algiers to know this assault would be on the massive side. Tomorrow, at the latest, the war for Fortress Europe would have begun at last.

Meanwhile, it was still possible to ignore that terrible certainty, to look down at the decks of the *Helen S Peters* and insist that time was a dream on a tideless inland sea that had seen its share of death and glory. While the illusion lasted, he would not have been too startled to see a Roman galley take shape on the horizon, in hot pursuit of a Greek trireme. Or, to reach still deeper, the black sail of a Phoenician gaoul, bound from Tyre to Carthage, nine centuries before the Christian era.

Verses came to him out of that blue mirage, and he spoke them aloud:

Quinquireme of Ninevah from distant Ophir,
Rowing home to haven in sunny Palestine,
With a cargo of ivory,
And apes and peacocks,
Sandalwood, cedarwood, and sweet white wine.

"Don't stop, please."

Bruce turned to face a barefoot Alice Stacey. During this off-duty afternoon, his chief nurse had exchanged her uniform for the briefest of sun-suits, a costume that did the most for a Rubenesque figure. Her smile—as she joined him at the rail—was a brazen reminder that war and death were springboards for the rites of Eros.

"Dismiss me if I'm de trop," she said. "You can't blame me for investigating, when a surgical chief speaks in verse. Were you composing—or quoting?"

"Quoting. From 'Cargoes,' by John Masefield. One of the burrs that stuck to my mind in college."

"Is there more?"

"The rest's in the same vein. Only the geography's different."

Stately Spanish galleon coming from the Isthmus,
Dipping through the tropics by the palm-green shores,
With a cargo of diamonds,
Emeralds, amethysts,
Topazes, and cinnamon and gold moidores.

"I like that even better."

"Try the last stanza. I hope I can remember it."

Dirty British coaster with a salt-caked smoke stack
Butting through the Channel in the mad March days,
With a cargo of Tyne coal,
Road-rail, pig-lead,
Firewood, iron-ware, and cheap tin trays.

"Is that your way of bringing me back to earth?"

"I hope the bump wasn't too severe."

"This afternoon I'd prefer to ignore the present."

"So would I, Captain Stacey. As you observed, I was trying hard. Unfortunately, we must both remember it's time for a boat drill."

"I came to ask about that. Eric says off-duty personnel must stand by. Does that mean full uniform?"

"By all means. The boarding detail would foul the davits, if they saw you now."

"Do you realize you've just paid me a compliment? As a woman, not as a nurse?"

"Perhaps the poetry brought it on."

"I assumed it was me, Bruce. I won't expect too much too soon."

"You *know* it was you, Alice—and you damned well know why. *Now* will you bring your detail on deck, after you've made yourself respectable?"

"We'll report on time, Major. Thanks for the glimpse behind the armor. It's nice to know you're vulnerable—though I'll admit my hopes aren't too high." Captain Stacey put one foot on the A-Deck ladder, a move that did no disservice to her *embonpoint*. "Not when it's common knowledge you're friendly with Shane McLendon—*and* a movie star. That's too much competition for a simple country girl."

"Churchill calls the Mediterranean front the soft underbelly of Europe," said Badger. "Somehow, I could never surround that metaphor."

"Why not—when we're about to show he's right?" asked Alice Stacey.

"My guess is the belly's a lot harder than Winnie thinks," said Captain Owen.

Bruce looked up at the exchange. Phil Owen, his new chief of medical service, was fresh from staff duty in London. He had boarded the ship at Gibraltar. Older than most Reserve officers aboard, and twice as misanthropic, he had been a valuable counterweight to optimism.

"Do you think we'll stub our toe tomorrow, Phil?"

"Not in Sicily—with the armor we'll be putting ashore. Later may be another story."

The boat drill was behind them now. The three male officers, and the captain of nurses, had adjourned to the lounge to compare notes before dinner. Badger, who had just added rum to his coffee—from the miniature piano that served as a cache for his bottle—moved forward to accept the challenge.

"I'll give even money the Italian war ends in a month."

"I'll take that bet," said Owen. "Name your figure, Eric."

"Everyone says they'll call quits, now we've kicked Rommel out of Africa. Mussolini will abdicate when we cross to the mainland."

"It's true the Duce's living on borrowed time," said Owen. "I expect the Italians to give up by fall. When that happens, the Wehrmacht will simply move in. We'll be lucky to take Rome by *next* Fourth of July."

"Fifty dollars says you're wrong."

"Done. Will you risk a bet, Alice?"

Captain Stacey shook her head. "You've taken me once too often, Phil."

"What about you, Bruce?"

The surgeon refilled his cup from the rack. A glance through a porthole revealed a tranquil sunset. Despite the aura below decks, and the clockwork realism of the boat drill, it was incredible that they had entered a combat zone—or that one of the greatest armadas to cross the Mediterranean was just down the horizon.

"Let's leave headaches to the high command," he said. "*We'll* have a long cruise, whatever happens in Italy."

"Is it true we'll be making medical history tomorrow?" Alice asked.

"This will be the first time an Army ship has backed a landing."

"Don't expect us to be too close," said Owen. "If I under-

stand the Geneva Convention, we'll keep six miles offshore."
As always, the medical chief spoke with the authority of a
man who has just emerged from a top war room. Bruce was
sure his omniscience was a pose, designed to extract bets
from brother officers. So far, the captain's winnings had been
phenomenal.

"Suppose Goering's sharpshooters can't read?" Badger
asked.

"Nothing's to be gained by worry," said Bruce. "Don't
you see you're upsetting Alice?"

"Alice is much too bushed to be upset," said the chief
nurse. "If you'll excuse us, Phil and I should check the B-
Deck pharmacy before dinner. Shall we lay below, Captain
Owen?"

"By all means, Captain Stacey—if your language is nautical,
not personal."

Badger sat frowning at a fresh coffee after the others had
departed.

"Come out of ambush, Bruce," he said. "You've been at
war. Phil's only a Grosvenor Square commando. Do *you*
think we'll need a year to occupy Italy?"

"We may—if Germany decides the factories around Genoa
and Milan are worth defending. Good or bad, this invasion
will take heat off the Russian front. Even if it turns into a
stalemate, Moscow will see we mean business."

"For my money, it's time we had proof of *their* intentions,"
said Badger. "Granted, we're stuck with them for the moment. I still wish we could shop for allies in a better market."

Bruce studied the man from Wisconsin narrowly before
he answered. The reaction was a familiar one. He had heard
it from others aboard.

"Phil was quoting Churchill just now. Remember what he
said last year, when Stalin and Hitler locked horns? How he
was prepared to welcome the devil himself—if he'd help
kill Nazis?"

"Churchill called Stalin by his right name, when he said

that. If Big Joe's on our side, why didn't he send a deputy to the Casablanca Conference? And why can't we get the real dope on the Eastern front?"

"Who says we haven't?"

"Both points were raised in the last Lowell Society *Bulletin.* I left my copy on your desk. This time, it makes sense all the way."

Bruce sighed—and reached for the rum. Two ounces of dark Jamaica, mixed with the still-darker shipboard coffee, now seemed a necessary antidote. . . . During the past month, bulletins from Derwent had saturated the *Helen S Peters.* Addressed originally to enlisted personnel, they had begun to reach junior officers as well. Signed by Hal Reardon's press agent—and bearing the same imposing list of sponsors— they were capsule reviews of the war, balanced with sermons on the virtues of a peace guaranteed by universal good will. Badger—who was ordinarily a saturnine observer of the passing scene—had accepted most of Derwent's slogans with this same pugnacious approval. So had many brother-officers in the complement.

"Apparently you feel that Derwent's called the turn again, Eric."

"The man's no fool. We'll knock off Germany a lot faster if the Russians begin trusting us—the way we *have* to trust them."

The notes of mess call put a period on the dogmatic assertion. Bruce set down his cup and turned toward the companionway.

"Do you really believe what you just said? Or are you letting an adman do your thinking?"

"Derwent may be a supersalesman. What's wrong with salesmanship, when the product's worth buying?"

"Peace? Or saber rattling?"

"Maybe you can't have one without the other. So long as they talk sense, I'm behind an outfit that can keep my kids from fighting another war."

The last Lowell Society *Bulletin,* addressed to Badger's APO, had been tucked into the blotter in Bruce's cabin. Hours later, fortified by dinner, and warning himself to throttle down his temper, he read it through at the tempo he assumed his second-in-command had followed—then at his own pace, with a deliberate search for traps between the lines. By now, the experience was a familiar one. And, though he had warned himself that his reservations were personal, the same doubts persisted when he crumpled the sheet of airmail paper and flung it at the porthole.

The *Bulletin,* deflected by a crosscurrent of air, floated to the blotter again. Creased as it was, it emphasized the paragraphs he had found most offensive:

> *A Thought for This Week:* The objectives of the James Lowell Society are harmony among nations and peace on earth. How can peace and harmony be attained—unless there is complete trust among *all* our leaders?
>
> Today, with American war aims clearly outlined at the Casablanca Conference, our strategists are concerned—*distressed* might be a better term—that Moscow, for reasons best known to itself, did not see fit to participate.
>
> As a result, our planning—in the field, as well as in diplomacy—is hampered at the source.
>
> *A Corollary to the Above:* How does Moscow explain an almost total blackout of events now taking place on the Eastern front?
>
> The founders of the James Lowell Society—and we feel sure our growing membership shares this view—believe that the first prerequisite to world peace is the free flow of information among *all* nations opposing the Axis.
>
> We suggest that the full weight of public opinion in America be exerted to assure such a flow.

Eric, it seemed, had quoted Derwent's lecture accurately enough. Viewed in this light, it seemed sincere: Bruce knew it would find a response in the Society's wide readership, just as it had won converts aboard the *Helen S Peters.* Who was he to suggest (on the basis of his instinctive mistrust of Derwent) that those well-balanced sentences, with their leitmotif of sweet reason, were hollow as the pipes in a circus calliope? Or that Derwent was merely exploiting two sides of an argument—a need for peace through understanding, and a veiled hint that the Russians, now or later, were preparing one of the greatest double crosses in history?

A second shot at the porthole was more successful. He felt better after he had watched the paper ball wing into the sea.

Brooding on the implications behind that apparently innocuous flyer, Bruce found himself pondering the enigma of Hal Reardon, and the part Hal had played in the chain reaction that had made the Lowell Society possible. Somehow, the *Bulletin* had been a fitting overture to the activities of Hal himself—who was now engaged in intensive maneuvers with the 75th Airborne, not too far from Algiers.

Hal, he reflected, would always be in the front ranks when news was breaking: the 75th Airborne had been slated for this push into Sicily, but Bruce had heard they were being saved for the even more important invasion of the mainland. . . . By the same token, this congressman-turned-paratroop-colonel could fade from view when an issue was in doubt, letting operators like Mike Derwent labor in his behalf while he was a whole world away. Their collision of wills at the Los Angeles Biltmore had been a prime example of Hal the phantom. From that moment, Bruce had suspected that Hal's refusal to attend Janet's studio party had had more than one motive.

Again, he forced discipline on his thoughts: it was dangerous to brood on Hal, and still more dangerous to remember Hollywood at this early hour. During the past months, he had saved those memories of never-never land as a kind of reward, a cushion for his weariness at day's end. Tonight, if only to provide an antidote for Derwent's *Bulletin*, he unlocked his attaché case to reread Janet's last letter from Puerta del Sol.

Mailed from California more than two weeks ago, the

letter was already outdated by events; it was brief, breathless, and warm with love. The early rushes for her second picture, she confided, had been scrapped: Brodski had ordered a complete rewrite of the script and a recasting of the male leads. Janet's father had spent part of the past month in Los Angeles, in another fruitless effort to persuade her to return to Washington. Hal had stormed off to Camp Jeff Davis for indoctrination, without even asking her to announce their engagement. . . .

Her best news had been saved for the last: *Pierrette* had already opened in America with great success and would soon be shown in North African base camps. The star herself, at the request of Army Public Relations, would make a personal appearance with each showing. Inevitably, the tour would reach Algiers. Once she had checked on the itinerary of his ship, she would work through channels for a reunion.

Skimming the words he knew by heart, feeling the expected clutch of desire at his throat, Bruce locked the letter away and left the cabin for his evening mile on the promenade deck. This, too, was part of the disciplines that ruled his day. During the Atlantic crossing, he had liked those hours the best—the eerie whiteness of the floodlit ship, the soft-voiced commands from the bridge, the tracery of masts and cargo hoists swinging against the stars. . . . Tonight, his appointment with the gods of war was a priority target that demanded all his reserves. Until that appointment was discharged with honor, he knew he must control his wool-gathering.

A review of the briefing he had just attended was a convenient escape from such wanderings in memory lane. As he continued to clock his measured mile, he forced his mind to go over each item Colonel Parker, the liaison officer from the Theater Task Force, had described in the chartroom.

The coverage had been based on a map of the shoreline the invasion force would attack. Only two other officers besides Bruce had been present: Colonel Stokes and the skipper of the vessel, a vintage mariner whose comments had given Parker's recital a needed leavening.

Captain Swenson had accepted tomorrow's task as a routine assignment, conditioned only by the state of the beachhead the Army intended to establish in the forenoon. Stokes seemed just as calm. . . . Bruce, attending the briefing as his CO's deputy, was keenly aware of his privilege. He had been careful to treat Colonel Parker with the deference a veteran campaigner deserved.

Dime Force was the name given to the landing. Its objective was Gela Gulf, on the southern coast of Sicily, a point directly north of Malta. Parker had warned the officers that beachhead action would probably be too heated, in the first hours, to make room for hospital units. After the landing barges had grounded, it was hoped, but not promised, that casualties could be ferried to the ship from battalion aid stations. At the start of the battle, the *Helen S Peters* might be expected to serve as a floating field hospital, receiving and treating wounded direct. Once the lines had moved inland, regular medical units supporting each division would come ashore. The ship, as its wards filled with patients, would then resume its primary function—the ferrying of casualties from one port to another, in this case from Gela to general hospitals in Algiers.

Their present position had been announced that evening on the radio—an open circuit accessible to both friend and foe. This, too, was standard procedure under the Geneva Convention. The liaison officer had shrugged off such protective acts as superfluous: in his opinion, the enemy had long since been alerted to each stage of the forthcoming attack. Such pickups had been reported during the African landings. Captured documents had revealed that the Afrika Korps had known the identity of every unit taking part—and, in some cases, the names of their commanders.

The fleet assembled for the Sicilian invasion was a formidable one: the overall operation, bearing the working title of

Husky, involved well over two thousand ships. The American Seventh Army would invest the southern beaches, striking at points from Licata to Cape Scalambri, with the town of Gela as its center. The British Eighth Army, including the First Canadian Division, would hit the eastern coast of the island from Cape Passero to the area south of Syracuse.

Thirteen divisions would be put ashore before the invasion was completed. Since Axis strength was estimated at twelve divisions, the Theater Task Force did not anticipate a picnic. However, with a large number of Italian troops involved, it was felt that the advantage lay with the invaders. From the start, Italians had shown a marked loss of interest in the war when forced to serve beside the Wehrmacht.

In Colonel Parker's view, the enemy would concentrate on the evacuation of his airstrips, once the tide had turned; with the Luftwaffe transferred, he would then retire across the Strait of Messina. During this rear-guard action—a running-wolf tactic for which the Germans were famous—Husky would secure all beachheads, extend its perimeters as rapidly as the local situations warranted, then proceed methodically with the total reduction of Sicily, and the creation of a vital base for the attack on mainland Italy itself.

Returning to more immediate problems, the liaison officer had repeated his warning: a delay, perhaps of hours, was to be expected—once the *Helen S Peters* had taken its station offshore. Since the Mediterranean was an almost tideless sea, its beaches were ill-suited to amphibious warfare. Allowances would be made for the slow pace of the LSTs and the LCTs, the efficient monsters that had delivered so much armor to Pacific islands. There would be traffic tie-ups with the infantry landing-craft, the smaller LCTs that would bring the actual fighting men ashore. At worst, Parker estimated that the last field hospital would be ashore by noon, and functioning at its peak of efficiency. With an efficient chain of command, the ship might even begin its return voyage to Algiers before darkness fell.

Procedure aboard had been reviewed once more before the briefing ended. Bruce would be in charge below, working with his team of surgeons, enlisted technicians and nursing personnel. On deck, as litter cases were hoisted aboard, an admitting officer and two assistants, the triage team made famous by the Spanish Civil War, would separate the wounded. Those judged critical would go at once to Bruce. Others would be put to bed to await their turn on the tables. Walking wounded would be processed on deck before admission to the D-Deck wards.

Captain Badger would handle this essential sorting: as Bruce's second-in-command, he had been intensively trained, both at Jeff Davis and at sea. The nurses under Alice Stacey would perform their traditional functions at all levels—bringing that indefinable touch of compassion which was the greatest gift the heiresses of Florence Nightingale could bestow.

Everything that could be foreseen had been provided, Bruce told himself, when he finished his evening mile and entered his stateroom. Only the imponderables remained: the height of the surf on the beaches if the wind freshened before dawn, the accuracy of the fire laid down to protect the first wave, the assumption that the hospital itself would be recognized as a mercy vessel and not a sitting duck. . . . Such worries, he added, were fruitless now the issue was joined. As he had told Eric Badger, anticipation could be excess baggage on a ship en route to action.

In his bunk, with a gooseneck lamp bent above his pillow, Bruce considered a letter to Janet, and abandoned the notion. Instead, he switched off the light and fastened his eyes on the open port—and the slow dance of the stars as the *Helen S Peters* rolled in the crosswind that had returned with the sunset. This was the time when it was useless to fight the tide of memory; this was the hour when he could surrender without shame to a recreation of his last night in California—

from the moment he had left Brodski's party to wait for Janet at the house she had rented in the Sierra Madre.

It was a vivid vision. Despite its revivals, it still retained the charm of an experience he could not quite believe, though his memory insisted he had lived it to the full.

That night in California, he had driven into the hills of Hollywood, pushing his rented car to its best speed on hairpin turns that led ever higher. A half-mile from his goal, he passed a delivery truck on a curve to roar toward Janet's villa, a tall, dead-white house whose facade could have passed for a castle in Spain.

His headlong pace, like that brief flirtation with death, had been deliberate—and, from a practical viewpoint, quite needless. Janet could not leave her studio party too soon, so there was no point in haste. Yet he knew that the pressure behind his eyes, and the thunder of his pulses, would drown coherent thought until he had unlocked the portals of this improbable paradise.

The first key turned the lock of a donjon-like outer gate— an ingenious mechanism that lifted the barrier, portcullis-fashion, to admit him to a closed courtyard. The door to the house itself was a huge redwood rectangle framed in vines: it opened to a towering foyer, where a blue emergency bulb was the only illumination. Ahead, a wrought-iron balustrade led to a fifty-foot living room, brought to instant life as his hand touched the switch. . . . The rest of Puerta del Sol was on the same grandiose scale: a *comedor* that could seat a score of diners and might have been lifted bodily from the Escorial, a study with clawfoot desk, carved throne-chair and stamped-leather walls, a terrace opening to a view of tumbled brown hills and the pinpoints of light that marked the Sunset Strip.

The feeling that it was part of a waking dream persisted, now that the dusk had deepened into night—broken at intervals by a moon that showed its face among fog banks. Each step he took in Janet's rented castle accented its empti-

ness. The view from the terrace seemed drained of life—the
lights of Hollywood too distant to be real, the Sierra Madre
bizarre as the mountains of the moon. Only a single house
on the next hilltop, remote as some bandit's eyrie, assured
him that this was a perfect setting for a tryst.

A second visit to the foyer brought additional evidence he
was alone: the note propped on a stair tread had obviously
been written by a butler, reminding Miss Josselyn that champagne was in the study, and thanking her for an evening off.
Wondering if it was too soon to open Janet's wine, he returned to the leather-walled den to seek out the cooler.
Opening the artfully concealed receptacle disguised as a
cassone, rotating the bottles in their bed of salted ice, he decided it would be wiser to wait, and fumbled along the walls
for another light switch. . . . It seemed grotesque to go
through the motions of reading, but he was badly in need
of some occupation to prove he existed.

The single open bookshelf in the study was a period piece,
filled with morocco-bound sets. Each volume was gold-let-
tered with the name of a classic—but *Don Quixote*, like
Hakluyt's *Voyages* and the *Decameron* of Boccaccio, resisted
his efforts to remove them. It was only when he examined
the sets in detail that he realized they were decoration and
nothing more.

He was still chortling at his discovery when the whole
house filled with the strains of "Siboney." Emerging from
the den, he found his hostess standing at the console of a
radio-victrola—still in the grisette's gown she had worn at the
studio.

"May I have this dance, *señor mayor?*"

Even after she had whirled into his embrace, he could not
be sure this was Janet Josselyn. Her response to the tango was
faintly teasing as she danced close, mournful to the point
of despair when they moved apart in the rituals of that love-
duel set to music. After a moment, he realized she was still
performing, that the flare of petticoats above those long,

sleek legs, and the flutter of kohl-dark lashes, were part of another impersonation—the exact look and gesture of Chita Miranda, a Mexican picture star whose conquests were the gossips' delight. . . . The mimicry, he knew, was deliberate, a touch of humor to counteract the strangeness of Puerta del Sol. Blessing her for that insight, he spun her from house to terrace.

"Why aren't the books real?" It was hardly the opening of an amorous duet, yet it suited the occasion.

"Nothing's real here," said Janet. "The violets are big as sunflowers, and there's music in every wall. It's a little like being on the set after hours. Eventually, I learned to adjust."

"Don't you get lonesome?"

"I might—without Aunt Hester. She loved this souped-up Alhambra from the first. So much, I find I can bear it too."

"She isn't here tonight?"

"Aunty's in San Francisco. I told you, at the studio. Tonight the Alhambra's all ours."

"It's still hard to take in."

"*This*, Bruce? Or the fact she won't be back until morning?"

"I can't get over the feeling we're acting another scene for Brodski."

"Perhaps we are." Janet held his hand at her back as she spun down the length of his arm, then returned for their next rhythmic embrace. "There's nothing I like more than playing a part. Especially, when I know my partner won't miss a cue."

"Would Aunt Hester approve, if she were in the audience?"

"I'm sure she wouldn't. Incidentally, with the servants away, she thinks I'm staying at the Ambassador. Hal does too. So you'll have to take me there, in a little while."

"After we finish this dance—and the champagne your butler left on ice?"

"I wanted you to see just how I lived here," said Janet.

"How silly it can be—and how exciting. There are days when I'm sure *I'm* dreaming, too."

"Perhaps you are. This may be a true castle in Spain. When morning comes, you may find it doesn't exist."

"A movie star built it thirty years ago," said Janet. "While he lasted, it was the final word in splendor. Did you know this is one of the highest foothills in the Sierra Madre? Or that the house on that next crag is the Eagle's Nest?"

"What was the eagle's name?"

"Rudolph Valentino. The Eagle's Nest was the place he went to be alone. Don't pretend you're too young to remember him."

"Valentino was the inspiration of my teens. You're making me feel a bit like him tonight."

"That's as it should be, Bruce. Why is it you never disappoint me?"

"Because I love you—and you love me."

"You mean that, don't you?"

"Of course I mean it."

"Let's put everything behind us, then—while the music lasts. Including the fact you're catching a plane for Charleston—and I must be on the set at eight."

"How long will the music go on playing?"

"Until we cut the switch. It's another feature of Puerta del Sol. The tango's nearly over, I'm afraid."

"It's over now," he said. "Shall we follow tradition, and end it with a kiss?"

"We'd spoil it if we didn't."

Play-acting was forgotten while their lips met and clung. His head was spinning when he released her. Even now, he saw he must await a final cue.

"*Muy buenos, señor mayor,*" said Janet.

"*Muy buenos, señorita.* Shall we go on?"

"The next number wasn't meant for dancing."

He turned toward the music that continued to pour from

the house—loudly enough to waken echoes in the surrounding hills. The tune had changed to Lizst's "Liebestraum," played by a concert pianist.

"Did you pick out the *records*, too?"

"Of course."

"Is this one part of our performance?"

"If you can translate it," said the star of *Pierrette*. . . .

Their night of love had begun on that note. It had ended hours later, in a fog-wet dawn, on the driveway of the Hotel Ambassador, before he had driven across Los Angeles to San Pedro—just in time to catch a plane bearing him to war. Begun with make-believe at a castle called Puerta del Sol, their night had ended with a last, wild kiss in the growing light of day, with avowals he had every intention of fulfilling. . . . Why could he still wonder where play-acting had merged with true rapture? How could he go on asking himself, even now, if that night was a figment of his fancy?

A hundred times, in the months that followed, that troublesome question had teased him out of thought. It was no less troublesome now, with Janet's last letter fresh in mind and the knowledge that their reunion in Algiers—in the event he survived tomorrow's action—would be only a matter of contacts, through established channels. . . .

On another, more tranquil midnight at sea, the playback of that scene on a Hollywood terrace would have eased him into slumber. Tonight, the weariness of a long day had done still more to numb his brain. His nerves, drawn taut since morning, relaxed slowly as he dropped into oblivion. The drop was not quite deep enough to shut out the roar of bombers, when the first wave swept north from Africa.

When he wakened, the ship's engines had stopped—and he knew the familiar thunder on the horizon was man-made. War, for the 241st Hospital Ship Complement, had finally begun.

"It's a lot less Italian than I expected," said Captain Owen. He lowered the binoculars and handed them to Captain Badger. "From here, it could pass for Southern California on a clear day."

The man from Wisconsin adjusted the lenses and studied the shoreline intently. "You'll probably have the same reaction at the pearly gates," he said. "For my money, it could pass for Paradise—if you overlook the smoke."

"You'll find Sicily a far cry from Heaven when we get ashore," said Bruce.

"Assuming we ever do."

"You read Colonel Parker's leaflet. This is one of the poorest islands on earth."

"Isn't that the real reason we're fighting?" Owen asked. "I doubt there'd be wars, once people lived up to their scenery."

"I, for one, am resigning from this abstract discussion," said Badger. "A boat is coming our way. Perhaps we're about to start behaving like doctors."

Bruce moved to a wing of the bridge as he took the binoculars and focused on the patrol boat that was attempting—so far in vain—to detach itself from the stream of invasion traffic. "You'd best go down with Eric, Phil," he said. "I'll join you in another moment."

As far as the naked eye could see, the Mediterranean was black with shipping. Transports continued to disgorge troops at a safe distance from shore batteries—and naval armor still poured salvos ashore to knock out the last defenders. The beach itself was obscured in a gray-white mist of small-arms fire, though its possession was no longer in dispute. . . . As battles went, this one had gone well but slowly. Judging by radio reports during the last hours, the Gulf of Gela would be secured for Allied forces before darkness fell.

Since dawn, the *Helen S Peters* had remained at its assigned station six miles offshore, while the 241st awaited its first casualties. Until midmorning, the action had been violent, with resistance far stiffer than amateur tacticians had expected. Now, in the late afternoon, with the enemy in retreat, the battle had a curious remoteness, as though ships and men were counters in a game played by unseen hands.

Sicily itself was a solid presence in the blaze of afternoon: Bruce could appreciate Owen's comparison to the oversubscribed glories of California. The binoculars defined the same white miles of beaches, the same humped hills, the same leprous files of eucalypti along the roads—and, to the north, the same gaunt sierras lifted against the blue.

The town of Gela, ringed by wheat fields and dusty olive groves, stood on a plateau well above the shore. It had no harbor, only a long steel pier, all but destroyed before the enemy had moved inland. . . . Despairing of his attempt to form a picture in the midst of confusion, Bruce turned to Captain Swenson. The skipper had not left his post for hours —but he seemed tireless and completely relaxed.

"You look puzzled, Major," he said. "Did things sound simpler at our briefing?"

"Colonel Parker hoped you'd be setting a course for Africa tonight. Apparently he was optimistic."

"Wars seldom follow the timetable set by their generals."

"What do you suppose went wrong?"

"The usual things, I suppose. Like barges grounding on sandbars, and batteries straddling their targets."

"Can we hold this position indefinitely?"

"If the good weather lasts, and the Luftwaffe seeks other goals."

"I wish I could borrow some of your patience."

"A sailor who runs cargo for a living grows used to waiting," said Swenson. "It hardly matters if the cargo is men or machines. I have ferried aviation gas to Pacific islands—and unloaded it under fire. Compared to such cruises, today's action seems a pleasant bore. Obviously, the picture can change at any moment."

"Assuming there *is* a snafu, I'd like to know the reason."

"Most battles are snafus—until they assume a pattern. By and large, this one is proceeding toward its goal."

"We were supposed to receive our first wounded by mid-morning."

"Eventually, your wounded will come aboard. You will salvage what you can—and I will ferry those survivors to Algiers. This time tomorrow—or the day after, if your load is heavy—our contribution to this holocaust will be an obscure footnote to history."

"Even though this is the first time a hospital ship has backed the Army?"

"Those who fight the battles get first mention in the histories," said Swenson. "Those who minister to the survivors are more easily forgotten." He raised his own binoculars to study the patrol boat, dodging through a file of transports to approach the ship at last. "There's an officer headed this way, with at least two casualties aboard. Perhaps he can enlighten you, in some measure."

Bruce reached the deck in time to join the group at the port rail, where ladders and hoists had been waiting since sunrise to receive wounded. Once their visitor had come aboard, the tale he told—in the staccato bursts of a man gray with fatigue—made the smoke screen ashore even thicker.

Medical Corps Colonel Meighan, attached to the staff of the Seventh Army, had been among the first doctors ashore. He had supervised the location of battalion aid stations a half hour after the beachhead was established; he had organized litter trains to bring wounded from the rapidly expanding battle line. By early afternoon, a viable chain of command had been established—and he had returned to the beach to find that crowded sea-lanes were gradually clearing. Further difficulties had been encountered when he had ordered water transport for his casualties—only to find that most of the barges were still lying well offshore with combat reserves to disembark. Extra DUKWs, and a few surplus LCIs, had finally been pressed into service. They would follow in the patrol boat's wake, whenever they could clear the press of invasion traffic.

Listening to this rapid-fire account—while Eric Badger stood by the hoists to watch their first casualties reach the deck—Bruce wondered if this experience was typical. Despite his weariness, the MC colonel seemed eager to return to the beach, now he had assured himself that the best possible help for his wounded existed.

"It was going well when I left," he said. "We expected delay. Gela is the key to the whole operation on this coast. They've begun to fall back—but I hear a panzer division is dug into the sierra to hold the passes."

"Do you think they'll succeed, sir?" Bruce asked.

"Not when we hit them again from the air."

"How many casualties may we expect before nightfall?"

"Plenty, Major Graham. Are you ready to handle them?"

"We've been ready since we left Charleston," said Stokes.

Meighan glanced down the deck, where his litter cases had already been evaluated, tagged for their sections, and rushed to the lifts.

"I can see that's no idle boast, gentlemen. One of those men's a flank wound that may involve a kidney. He happens to be my master sergeant."

"Major Graham will operate on him at once," said Stokes.

Ten minutes later, holding his dripping arms above a sink in Operating Suite Two, the surgical chief watched his group take their stations. Gloved and gowned, he moved out of the scrub room to evaluate the operative area—nodding his approval when he saw the kidney clamps were ready, in case that organ was damaged beyond repair. Here, despite the melee ashore, the last precious second would be wrung from the timetable.

"I wish we'd had him sooner—but his chances seem good. We'll make a transverse incision for maximum exposure."

It was only when the scalpel came into his hand that

Bruce realized Colonel Meighan's discourse had left him no wiser than before, so far as events ashore were concerned. The omission seemed unimportant, now his own battle was beginning.

When it was over, Bruce found that two impressions were dominant. One was the sense of profound relief that had come with his first scalpel stroke, like the closing of a door on chaos. The second was the discovery that his command was now absolute. A world where death was king—the world of war—had been replaced by a universe whose watchword was salvation, whose tools were equal to its tasks.

Operating in a combat zone, he had visioned flashes of drama to match those months in Spain—a roar of guns, a reek of powder, a call from the lines to save men under fire. Once the tempo of the operating rooms had settled, it had not seemed too different from its counterpart at Lakewood.

When it was really over, he knew what the Gela invasion called to mind—an all-out emergency in Baltimore during his intern year, when an explosion in the railroad yards had coincided with a five-alarm fire, jamming the wards with scores of cases, and driving his entire service to the brink of exhaustion.

Some of the crises aboard this floating hospital had tested his skills to the utmost: inevitably, there had been failures to balance his success. His first operation—the flank wound that had begun his incarceration below decks—had been a touchy affair, before he could pull Meighan's sergeant through with no greater loss than one-fourth of a kidney. That same afternoon, a cerebral laceration had required the combined techniques of his team, and a touch of pure luck, to save the patient. On the second day (when it seemed he had been operating forever), he had received two multiple intestinal perforations within an hour, had lost the first, and saved the second with a lightning-fast resection, anastomosis, and a half-dozen pints of whole blood. . . . For the most part, he was home again—functioning with the same precision, receiving the same help from the willing hands that appeared and vanished and appeared again in the hard white circle of his work lights.

When the agony of blood and sweat had slackened, when the last bleeder had been tied off and the last incision closed, when the last wounded GI had dropped into a nirvana of drugged repose, the score sheets had shown the same predictable results. Thanks to the help they had received aboard, scores of men had been snatched back from death. Others had died under the surgeons' knives. Many more, ranging from walking wounded to litter cases not classified as urgent, would recover with a minimum of pain, to rejoin their units on another field.

Now and again, he was reminded that he was functioning on the edge of a great battle. Stealing a moment on the boat deck in the second dawn, when bad weather had slowed the barges, he had watched a savage dogfight between enemy aircraft and carrier-based fighters, sent to screen a new wave of bombers sweeping over Sicily.

He recalled the vivid curses of Eric Badger, when other delays ashore had cut his case load to a trickle, and the deck teams were forced to mark time. Colonel Stokes, operating steadily on routine cases, had emerged at times from the fog to murmur words of commendation. More than once, he had looked up into Colonel Meighan's eyes, to read the same message there as another case left his table. . . .

From the first, the 241st had functioned according to plan. Since the flow of wounded had been constant—save for an occasional roadblock—it had functioned at its peak. Once aboard, the injured were logged in swiftly, including a recheck of their wound tags. Less serious cases were led to a rest area on the boat deck, where broad awnings sheltered them from the sun. Working under floodlights when darkness fell, nurses and medics checked each man for tetanus injections, changed each dressing as required, and dusted fresh sulfa powder into wounds.

Patients in shock were brought to a special ward, where both plasma and frozen blood could be administered, and body heat preserved with blankets and electric cradles. Those who could withstand immediate surgery were taken to the operating theaters, where still other teams prepared them for the table. Auxiliary operating rooms were opened before this case load could fill the corridors—and one of the stand-by surgical teams was called from deck duty to join the fight for life below.

At no time in two long days did the lines get out of hand. It was a tribute both to the hospital ship designers and to the complement's training at sea.

After his years on emergency at Lakewood, and the brutal revelations of Spain, there was little left to surprise Bruce in that steady flow. A few cases stood out—among them, a sailor thrown twenty feet in the air when a direct hit had blown up the barge he was steering. The patient had shown inescapable signs of internal damage, though there was not a mark on his body. Opening the abdomen with a long incision, Bruce had uncovered a ruptured intestine—burst as effectively by the concussion as though a shell fragment had cut into the man's body.

Aided by Alice Stacey (whose skilled fingers helped often with difficult sutures) he had closed each break with catgut and a single line of silk. The peritoneal cavity had been cleansed with saline solution; crystalline sulfa powder had been poured in, before a closure without drainage ended the procedure in record time. . . . With a minimum of post-operative shock, the instant diagnosis had made chances of recovery better than even—though an adequate supply of penicillin, the new miracle drug celebrated in each issue of the *Military Surgeon*, had not been available to clinch the victory.

Even more harrowing was the teen-age soldier whose jaw

had been sheared away—as cleanly as though by a scalpel. The patient had come to the table in a semicoma, already half-drowned by his own body fluids, with blood and saliva bubbling in what had been the mouth. Depressing the boy's head so the deadly flow could be reversed, Bruce had inserted a tracheal tube—to insure an open airway to the straining lungs—before he proceeded with his salvage. . . . Inured though he was to the senseless waste of war, he could not help noticing that this had been the handsomest face to come under the lights.

At the moment, only routine repairs to severed vessels could be attempted: the mouth would be left to the deft repairmen in a general hospital. Curiously enough, the injury was less drastic than it seemed. Because of the extra-rich circulation in this area, tissue would still be viable when the plastic surgeon took over. The boy's good looks were gone forever; tailor-made dentures and jaw would be workable substitutes for the originals left in Sicily.

As always in war surgery, limbs suffered most. When the final returns were in, the deck force reported that it had listed almost four hundred simple and compound fractures. There was a racking sameness to the techniques employed on the table—the slash of the knife that removed hopelessly-damaged tissue, the rasp of the saw that excised shattered bone, the alignment of still-operable fractures before the wound was packed in vaseline gauze, the application of casts in what was now known as the closed-plaster treatment. . . .

There were other, even more terrible memories of those days below decks, but Bruce could close most of them from his mind. When it was over, a full shipload of patients were convalescing in his wards. On deck and in companionways, in every corner where his staff could swing a hammock, less critical cases were awaiting transfer. Most of his patients would recover, thanks to the combined efforts of the 241st—and he knew that his training had been largely responsible for that result.

It was a good thought to take to his cabin, a precious inventory to sort while he settled in his bunk. Three full days after he had heard that first man-made thunder on the horizon, he could still wonder if he had really been on the fringe of war. There was no doubt that he had done his part to rescue over a thousand wounded warriors.

The certainty was established in his mind, not his heart. Had his heart remained open to the realities of that war, it would have long since broken.

Ten hours later, Bruce opened his eyes to the sunlight pouring through his portholes. Outside, the air was still. On shipboard, the public address outlets had just spread the sound of bells, announcing the start of the noon watch. Relaxing an instant longer in a delicious sense of non-being, he felt a hand on his shoulder and looked up into Eric Badger's wide-awake eyes.

"I wouldn't do this to my worst enemy, Bruce—but we've got problems."

The surgeon sat up, with a vast yawn. Expecting to feel the vibration of the ship's diesels, he realized the *Helen S Peters* was motionless.

"We can't handle another patient, unless you put him in the crow's nest."

"This seems to be a shorebound problem."

"Why aren't we headed for Algiers?"

"Three other ships beat us back. We can't unload until they've been cleared."

"Where are we now?"

"At a mooring offshore. Directly opposite that blown-up pier. Stokes wants you to come topside to admire the view."

"Can't *you* tell me what's up?"

"No, Bruce. On the rare occasions when our CO breathes out fire, I don't ask questions."

After days of blood-soaked operating suits, it was a pleasant change to don Army suntans. With Badger in tow, the surgeon found Stokes on the top deck, glaring down at the sea. Mei-ghan's patrol boat was racing toward land, in a patina of spray that boasted its own small rainbow.

"Take a hard look at that beach," he said. "By now, we've put a dozen divisions ashore. Why must they ask *me* for help?"

Bruce moved to the rail. The ship was moored to buoys less than two thousand yards from shore, where the bustle of war's aftermath continued. Most of the activity centered on such tasks as road repair and the collection of debris. Across the clear water-lane between the *Helen S Peters* and the shat-tered pier, a trio of DUKWs were wallowing in Meighan's wake, to converge on an LCI that had just been secured to the dock, at a point where a series of improvised catwalks con-nected the fragments with the land.

"That rusty tramp arrived from Licata at sunup," said Stokes. "For the past seven hours, we've been converting it into another hospital unit—donating whatever surplus stores we have below."

"*We*, sir?"

"Meighan chipped in too, of course. Until further notice, it will serve as a focal point for casualties."

"Who's in charge, Colonel?"

"You are—with assistance from Phil and Eric. With luck, I'll pick up your case load before the week's over."

"Should we be honored, sir?"

"If you ask me," said Stokes, "it's a bare-faced raid. You'd best go in now, and make sure your equipment's assembled."

"Won't you join us?"

"I haven't the time, Bruce. What's more, I wouldn't trust my temper."

A second patrol boat waited at the boarding ladders; an ensign stood on the coaming to hand the two doctors aboard. At the rail above them, the commander of the 241st shouted a last sulfuric oath to send Bruce and Eric on their way. When they reached the gutted pier, the LCI had been completely secured; its ramps had been lowered to admit a file of technicians, each bearing his quota of supplies. Thanks to that open-end view, Bruce realized the vessel had already been equipped for its mission.

Descending the ladder amidships, he saw that extra bunks had been added to those already lining the hull. Still others were set up on deck, where awnings marked with white crosses shielded the cavernous interior from the sun. Two operating tables, and the equipment surrounding them, were illuminated by bunched floodlights, giving the hold of this oddly-proportioned craft the look of a surrealist torture chamber.

A scattering of patients were already resting in their bunks. At one of the tables, a pharmacist's mate was changing a dressing on the forearm of a Navy chief, who observed the procedure through a cloud of cigar smoke and seemed only mildly concerned with the pain.

"Who's in command here, sailor?" Badger asked.

"Colonel Meighan, sir. You'll find him on the afterdeck."

"Is this an Army show, or the Navy's?"

"When I take this patient ashore, Captain, it's all yours."

Phil Owen emerged from the forward locker with a clipboard in his hand. At his nod, the newcomers turned toward the ladder that led to the constricted afterdeck—where the staff colonel's voice was booming orders.

"The takeover's complete," he said. "Our new boss is waiting to describe it in detail."

"Can you explain how this happened, Phil?"

"Nothing could be simpler. The complement gave a sellout performance in its first run. In fact, it was so outstanding Meighan's drafted three of its performers for his road company. Don't look so stricken, Eric—it's only TD. Stokes will see to that."

"Would you say we're operable?" Bruce asked.

"Present equipment's adequate. More's on the way from Meighan's division—including extra personnel. We'll be kept busy, but we won't be worked to death."

"How does it feel, being kidnapped by the Seventh Army?"

"I expect to survive, if there's no rough weather. I'd hate to be aboard an LCI in a storm, with every patient puking out his guts."

"It may not come to that," said Bruce. "Let's leave this scene from Dante, and learn the worst."

After he had adjusted to operating in a steel hull below the water line, Bruce admitted that his new assignment was not really unpleasant. Sunny days were followed by windless nights during the next week. The specialists he had brought ashore, augmented by an experienced surgical team from Meighan's own outfit, were more than capable of handling each case as it came aboard.

Casualties continued to build for the first days of his temporary duty. There were times when the lines, winding down from hastily repaired roads, threatened to overflow the rusty flanks of the landing ship. After a second LCI had arrived to accommodate the walking wounded, the surgeons found it was possible to spell each other in four-hour watches.

Even here, within touching distance of land, Bruce felt detached from the war, a patient gnome who was content to sling his hammock under the stars and drop into a dreamless pit when his day ended. On the fourth morning, when freshly-arrived wounded reported that both the Germans and their foot-dragging allies had been blasted from the perimeter, he felt no impulse to cheer. On the fifth, when the hulls of the two LCIs were shaken by bomb blasts, and he realized the Stukas were making a final run to cover the retreat of the panzer unit in the mountains, he had been busy with a difficult fracture. There had been no time to wonder if those white crosses on the awnings were a guaranteed protection. When the suicide run had been shot down, or had retreated to Italy, he listened to eyewitness accounts with a flash of resentment (like a passerby who has missed a street brawl), and an inward delight that he, at least, had not stopped one of those wildly delivered blows.

On the sixth day, Meighan appeared in person, to square rumor with fact. Sicily, while not yet conquered, was yielding to Allied thrusts. Gela Gulf had been one of the more hotly contested sectors. The British had had an easier time in Syracuse—and the whole coast road was now open to troop movements.

"I can't thank you enough for your contribution," said the staff colonel. "If I could, I'd steal you permanently—but that's hardly fair to Jerry Stokes."

"Is our temporary duty ending, sir?"

"It ends officially tomorrow—when Jerry reclaims you."

"We'll have only half a load."

"I've already radioed that fact to Theater Headquarters. The ship will proceed to Syracuse to fill your berths, then head for Africa."

"Does that mean I won't set foot in Sicily?"

"A truck and jeep convoy is moving supplies tomorrow, by the coast road. Regulations say a medical officer must accompany them. With your CO's permission, I can extend your TD another day, and give you that assignment. Once you're in Syracuse, you'll be ordered back to your complement."

"May I take Badger with me?"

"Sorry—but the rule says one doctor to a convoy. This is a time I'll expect you to pull rank."

When the hoot of a whistle roused Bruce at sunrise, the *Helen S Peters* was approaching a new mooring, less than a quarter-mile from the pier. There was still time for a pickup breakfast in the galley before he boarded the first barge, to supervise the transfer of the wounded.

Stokes was waiting at the rail—looking rested and far less grumpy.

"It seems you've all been God's gift to the Seventh Army," he said. "Your stock with Meighan couldn't be higher."

"I'm glad we were useful."

"First, he radioes a commendation for your service record. Now I hear you've scrounged a tour of Sicily."

"With your permission, sir."

"You've earned a day off, God knows. Just be sure you come aboard at Syracuse."

"How did the crossing go?"

"We had a millpond voyage. The Tenth General Hospital passed three-fourths of our patients directly to their convalescent area. They didn't even need an overhaul."

"*That's* good news."

"Go down to Cabin C. You'll find even better news is waiting."

"Is the news named Janet Josselyn?"

Stokes observed his deputy under raised eyebrows. "You've overshot your target, Major. Miss Josselyn is touring the camp circuit—but she'd hardly be permitted to visit Sicily. Our passenger is a journalist named Shane McLendon. She claims you're friends of long standing."

Shane was seated at a table in the cabin on the luxury deck, with a typewriter before her and the recorder at her side. The tips of the playback apparatus were on her ears, and she was composing with her usual concentration. It was the first time Bruce had seen her in the uniform of a war correspondent, with the identifying green tabs at her shoulders. Had they parted an hour earlier, her smile could not have been more casual.

"Come in, Major," she said. "This is my final last line."

"Couldn't we manage a more personal greeting?"

"We might, if you're sure we're alone."

"At this moment, the deck's deserted."

Shane lifted her lips for his kiss. The contact was unhurried—and impersonal. He could see her mind was elsewhere.

"Welcome aboard, Bruce."

"*I'm* the one to say that."

"It doesn't matter, if we both mean it. You're looking

well, for a man who's survived his first invasion beach."

"How did you manage this ferry ride?"

"Easily enough, once I'd convinced the Theater PRO that war from the distaff side would be good home-front publicity."

"Have you been in Algiers long?"

"Long enough to exhaust the headquarters beat. The *Helen S Peters* is a new approach. Covering a hospital ship at sea will be my first scoop. When I've interviewed your patients, I'll have another."

"If you're properly grateful," said Bruce, "I might supply a third."

"Don't try to smuggle me into a combat zone. I've sworn to keep clear, this time round. Your Task Force Command has old-fashioned ideas about women in foxholes."

"Assuming my CO's in a good frame of mind, would you like to go ashore—with a jeep convoy to Syracuse?"

"Would you be part of that convoy?"

"Of course. Why else would I ask you?"

"What would you expect in return?"

"Bring me up-to-date on what I've missed back home."

"When does this convoy leave?"

"At eleven hundred. You'll have time to interview my patients. And I needn't warn you we must travel light."

"My typewriter's lap-size," said Shane. "If your offer includes a bed, I'll tuck in a toothbrush."

"I'm billeted at the Pensionare Margherita. We'll radio ahead, and reserve a room for my assistant. They'll put your recorder ashore at Syracuse with your luggage."

"I'd planned to leave it—as a bread-and-butter present for the colonel. You'll find I don't take up too much room."

Studying the war correspondent's slender figure, Bruce shrugged off second thoughts. His invitation had been spontaneous. A bit tardily, he realized it might have been unwise.

"We'll manage to fit you in," he said. "Before I speak to the colonel, do I have your word you won't go kiting off to the north?"

"I gave my word in Algiers. Must I give it a second time?"

"I'm afraid so—for my peace of mind. Otherwise, the deal is off."

"I'll stay with the convoy, Bruce—and trust you to protect me." Shane got up briskly, as the whine of a winch was heard amidships. "They're beginning to hoist your wounded. Thanks to mutual friends, it seems I'll have a busy day."

Circling the outskirts of Gela—where a whole dwelling was the exception that proved the rule—the convoy had picked a cautious path through the rubble, to gain the dust-white ribbon of the coastal road. The going had been rugged for the first hour, though repair crews had filled each bomb crater on the right of way. Once they were outside the beachhead perimeter, it was possible to make good time. At midafternoon, the sergeant driving the lead jeep—a six-foot cowboy from Wyoming—swung into a seaward-facing meadow flanked by wheat fields, and motioned to the convoy to follow.

"This is halfway, Major," he called back to the personnel carrier where Bruce was riding. "There isn't a better place to stop for chow."

Shane had already stepped to the greensward with a cry of delight. The meadow commanded a panorama of coast and sea and steeply-terraced farms. To the right, a brook changed to a torrent at a cliff's edge. To the left was yet another olive orchard, inhabited by foraging goats. Beyond it, a village surrounded a snug harbor: fish nets spread on frames, and the faded, pastel-tinted walls seemed older than time in the blazing sun.

During the drive, the journalist had been busy snapping action shots of the convoy. Now, she lifted her Leica for a close-up of the boy from Wyoming, before she moved on to the corporals assigned to the portable oven. Bruce had noted

her easy intimacy with the caravan personnel—and the way
she had shifted transport at each halt. . . . This, he realized,
had been an essential move, permitting her to cover their
journey from several angles. Assuming his own turn was due,
he collected a mess kit at the oven and took it to the cliff's
edge, to settle on the roots of a gnarled cedar that seemed to
cling there in defiance of gravity.

Chow, he discovered, was more substantial than inspiring
—Spam and bacon bun, and a mug of the scalding, corrosive
coffee that is brewed only on Army grills afield. He was still
eyeing it doubtfully when Shane crossed the meadow to join
him, closing her camera case en route.

"I know you're being exclusive for a good reason," she
said. "We can probably risk lunch together—if we're in full
view of the convoy."

"Sergeant Drury's a romantic. I'm sure he thinks we're on
a one-night honeymoon."

"Shall I tell him you're spoken for by a picture star?"

"Who told you I was spoken for by anyone?"

"A good newspaperman never reveals his sources."

"Was Hal Reardon your informant?"

"I won't deny I've seen Hal in Algiers. He gets into the
city quite often—when he isn't making practice jumps in the
bled."

"Spare me Hal's doings, please. I'm sure they're pictur-
esque."

"Three hours ago, you asked me to bring you up to date,"
said Shane. "We can't back away from the past forever."

"I didn't mean to sound bitter. Just how often have you
seen him?"

"Three times, to be exact. We discussed your situation at
some length, as well as our own."

"Do you have a situation, where Hal Reardon's concerned?"

"Back at Gulfview, I told you I had hopes. He needed a
dancing partner, and I was glad of an escort. Algiers is quite a

town, now the Army's taken over. Be sure to make the rounds with Janet, when you have *your* reunion."

"This is getting more like Old Home Week by the minute."

"Janet's still in North Africa with *Pierrette*. Sooner or later, you'll make contact."

"I'm looking forward to seeing her."

"So are a million other homesick GIs. Not all of them have your entree."

"Are you trying to back me into a corner?"

"Not at all. As an interested spectator, I'm checking your wedding plans, if any."

"I've been neither accepted nor rejected. The question's in the deferred file. Now may we drop the subject?"

"Why so abruptly? I'm willing to discuss my plans for Hal."

"Do, then—by all means."

"Only if you'll stop sulking."

"Sulks are over—word of honor."

"First and most important—it's no secret I'm prepared to bet on your classmate as the man of tomorrow."

"So would I, if I were a betting man."

"He'll be part of the first Italian airdrop, before the summer's over. If he survives the war—and he has the knack for survival—he's bound to take over Lucius Josselyn's place in the Senate. Even if the senator's daughter makes your present love-affair official—"

"We're discussing Hal, not Janet."

Shane waved the interruption aside. "I won't predict Hal Reardon's headed for the White House. That, I'll admit, is wishful thinking. Assuming he comes out of Italy a hero— and uses the James Lowell Society properly—he could have a shot at the office. In the first postwar election, or the second."

"*Now* who's being an opportunist?"

"Politics is the science of opportunity."

"Legitimate use of issues is one matter. Shaping another man's ideas to suit your ends is another."

"Hal warned me you wouldn't like the way the Lowell Society is developing."

"I've objected from the day Mike Derwent showed me his first form letter. His *Bulletins* get worse with each number. How many have you seen?"

"I've seen them all. When I've had time, I've helped Mike write them."

"Don't tell me you *approve* his brand of double-talk."

"Double-talk has its values. In fact, it's essential to most careers."

"Surely Hal doesn't think the Russians are stalling—with half their heartland overrun, and the Nazis butchering them by the thousands?"

"A good many Americans believe they are," said Shane. "History may bear them out. Meanwhile, the views of the Lowell Society are on the record."

"If Hal shares those views, why doesn't he back them openly?"

"An officer in uniform must keep clear of politics."

"The *Bulletins* go to men in uniform."

"There's nothing illegal in that—so long as they support the war."

"I suppose Derwent got his mailing list through Hal."

"What if he did? Hal's the official heir of the Lowell credo. It was Jimmie's own idea to begin at barracks level."

"Derwent's pitch isn't even remotely related to world peace. Not as Sergeant Lowell saw it."

Shane put a soothing hand on Bruce's arm: it was a gesture that begged for tolerance in advance. The warmth in her eyes warned him to mute his anger. This, after all, was a friend—who had proved her friendship in the strongest terms.

"Mike Derwent's a smart operator, Bruce. At times, I'll grant you, he's too smart. You can hardly deny he gets results. At this stage, he's damned useful."

"To Hal—yes."

"What has Hal done so far that's against the country's interests?"

"Is it right to make Americans doubt their allies, before the fighting's over?"

"If you're referring to the last *Bulletin*, you have a point. Mike went too far with that one. For the most part, his criticisms have been reasonable—and they *have* helped build the Society. Do you know how many members it has today?"

"The last figure I heard was three million—which isn't too remarkable. A country as big as ours can spawn that many crackpots, without half trying."

"Today, the figure's nearer five than three," said Shane. "A good many of those five million are decent people who want to build a better world. Don't dismiss them in advance, just because they chose a different blueprint."

"Where does this leave us? You say Hal's a patriot, with sure-fire nostrums in his briefcase. I think he's playing both sides of the street until he's sure of his ground. Let's pick a safer topic—like ourselves."

"Are you sure we're the safest topic in the world?"

"I'm sure we've been good for each other. At least, until we start arguing about Hal."

"Or Janet?"

"Or Janet, if you insist. Let's get back to you and me, and see where it takes us. Are you enjoying your tour of Sicily half as much as I am?"

"I've enjoyed every moment," said Shane. "Thanks again for making it possible. By now, my debt must run into five figures. I only hope I can repay it."

"I wasn't aware of a debt."

"Wasn't it you who reminded me that I'm a woman—with a certain attraction for the roaming male?"

"If you refer to a night on S Street—"

"*And* a night in West Florida," said Shane. "When your scruples overcame your instincts. Even then, you were a tonic for my ego—at a time when I needed tonics badly."

"You'll need no tonic tomorrow, with Hal in Algiers."

"So we're back with Hal and Janet. From where I'm sitting, you seem recovered too. Let's congratulate each other on good health, and move on to Syracuse."

The Pensionare Margherita turned out to be a rambling, pink-walled inn on the heights above the bay—commandeered, for the most part, by British staff officers from the Eighth Army.

Bruce and Shane had arrived in the dusk, in time to join the group at dinner—a surprisingly well-served repast, considering the fact that Syracuse had barely emerged from a state of war. There had been toasts—in *Asti spumante*—to the success of the Allied arms. There had been fervent discussion of Allied war aims over other bottles of *Asti*—after the diners had moved from inn to garden. Midnight had struck from the hallway before the two Americans had gone to their rooms— and Bruce had admitted his senses were balanced between meaningful recall and the nepenthe of true intoxication, when they ascended the narrow stair.

Shane (he remembered, not too resentfully) had seemed sober enough when they said good night at her door. They had agreed to rise in time to see each other off: his ship would come in with the dawn, and Shane had been promised an early plane-ride to Algiers.

In his own room, in the cloying midsummer heat, he had stripped to his shorts and composed himself on the *letto matrimoniale* that seemed an odd note of luxury in the tall, bare chamber. His last coherent memory had been a sound of rustling sheets. Shane, no less than he, was finding slumber an elusive goal in the adjoining bedroom, whose partition seemed more a ghostly illusion than a wall.

Eventually, he had dropped into an uneasy doze. Now, wakening in deep darkness, he knew he had been roused by the same thunder he had heard at Gela.

The luminous hands of his wrist watch told him he had

slept less than an hour—and he had identified the thunder
before he could sit up in the huge bed. At dinner, the officers
had admitted that the Luftwaffe, though it had withdrawn to
safer fields on the mainland, had not been driven from the
sky. It was apparent now that enemy bombers had returned to
strike at the airstrip north of Syracuse.

At the far end of his room, open glass doors gave to a
terrace masked in bougainvillea. Beyond, above the umbrella
pines in the garden, he could glimpse the harbor, like a dim
plain beneath the stars. Farther still, he saw orange flares
against the sky, as an antiaircraft battery went into action.
The salvo was followed by the *crump* of falling bombs.

So far, the threat seemed remote. That afternoon, leaving
Ragusa to approach the city from the west, he had noted that
the airstrip now under attack was at least five miles from the
inn. Standing at the terrace rail, he concluded that the enemy
had swept in from the north, to circle its target. A babble of
voices from the garden told him the British were still at their
wine: judging by their comments, he gathered that the raid
had inflicted no great damage, thanks to the alertness of the
defenders. He was still leaning far out from the rail—and
cursing a patchy cloud cover that obscured his view—when
Shane appeared on the terrace.

She was draped toga-fashion in a sheet. He saw that she
was still only half-awake, and realized she had joined him for
just one reason—the primitive need all humans share to
draw closer when a sound that spells danger in any tongue
intrudes on their slumber.

"Are they coming closer, Bruce?"

"I think so. It's hard to be sure."

A salvo from the ground, near enough to torture the ear-
drums, was climaxed by the detonation of a gas tank on the
heights above the inn. Shane moved quickly to his side, as
the flare outlined each leaf in the canopy of vines above them.
It seemed only natural to put an arm about her shoulders, to
ignore the fact that she had used a sheet for a nightgown.

"They *are* heading this way," she said. "It must be their escape route."

"They probably won't bomb civilians—when they've already lost Sicily."

"Who knows what a bomber pilot will do, when he's been driven off his target?"

"I gather this isn't your first air raid."

"We had our share in London. Somehow, this one is different. Are you afraid?"

"Of course I'm afraid. Aren't you?"

"I'd be shaking in my shoes, if I'd stopped to dress."

Neither of them stirred while a second gas tank, less than a mile away, painted a crimson arc against the night. Already, he could see that Shane was right. Now they had found the airstrip well-defended, the raiders were pinpointing other targets as they fled. Flying low to make sure of their aim, they were roaring toward the harbor as their final objective. Even from this limited vantage point, Bruce knew it would be a suicide run, now that scores of naval guns were pointed skyward.

"*Here it comes,*" said Shane. "If you know any prayers, say them."

"It might be wiser to go inside."

"If my number's up, I'd like to hear the news outdoors."

Another bomb, falling in a garden a block away, cascaded a green wave of branches above the wall. Shane moved into his arms with the blast—and, once again, their mouths seemed to meet by instinct. The kiss had the same wild hunger they had shared at Gulfview—a hunger it was too late to hide.

"There are worse ways to die," she whispered against his lips.

"No one's dying tonight. They've headed for the docks."

His prediction, it seemed, was accurate: the blasting of the garden had been the nearest threat to the inn—and the suicide wing of the Luftwaffe had already swept down on the bay, into an enfilade of guns. A final explosion, when a crip-

pled bomber crashed at the water's edge, did no more than
rock the building gently, though it pinned Shane even closer
in his embrace.

"I've lost my sheet, Bruce. Do you mind?"

They did not speak again, while he carried her from the
terrace to her room.

The morning after, when he had settled their bill with the
padrona, revealed the scars of last night's raid. His ship was
moored at the quay below the Ospedale Maggiore. For a moment, they stood at the garden's edge, then linked hands to
move toward the stairs that led to the driveway of the inn—
and the jeep that would deliver Shane to her airfield before it
dropped him at the harbor.

"The driver will wait," he said—and halted in the shade of
the last umbrella pine.

"It's time to go, Bruce."

"We've another minute. Perhaps two."

"All our good-byes seem to be rushed," said Shane. "I wonder why."

"Perhaps we can meet in Algiers. I'll dock there on Friday."

"I'm stopping just long enough to clear my copy. Then I go
on to London."

"I wish we could fly back together."

"This way is better," said Shane. "Don't forget I'm the
other woman now."

"There's no need to say that."

"Even when it's true?"

"It wasn't true last midnight."

"Last midnight belonged to Sicily. This morning, we're
returning to the mainland."

"Can you tell me how it happened?"

"We were alone—and afraid. A bomb blasted us together."

"Most bombs blast people apart."

"This one performed a special function. It reminded us we
were still alive."

"It's good to know the service was mutual."

"Of course it was mutual," said Shane. "You've been lonesome as hell—since you said good-bye to *Pierrette* in California. So have I. There've been times—like last midnight—when you weren't even sure she existed. Why shouldn't you welcome a stand-in, when the Stukas came calling?"

"It's hardly an excuse for using *you* to shut out death."

"I used you too, Bruce. While we were together, we were less afraid. And a lot less lonely. Isn't it better to leave things there?"

"Much better, if you'll let me off so easily."

"Put things another way," said Shane. "Last night, a debt was canceled—and the ledger's clean. *Now* will you take me to the airport?"

Their hands were still linked when they went down the stairs to the driveway—and the iron band that had choked off thought had ceased to constrict his brain. The voice of conscience had not been stilled. He would hear it again when he had left her at the airstrip—but this moment of parting, which he had dreaded, was magically tranquil. As always, Shane McLendon had put the future into gear with the fewest words.

It was a gift beyond price—but he had no way to thank her while he handed her into the jeep, stepped in beside her, and told the driver to hurry.

In Algiers, Bruce's ship discharged its second full load of wounded at the Tenth General before crossing the harbor to take on supplies at the quartermasters' docks. Here, he found a message from Janet. She had given performances in camps outside the city. She would give another tonight, at the staging area near the harbor—and she hoped he would join her.

The certainty that he was still living a dream—a hectic double vision that had its own perils—had persisted during the discharge of his patients; it had not lessened while he stood on the quay in the steaming afternoon to log in his stores. Algiers was part of it, a city of glaring whites and mud-dark browns, crowned by its famous Casbah—the High Place that had once been a fortress and was now the core of the Moslem quarter. . . . Four hours later, wearing his best trop-ical worsteds, he arrived at the Grand Hotel to escort the star of *Pierrette* to her performance.

Janet's show was an echo of her triumph at Annapolis, down to the wolf whistles of ten thousand happy young war-riors. The audience had loved the picture preceding her act, a musical done in Brodski's best style. It had loved Janet even more when she had come onstage with other members of her troupe to repeat the hit numbers.

Watching from the runway that led to the impromptu stage, Bruce had loved her most of all. He had applauded busily with the others—but the dormant critic far back in his brain was even busier, whispering that tonight was the sum total of Janet Josselyn's talent, that the letter he had received today from her director was a true prophecy for the fu-ture. . . .

At the show's end, he had said nothing of Brodski. He had been careful to leave his doubts unmentioned while they took a taxi—a diminutive Renault, specially designed for the alleys of the native quarter—to dine at the Café Rif.

The famous restaurant, at the very summit of the Casbah, was crowded to overflowing. He had already bribed the maître d'hôtel to hold a table on the terrace; he had insisted that Janet sample the couscous and the aromatic lamb ragout, which were specialities of the *maison*. A second bottle of Pommerey dissolved the worst of his nerves. But it was only with the arrival of the thick Arabian coffee, and a superb brandy, that he dared ask the first significant question of the evening.

"Have you seen Hal since you've been here?"

"He called me at the hotel, last evening. That's all he had time for. His general's a very busy man these days."

"You're still on good terms, then?"

"Hal and I will always be on good terms."

"What did he say about me?"

Janet twirled her brandy inhaler, with her eyes on the white-roofed city below them. She had never been lovelier than tonight—and, from all outward signs, never more confident of her goal. Recalling the part he had played in creating that confidence, Bruce wondered why he did not feel more guilty—and why he found it easy to leave Shane McLendon, and a certain Sicilian interlude, unmentioned.

"Hal knows I intend to marry you," she said. "He knows you've promised never to interfere with my acting—as he would have done."

"How did he take the news?"

"Quite as gallantly as you'd expect."

"Did he tell you I was luckier than I deserved?"

Janet smiled down again at her glass. "No rejected suitor could omit that observation."

"I'm glad he's adjusted to losing you. In his place, I wouldn't have been so tolerant."

"After all, he'll have Shane to console him."

"You knew about Shane?"

"It's hardly a secret. He saw her often—when they were in Washington. Shane's done a great deal to advance his career. Apparently, she expects to do even more in future."

"If she does, will you mind?"

"Why should I—now? Do you?"

"Of course not—if they were made for each other."

Janet studied him for a moment, before her smile banished the last of his doubts: the exchange had brushed far too close to truth for comfort.

"Do I still hear a note of disapproval, Bruce? Actually, it's Shane's privilege to help."

"Frankly, I wish she'd picked another politician. The fact she's behind Hal—and his ideas—is something I still can't grasp."

"Nothing could be simpler," said Janet. "She's in love with him."

"Is love a word that explains everything?"

"It generally does," said Janet. "Even when it's applied to a hardheaded lady journalist. *You* aren't in love with her, I hope?"

"I'm in love with you. And I *am* far luckier than I deserve."

"Hal tells me she has great plans," said Janet. "With her column behind him, he fully expects to be President someday. I'd have settled for a Senate seat, if we'd stayed together."

"What will you expect from me?"

"A flourishing practice in Los Angeles, and escort service to all my premieres. We'll have a good life together, Bruce. I promise you that."

Brodski's note, folded in his pocket, burned with a flame all its own—but he ignored its presence. Clearly, this was not the moment to suggest that Janet's tenure in Hollywood might soon be ending. Or to ask if she would be content to share the life of a surgical research specialist in Baltimore.

"Thanks for that look in your crystal ball," he said. "I'll work hard to see it comes true."

"Why shouldn't it? You heard the applause tonight."

"No one applauded louder than I. Your director should have been in the audience."

"Leo's far too busy with my new script to come to Africa. He wants me back next month, to start shooting."

"How is the rewrite going?"

"Well enough, he tells me." Janet made a quick gesture of dismissal. "Don't make me talk pictures, Bruce. I've done nothing else for months. Let's talk about you."

"I'm afraid I'm a rather dull subject."

"Not to me. Are you going to take part in the Italian invasion? Or is that top secret?"

"The cruise of the *Helen S Peters* is an open book. If the Army moves to the mainland, we'll be six miles offshore in the next landing—*and* the next."

"Can't you tell me more?"

"I'm afraid one invasion beach is like another—if it's viewed through a porthole. Sure you won't have more brandy?"

"Only if you can't exist without it."

"If you like, we can have our next drink at the Cabaret de l'Enfer. It's the *dernier cri* in Algiers."

"Will you think I'm completely shameless if I ask you to take me to my hotel? We'll have our next drink there."

Next morning, on one of the new military airstrips south of the city, he watched another DC-3 dip its wings at the control tower before setting a course for Oran. The plane was bearing Janet Josselyn and her troupe to a final performance of *Pierrette*, before her return to the States. Their farewell kisses —in the doubtful shelter of a thorn tree where his car was parked—had had a familiar fervency, a faintly desperate promise of a tomorrow when all things would be easy for them both.

Moving slowly toward the car, he stared up again at the empty sky—and cursed his fluency, even as he rejoiced in its apparent success. Memory assured him that his deportment had been flawless in the long night hours—at the Café Rif, and later, in the bedroom of the Berber Suite at the Grand Hotel. . . . The rapture he had shared with Janet had been genuine. Nothing of consequence had been left unsaid: no promise had been made that he was unwilling to fulfill, if Janet should ask later for its redemption. There would be time to spare for another debate with his conscience.

Overhead, a wedge of Spitfires roared back to base after a dawn patrol. The sound reminded him that he had duties to perform aboard a floating hospital, decisions that could be postponed no longer—but he was still unprepared to face his brother officers aboard. Already, he could anticipate the teasing of Eric Badger, Alice Stacey's sidelong looks—and Phil Owen's refusal to believe that he had dined last night with a picture star. He was still less prepared to excuse a nightlong absence to Colonel Stokes. . . .

Under the wheel of the jeep, he delayed turning the ignition key. Instead, he opened his wallet to extract the note he had been so careful to ignore during his evening with Janet.

Brodski's prose, like his conversation, was on the aphoristic side:

> When you read this, you will almost surely have seen an overseas screening of *Pierrette.* I know you will applaud its merits, including my bravura touches and the ability of its star to mimic her betters—in a fashion audiences will find entrancing.
>
> Unfortunately, mimicry can be exploited just so far by the camera.
>
> To establish my point—and to give Janet herself a chance to grasp it—I am, as it were, "producing" her second starring vehicle. Here, as in the Army, we have our high brass whose blockhead orders must be obeyed. At this moment, our Supreme Command is clamoring for a new comedy-with-music to match her first—so I must belabor them with the obvious. The first start, as you may have heard, has been abandoned. I am about to begin from another angle, knowing my attempt is doomed.
>
> Janet Josselyn, alas, is a super-amateur at best—a *performer,* not an actress. When she makes that discovery, I am confident that pride will force her to cancel her contract. When they see our new rushes, I am equally confident that our studio head will be more than willing to let her go.
>
> Thereafter, Janet will be badly in need of consolation. I give you this advance warning, in the hope you can supply it. If my psychic antennae are in order, this charming but basically shallow girl has already offered you what devotion she possesses. With proper training, she may make you a good wife.
>
> When the crisis is upon her, and she must search elsewhere for fulfillment, will you do what you can to make that search rewarding?

Bruce looked up as a shadow fell across the paper. Brooding over Janet's impasse—and his own—would serve no valid purpose, now that Brodski had confirmed his own judgment. . . . He could almost be grateful his train of thought had been shattered, even though the interloper was Colonel Harold Reardon.

In Los Angeles, preening at a hotel mirror, Congressman Reardon had seemed a hero from a nobler age in his Brooks Brothers pinks and tunic. Today, wearing the fatigues of an officer on field duty, complete with parachute belt and high-laced boots that gleamed like chestnuts, Colonel Reardon was part of the African landscape. Glancing down the tarmac, Bruce saw he had arrived in his general's own car. The smartly painted vehicle, flying the pennons of the 75th Airborne, had parked at a respectful distance.

"So far, we've missed connections," said Hal. "You might pretend you're glad to see me."

"What are you doing here?" Even as he barked the question, Bruce felt his skin prickle with the gooseflesh of memory. At Bolling Field, he had used those exact words to express his resentment of Hilary Manning: today, Jake Sanford's lawyer and General Leonard's aide had affinities he could not ignore. Hal's manner, for all its airy friendliness, had the same aura; Hal's eyes had narrowed to the same opaque slits at this hostile response. . . . Today, though they wore the same uniform, it was clear they were potential enemies.

"I've the right to visit the Boukhalf airstrip without a pass," said Hal. Now that the flash of anger had passed, his voice was as carefully measured as his smile. "Obviously, you're here to see Janet off. I intended to do likewise—"

"You're a bit late. She's been airborne for a quarter hour."

"As you see, I've been running errands for my general."

"Your timing's usually better."

"To be frank, I knew I'd missed Janet when I phoned the Grand Hotel. I came to Boukhalf regardless—on the chance I'd catch up with you. We should have met long ago."

"Didn't we settle everything in Los Angeles?"

Hal circled the jeep and lifted a gleaming boot to the

bumper. Viewed from this angle, he seemed even more appropriate to his background. The silver eagles at his collar were a reminder of his first promotion, made in the field before he had tasted combat; the deeply tanned face beneath the crash helmet could have belonged to a combat veteran older than Hannibal.

"Good friends are never talked out, Bruce."

"Do we have that status?"

"In Los Angeles, we agreed on an armistice—until we could find out where we stood. I, for one, don't intend to break it."

"I still wonder what you really want."

Hal pushed back his helmet, to reveal a wrinkled brow. "Will you drive me to the practice range? It's in the *bled*, less than five miles. My orderly can follow—and we can talk on the way."

"I'm due on the ship by noon."

"You can make it easily. This may be our last chance to agree on fundamentals. The 75th leaves for maneuvers in Libya tomorrow."

"Aren't you crossing to Sicily?"

"Our mission is classified," said Hal. "However, it's no secret we're troubleshooters. We're training to spearhead the mainland show."

"My job isn't that mysterious—or that important. I go back to Syracuse tomorrow, to pick up another load of wounded."

"So we must talk here, or not at all?"

"If General Leonard can spare ten minutes of your time."

"I won't need ten minutes, since you insist on cutting corners," said Hal. "As you probably know, Shane and I have decided we can advance each other's careers by teaming up. Can you say as much for Janet—and yourself?"

"I think so, Hal."

"Have you wondered what's to become of her, after her contract with Brodski ends?"

"Who told you she's parting company with Brodski?"

"I've always known that Janet would be through with pictures—once she'd finished *Pierrette*."

"I intend to make her happy, with a career or without one. After all, I happen to be in love with her."

"Try to think clearly, Bruce—for all our sakes. Forget romantic words like love and happiness. How long could you have lasted as the consort of a movie star—if Janet *had* made good on the Coast? How long would Janet endure Baltimore—pouring tea at your Faculty House, and listening to your triumphs in the lab?"

"Are you trying to say we won't make a success of marriage?"

"Janet never really intended to marry you," said Hal. "It wasn't part of her timetable, or of mine."

"You've no right to say that."

"I'm the man Janet's father chose as her husband—after she'd had her fling with a few knights in armor like yourself. I'm the man who will give her the life and the prestige she's been trained for. You'll never play ball in our league. Go back to a game you can handle."

"Do you expect me to follow that advice?"

"You'll be forced to follow it, before the year ends."

"Janet's broken your engagement, to marry me."

"Our engagement was never broken." Hal's voice was completely serene—the tone of the relaxed worldling, instructing a barbarian in words he could understand. "It was merely postponed—because of my obligations to the 75th Airborne. We can pick up the threads when we like."

"What about Shane? Or are you planning to be a bigamist?"

"Shane realizes I have certain obligations to the Josselyns. We can still be useful to one another."

"*She* expects marriage too."

"Perhaps she did, not too long ago. Once she realizes how deeply I'm committed, she'll accept the situation."

"And go on serving your career?"

"With all her considerable talents—because she thinks the service is worthwhile."

"You feel you can't lose, then—no matter how the game turns out?"

"I was always bound to win, Bruce."

"Not when the game is playing God."

"That, too, is a familiar accusation," said Hal. "Why not accept me as a mere mortal—with your best interests at heart?"

"Someday you're going to discover you can't wrap up people's lives—and expect them to stay inside the package."

"No one is being packaged," said Hal. "I'm only stating a few home truths you're too blind to face. I hope you'll accept them in time, before you're too badly hurt."

His foot dropped from the bumper just before Bruce drove his jeep across the airstrip at a roaring speed that missed the general's car by inches.

A half hour later, when he crossed the quartermasters' quay that served the Tenth Base Hospital in Algiers—and picked out the silhouette of his ship against the bustle of the harbor—he had no memory of his drive from Boukhalf. His only feeling was the relief of a man about to enter a sanctuary where familiar tasks awaited him, and the confusions of the world could be left on the threshold.

Salerno

The wounded man, Bruce hoped, would live. With time on his side they might even save his leg, despite the injury inflicted by the explosion.

With both thumbs deep in the sailor's groin to stop the flow from the severed artery, he had made no attempt to judge the damage aboard. He had looked up when Captain Swenson crossed the deck to announce he was beaching the ship to save it from sinking—and wondered why the skipper had been at such pains to make this report in person. . . . It was only when he faced Eric Badger across the operating table that he grasped the import of that detour, and the terse announcement.

Colonel Stokes had been on the forward deck, watching the raising of an awning to shelter walking wounded. Bruce himself had just come topside, to confer with the team waiting to receive new arrivals at the boarding ladders. What happened thereafter remained a jumble in his mind: a rush of wings as a crippled bomber swept across the ship's bow, an ear-shattering detonation as it crashed into an LST a hundred yards away.

The plane and the LST, he knew, had exploded together in a burst of flame and flying debris. Before the smoke could settle, he realized that the *Helen S Peters* had also taken punishment. Again, the actual events had been hidden from his view. He had heard only a second, far closer explosion, after he had spread-eagled on the deck to dodge a geyser of flying steel.

At first glance, the entire forward deck seemed buckled; the bow, mantled in steam as the automatic fire extinguishers gushed into the bulkheads, was a crater of twisted metal. The only visible casualty was a sailor, thrown into a scupper by the explosion, with blood pumping from a wounded thigh. Stokes and the three-man awning detail had simply vanished.

The emergency crew had sprung into action before Bruce could kneel beside the injured man. He had not looked up again until the stretcher-bearers answered his call. Thanks to the iron discipline aboard, he knew he must trust such control—if control was still possible—to others.

Captain Swenson's words, spoken across the litter, had reached his brain belatedly, just before a scalpel came into his hand. The explosion that had just crushed the bow had taken the life of Colonel Gerald Stokes. As the colonel's deputy, he was now in charge of the 241st Hospital Ship Complement.

Even with a tourniquet in place, the task of locating a badly lacerated blood vessel had been formidable. Eric was working hard to provide exposure, and Bruce was in the midst of a difficult suturing, when they felt the deck vibrate as the screws reversed. The gentle bump, after the bow had made contact with a shelving beach, had hardly been felt below. The realization that the deck had remained blessedly level had lifted a weight from each mind in the operating room.

Another half hour passed before the patient was out of danger. The surgeon remained at the table until both the vital femoral artery and its accompanying great vein had been secured. Only then did he step out of the cone of light, leaving the closure of the wound to other hands.

"Go to the bridge, Eric. Tell the captain we've saved Seaman Hebard, and ask the extent of damage forward. I'd also like a report on the situation ashore, since we now seem part of it."

"Did they get Jerry Stokes?"

"I'm afraid so."

"I was on D-Deck when I heard the bang. What caused it?"

"That's what you're going to find out—while I make sure *this* part of the ship's in one piece."

During the emergency the reports that had reached the table had been reassuring—but Bruce needed the evidence of his own eyes. He found that some three hundred patients—brought in during the initial assault on Salerno—were reasonably quiet in their berths, now that news of the beaching had been confirmed. In an adjoining operating theater, a compound fracture was proceeding to its conclusion. In another, a sailor with a shoulder wound was slipping into oblivion under the drip of a sodium pentothal needle inserted in his arm vein. Both procedures were tangible evidence that the training of months was its own reward. Standard operational procedure had prevailed below decks, even while the *Helen S Peters* steamed toward a grounding with a ruptured bow.

The setting of the fracture, he saw, was now virtually completed. In the sailor's case, two of his assistants had begun the needed surgery. In an alcove, an enlisted technician was seated beside Shane McLendon's recorder, noting the patient's babbling in shorthand, for later comparison with the recording itself. . . . Since the ship had left Gela, the routine had been followed often with wounded patients suffering from the reaction to trauma known as neurogenic shock. The value of such recordings had often been negative. Occasionally, they had given valuable insight to a man's mental state at the moment his injury occurred, and to the likelihood of postoperative complications in the brain and nervous system.

Badger was waiting in the A-Deck office that served as Colonel Stokes's command post. The man from Wisconsin had been thoroughly briefed. With a member of the salvage crew, he had gone down to the blasted forward bulkheads to assess the damage. The story he told confirmed Bruce's estimate.

An enemy plane, apparently a fugitive from the battle that continued north and east of this invasion beach, had appeared like an unwanted banshee, to make its last doomed run before its engines failed. Only blind chance had prevented a direct collision amidships. Some observers on the bridge felt this had been the pilot's original intention; as it was, the plane had barely cleared the radio antenna before striking the LST dead center.

The Landing Ship Tank had been ferrying ammunition to the beachhead. The two-way explosion had occurred on contact.

Opinions differed on the exact cause of the damage the *Helen S Peters* had taken on its bow. Captain Swenson was reasonably sure that a shell aboard the LST, flung skyward by the explosion, had struck his forward deck. The first officer insisted an enemy bomb, dislodged as the Stuka passed above them, had performed the same function. . . . The entire bridge agreed that the prompt grounding had been all that had saved the ship. Fortunately, the pumps had controlled the sea intake during the run to the beach. Here, skillful handling on Swenson's part had driven his shattered prow deep into a mudbank, steadying the vessed on an even keel— and permitting the rigging of jury anchors to maintain that position until a Navy survey team could come aboard.

"Will we float again?" Bruce asked.

"The skipper's taken worse gougings in the Pacific, and completed his mission. This time, he says we've been lucky."

"Not if we lost Jerry Stokes."

"There isn't a trace of those men forward. The boys in salvage think they were incinerated when they pitched into the crater."

"What about the LST?"

"It went down like a stone. Like the Stuka, it was a ball of fire when it sank. Thank God that problem's outside our concern."

"Are we in a position to receive wounded?"

"They can't reach us direct. We're on a marshy neck, with gumbo between us and the beach. But there's open water to starboard. Once we've shifted our hoists, barges can come alongside again."

"Just where did we ground, Eric?"

"Directly below Paestum, on the south end of the Gulf of Salerno."

"Is Phil Owen still ashore?"

"He just radioed that he won't be back before nightfall. Apparently he's had a rough day in the hills. Do you have special orders for his section?"

"Why should I?"

"You're in command, with Stokes gone."

"I may not be for long."

"This is no time for modesty," said Badger. "I saw your last efficiency report. Jerry Stokes was a fine CO—but you'll be even better."

The man from Wisconsin, with his matter-of-fact responses, had helped to put the situation in perspective: Bruce found his thoughts were clear enough when he sat down to prepare an evaluation for the Task Force Command.

One picture was fixed in his mind as he began writing, and no concentration on facts and figures could erase it. He had not been an eyewitness to the grotesque mischance that had snuffed out four lives—but he could recall his own part in the events all too clearly. That morning, when he had left the wards for his check at the boarding ladder, he had fully intended to oversee the rigging of that awning. Instead, he had continued with a more important chore—and the CO had gone to watch the work detail. Save for that change of roles, Jerry Stokes would be seated in this command post tonight. His deputy would have been a lost cinder in the Tyrrhenian Sea.

It was sunset when Bruce came on deck again. The Navy team had long since assessed the damage and established priorities for its repair. The officer in charge had assured the new complement commander that his hospital would be seaworthy again—in ample time to fulfill its present assignment, the ferrying of a full load of Salerno wounded to the hospital quay in Algiers.

A memorial service had been scheduled to honor the four men who had given their lives—the first casualties the Merchant Marine and Medical Corps personnel aboard had suffered in more than two months of mercy steaming. At the roped-off crater, Bruce paused to murmur a prayer for Jerry Stokes and the three sailors who had joined him in death that September morning. The words, he knew, would have seemed on the sentimental side to most of the case-hardened seamen aboard. He was glad the pause had gone unnoticed when he ascended the bridge to sweep the shore with his binoculars.

Like his first view of Gela, the landscape in his lenses had the same affinity with an encyclopedia plate come alive. Except for the marsh and mud flats between ship and beach, it was the Italy of legend—an indigo-blue gulf, sickle-shaped beaches, green farmlands sweeping north to a wall of mountains. Despite the bustle of shipping and the blinker signals, it was hard to believe a full-scale invasion called Avalanche had just rolled toward those mountains. Or that Allied troops were now hotly engaged there, with an enemy who had yielded the beaches to stand and fight again, on a new front between the Gulf and Naples.

Salerno, at the end of the arc, was only a white presence in the gloaming; the smaller town of Agropoli, at the opposite end of the bay, was lost to view. The war itself, a duel of guns in the north, seemed remote as summer thunder. . . . Hearing a launch bump the boarding ladders, Bruce lowered his binoculars. There was time to descend to the lower deck before Captain Philip Owen appeared at the check-in desk—looking too tired to stand after his liaison duty ashore.

"It's good to know you're safe, Phil."

"At this moment," said the medical chief, "I'm not quite sure if I'm alive or dead."

"You must have had quite a day."

"So, I hear, have you."

"Things could have been worse. If you like, you can make your report in the morning."

"I'd rather talk now. It may help me unwind. Is it true you're our new CO?"

"Theater Headquarters has confirmed the command. I still can't believe Jerry Stokes is gone."

"I find it easy to accept, after what I've seen."

"Are things going badly?"

"Don't be misled because the beach perimeter's quiet," said Owen. "It's another story in the mountains."

"Were you at the front?"

"I didn't go quite that far—but even the field hospitals are too close for comfort. Apparantly the Wehrmacht decided to let Avalanche roll awhile—then closed in with all they had."

Bruce studied the medical chief's drawn face in the dusk. Recalling his tendency to pose as a strategist, he had been prepared to discount his tidings. Tonight there was a note in Phil's voice that compelled belief.

"At least Italy's backing out of the war."

"I don't think the Nazis mind too much. From now on, they can handle the action their way." Phil reached for a cigarette with shaking hands. "Our friends from Jeff Davis took the worst beating. It started even before their drop."

"The 75th Airborne?"

"The famous trouble shooters—" Owen bent to the match Bruce offered. At that precise instant, the ship glowed with light from stern to shattered bow: had the new commander touched a switch, the effect could not have been more startling. . . . Understanding the medical officer's recoil, Bruce steadied him with a hand at his elbow, then led him to Stokes's former cabin. Phil settled in an armchair and continued to stare wildly at the brightly lighted deck outside.

"Are you sure we should light up, Bruce? When we're almost on the beach?"

"We're a hospital, afloat or ashore. Any risk is better than a blind hit in the dark."

"I hope you're right. I could use a drink, until I'm sure."

"You'll find brandy in Jerry's locker. What's your story on 75th Airborne? Is it fact or rumor?"

"This is straight dope," said Phil. "They were supposed to occupy a pass, and block it. The drop missed its target completely. What's worse, some of them were mauled by our own ack-ack offshore."

"There's always that kind of talk after an airdrop. The Army likes to blame the Navy for its mistakes."

"Whoever's to blame, there *was* a foul-up—and some pretty bloody results. I saw examples at the clearing stations."

"Why weren't they evacuated sooner?"

"They couldn't be reached until our infantry moved north and dug them out. The whole operation scatter-gunned among those mountains. The lucky ones got first aid from their own medics. Lots of others died before they made the clearing stations."

"Any estimate of the casualties?"

"We should get at least a hundred as our quota. They're coming to the beach by special convoy. Quite a few officers were involved, including a staff colonel. An ex-congressman named Reardon."

"*Hal* Reardon?"

"I talked with his orderly at the field hospital. Reardon wasn't hurt badly. A wounded foot, plus shock from exposure." The medical chief put down his glass. "What's wrong, Bruce? Have you seen a ghost?"

"I've known Hal Reardon all my life."

"I'd forgotten he was your congressman."

"And my college roommate."

"Don't you want to hear more?"

"Not if the case isn't serious. If you don't mind, we'll check him out later, when he comes aboard. You can finish your report in the morning."

When he left Owen on the promenade deck, Bruce did not return at once to his quarters. Now that he had absorbed the news, he was not too startled. In war as in peace, friends and enemies turned up on one's doorstep without warning: now that he had granted Hal's ability to land on his feet like a cat, he would take his arrival aboard in stride. . . . And yet, it was quite true that he had just stood eye-to-eye with a ghost—the last, phantom hope that he might win Janet Josselyn.

Hal Reardon as a paratroop colonel had been competition enough. Hal as a home-front hero in the making, ready to recapture a fiancée after her break with Hollywood, was an adversary without peer.

It was well after ten when the first units of the ambulance train appeared on the beach. Alerted by radio of its arrival, the 241st had readied all its operating theaters. The precaution had been well advised: the first hoist brought a severe hemorrhage case aboard, a corporal from the 75th Airborne who was almost exsanguinated when he arrived on Bruce's table.

The man's injuries involved a broken femur—and a deep wound adjoining the break. It was midnight before he could pack the wound and stand back to estimate the value of the last transfusion. Despite the long delay, he was reasonably sure he had saved his patient.

The emergency, while it lasted, had driven all other thoughts from his mind. The rest of his stand-by teams had performed on schedule: this time, unfortunately, the mortality rate had been far higher than usual, due to the time lag on a highly fluid front. When he had checked the last chart, and conferred with Alice Stacey on the disposition of the walking wounded, Bruce went in search of Eric. He found his second-in-command on the empty deck, at the check-in table.

"Everything's in control, it seems."

"We managed easily," said Badger. "This was the same outfit Phil saw assembling at the clearance station. From what I hear, they've been through triple-deck hell."

"Is a Colonel Reardon on your list?"

"Your classmate was on the second barge," said Badger. "He came aboard at twenty-three hundred." For a moment, he stared down at his admissions book without speaking. "I put him in a private room and started shock treatment. Do you want to handle this one yourself?"

"How severe is the shock?"

"Bad enough—but not likely to be fatal."

Something in his deputy's tone had sounded its own warning. Bruce hesitated, then sat down at the admissions table.

"All right, Eric—give."

"He's in what I'd call acute catatonic shock. It's too soon to be sure, of course, but my guess is that he's a psycho casualty."

"Since when did you set up as a psychiatrist?"

"I've learned plenty from our wire recordings on acute cases. When you see him, I think you'll agree."

"Catatonia's a big word."

"Not for Reardon. I've assembled a whole clinical pattern —put together from what his men have told me. It goes back to his training at Jeff Davis. Even then, he seems to have been jump-crazy—"

"Hal was a four-letter man at the university. Why shouldn't a fine athlete make a fine paratrooper?"

"No reason at all—especially when it adds a touch of drama to his record. From then on, unfortunately, the Reardon saga begins to develop some pretty fantastic angles."

"Were you there to see them develop?"

The man from Wisconsin glanced down the deck, to make sure they were still alone. "I was skeptical myself—until I

talked with paratroopers who *were* on the spot. One was
Reardon's own orderly. The other was a staff sergeant. Both
of them jumped behind the hero who couldn't wait to yell
'Geronimo!'"

"Were they struck by Navy ack-ack?"

"Their plane got through, after evasive action. They
dropped among a German outpost company with commando
training. Half that jump was knifed before morning. The rest
dug in."

"Including Hal?"

"The men I interviewed lost him in the dark. In the morning, when the Germans pulled back, they found him under
a tree. With a foot wound, and unconscious. The EMT de-
scribes his injuries as brain concussion, plus that gunshot
wound. A compound metatarsal fracture."

"Are you suggesting it was self-inflicted?"

"It's what an Army forty-five would do at a three-foot
range," said Badger. "For *concussion*, read *catatonia*—and
you've got the missing link. Obviously, no battalion surgeon
would put a psycho tag on one of his own staff officers."

"The battalion surgeon put down what he saw. You're
jumping to conclusions."

"Don't tell me you're going to let that tag stand, Bruce."

"I'll have to—unless this patient confirms what you've con-
jectured."

"Why? Because you still feel obligated?"

"No, Eric. Because your clinical pattern, as you call it,
can't be accepted without evidence."

"What more do you need? The drop was Reardon's big
test. He flunked it cold. For the first time—since he threw
those winning touchdown passes—he had no one to cheer
him on. The best he could do was lie doggo in his tree, while
the enemy stabbed his men on the ground. Sometime before
the Germans started pulling out, he decided he'd had enough
paratrooping, gave in to his nerves, and fired his one shot of
the war—at an easy target. When he saw help on the way, he

tumbled from his hiding place. He knew he'd pull an honorable discharge, if no one asked questions. Nothing could be simpler, or neater."

"Are you claiming the catatonia was self-inflicted too?"

"Catatonia's a logical aftermath of cowardice. Call it a fugue state, a withdrawal from reality. We've treated identical cases on this ship."

"Is this your whole bill of indictment?"

"Signed and sealed. And I'll repeat it before a court of inquiry."

"I hope you interrupted your analysis long enough to get an X ray."

Eric flushed. "You'll find it clipped to his chart. An in-and-out bullet puncture of the right foot—made *from above*."

"Did they bring his pistol with his gear?"

"The holster was empty when they found him. A service revolver was an item he couldn't risk keeping."

"You're overlooking one thing," Bruce said. "It could have been accidentally discharged when he fell into the tree."

"Meaning that you're about to apply the whitewash—and to hell with accusations?"

"Meaning you'll forget what you said tonight—unless we turn up other evidence. That's a direct order."

"As you wish, Major Graham. Colonel Reardon's a minor-wound entry in our admissions book, and nothing more. Is that correct, sir?"

"That is correct, Captain."

"I've put him in Cabin F. Do you want to examine him?"

"I'll make my evaluation now."

On the deck above, where the cruise ship's luxury cabins were reserved for patients needing special care, Bruce picked up Hal's clipboard and dismissed the corpsman who had been sitting at the bedside. Prepared though he was by Badger's recital, he was appalled by what the cabin lights revealed. Combat-zone duty had accustomed him to most injuries the human body is capable of enduring—yet, as he began his examination, he had the uneasy certainty that death itself was grinning at his side.

Hal's breathing was almost too shallow to disturb his rib cage. A bruise above his right temple showed beneath its antiseptic coating. His face seemed gaunt as the skull behind it, and the hands that lay on the coverlet resembled the curved talons of a bird. In Algiers, in his fresh fatigues, Hal had been a figure to remember, a latter-day centurion ripe for his first honors. Here, in a bare cabin aboard a hospital ship, he might already have been ticketed for the grave—though both heart and breathing were close to normal, along with body heat and pulse.

The gaunt look, Bruce well knew, was a common side effect of the catatonic state. So were the wide-open eyes that stared unwinking into space—and gave no reaction to the pencil flashlight he snapped on above them. The possibility of brain hemorrhage was all but ruled out. The bruise did not include a fracture—and whatever concussion existed beneath it could be left to self-healing.

A complete neurological check produced only negative results. The surgeon performed it by instinct, certain that he would find nothing to contradict the notations on the chart. The wound itself was not serious. The X ray revealed that the bullet had bored its path between the second and third metatarsal bones, passing through the top of the foot and emerging from the sole. Small portions of each bone were fragmented, but there was every reason to hope they would heal with no marked deformity. Close examination revealed that the bullet hole was free of dirt and clothing fragments, the most dangerous fellow travelers in wounds of this sort. Bleeding, as the EMT had noted, had been minimal. There had been no need for a tourniquet—which might have damaged circulation during the time Hal had spent in transit.

Badger had posted the patient for the relatively minor surgery required before a cast was applied. About to put down

his own name as the doctor in charge, Bruce left the space
blank and contented himself with initialing the report.

In his own cabin at last, settling into his bunk, he could
still not adjust to Hal Reardon's presence aboard—or to the
nagging certainty that Eric had diagnosed the case correctly.
Tonight, at least, he could welcome the weariness that
blacked out such problems in advance, seconds after his head
touched the pillow.

Eight hours of unbroken sleep did much to lighten the
pall of depression that had settled on Bruce's spirits—though
it was still a shock to enter the officers' mess and find Jerry
Stokes's seat vacant. On deck, he was greeted by the tattoo
of welders' drills as a detail of Navy repairmen, swarming
on work-hoists at the ship's bow, fitted new steel into the
damaged bulkheads. Their speed seemed an excellent augury.
He was almost cheerful when he went below again, to check
on activities during the night.

Forty new cases—all transferred from a field hospital, where
initial surgery had been performed when needed—had come
aboard while he slept. The admissions ledger showed that
less than a hundred empty beds remained—and experience
told him the ship would be loaded to capacity by nightfall.
Reading through the record of operations, he saw that Badger
had performed a routine débridement on Hal's injured foot.
The surgery had proceeded without complications. . . . He
reached for the phone to summon his assistant, when Eric
himself appeared in the doorway of the record room, his
mouth set in a schoolboy grin.

"We decided to let you sleep this morning, sir."

"Skip the formality, and the smoke screen," said Bruce.
"I wanted to operate on Colonel Reardon."

"Why should you be wakened to repair a routine foot injury? Phil and I did the job between us." The man from
Wisconsin opened the cabin door to admit Captain Owen,

who marched in behind an even broader smile, bearing Shane's recorder.

"As you see, Major, our technique was strictly SOP," he said. "Including verbatim remarks from a patient in severe neurogenic shock."

"Did you run a *recording?*"

"Loud and clear, Bruce. While he was under anesthesia." Owen placed the machine on the desk. "This time, we omitted a stenographer—and a nurse, since we had to do practically nothing to the wound. Eric preferred to operate with just one witness. Myself."

"Both of us will vouch for the information the patient volunteered while in a state of narcosis," said Badger. He nodded to the medical chief, who closed and bolted the door.

"What made you so sure he'd say a word?" Bruce asked.

"It's a temptation no politician can resist," said Owen. "Even when he's supposed to be in coma." His hand was on the playback switch. "This is probably the most sincere speech he ever made."

"I'm not sure I care to hear it."

"It's part of my report," said Badger. "Since it supports the conclusions I reached last night, it deserves your attention."

"Do you agree, Phil?"

"Completely. We've followed identical procedure with other shock cases. The spools are part of this hospital's records. Why should a congressman be an exception? He can't cry immunity when he's in uniform."

Bruce settled behind the desk, with a gesture of resignation. Guessing what he was about to hear, he felt a chill run down his spine at the sound emerging from the softly whirring recorder—a high-pitched wail of terror, old as the caveman's first howl beneath the moon.

"As you'll observe," said Badger, "this went on for quite a while. You might call it an overture to the main attraction."

Owen chuckled, and perched on the edge of the desk to

adjust the volume. "While it lasted, it took both of us to keep the pentothal needle in his arm. You'll hear quite a change, when he starts to go under."

The wailing died as the recording purred on. It was replaced by an incoherent babble that changed, by degrees, to a few shouted phrases. These yielded, in turn, to a soft-voiced yet passionate declamation, as though Hal were defending himself before a jury. Feeling his fingers itch to cut the switch, yet knowing he would listen to the end, Bruce heard the wounded man's review of the events that had preceded his blackout: the jump into darkness, his sudden, jarring immersion in tree branches, the knowledge that he had plummeted into a nest of mortal enemies. . . . The whispered recital rose and fell, as the patient recalled his rising panic, his determination to survive at all costs—and, finally, the uncontrollable need to escape his terror.

"He even acted the business with the gun." Eric's voice cut through the recital. "Right down to the bead he drew on his boot—and the way he squeezed the trigger."

"Luck was with him to the end," said Owen. "Dawn was breaking when he bought his ticket home—and the enemy had begun to pull back. Two minutes later, he fell from the tree, and banged his head."

"Cut that switch, please. I've heard enough."

The medical chief disconnected the recording. "You asked for additional evidence, Major Graham. You have it."

"We'll both be your witnesses, if it comes to a general court," said Badger.

Bruce leaned across the desk and opened the recorder. The wire was coiled on its spool, between the reversible microphone and the amplifier. Lifting the reel from the machine, he tossed it on the blotter. The move stirred a dismal echo in his memory: he could vision Jake Sanford's office in Washington, all too well.

"As I see it," he said quietly, "I have two choices—thanks to your efforts. The first is simple: to destroy this reel, and let the field diagnosis go in our records. The second choice is to send our findings to the Task Force Command. Frankly, I don't think either of you has considered what that would involve."

"Unmasking a coward is always a pleasure," said Owen.

"The facts of Army life aren't quite so simple, Phil. Colonel Reardon's a national figure. He's the President's friend, and he's heir-apparent to a Senate seat. Suppose he denies every word in that recording? Are you prepared to challenge him at a court-martial?"

"Why not—if the evidence stands up medically?"

"This evidence, as you call it, is still experimental. A court-martial must be preceded by a board of inquiry. Suppose they throw out your recording? Then it's your word against the colonel's."

"I still think it's worth the chance," said Badger.

"And I'm warning you that your chances are minimal. One thing's for sure. Win, lose or draw in court, the heads of three MC officers would go on the block."

"You're making *us* sound guilty, Bruce."

"Only of being indiscreet."

"Maybe we have a third choice," Badger persisted. "Call this reel a time bomb, tuck it in a file-and-forget drawer—and save it for use later."

"What would be your choice, if you were I?"

"I'd call number two the most intriguing."

"Phil?"

"File for future reference, Bruce. It's the easiest out."

The surgeon weighed the spool on his palm before he tossed it in Badger's lap. "I appreciate your help—and the intentions behind it. Captain Badger will destroy this portion of the special pentothal file the moment he leaves this office. We'll do our best for Colonel Reardon while he's aboard—and hope he stays on the ground in future."

When the deputy CO spoke again, his voice was spent. It was the tone of a man who has just crossed a crowded room to hail a friend, only to find himself facing a stranger.

"We came here in good faith, Bruce—"

"I'm sure you did."

"We were thinking of your interests, where this fellow's concerned. In your place, I'd hit him with the book."

"I've told you why we can't, Eric. My order's been given, as commander of this complement. See it's carried out."

"Would your thinking be different, as a civilian?"

"The question's pointless. I can't imagine a similar condition in civilian life."

"Cowardice isn't confined to war," said Owen.

"Have you never been afraid, Phil?"

"I've been scared blue lots of times. I've yet to blank out and shoot away a toe."

"What about you, Eric? How did you react when we took that blast at the water line?"

Badger grinned as he picked up the recorder. "If you must know, I almost wet my pants."

"Suppose you'd fallen in a treetop, with wolves below. Suppose you'd hung on until daylight, expecting to feel those fangs at your throat? What would *you* have done, with a forty-five in your belt—and help on the way? Wouldn't it have been a tempting exit from the war?"

"It's something no man can answer, Bruce. Not until he's tested the color of his liver. Reardon's, it seems, was paper-white."

"This summer I was on a terrace in Syracuse, with bombs falling next door. I'm not sure what escape I'd have chosen— if I'd been alone."

"You didn't cut and run, Bruce."

"True—because I had someone to share my fear—and the bombing was soon over." Remembering that night at the Pensionare Margherita, Bruce wondered if the others had noticed his blush. "Most of us have company when we're face to face with terror. It isn't often that our testing comes in solitude, and goes on for hours. Colonel Reardon was alone in his treetop. And he had lots of time to think."

"Does that excuse him?"

"Not entirely. But it's a point in his favor—and one you shouldn't forget. After his drop, he was stranded for God knows how many hours, face to face with death. Eventually, he cracked. In his place, I'm not sure I'd have acted differently. Since I *am* unsure, I refuse to damn him."

After he had dismissed his two assistants, Bruce picked up the phone to call Alice Stacey. At his request, a nurse was assigned to watch Colonel Reardon, with instructions to summon him at once if the patient required his presence. No call had come by afternoon, when his routine chores were behind him and he could spare a moment to stop at Cabin F. A nurse was changing the bed.

"I was about to send for you, sir. He seems to be coming out of shock at last."

"Has he been talking?"

"Only a few words I couldn't catch. But he's been moving about—and he opened his eyes just now. He's been perspiring a great deal, so I thought I'd make him comfortable."

The chart showed no significant change—save for the notation that the patient had been intermittently conscious and able to take some fluids. The cast, Bruce observed, had been expertly applied. The pulse count was normal, as were other vital signs.

"I'll stay with him awhile. I don't think he'll need red carpet treatment after today."

"Why is he taking so long to come round? Is it an aftermath of the concussion?"

Bruce glanced again at the chart. Eric—complying with his orders—had let the EMT diagnosis stand. It meant the situation was under control—at least, until Hal wakened in earnest.

"It could be a side effect," he said carefully. "My guess is he'll improve fast, from now on. There's nothing here to suggest intracranial complications."

"I hope not. We need more men like Colonel Reardon in Congress."

"Then you think he should go back to Washington?"

"I think he's done his bit, Major. Don't you?"

"He's been through a rough experience. There's no doubt of that." Bruce stood aside to permit the nurse to leave the room. When the door was shut behind her, he bent above the sleeping man, to pinch the skin behind his ear.

"Time to wake up, Hal. Can you make it?"

The patient's eyes opened slowly. The blank, unseeing stare was almost gone. Only a hint of wariness remained. In another moment, even that residue of fear had gone, as Hal's lips relaxed in a drowsy smile.

"Is it really you, Bruce?"

"It's really me."

"At least I needn't ask 'Where am I?' Since you're here, I must be aboard the *Helen S Peters*."

"They brought you aboard last night. You were wounded in the drop behind the beach."

"In the leg? I can feel the cast."

"The right foot."

"Is it serious?"

"The injury's minor. Two of the metatarsals were fractured. They should heal completely in a few months."

"A few *months*? Does that mean I can't go back to my outfit?"

"I'm afraid it does. Do you remember how this happened?"

"Only the beginning. We'd gone in on our flight plan—and we were still short of our objective. We'd lined up for the jump, when AA shells began exploding around us." Hal closed his eyes and leaned back on his pillow. "I know it's ridiculous—but that's where I black out."

"Completely?"

"Until I recognized you just now. Can you fill me in?"

Hal listened with deep attention while the surgeon described the aftermath of the drop behind Salerno.

"I don't even recall leaving the plane. Judging from your story, we must have bailed out at discretion. You say I had a wounded foot when the medics found me—and this head injury?"

"It's only a mild concussion."

"Apparently it was severe enough to take away my memory."

"Such cases aren't uncommon. Including a temporary blackout."

"Are you sure it's temporary, Bruce?"

"You know who and where you are. That's always a good sign. The rest should come back later."

"Isn't there some way to jog my brain?"

"You'll help yourself most by relaxing completely. I'll give you a hypo to make sure you sleep until morning."

Hal did not stir while Bruce injected the morphine.

"Can you send a cable in my name?"

"Of course. To your family?"

"What's left of my family is unimportant. They'll hear soon enough that I came out of this show alive. I'd like Senator Josselyn to get the news promptly."

"We'll radio Algiers tonight."

"He'll pass the word to Janet," said Hal. "Have you heard from her lately?"

"I had a letter last week. She's still making that second picture."

"I'm sure she is," said Hal. His voice had begun to slur under the morphine. "Some illusions die hard, Bruce. I've no intention of destroying hers ahead of time. Nor, I'm sure, have you."

"Brodski may be mistaken about her talent."

"Leo has yet to guess wrong about an actress. Weren't you taught that a doctor never argues with his patient?"

"I thought it was the other way round. Shall I send a separate cable to Shane?"

"I wouldn't know how to reach her. Besides, there's no need. Shane realizes I'm hard to kill."

"We're in agreement there. Take things easy. I'll look in on you before noon, tomorrow."

In the radio room, Bruce filed the message to Senator Josselyn's Washington office, along with a score of similar wires the Red Cross would relay to Algiers. There was no need to wonder why Hal had chosen to address Janet through her father—or why he had made no attempt to reach Shane McLendon. Even in a hospital bed, he was already sure of his ground, and preparing to call the next tune.

Eric Badger was already in Bruce's office when he came in from breakfast. After the new CO had settled at his desk, the visitor made a point of closing the door—and dropped the bolt in place.

"Any afterthoughts on your orders?"

"None whatever. Our most famous patient is progressing well, according to the morning report."

"I looked in on him myself just now. He tells me a good night's sleep was all he needed to swing the pendulum back. When I left, he was demanding a steak for lunch."

"How's the memory?"

"He's saving that part of the prognosis for you. Shall we see him together?"

"Is this a consultation?"

"I've earned the right to hear his cover-up. After all, I'm the surgeon of record."

"Come with me, then. Just remember your name is Badger, not Freud."

They found Hal chatting with Alice Stacey. When the chief nurse had moved on, Bruce sat at the end of the berth to check the patient's chart. The improvement wrought by sleep and solid food, he saw, had been amazing.

"When can I leave this cabin, Bruce?"

"Things are going well, I'll admit. But you could use more rest."

"I'd much rather join the walking wounded."

"If you're in good shape tomorrow, we may give you a few hours in a deck chair. I'd rather keep you here until all your tests are normal. Especially your memory."

"*That's* back on full-time duty."

"Can you tell us what happened in the drop?" Badger asked.

"In somewhat painful detail, Captain. Including my private fiasco. At least, I think I have the high points in order."

"Are there still gaps?"

"Here and there. Shall I begin with the AA bursts?"

"You remembered that much yesterday," said Bruce.

"The *jump* was blotted out—and what came after. You put that down to concussion." Hal considered his next words carefully. "At first, none of us could believe those salvos were from our own guns. When we realized the truth, the best we could do was bail out fast."

"Have you compared your experience with others on the plane?" Badger asked.

"Of course not. How could I?"

"Two of those men are aboard, Colonel Reardon. Your orderly and your staff sergeant. I've already questioned them."

"Let's hope my report fits with theirs," said Hal easily. "The rest happened fast. So fast, I can't expect either of you to follow me—unless *you've* jumped too."

"Try it for size, Colonel. We'll stay with you."

Hal favored the man from Wisconsin with a long, cool stare before he turned to Bruce.

"Actually, my story's commonplace. I landed in a treetop —a fact that saved my life. After I hit the top branches, I realized I'd been wounded. I cut away my chute and stayed in hiding until daybreak. By then, I was too exhausted to hang on—and knocked myself out when I fell. My next memory was wakening in this bunk."

"Just how were you wounded?" Badger asked.

Hal's smile, Bruce noted, had grown a trifle strained, but his voice retained its easy urbanity.

"If you'll pardon the wordplay, Captain, you're as persistent as the animal whose name you bear."

"I need the facts for my report, sir."

"As you may know," said Hal, "I'm a member of General Leonard's staff—one of several officers who volunteered for the Salerno jump. In that capacity, I, too, must keep records. Before you arrived, I was preparing a personal letter to the general, with Nurse Stacey's help. You'll find it on the back page of the clipboard. Use as much as you wish."

Bruce took up the clipboard and read the last page through before he passed it to Badger. Couched in purest Army prose, it described the first combat experience of Colonel Harold Reardon, in the colonel's own words.

As Hal had reconstructed the episode, he had jumped just after midnight, with the unit he was commanding. He had maneuvered his chute toward a hillside, planning to take cover there until he could check the terrain. Landing in a treetop, he had heard a sharp report at the moment of impact; his service revolver, ripped from its holster by the clawing branches, had somehow been discharged. This, to the best of his knowledge, accounted for the bullet hole in his foot.

Immediately after his landing, he had cut the chute with his ranger knife, freed it from the branches, and sent it kiting off into darkness. During this vital maneuver, he had heard shots on the ground below, and realized his group had fallen near an enemy strong point. Because of his wound, he could not risk leaving his ambush. He had dressed his foot as best he could, from a first-aid pack—and waited through hours of darkness, hoping for an enemy withdrawal or a counterattack. At dawn, already lightheaded from the pain of his injury, he had fallen twice—first, to a lower nest of limbs, then to the ground itself, where his head had struck a rock.

Hal's last clear memory—according to his account—was a burst of gunfire from the slope below, suggesting that the enemy was retiring under pressure. The concussion had brought a complete blackout thereafter, until he found himself aboard the hospital ship.

"Was your pistol recovered, Colonel?" Badger asked.

"I've no way of knowing."

"You're sure it caused your wound—not enemy fire?"

"If the enemy had seen me in that treetop, I would hardly be telling you this story now."

"There were no snipers in the tree itself?"

"Of course not. Why do you ask?"

"The bullet entered your foot from *above*. Your report leaves that fact unmentioned."

"Are you implying that I should prepare for a general court, because of a self-inflicted wound?"

The captain's and the colonel's eyes clashed. Bruce knew the captain's would be the first to drop—now that Badger had established his competence, both as a doctor and a sleuth.

"We've covered the situation, Eric," he said. "Perhaps you owe Colonel Reardon an apology."

"No apology is expected," said Hal. "Your colleague's on the zealous side—but I appreciate his thoroughness. The facts are as I've stated them. The pistol was wrenched from its holster when I struck the tree—and discharged by accident."

"My record's complete, sir," said Badger. "If my language was intemperate, I'm sorry. With your permission, I'll add this report to our files, verbatim."

"Of course, Captain Badger."

Again, Bruce took control. Eric, he knew, had shot his bolt—but the tension in the room was still palpable.

"I'd suggest we let our patient rest, Captain. We agreed to make his ordeal brief."

In the hall outside, the deputy CO marched to the deck without speaking. Here, he turned to Bruce with a gesture of pure despair.

"Why call it an *ordeal?* He loved every moment."

"You were licked from the start. No mere captain can grill a full colonel and stay alive. I'm glad I got you out in time."

"I still wish I'd crowded him harder."

"Do you see now why I refused to let you sound off?"

"I see all too well. No casualty in my memory has staged a faster comeback. The man in Cabin F is a far cry from the psycho we heard yesterday—on Miss McLendon's recorder."

"Are you sure that was Hal Reardon? The patient we just questioned has been around a good deal longer."

"Don't tell me you accept *him* at face value."

"You've just admitted it's a public image you can't destroy."

"I wonder if Reardon himself knows where the public figure leaves off—and he begins."

"I think not, Eric. If his luck holds, he never will."

"Even he can't believe that Boy Scout version of Salerno."

"Give him time. He'll blot what really happened from his conscious mind—and live with the scar tissue. It will never show."

"Only because you've given him the last word," said Badger.

"Colonels usually have the last word in this man's Army. How else can he go on serving his commander? Or the electorate—when he gets his honorable discharge? He won't be the first man to come out of a crack-up stronger than before."

"With the electorate—or with himself?" asked Badger.

"With both, perhaps. We all have scars to live with."

Since the *Helen S Peters'* last call in Algiers, the quay of the Tenth General Hospital had been extended, permitting the ship to unload its wounded directly to their waiting transport. As a result, thanks to an early-morning arrival, the ship was cleared of its human cargo by midafternoon.

While the unloading proceeded, a swarm of engineers from the naval repair base had investigated the situation below decks, pronounced the Salerno patch job adequate, and cleared the ship for an Atlantic crossing, after it joined a convoy at Gibraltar. Rumors of a return to the States for more extensive repairs had been rife. That noon, with Bruce beside him on the bridge, Captain Swenson had made the rumor official on the public-address system. They would sail for Charleston as soon as a thousand convalescent patients and the necessary supplies could come aboard.

Hal Reardon, who had moved from chair to crutches before the ship could leave Italy, was almost the last casualty to go ashore. His day had been a round of farewell visits: as Bruce had expected, he had become the favorite patient aboard. When he was wheeled from ship to quay, only the complement's ingrained discipline prevented a procession from forming in his wake.

Bruce had managed his own good-bye in offhand fashion, while the wounded colonel was still surrounded by nurses and orderlies; he had gone to the bridge to observe Hal's departure from a safe distance. The still-unofficial hero of Salerno had descended the gangway with the aid of a corpsman. On the quay, he had assumed his crutches, to move with surprising speed to the staff car awaiting him. The handshake he gave the corpsman at the gangway had been the essence of democracy. The salute he exchanged with the sergeant who sprang forward to open the car door was part of the well-bred poise of an officer born to command.

"Join me in the wheelhouse, Major—if it is more than you can bear."

Bruce turned toward the skipper's voice. Captain Swenson, looking even more saturnine than usual, stood in the doorway that opened to the bridge.

"Was my distress that obvious, sir?"

"Distress is not the exact term. Is it not more accurate to say you mistrust Colonel Reardon's popularity—even though you've trained yourself to accept it?"

The complement commander knew he was smiling when he followed the captain to the privacy of the wheelhouse. His confidence in Swenson had been complete, from their first encounter. Today, as always, he knew it was safe to speak his mind in this modern Viking's presence.

"So you don't care for Colonel Reardon either?"

"Let me confess, in confidence, that I, too, mistrust him. The colonel and I had quite a chat last evening. Before it ended, he had given me the essence of his philosophy. You might call it one of his pretested speeches. I gather he has delivered it often on this cruise."

"Something about America's mission when the war ends?"

"Exactly, Major. A *Pax Americana*, to be enforced by any means at hand."

"In other words, the current line of the Lowell *Bulletins*."

"I mentioned the analogy, of course. He denied all connections—even though he preaches the same gospel."

"World peace, with the accent on American enforcement?"

"Colonel Reardon feels we will emerge from this war the strongest nation since Rome. He believes we should use that strength as a club to keep the world in line."

"The fallacy is familiar, sir."

"So I reminded him," said Swenson. "Rome, after all, was centered in the Mediterranean, where its arms were supreme. When it reached too far beyond, its legions failed. Just as the so-called *Pax Brittanica* is failing now—since it is based on powers that exist no longer. Granted, it is tempting to think of America as the next world pacifier. But no nation is big enough to act as global policeman tomorrow. Peace must be a universal project, or it is nothing."

"Did he concede the argument?"

"In principle, yes," said Swenson. "He still insisted America's voice must be dominant. In his opinion, that is the ideal for which Sergeant Lowell lived and died."

"Nothing could be further from the truth. Jimmie would disown the Lowell Society completely, if he were alive today."

"I'm sure of that," said Swenson. "Unfortunately, Colonel Reardon thinks otherwise—he, not us, can make his voice heard. Which brings us back to the man himself, to what he feels is a God-given mission. Colonel Reardon will always be convinced his logic is supreme. In his view, the credo he defends—in any ear he can find—is the only salvation for mankind."

"Even at college, he was the debater who never lost an argument."

"Such men are often fortunate in their timing and their goals," said Swenson. "Naturally, they expect the world to approve those goals on sight. It is a trait dictators share with messiahs."

"Perhaps he'll earn the second title before he's done. Had you thought of that?"

"All things are possible, Major. If he does, we deserve to be banished to outer darkness."

"I, for one, refuse to be exiled without fighting back."

"I take it you were friendly enemies in college, when the mold was taking shape. Even then, did you refuse to worship the campus god?"

"More or less. Most of my classmates thought I was off my rocker."

"Naturally, your distrust has rekindled aboard my ship—where he has won over your staff, with the simple exercise of his charm."

Bruce shrugged a silent agreement. For a moment, he could wish that Swenson had heard the tape recording. He wondered what the skipper's reaction would have been.

"Eric wasn't won over. Nor was Phil Owen."

"Your deputies are home-grown cynics. A stubborn breed that finds pleasure in dissent. They are exceptions to the average. Unless there is a change from the past, your countrymen will emerge from this war eager to swallow a ready-made cure for their ills."

"With Hal to deliver the sales talk?"

"Already, he has persuasive supporters. Including the wonderful woman who sailed with us on our second cruise to Gela. As you'll observe, she's here to meet him. From this vantage point, her welcome seems a warm one."

Following the captain's gesture, Bruce turned to the starboard window of the wheelhouse, a wide glass panel that permitted a sweeping view of the quay. Hal's staff car, he observed, had been detained by a resplendent admiral, who had just turned back to the battlewagon berthed in the next slip. Shane McLendon had burst from a taxi, to rush toward the staff car before it could pull away—and Hal, with a booming shout of welcome, had opened the door to receive her.

The vignette, brief though it was, had a stunning impact. Bruce turned aside before he could witness the actual meeting; it was enough to note the joy that crowned Shane's head like a halo, to realize, with a sinking heart, that Hal had accepted it as his due. . . . For the last time, he told himself that his classmate had won. Already, he could curse the tolerance that had forced him to reject Eric Badger's recording. Yet even now, he knew he could not have used so cruel a means to destroy Shane's happiness.

"It is never pleasant, watching a woman one loves make a wrong choice," said Swenson. "It is even more troubling to wonder if she will see the light in time."

"I'm not in love with Miss McLendon. I *am* distressed that she can't see through a handsome facade."

"Why should she? Women have always been poor judges of men. Are you sure you aren't in love with her?"

"I have a girl back home, Captain. I still hope to marry her, now we're bound for the States."

"It's a shame you aren't a sailor," said Swenson. "Tradition allows us a girl in every port. So you can see why we prefer the sea to the land."

At Charleston, two months to the day after that interlude in Algiers, Bruce sat in the lounge of yet another BOQ, with a newspaper on his knee. Watching a November downpour streak the panes, he was discovering—one more time—that he could survive a morning with no clear memory of its passing. . . . Until now, those two months had been busy enough—but he could bring back only a jumble of experiences repeated, a review of acts that seemed no more significant today than the dim vistas of his boyhood.

His conscious mind assured him that he had completed an important mission, the transport of nearly a thousand wounded men—from a base hospital in Africa to specialized care in the States—without losing a patient. Today, the return voyage was a blur of routine below decks, while the *Helen S Peters* wallowed westward through autumn gales. His hours off duty were no clearer. Most of them had been spent alone—staring into wind and rain, closing his eyes against the one picture he could not avoid, a dusty quay in Algiers, an Army staff car moving from his range of vision, and Shane McLendon on the back seat, talking eagerly to Hal Reardon. . . .

He could take little comfort in the knowledge he had been powerless to prevent that rendezvous, that he could not have denounced Hal without far stronger reasons than he possessed at the moment. If Shane was determined to collaborate in Hal's career, if she truly believed that this was the voice of tomorrow, he had no choice but to stand aside.

When the ship had gone into dry dock at the Charleston Port of Embarkation, marine experts had discovered that the plates in the forward bulkhead had been strained by the

rough crossing. One of the diesels had needed replacing—
and, during the overhaul, it had been decided that a more
efficient ventilating system should be installed. All these
facts, in Captain Swenson's opinion, meant that the *Helen
S Peters* would see service in the Pacific—but the plans of the
Transportation Corps were still veiled, and Bruce had not
pressed for details.

His first weeks at Charleston had been active. Because
of his experience in Italy, he had been called on to address
groups of trainees destined for similar duty. When a sister
ship arrived from Norfolk, he had joined the trial run, instructing the technicians below decks and advising the complement commander on his duties. . . . Again, he had been
willing to live from day to day, doing the tasks assigned him,
volunteering for extra duty, and slipping into exhausted sleep
when his duties were behind him. Even the discovery that
he had become a lieutenant colonel—the promotion had come
to him direct, via the Transportation Corps Command in
the Mediterranean Theater—had left him unmoved.

Eric Badger, Phil Owen, and most of the other officers
under his command had gone on leave—but he had refused
to do likewise. Like the skipper, he had preferred to spend
his time at the base, awaiting a phone call that did not
come. A sense of impending change had never left him,
from the day he had seen the Carolina coastline lift from a
slate-gray sea. Until he received that call, he knew this state
of inertia would persist.

During the last weeks, it would have been easy to lift his
own telephone, to make one of several contacts that would
set his doubts at rest. Pride had stayed his hand, since his
first attempts to reach Janet Josselyn had crashed into a
blank wall of silence.

As for Hal and Shane, it was even easier to remind himself
that he had burned his bridges. They, at least, had made
their intentions clear. Silence was the price he had paid for
self-respect.

Again, he looked down at the paper on his knee—a copy of the Charleston *News and Courier*, salvaged from a stack of back numbers on the reading table. The paper was eight weeks old. The column by Shane McLendon was a replica of the one he had first seen in the *Times* of London, when the *Helen S Peters* had called at Gibraltar. If he was rereading it now, it was only to rub salt into old wounds, to use a page from a newspaper as an excuse to damn Hal Reardon once again.

The column was still titled *As I See It*—and Shane's profile was still a decoration beside that standing head. Below, in type almost as large, was the subhead that introduced her story:

I Jumped to Nowhere

Filed from Algiers months ago, the column was a replay of the 75th Airborne's run over Salerno, with Hal Reardon as narrator and star performer. Hal's account of the jump was given in his own words—with enough comment from Shane herself to make the column a classic of wartime journalism, a cameo-clear portrait of a civilian paratrooper who had risked his life for his country.

Shane had highlighted the black terror of the jump itself, the unplanned landing in the treetop—with seconds left to cut away a chute that would have revealed Hal's presence to the Germans. She had continued with an hour-by-hour playback of his calvary among the leaves, as he had clung to his precarious refuge and fought the pain of his wound. She had described his delirium at daybreak, when his senses had left him at last, and he had tumbled from his perch. . . . Finally she had told of Hal's mute despair, when he found himself in a hospital bed, and realized that his contribution to the war was over, hours after it had begun.

The column ended on a note of simple dignity, when Colonel Reardon—accepting a Purple Heart and the Silver Star from his commanding general—had agreed to return to the States to serve the cause in other fields. Relying on the impact of understatement, letting the inherent drama shine through on its merits, Shane had achieved a tour de force of reportage. Here, in sober truth, was the hero in his purest form, the man from the American mainstream who had risen above fear in the lonely darkness, to solve the problem of survival.

The column had been reprinted a score of times, at home and abroad; it had appeared in one of those all-purpose anthologies of combat journalism, guaranteed a million copy sale. Its author was already being mentioned as a candidate for the Pulitzer Prize, with this story as the capstone of her career. And her subject, touring America at this very moment on a new war-bond drive, had grown in stature with each passing day.

At Gibraltar (reading these same words in the London *Times* while he stood at the ship's gangway), Bruce had dropped the paper overside with a muttered imprecation. While the ship remained at anchor, he had written an angry letter to Shane—and destroyed it, after reminding himself that he had no visible cause for his rage, no right whatever to censure her wish to celebrate Hal's baptism by fire—or, if she chose, to worship false gods. . . .

Janet Josselyn, of course, was another story. Her long silence had made his isolation complete—and he had refused, so far, to break it by his own efforts.

En route from Algiers to Gibraltar, he had composed a long and loving missive, repeating his offer of marriage and begging her to arrange an early reunion in Charleston. He had mailed his letter, via the International Zone of Tangier, with special air-mail priority. Expecting an answer when he reached his port in Carolina, he had been shocked to find none waiting. His dismay had grown after a long-distance call to California had failed to reach her.

Part of the mystery had solved itself during his first week in Charleston, when a New York gossip column had stated that Janet Josselyn had left Brodski's studio, after her contract had been terminated by mutual consent. Bruce had understood still more when a news item from Tampa confirmed the rumor—adding that Janet had returned home to attend her ailing father, who had suffered a coronary attack on the Senate floor and gone to Florida to recuperate.

Hesitating to put through a second long-distance call when he had received no direct word, Bruce had sent a brief note to Tampa, asking if Janet had received the letter from Tangier, and expressing his regret at her bad news. The sense of doom had persisted when days passed with no acknowledgment of the second letter. It had deepened when he picked up a copy of the Miami *Herald* picturing Colonel Hal Reardon and the senator's daughter as participants in a war-bond rally in that city.

A week ago he had received a telegram from Janet, stating that her father's illness had occupied her steadily, and promising direct communication when the situation clarified. There had been no further word.

It had been a bad two months, a limbo where he had waited without plans and with no clear hope. Now, this rainy morning in Charleston, he felt the time of indecision was behind him, when he heard his name called from an adjoining barroom in the BOQ. . . . Perversely, he was reluctant to answer the steward's summons.

"Are you there, Colonel Graham?"

"Coming. Is it long distance?"

The steward had already appeared in the doorway with an envelope. "It's a telegram, sir. They just sent it up from headquarters."

Bruce damned his prescience as he ripped open the envelope. Because of continuing crises aboard his ship, wires were no novelty. . . . This one, he found, was a thing apart, a day letter from Tampa asking him to call a number in that area between noon and three. Save for the initials J.J., there was no identification of the sender.

Captain Swenson's office ashore was a lean-to adjoining the dry dock, with a distant view of Fort Sumter and an agreeable sense of isolation. As Bruce had hoped, it was deserted in the lunch hour. Cradling the phone on one shoulder while he settled in the captain's chair, he put through his Tampa call—and found it absurdly easy to avoid conscious thought while he awaited the connection.

When a strange voice answered—a woman's tone, high-keyed and petulant—he could almost hope he had misunderstood the wire.

"I was asked to call Miss Josselyn at this number—"

"Who is speaking?"

"This is Colonel Graham."

"Miss Josselyn was expecting a *major*."

"Will you tell her I've had a promotion?"

Janet came on the wire—so abruptly, he was sure she had picked up an extension.

"Is that you, Bruce?"

"I'm answering your telegram. Where are you?"

"That was Aunt Hester. I'm at her house on Davis Island, to get away from reporters." Janet's voice was strangely indistinct, as though she had risen from sleep. "You've heard the news, of course?"

"I'm afraid not—"

"Dad died in his sleep last night. That's why I sent that second wire—to keep you from calling me at home."

"Is there anything I can do?" It was not the exchange he had imagined in his weeks of waiting. And yet, now he had grasped the import of that strange telegram, each word seemed entirely natural. It was as though he were hearing Janet Josselyn's voice for the first time—as though he were seeing her, despite the miles that divided them, more clearly than ever before.

"You've done so much for me now, Bruce. Will you do me one more favor?"

"Of course, if it's in my power."

"Listen carefully," said Janet. "Try to see my problem."

"I'll do my best."

"There's just one way to tell you this. I'm going to marry Hal Reardon."

"Because of your father?" He had asked the question mechanically: the shock had been astoundingly light. Two months of silence had prepared him well enough.

"Dad's part of it, of course. Before he died, I promised to respect his wishes—and I'm keeping that promise. But *you're* the real reason I made up my mind. While I was having what Leo Brodski called my picture career, I honestly hoped to make you happy. Now I've no career left, I could never match your gifts—"

"Do you know you're talking nonsense?"

"Please don't be gallant, Bruce. It happens to be true. Sometimes a failure in one field gives you perspective in another. When I was the toast of the camp circuit, I thought there was no part I couldn't play. I could even pretend I deserved a doctor-consort after Leo had made me a full-fledged star. That was part of the illusion. I'm glad I've outgrown it—"

Hearing her voice go on—as gliby as though this were a set speech for a tryout audience whose approval was assured —Bruce forced a protest.

"I can't believe this decision was based entirely on my welfare."

"You'll remember my father never quite approved of you," said Janet. "I fought him while I still had hopes at the studio. I began listening again—after I'd given up on Brodski. Marriage to Hal was part of my life from the beginning. I can't pretend it was made in heaven—but it's bound to succeed."

"How soon will you make this official?"

"Naturally, there can be no formal statement now. Aunt Hester will announce our engagement in the spring—when Hal is back in Washington."

"I thought he'd resigned his seat in the House."

"The governor's appointing him to fill out my father's term. That was also in the stars."

"Probably it was, now you mention it. Hal's a lucky man, on more than one count." Again, Bruce was astonished at the ease of his acceptance. Now that the words had been spoken, he knew he had been rehearsing them as diligently as Janet. The kisses they had shared at Five Oaks, their operatic love-making in a Hollywood hacienda and a hotel in Algiers, had been part of the same *commedia dell' arte*—a scenario that Janet herself had composed, to postpone the duty she was discharging now. He, too, had played his part in that scenario—and his performance had been more than adequate. He had never hoped to leave the set so tranquilly, once it was time to forget make-believe.

"I tried to write you this morning," said Janet. "It seemed fairer—telling you this way. Think what you like of me, I'm not a coward."

"You were never that."

"The moment I heard your voice, I knew you'd understand." Janet's own voice seemed to come from a great distance, though it was clear enough.

"Of course I understand. And I wish you every happiness."

"Wish it for both of us. For Hal as well as me."

"Isn't that asking a lot?"

"Shane did—and she's been in love with him for a long time."

"Perhaps we should cry on each other's shoulders."

"She's in New York. Would you like the number?"

"I'll write it down, if you like."

"It's Murray Hill 1-5890. Good-bye, Bruce. I'm sorry things turned out this way."

"So am I, Janet."

He stared for a while at Swenson's phone after he had hung up on his call. Then, obeying an impulse he did not pause to question, he took it up again, to ask for the New

York number Janet had given him. . . . The white light in his brain was still blinding, but he had begun to adjust to its radiance.

It was strange he had needed the full impact of this rejection to open his eyes at last, to show that it was Shane he desired with all his being—that he had loved her from the moment they had sought to cheat each other's loneliness in a walk-up on S Street. It was stranger still that he felt the need to hold back even now. Did he hesitate because Shane herself had not asked him to make this call? Or did he wonder if he had found his true reason for being, only to lose it?

His heart was thudding painfully while the number went through the station switchboard. Something alerted him instantly, when he heard the sharp double *ting* in New York. Long before another woman's voice had answered, he knew his worst forebodings had come true.

"The James Lowell Society."

"Perhaps I have a wrong number. May I ask your address?"

"We're at 247 Park Avenue, sir."

"Are you part of Michael Derwent's firm?"

"We're on the floor above Mr. Derwent, sir. Who is calling, please?"

"Do you have a Miss McLendon in your office?"

"Miss McLendon is working here on a special project. *Who is calling?*"

"Will you tell her that Colonel Bruce Graham will be in New York tomorrow?"

"If you wish, Colonel, I'll connect you now."

"Tomorrow will do nicely."

He sat for a long time at Swenson's desk before he picked up the phone for the last time, to dial the Transport Service at the base and ask for an overnight berth to New York. Not since a night in Washington—when he had turned into a bar for a dash of Dutch courage before taking his bus to Camp Bruckner—had he felt so alone.

"If you don't unbend a little," said Shane, "I'm not sure we can talk at all."

"We've always been able to talk before."

"Up to now, our minds have met—even when they've collided. Why don't we back up and start over?"

They had been sparring in this vein, not at all gently, from the moment Bruce had entered Shane's office. Ever since he had taken the visitor's chair—to face her across a wide, glass-topped desk—he had found her more desirable than his wildest dreams. And yet, after the first words they had exchanged, he had never felt more deeply hostile. The need to declare his love despite the barriers dividing them was matched only by the need to wound her—to show, beyond all doubting, that he had reached the limits of his patience.

"Stop behaving as though I were your worst enemy," said Shane. "How can I explain what I'm doing here, if you won't even *pretend* to listen?"

Bruce got to his feet and crossed to the window. Outside, the canyons of Manhattan were beginning to darken. He spoke with his eyes on the shrouded concrete mass.

"It's true, then?" he asked. "This *is* the nerve center of the James Lowell Society?"

"These are national headquarters. Would you like a guided tour?"

"I'd loathe it."

"They've expanded, to take in a whole floor. The *Bulletin* alone employs ten copywriters. We've a psychiatrist from Columbia to set its tone—"

"Spare me the mumbo jumbo. Just explain where you fit in."

"Mike's on another job this month," said Shane. "I agreed to sit in, when I wasn't chasing copy."

"How are you helping?"

"Actually, it's a special project—a brochure for Hal's campaign. He wanted me to see it through the press."

"Hal was only appointed this afternoon to fill Josselyn's

place. He has a year to serve. Isn't it a little soon to start campaigning?"

"Not for a Senate seat. We knew this appointment was coming, after Lucius became ill. Here's the result of our thinking." Shane opened a desk drawer to take out a glossy pamphlet. It featured an eye-catching cover, showing Hal's profile against a backdrop of Allied flags, a chromatic montage in which the Stars and Stripes dwarfed all the others.

"Was this printed in *anticipation* of the event?"

"Of course," said Shane. "Senator Josselyn would have retired in any case, before Congress convened. Our format's still tentative. We'll improve it later."

"Starting with the cover art, I hope."

"The cover's a bit theatrical," said Shane. "It's on the right track. At least it makes its point—and Hal's."

"America forever—with a good man the flag-bearer, and instant death to the bad guys?"

"Yes—if you must oversimplify."

Bruce accepted the pamphlet and turned its lavishly illustrated pages. "Did you put this together?"

"The layouts are Mike's," said Shane. "I did most of the writing."

Flipping the pages, he was only faintly ill at what he saw: Derwent's style, after all, was familiar. The brochure summed up Hal's career: the big man on his campus, the hard-hitting young district attorney, the congressman who had done so much to put the American war machine in gear. Two facing pages showed Hal in uniform: the section was climaxed by Shane's now-famous column describing the Salerno jump. The final pages pictured Hal and Senator Josselyn at the last bond rally the senator had attended. It was followed by a paste-up of today's headlines, announcing Josselyn's death and Hal's appointment to the vacant seat.

"As you'll observe," said Shane, "we've several gaps to fill before the show hits the road."

"It seems complete enough, as advertisements go."

"Mike plans to send it out this spring. The day after Hal announces his candidacy for the full term."

"There's no mention of a tie-in with the James Lowell Society."

"No tie-in is planned, Bruce. The Society is staying out of politics completely."

"Surely it's giving Senator Reardon its endorsement."

"It can hardly do less. It has far bigger goals than a Senate election."

"Are you still pretending there's no connection between Hal and the Lowellites?"

"The Lowellites are dedicated to world peace—with a strong America behind it. So is Hal. The connection ends there."

"I've heard that argument *ad nauseam*. Granted, the support of the James Lowell Society is valuable to a politician. What I can't swallow is your belief that its big-stick approach will work."

"Are you sure it's the Lowellites you're against, and not Hal?"

"I'm against both—since he's been their cheerleader from the start."

"And I'm supporting both," said Shane. "I'm giving Hal Reardon my best, because he deserves my best. I think he'll sweep this fall election—and become a significant figure in postwar America."

"Providing Mike Derwent merchandises him properly?"

"Ideas and men need marketing, if they're to reach the public. I wrote that brochure to offer America a citizen-soldier who believes he can outlaw war. I'd call it fair comment—and I'll expect him to justify every word."

"Even if he and Janet go into the White House? The one place *you* can't follow him?"

Bruce had used the question as his trump card. Expecting

an explosion, he was thrown off balance completely by Shane's peal of laughter.

"Are you under the delusion I'm about to become Hal's mistress? On a full or part-time basis?"

"What else could I think, after what happened in Algiers?"

"Who told you what happened in Algiers? What's the basis for this slander—beyond your romantic imagination?"

"You can't deny you were seen everywhere."

"Of course we were. Usually en route to dine with officers of the Theater Command. In Algiers, Colonel Reardon was much too busy to think of making love to me—even if he'd been so inclined. His off-duty energy was used to mend fences with Lucius Josselyn."

"Are you pretending that your relations with Hal have always been platonic?"

"I said nothing of the sort, Bruce. It's none of your damned business, but I did hope to ignite a spark—before he closed in on his true objective. It's quite another setup, now his marriage plans are official."

"Have you surrendered all personal claims?"

"I never had personal claims. Just as you had no lease on Janet's future. From where I'm sitting at this moment, I'd say you'd begun to get over that delusion. I've got sense enough to give up mine."

"Then you're supporting Senator Reardon, with no hope of reward?"

"To my mind, he's what this confused, big-rich country needs. Granted, he can be a poseur when it suits the occasion. Granted, he has a will like a juggernaut. What great man doesn't?"

"You honestly think he belongs with the great?"

"I think he could—someday. If I'm right, my reward will be the knowledge I helped to put him there."

Bruce breathed deep before he tossed the brochure on the desk. "I'm sorry we've come to the parting of the ways," he said. "If I could, I'd buy what you have to sell. The effort's beyond me."

Shane put out her hand to touch his arm with a restraining —and oddly compelling—gesture. "You knew Jimmie Lowell —and admired him. There's one thing you *can* do to keep his memory green. Whether you agree with the Society or not."

"It's hard to believe, but I'm listening."

"I'm sure you heard they plan to found a rehabilitation center near Concord. The Lowell Sanitarium. If the Society continues to grow at its present rate, the cornerstone will be laid next year. Would you accept the post of director?"

"Is this idea yours or Hal's?"

"He asked me to mention it. Apparently he made you a similar offer in Los Angeles."

"So he did. I'd half forgotten."

"Once this center's in operation, it will help far more veterans than you could save in the Army. With your war record, you'd be the ideal man to run it—"

"And the ideal front for the Lowellites? Or should I say, for Derwent's sick brainchild?"

"Won't you at least think it over?"

"You can have my answer now, Shane. I prefer to fight this war in uniform—and to go back to Lakewood when it ends."

"This is good-bye, then?"

"A long good-bye."

"Not if you'll see the light," said Shane.

"I'll leave you with the same forlorn hope."

They did not speak again, while their eyes met and held. The urge to take Shane McLendon in his arms—and kiss her unhappy frown away—had never been greater. Love was a dull knife at his heart, probing without pity. But his anger and disappointment were still greater as he turned to the door that opened to the corridor.

When he stepped into a waiting elevator, he realized that the glass panel had shattered under the force of his closing.

San Francisco

Bruce had not been on deck when his ship steamed under the great new bridge spanning the Golden Gate. Using canvas slings to supplement regular berths, he had taken nearly fourteen hundred casualties on this voyage to the States— and last-minute tasks had kept him at his desk. . . . He had heard the news of the German surrender during his morning rounds. When he joined Captain Swenson on the bridge, the *Helen S Peters* had crossed San Francisco Bay to its moorings. The city itself and the hills on which it sat were drowned in fog. May in California seemed almost cold, after the crossing from Okinawa.

The unloading had become second nature to the 241st, after eighteen months of mercy steaming. In the far places of the Pacific, in Sydney and Auckland and Manila, Bruce had seen identical files of stretcher cases and walking wounded move from ship to shore. It had not been too different at Pearl Harbor and San Pedro and Seattle, while he had cruised on courses that now seemed as well-worn as the grooves of his palm.

This morning, the ambulances and buses were even more efficient than usual: in another hour, these patients would begin their next stage of recuperation at the Army's famous Letterman General and other installations in the Bay area.

The surgeon's quiet pride in that knowledge was far more real than this latest view of an America shrouded in gray-white vapor. For a long time, the country of his birth had been remote from his daily round, if not from his concern. He was none too eager to resume contact.

"The morning papers are aboard," said Captain Swenson. "Do you want to read them now or later?"

"Later—when I've realized I'm home again. I still can't believe the future of the world is being settled in that fog bank."

"Nor can I, if you refer to the architects of the United Nations. Do you plan to attend the Conference?"

"I'd like to."

"Its methods should be worth observing," said the skipper. "What's happening now in San Francisco *could* be more significant than today's news from abroad." He looked down at the diminishing bustle on the quay, and the wisps of sun that had begun to outline the streets beyond. "I wish I could be more sanguine of the outcome."

"The Allies have just ended one part of the war. This time, they may have luck at the peace table."

"Perhaps they will, Colonel. To my mind, it's unrealistic to plunge into peacemaking so quickly."

"Even to create a parliament of man?"

"The war is not yet over. Japan is still alive. The peacemakers themselves are far from agreement, if we can believe the reports."

"Today's news may be better."

"I doubt it," said Swenson. "America lost its strongest voice when Roosevelt died. The British are divided, with a change of government impending. The Russians have never been more truculent—"

"At least, they're conferring."

"What's your real opinion, Colonel Graham? At this stage of human evolution, is world peace a pious slogan—or a hope?"

Bruce shook his head—and turned toward the bridge ladder. "I have no opinions this morning. Before I can set a course, I'll have to stay topside awhile, and take fresh bearings."

"San Francisco is a good place for that," said Captain Swenson. "To my mind, it's one of the world's most civilized cities. Give yourself time to enjoy it before you sail again. You'll find it excellent medicine."

It was after twelve when the surgeon left the record room—but the log of the voyage was a closed book.

He had just put a fresh star beside the complement's record, another ocean crossing without the loss of a single patient. As always, a first-rate performance had carried its own penalty. Word had just reached him that the ship had been ordered west again as soon as fresh supplies could be loaded, to serve a battle station half a world away.

Knowing he could postpone contact no longer, he picked up copies of the *Chronicle* and the *Examiner* in the lounge, carried them to his cabin, and bolted the door against interruptions. Shane McLendon's column sprang out of the *Examiner*'s front page. He had seen these examples of her reporting whenever American papers reached the ship. It had given him an illusion of continuity to read her coverage of the European war before and after D day. Later, as the first woman journalist ashore in the Philippines, and one of the first at Okinawa, she had seemed even closer.

During the last national campaign, when Hal Reardon had run for a full Senate term, Shane had returned to support him. She had followed him down the campaign trail. Today, as Bruce had expected, she was reporting from San Francisco, where Hal was serving with the American delegation to the United Nations Treaty Conference. It was an honor he had richly earned—as a ranking Democrat, a distinguished veteran, and a statesman whose views on foreign affairs commanded wide attention. Returned to office last fall by a landslide vote, he had stumped the country ever since to expound those views. Today's *As I See It* was a restatement of the senator's credo—and a ringing endorsement.

On surface, Hal's formula for peace with honor seemed entirely reasonable. Bruce was positive it had already been hailed by a sizable minority of the electorate—including the James Lowell Society, which had given the senator blanket support at the polls. America, in Hal's view, must dominate the emerging union of nations—because of its present muscle, and its contribution to victory in Europe. Once again, he insisted that the proposed Security Council—the power core of the UN, an eleven-nation body with the five great powers as permanent members—must be organized to make the American vote decisive.

Since it was unlikely that an international police force would emerge from the UN Conference, Hal repeated his now-familiar demand that America's strength be used as a workable substitute—at least, until world peace was more than an idealist's dream. Last and most important—so far as the San Francisco meeting was concerned—Hal issued a stern warning, a direct quote that formed the climax of Shane's column. Unless there was some compromise on the veto power of the Security Council, he would vote for an American boycott.

As I See It was careful to note that Senator Reardon spoke only for himself, and the body of public opinion behind him: by and large, his stand was opposed to that of the White House—though he had every wish to remain loyal to the new President in these trying times. However, considering the strength of his public support, outright rejection of his views could have unfortunate consequences. . . . Shane hinted that such consequences would be spelled out later—if the treaty-makers failed to meet this all-American firebrand half-way. . . .

The *Chronicle*, like the *Examiner*, blossomed with head-lines proclaiming the collapse of German resistance. There was still room for a story announcing that Senator Reardon's wife (the former Janet Josselyn) had arrived in San Francisco to join her husband at the Mark Hopkins. She would entertain the treaty-makers that afternoon at cocktails.

Cheek-by-jowl with this item was a column even better known than Shane's—the syndicated *World Beat*, by Lewis Carleton. A former theater press agent, Carleton had made giant strides in journalism, thanks to the new horizons the war had offered him. Over the years, his barbed wit had grown sharper—and, though he still discussed world affairs with the same vocabulary he had used to describe the passing Broadway scene, he had won readers by the million. A tireless drum-beater for any cause that displayed his ability to bore from within, he was also in San Francisco. Today's column took the opposite tack from Shane's.

Reporting from ringside at the UN Conference, *World Beat* admitted the portents were dire. However, it reminded the public that most treaty-makers had found it easier to come to blows than to agree—especially when dissenters like Senator Reardon were on hand to sound off. In Carleton's view, the proposals Hal had offered deserved a loud rejection, not only from his counterparts at the Conference, but from supporters at home. His demand for American police power, said Carleton, would only create enemies among our present allies. His posture as a guardian of American privilege was an echo from an isolationist past, as grotesque as the struttings of the European dictators who had drowned their continent in blood.

The column, like most of Carleton's efforts, created more heat than light. Bruce could see that this polemic, skirting libel by a hair, had been inspired more by spite than by solid disagreement. *World Beat*, though it demolished the Reardon formula, produced no alternate of its own: its hint of Götterdämmerung had been tossed in as window dressing. It was a travesty of logic that this former gossip-peddler should speak with the tongues of angels on one front page—while Shane McLendon echoed Hal's jingoism on another.

Flinging the *Chronicle* across his cabin in the wake of the *Examiner,* Bruce settled in his bunk: it was a long time since he had felt quite so helpless, or so exhausted. Already, he wished he were at sea again—leaving a troubled world down the horizon, putting his long duel with Hal Reardon from his mind. . . . And yet, even as he groped toward sleep, he realized escape was useless. Foggy though his mind was at the moment, he saw that this cruise to San Francisco had been foreordained.

Before his ship turned west again, he would settle that duel, for good and all. Despite their long separation, his love for Shane had never been more steadfast. Until he convinced himself that Hal Reardon was her true lodestar, he had no other course.

It was night when he wakened—clearheaded, if not too refreshed—to answer Eric Badger's knock. His deputy entered the cabin breezily, behind a cocktail shaker.

"Alice Stacey and I are having dinner in Oakland—at Trader Vic's. Why not join us?"

"If you don't mind, I'll take a rain check."

"The log is closed, Bruce. I've just come from the record room."

"We'll be taking cargo tomorrow. Make sure you're back by reveille, in reasonable shape. Phil Owen's on a two-day pass. We'll have to make up the pharmacy list between us."

"Don't tell me you're going to sit and brood—just because you're in the same town with Hal Reardon."

"Forgive me—but I'm in no state to discuss Senator Reardon."

"There's nothing I'd rather skip—as you well know," said the man from Wisconsin. "I still feel it's my duty to tell you he's speaking on the Blue Network at eight o'clock."

"What's the occasion this time?"

"A hundred-dollar plate dinner for the local chapter of the James Lowell Society."

"There must be some way to avoid exposure."

"You can try Oakland with us. He'll be on the PA system, if you stay aboard. Most of the complement's planning to listen."

"Even the ones who disagree with him?"

"Most of them enjoy the sound of his voice," said Badger. "So does most of San Francisco. This morning at Letterman, I discussed him with three medical officers. Two of them thought he made more sense than any politician since the late President. The third—with no prompting from me—called him the devil's advocate behind an all-American mask."

"Too bad the percentage wasn't reversed."

"That isn't all," said Badger. "On the way back, my taxi driver informed me that Reardon did more to liberate Europe than most of our generals. I needed self-control to forget Operation Treetop at Salerno."

"Salerno's well-buried, Eric. You'd better collect your date, before someone else does."

When his second-in-command had departed, Bruce took out his best uniform, though he had no destination in mind and his mood was anything but festive. It was well after eight when he followed the boat deck to the radio room. Hal's voice—vibrant, with sincerity—reached him at once. Expecting that rich baritone to raise his hackles, he had braced for its impact. He was unprepared for the cheer that greeted Hal's proclamation of America's sacred mission to make the war worth fighting—a duty more solemn than ever, now its European phase had ended.

When he paused in the shadow of a stanchion, he saw that a dense crowd of listeners was grouped at the door of the radio room, where the broadcast could be heard most clearly. Feeling his mind sink in a black pit of doubt, he marveled anew at the spell Hal Reardon could weave with no apparent effort—at the well-timed pauses, the thundering *crescendi*, the overall sense of rightness. Measured against these forensic gifts, the speaker's actual words seemed unimportant. There was no doubting his deep emotion as he berated the men of little faith, in Washington and abroad, who already seemed willing to settle for a cut-rate peace. . . .

Minutes after he had descended the promenade-deck ladder, Bruce had forgotten the thread of Hal's discourse. A final burst of applause, when he ended his last, towering challenge to his country's enemies, was chilling evidence that communion with his audience had been complete.

The need to leave the ship was now overwhelming. At the gangway, Bruce heard his name called. The radio operator was hurrying toward him with a message.

"I didn't know you were aboard, sir. This just arrived. I was listening to the Senator's broadcast and nearly forgot it."

Taking the wire to the check-out desk, Bruce swallowed his reprimand: the ship was in port, and the operator's lapse excusable. He had just seen fifty people—many of them intelligent, some highly educated—spellbound by Hal Reardon.

The telegram was from Shane. She would be at the Top of the Mark at nine thirty, and hoped he would join her there.

With an hour to spare, he took a taxi to the Embarcadero and wandered among the boat sheds, where stevedores were sweating under the arc lights to load supplies for battlefronts in the Pacific. The feeling that he was part of this activity restored his detachment. He was calm enough when he left the waterfront and entered a bar on Powell Street— an oasis whose outer wall, built to resemble the beam of a whaler, suggested it was a local rendezvous.

The Snug Harbor was empty at this hour, save for a broad-shouldered barman—who, to the visitor's surprise, was deep in a book beside his cash register. Cauliflower ears and a badly repaired nose suggested the prize ring. They were strange contrasts to the volume on the bar, Veblen's *The Theory of the Leisure Class*.

"What'll it be, sir?"

"Bourbon and water, please."

The man's eyes, alert as black mica in their sparrow-pouches, studied his only customer intently while he filled a glass. The scrutiny included the double row of campaign ribbons—and the silver eagles Bruce had received a month ago.

"You've seen a lot of war, Colonel."

"More than enough."

"Do those snakes mean you're a doctor? I'm never sure."

"I'm commanding officer of a hospital ship."

"The big one at Pier Twelve? If we weren't still fighting Japs, I'd have sworn it was the *Lurline*."

"You aren't too far off. The *Helen S Peters* was a cruise liner."

"Where did you come from—if that isn't classified?"

"Nothing we do is classified. We crossed direct from Okinawa."

"Is it true you're painted white to warn off subs?"

"That's the general idea. It's worked so far—except for a freak hit at Salerno."

"What about those suicide planes? The kamikazes?"

"Two of them made runs at us on our last voyage—then veered off." Bruce found himself relaxing a trifle; the man's interest was too deep to be contrived. "When hospitals are involved, most nations respect each other's rights."

"Wouldn't you think they'd try respecting each other all the way?"

"The UN Conference is working on that angle."

"So the papers tell us, Colonel. Course, that depends on what paper you read."

"Some of the columnists say you can't abolish war with a debating society."

"The UN will do better than that," said the barman. "I've

listened to sessions at the Veterans' Building—where they're hammering out the charter. They may come up with results, if they stick to the rules."

"I hope you're right. It seems a tall order to a man who's just come ashore."

"Writing a peace treaty is a headache in any language," said the barman. "Specially, if they start arguing *now* about who's going to settle the first quarrel."

"It seems you've been sampling opinions on Senator Reardon."

"Did you hear his speech tonight?"

"Only the end. I'm afraid I've heard that speech before." Again, Bruce was surprised at his sense of ease. On shipboard, he had found Hal Reardon's rocket-bursts of rhetoric more than he could bear. In a Powell Street bar, it seemed natural to speak his mind. "Do you approve of his views?"

"Reardon's on the ball when he says we'll have trouble with Russia. Just the same, we have to live in the same world with Moscow—even if they're itching to backstab us. So long as we both stay inside the United Nations, we've a chance to knock down that knife."

"Reardon thinks we should run the show—in the Security Council."

"I know he does, Colonel—and he's way off base. Nowadays, no country on earth can make the world behave. Just as there's no bartender strong enough to double as his own bouncer."

"I take it you speak from experience."

"I own the Snug Harbor, free and clear. When the Embarcadero closes, we'll have longshoremen stacked at this counter three deep. Mostly, they blow off steam without quite swinging on one another. When they do start trading punches, I'll have friends in the crowd to break things up, before blood gets spilled. Then the house buys a free round—and sweeps up the broken teeth. It's a rough system, but I've yet to lose my license."

"How did you figure it out?"

"You might say I'd had special training. In my younger days, I was a hot club fighter—one of the fastest middleweights in town. When I turned twenty-five, I decided to quit the game before I got punchy. I'd already bought a half-interest in this gin mill, so I decided to go into the saloon business full time. Since then, I've found you can't beat selling liquor across a counter. Nothing on earth makes people better company—until they hoist too many."

"I gather the Snug Harbor's a good investment."

"Tending bar can be fun—if you don't lose your sense of humor. When things are slack, I read books I never had time for, and pretend I understand them. When things are jumping, I wouldn't trade this bird's-eye view of the human race for any job you could offer me—providing I stay on my own side of the mahogany, and don't have to break up fights."

"How did you operate in the old days?"

"Like a high-school coach cooling a locker-room argument. If it was a two-man beef, I'd take both men by the scruff, and bang their heads together. Usually they piped down afterwards. Sometimes they even shook hands."

"Isn't that Reardon's formula for America, if we're elected world policeman?"

"If we're offered that job—and take it—we'll be the fall guys of our century. The boys in Washington would only get their lumps—like I got mine."

"What happened?"

"It was an offbeat fight, Colonel. One man was nearly as big as me. The other was runt-sized. I banged their heads extra hard, to make sure they behaved. They were meek enough afterwards—or so I thought. When I locked up for the night, they were *both* waiting in the alley. Broke my arm, and caved in my face with a manhole cover. After I left the hospital, I decided to quit peacemaking."

"Maybe Senator Reardon could profit by your example."

"I think he could. Right now, he figures he can wade into

any Donnybrook from here to Zanzibar and come out alive—
if they give him a big enough blackjack. Maybe he *would*
stop a few fights among the runts. Sooner or later, the runts
would gang up on him, and he'd finish like me—on his back
in the gutter."

"Unfortunately, Reardon hasn't had your experience," said
Bruce. "He's yet to start an argument he can't finish."

"Let's hope he loses this one, and loses fast. The way I
see it, we have just one choice—to go into this world parliament as an equal, not as the big boss."

"Not even the big brother?"

"Naturally, we want our fair share of the future—but that
still means one vote for one country. And God help us all,
if too many hoods stay outside in the alley."

"One vote for one country makes sense today," said
Bruce. "The UN won't have much over fifty members at
the start. What happens ten years from now, or twenty?
When things get really crowded?"

"That problem can be handled—if there *is* a UN in twenty
years. We've broken up worse logjams in Congress, and got
the right laws on the books."

Bruce put his empty glass on the bar and shook his head
at the offer of a refill.

"Has it occurred to you that you could pass for a philosopher?"

"All barmen are philosophers, Colonel. How else could
we face our customers without gagging?"

"Present company excepted, I hope."

"Present company's always excepted. That's how we stay
in business."

"Would you mind, if I tried to get your ideas in print?"

"I wouldn't mind at all. Like you see, I'm happy to sound
off to anyone. Some of my best friends are reporters."

"This is a rather special reporter. I'd like to send her
round, if she'll come. Her name is Shane McLendon."

"Miss McLendon's one of my favorites. We've had some

good talks right at this bar—before she began touting Reardon."

Bruce held out his hand. "My name is Graham."

"Henry Morgan, Colonel Graham. Same as the well-known buccaneer. They christened me Enrique Martinez—but I changed when I opened my first saloon. It doesn't help, being a Mexican in California. Not if you sell booze."

"I'll keep your secret, Mr. Morgan. And thanks for everything."

"What have I done for you—besides bend your ear?"

"You've put me back in the mainstream. Whatever that means."

The Top of the Mark, at the summit of the famous hotel, was a vast circular room whose windows commanded four quadrants of the horizon. Tonight, one of the world's most spectacular views was blanketed in fog—but the crowd that jammed each inch of space, intent on celebrating the news from Europe into another dawn, seemed unaware of the looming dark. Caught in the press at the door, Bruce saw Shane at once at a table beside a picture window—on a dais that set it apart from the others.

He had expected to find her changed after their long separation—but that first glimpse was shocking enough. She was far thinner than he remembered. The gaunt planes of her face were accented by the lighting, and her manner seemed almost feverish as she argued a point with the man at her table. The change, Bruce knew, was Hal Reardon's work. This, he thought grimly, was the reward she had reaped from a free-wheeling operator, who made no distinction between means and ends.

The revelation was all he needed to harden his resolve. He could even smile as he pushed through the crowd, stepped up to the dais, and bent to kiss her.

"Don't tell me it's been a long time," he said. "My luck's been bad until tonight."

Deep in discussion, Shane had not noticed his approach. The blush that stained her cheeks was an added confirmation of his diagnosis—and a reason, however slight, to hope that a cure was possible. It told him that the girl he loved had anticipated this meeting—and dreaded it—as much as he.

"This is Lewis Carleton, Bruce."

The columnist fitted his legend. He was small enough to pass for a retired jockey. The bright bow tie he wore, the enormous black-rimmed spectacles, and a perpetual smiling pout completed the outlandish pattern. Even after his damp handshake, Bruce needed a second look to realize the man was reeling drunk.

"Give me time, Colonel." Carleton's voice was low-pitched —a half-snarl, half-purr that combined the worst of both sounds. "I know the name's familiar."

"Lots of people have it, Mr. Carleton."

The columnist struck his temples with both palms: his domed head was dead-white, suggesting that he functioned far from the sun. "You're the surgeon from Scranton General—who tangled with Jake Sanford, back in forty-two. Am I right, Shane?"

"You usually are, Lew."

"The story Hal Reardon hushed up, for reasons of his own," said Carleton. "What really happened?"

Bruce glanced quickly at Shane. Her face was a patient blank. "Nothing of importance, I assure you," he said. "Sanford was planning a standard-brand persecution. You might say the fight ended in a draw."

"Jake's dead," said Shane. "Let him rest in peace."

"When did Sanford die?"

"Last week, in the Federal pen at Atlanta—where he'd gone for income tax fraud," said Carleton. "I can assure you that few of us shed a tear. Forgive me, Shane. It's obvious your friend won't enlighten me—and I'm sure you've better things to discuss than dead witch-hunters."

"You're quite right, Lew."

"The reformer who has lost contact with reality remains a fascinating topic. Don't you agree, Colonel?"

Aware of what was coming, Bruce answered steadily. "If you're asking my opinion as a doctor, I'll repeat what I once told a Sanford admirer. The man needed a psychiatrist."

"My sentiments exactly," said Carleton. "Even so, I doubt if psychiatry would have helped Jake much. There's no known cure for elephantiasis of the ego. Such men carry the seeds of their own destruction. Whether they're called Sanford or Reardon."

Shane took the broadside calmly. "Can't you stop slandering Hal for a minute?"

"Not for a minute, my dear. Even though you refuse to take the dare."

"I've already asked you to go, Lew."

The columnist rose with tipsy dignity. "I'm on my way, before we come to blows. I did plan to have my nightcap here—with a man who's seen war firsthand. Instead, I'll proceed to the Snug Harbor. Good-bye, Colonel."

Bruce accepted a second damp but clinging handshake. "Do you know the Snug Harbor?"

"And its loquacious owner, Henry Morgan."

"I've just come from there."

"Henry's famous in Frisco. Visiting reporters call him the Powell Street Plato."

"I was about to ask Shane to interview him."

"Don't. She has other uses for her column these days. I won't elaborate—since you're part of her loyal public."

"Don't wear out your welcome, Lew," said Shane.

"Before I go, Colonel Graham—will you give *me* an interview?"

"I'm afraid I've no story you'd find quotable."

"Don't be too sure of that. Call me at this hotel tomorrow, if you change your mind." Carleton took a quick step backward, as Shane's chin rose higher. "Turn off the deep freeze, my dear. This time I'm really going. Thanks for the visit—even though you were better company in your pre-Reardon phase." He left the dais, working his way among the tables with the painful skill of the intoxicated.

"I never planned to expose you to that rumpot," said Shane. "Sometimes he's even more offensive."

"I wish he'd stayed. Much as I hate to agree with Lewis Carleton, he may be right."

"About me? Or Henry Morgan?"

"Actually, I was thinking of a girl I met three years ago—in a Washington bar. She'd have jumped at the chance to interview a man like Henry. Whatever happened to her?"

Shane's lips tightened. "I asked you here to find out if we speak the same language, Bruce. Don't give me too rough a time."

"At least there's hope for us—if this *is* a reunion."

"If you'll meet me halfway, it will be."

"That bartender on Powell Street is an American citizen. An ordinary man, who wonders how the peace is shaping up. Doesn't he deserve a column? Or have you lost touch with ordinary citizens?"

"I've talked with Henry often. I know his views by heart. They don't have much relevance to you or me."

"Because he happens to differ with Hal Reardon? Is that already a crime?"

"I was wondering when we'd get back to Hal."

"We've never been away. He's the real reason I'm here."

"We want you on our side, Bruce. Both of us. You've been away much too long."

"What possible use can Hal have for me now?"

"He wants to go on being your friend. You've had eighteen months to make up your mind about him—and his ideas. That's time enough to form a judgment."

"It's been more than enough—thanks to the Lowell *Bulletins* and your columns."

"History's on our side," said Shane. "So are the voters."

"How many voters, and what kind? The Lowell Society

has a different breed of sponsor these days, as you well know."

"I was waiting for *that* objection too."

"It's well worth making, Shane. Look at the names on Derwent's letterhead nowadays. Fossils who wish McKinley were still in the White House. Fat cats who give their tax-free dollar to keep the *status quo*. I was hoping to find you in better company."

"Won't you be fair—and let Hal answer your doubts?"

"We sail day after tomorrow. Judging by the papers and the radio, Senator Reardon's the busiest man in San Francisco. I hardly think he has time for a hospital-ship doctor."

"Hal is waiting for us now, one floor below."

"So it was he who sent that wire."

Bruce had half-risen with the words. He settled in his chair again, after Shane's pleading gesture.

"This is the last favor I'll ask of you," she said. "It's also our last chance to make contact. Let Hal defend the kind of America he believes in. Or walk out now, without seeing me again."

"In other words, put up or shut up?"

"Speaking bluntly—yes."

"I'll listen—if *you're* asking me."

"Shall we go straight down?"

"Senator Reardon can wait. Is that the suite he engaged for Janet?"

"She won't be back for a while, if you'd prefer to avoid her. At the moment, she's entertaining the California branch of the Lowell Society, at the St. Francis. Hal was the guest of honor, but he left after his speech."

"Shouldn't Janet be on hand, since this is his final effort to convert me?"

"She's been a good wife—but she doesn't follow Hal's politics. I'm not even sure she understands them."

"Are you sure *you* understand?"

Their voices had not quite reached the shouting stage—but

Bruce knew that heads had turned to hear their quarrel. Forcing himself to remain calm, he leaned across the table and took Shane's hands. Now that he was sure of himself—and his mission—he could afford to yield ground.

"Since it's what you want, we'll go downstairs in a moment," he said quietly. "Before we do, it's my duty as a doctor to say you've behaved like a damned fool."

"If you think I'm emotionally involved with Hal, you're wrong. I told you that was over in New York."

"I'll believe you faster, if you withdraw your backing."

"Has it occurred to you that Hal Reardon's career is partly my creation? That I might take pride in that creation—even after I'd surrendered the man himself?"

"I don't believe women give men up that easily."

"Believe what you like, then. Just promise to listen with an open mind."

"I'll risk it, Shane—for your sake. But I still think you're in a souped-up jalopy, riding for a crash."

"And I think Senator Reardon's headed for the top. If I'm wrong, I can always climb out of the wreckage."

"Not if you discover you're part of it."

"Just what does that cryptic remark signify?"

"Look in your mirror for the answer. You'll see what this demagogue has done to you."

"Hal isn't a demagogue. He never was. Why do you hate him so much?"

"Because I'm in love with you. And being in love, it hurts like hell to see you fall apart."

Shane drew in her breath sharply. "You might have told me this sooner."

"How could I, when your political masterpiece was always in the way?"

"May I ask when this great emotion began?"

"Don't ask me for dates. In the bar at Union Station—in your flat on S Street—does it matter? As you've remarked more than once, I'm a stubborn Scotsman. It took me quite awhile to sort things out. To admit I'd been snowed by an opportunist I once called a friend. And by a girl trademarked from birth to be his wife. What really hurts is the way *you've* drifted into his shadow. I can't stand by and watch you die there."

"Does this mean you won't go downstairs with me?"

"I've already promised to go. Suppose you lead the way."

On the residential floor below, Shane turned into the entry serving the Reardon suite and entered without knocking. The foyer, an ivory-and-gold rectangle, opened to a half-darkened salon. Tossing his cap on a table, Bruce saw that a life-sized photograph of Jimmie Lowell, framed in heraldic vine-leaves, hung on the wall above. The boy, dressed in the olive drab of his rifle company, glowing with the innocence of youth, seemed an odd intruder in this setting. An identical photograph, Bruce recalled, was now used as a frontispiece for each issue of the Lowell Society *Bulletin.* There was no identification beyond a blood-red caption.

America's First Sacrifice at Pearl Harbor

"Does Hal carry this icon on his travels?" he asked.

Shane, who had gone into the salon, spoke with icy precision before she touched a light switch. "Stop snapping, and make us a highball. Hal's on the phone. I'll tell him you're here."

It was the first word she had spoken since they left the Top of the Mark. Baffled by her reserve, unsure whether she had been stirred, however faintly, by his declaration, Bruce said nothing while she moved toward the inner rooms of the suite. He could hear Hal's voice clearly now, ending a call to an important personage he was addressing by his nickname. . . . At the bar, pouring two drinks without pausing to measure, he had all the sensations of a back-somersault into the past—to a hallway at Five Oaks, where he had stood before another door and heard another senator use the same tone.

He was still frowning at the memory when Shane emerged from the inner room and took her glass. Hal followed, so quickly it was impossible to doubt the entrance had been planned.

"I told you he'd come, Shane. Doesn't it show he loves us both?"

The senator was still in full evening dress, a garb that suited his greyhound slimness. On his left lapel, he wore the rosette of the Legion of Honor. Above it, a smaller ribbon signified that he had been awarded a Silver Star by his grateful government: Bruce recalled that each member of his unit had received the same decoration after Salerno. When Hal crossed the room with his hand extended, it was evident that he favored his right foot slightly. The shuffle did not impair his grace. Even the surgeon's trained eye could not be sure the limp was feigned.

Much later, reconstructing his first impression, Bruce realized that Hal's splendor had put the capstone on his resolve—the lines of that perfectly cut tailcoat, the gleam of a military decoration as precious as it was unearned. His response was primitive, the recoil of the hunter from the diamondback's rattle. Already, instinct had told him it was too late for compromise. Putting down an untasted drink, ignoring his host's hand, he turned toward the window—aware, even as he moved, that he resembled a sullen child rebelling at the tolerant wisdom of his elders.

"Is that limp a souvenir of Italy?" he asked.

"Only when the weather's damp," said Hal. "You're letting good whiskey go to waste, Bruce."

"I've changed my mind about a drink."

Hal stepped behind the bar to pour himself a brandy. "Let's not begin with a dogfight," he said equably. "We're here tonight to make peace."

Again, Bruce forced himself to ignore his classmate as he

turned to Shane. "I promised to hear one more speech from your alleged statesman," he said. "I'm keeping that promise. First, I'll ask a few questions."

"That's your privilege," said Shane. "It would help, if you remembered your manners."

"Our visitor's manners are above reproach," said Hal. "He knows I'm at his service."

"Question one's the hardest," said Bruce. "What's your game here?"

"If you mean the UN Conference, the answer's simple. I'm working night and day—to bring back a treaty the Senate can ratify."

"According to Shane's last column, you want the last word in the Security Council."

"That's always been my purpose," said Hal. "America alone can enforce peace."

"And blow the police whistle?"

"The United Nations will collapse unless mavericks are kept in line."

"Including the Soviet Union?"

"Naturally, Bruce. Millions of troubled people share that belief."

"Don't you mean misguided members of the Lowell Society?"

"It's easy to damn reactions you don't like," said Hal serenely. "Easy—and a trifle juvenile."

"Do you have real support in the American delegation?"

"Of course."

"Who—and how many?"

"Their names are secret."

"Because they happen to be your stooges? And Derwent's dug up enough dirt to keep them in line?"

Hal shrugged, but did not answer.

"Meanwhile, you're trying to stampede the others."

"I object to that description of my methods," said Hal. "Naturally, I'm using every persuasion at my command."

"Isn't it true your program would go down the drain, if you lost the support of the superpatriots? The fanatics who'd vote for anything that's wrapped in the right slogan? In a word, the Lowellites?"

"My support isn't confined to the Lowell Society," said Hal. "At this moment, I express America's best hope for tomorrow. Time and social evolution will show how right I am."

"Those are empty words, and you know it. Without the Lowellites, you'd be just another Deep South diehard."

Hal held up both hands for silence. "Surely we can spare Shane this absurd invective."

"Do *you* think it's absurd, Shane?"

"I think you're blinded by your prejudice." Shane had spoken slowly, with her eyes on her glass. "In your way, I'd call you as one-sided as Lew Carleton."

"Because I've told you who's supporting Hal—and why?"

"Because you've done nothing but call our host names, since you set foot here. After all, you were invited to listen."

"The floor is yours, Senator," Bruce said quietly. "You consider yourself a statesman-messiah. I've called you a state-house politician. Obviously, one of us is mistaken."

Hal leaned against the bar. Even now, his smile was as warm as his manner.

"Suppose we leave out personalities and stick to facts. Do you realize Poland and Rumania are already well on their way to becoming Soviet satellites? That others are sure to follow?"

"We heard that news in Okinawa. It isn't surprising. Communism is a devourer of others. It must go on devouring to survive."

"And you'd admit such monsters to the UN, as your *equal*?"

"A world organization should include the world."

"Moscow will be our next mortal enemy—now we've knocked out Hitler, and are ready to knock out Japan. We must keep the upper hand. It's part of the logic of survival."

"Admittedly, the Russians are a century behind us. They still deserve membership in the United Nations. It's the job of *all* the members to make them behave. We can't handle them alone."

"In my view, naked strength is the only argument a beast respects."

"So you're demanding the club for American hands? And the police whistle?"

"Someone must use them. There's no other way to peace."

"Isn't it true you want them for yourself?"

"So we're back to you and me again," said Hal. "I've told you I refuse to take second best for my country. Does that make me a dictator?"

"You'll take a giant step in that direction, if you get your way here." Again, Bruce turned to Shane. This time, he made no effort to mute his desperation. "Can't you hear me either? Won't you even try?"

Shane did not lift her eyes from her glass. "You've said your piece, twice over. If you've lost all sense of proportion, you might as well go."

"Your mind's as closed as his, then?"

"I'm supporting Hal and his program."

"Can I take you to your hotel?"

"It's a little late to be chivalrous. *I'm* at the Mark Hopkins too—and I must wait for Janet. She's promised to set up an interview with Sergeant Lowell's mother."

Hal's voice cut in smoothly. Stunned though he was by his utter failure, Bruce could still marvel at his enemy's sang-froid.

"Stay a little longer, Bruce. Janet will be heartbroken if she misses you."

"Shane feels I should leave—and she's right. Give Janet my best."

"As you wish. I'll walk you out."

Bruce turned to Shane—still in her armchair, and staring at her drink.

"If I thought you'd believe me," he said, "I'd tell you I was sorry. It was a waste of time to bring me here. A fearful waste—for us all."

Expecting no answer, he was surprised when he saw her cheeks were streaked with tears. Treasuring his one small triumph, he left the room quickly—afraid, even now, that he would yield to that unspoken plea for a truce.

In the foyer, Hal had opened a closet to extract an odd but familiar object, a satchel-shaped box covered in cowhide.

"Remember the recorder you brought into Jake Sanford's office? I've taken it everywhere, since I came back from the war. Janet calls it my good-luck charm."

"You don't need charms. You've made your own luck from the start."

"I promised to give it back when the war ended."

"The war isn't over yet."

"*Our* war is ended, I trust. I won't bear down on the fact I've won the final battle."

Bruce had already turned to the foyer table to pick up his cap. Looking at the giant photograph of Sergeant James Lowell, he had the eerie conviction that the boy's lips had just moved to convey a message. Before the fantasy died, he felt his brain come alive with a thought he could share with no one—least of all with the urbane man in evening dress who continued to face him, with a wire recorder extended in lieu of an olive branch.

"Sorry to contradict you one more time," he said. "But our war is just beginning."

Taking the recorder, he stepped into the hall. Before the door closed, he had a final glimpse of the suite. Shane McLendon had not left the armchair, and her head was still bowed.

It was the only memory Bruce took into the night. The

junior senator from Florida had merged with the furniture—
now that he had stumbled on a way to reduce him to his
proper size.

The hands of his wrist watch stood at noon when Bruce
wakened in his cabin, and his head had never been clearer.

The only confusing item was the cowhide-covered satchel
he had dropped on his desk after his return from the Mark
Hopkins. He stared at it owlishly before he rose: in a way,
that box summed up Hal Reardon's arrogance. . . . This
morning, he could regret that the dynamite it might have
triggered was no longer available, thanks to the order he had
given at Salerno. Now that another weapon was at hand,
the lack did not seem too important.

It was almost one, and he was finishing a quick check of
his supply lists, when the OD appeared to announce a
visitor.

"It's Lew Carleton, sir. I checked him against his police
card. He says he has a noon appointment."

"I left a note at his hotel, asking him to stop by. Take him
to my cabin. I'll be there in a moment."

The columnist was pacing Bruce's quarters when he
entered, with his attention riveted on the recorder. In the
bath of sun at the ports, he seemed more than ever a creature
of the night—but his handshake was firm, and his bloodshot
eyes did not waver.

"You're late, Mr. Carleton."

"My hangovers need time to subside, Colonel. The one I
had this morning would have shamed Nero. Do you have a
top secret in that recorder?"

"The recorder's empty. The story I promised you begins
in Washington almost three years ago. It can be verified
easily, with your connections there."

"May I use this desk to make notes?"

"Of course. I hope you can take shorthand."

"I was a stenographer before I decided to be a writer."

Bruce took a turn of the cabin, while the columnist settled at his desk. Clear-cut though his plan now was, he was uncertain how to begin.

"The purpose of this meeting is to head off Senator Reardon. Until I know more about you, I'm not sure I'll give you the facts."

"My views are an open book, Colonel Graham. I'll admit some pages are on the murky side."

"Do you really support the concepts of the United Nations? You weren't just baiting Miss McLendon last night?"

"Baiting Shane is always a pleasure—but my argument was sincere. I'm all for world government, even if it never happens."

"A one-country, one-vote UN? The kind that's shaping up at the Conference?"

"It's the only deal that has a sporting chance, Colonel."

"May I have your reasons?"

"Don't think this is a *non sequitur*—but they tie in with my analysis."

"Somehow, I can't see you on the couch."

"It goes back to my first year on *World Beat*. Everyone loved me—when I was a press agent. Now that I was cutting their hearts out, those same people had begun calling me nasty names. So I went to the headshrinker. I told him I *enjoyed* being a schlemiel—and asked him if I was worth curing."

"Don't pretend he stopped you from being one."

Carleton leaned back in his chair with a deep guffaw. "On the contrary. Dr. Krantz is tops in his profession. After three months, he convinced me that I was meant to be tops in mine—that I'd stumbled on my salvation. In other words, being a Grade A bastard was my natural calling."

"So you've worked at it harder than ever—until you're the biggest one around?"

"You're with me, Colonel Graham. Whenever I feel a destructive impulse coming on, I put it in my column—and my tensions vanish. Repeat my experience on a global scale, and you have the United Nations. Persuade fifty-odd countries to meet under one roof, let them yap at each other in public, and you'll burn up some of the excess bile that leads to war. It's worth a tryout, even if the show flops on opening night."

"Hal Reardon has somewhat different views."

"Senator Reardon's a bigger bastard in his field than I am in mine. A wheel horse from away back who thinks he belongs in the Kentucky Derby. An operator who's yet to latch onto an idea that isn't secondhand."

"Some people think he's done a fine job in Congress."

"Only because he's been smart enough to con the right people—and smooth enough to star on every committee he's joined. Naturally, he's trying to star at this San Francisco clambake. So far, he's been making too much progress for my peace of mind. Do you *really* have a way to head him off?"

"I think I do, Mr. Carleton—with your help. We'll see, after one more question. Hal wants America to run the world, after the shooting stops. Why is he so positive we can?"

"I can make an educated guess," said the columnist. "You've been out of the country for a while. Probably you haven't heard of a Sunday punch our government has in reserve—"

"Rumors of that sort come out of every war."

"Originally, it was Germany that had the big bang. Now it's supposed to be us. If the story's true, Hal's in on the deal—through the Armed Services Committees in both Houses."

"The big-stick argument's real, then?"

"If he wins this power play at the UN Conference, it could be his selling point. You might even say he has demented logic on his side."

"Why demented?"

"Because if there *is* a big bang in our arsenal—and we use

it to end World War II—other countries will copy the formula for World War III. If that happens, we'll need this world debating club more than ever, to keep from using it on each other."

Studying Carleton's pout, and the steady eyes above it, Bruce made his decision swiftly. The man was a rusty instrument for the operation he had in mind, but he would serve.

"You've passed your test," he said. "I think you understand Hal—and the harm he can do, if he isn't tripped up hard."

"Give me the trip wire, Colonel. I'll do the job."

"Actually, Hal himself isn't to be mentioned in your story."

"Why not, if I'm to preside at his execution?"

"You aren't being asked to kill Senator Reardon. Only to draw his fangs."

"Give me the pliers, then. I'm a good dentist too—with or without novocaine."

"I want you to destroy the group that's supporting him. The James Lowell Society."

"Do you have the goods on that clutch of psychos?"

"All we need, I'm sure. You can start taking notes as soon as I've locked my cabin door."

After the columnist had departed, Bruce stood at the port to watch him leave the pier—and poured himself the first drink of the day. He was swallowing his second when Badger entered.

"The pharmacy lists are ready. Shall we pitch in?"

"You'll have to do a solo job, Eric. I'm planning to get quietly drunk."

"Wait until six bells, and I'll join you."

"Sorry. I'm tying this one on alone."

"Without telling me why?"

"You'll know why soon enough." Bruce poured his third bourbon, discovered he did not want it after all, and put the glass down. "How would *you* feel, if you'd just thrown mud on an American idol?"

"That would depend on the idol. Some are natural targets."

"Suppose you'd called in Lew Carleton to help you. Could you stay sober, with him on the team?"

"I wondered what he was doing aboard."

"I sent for him, because I needed a scavenger to handle details. Between us, we've just torn the James Lowell Society apart."

"No wonder you're getting drunk. Want to go back to the beginning?"

"It started in Manila, months before the war. When a nice kid in a rifle company made the one bad mistake of his Army career."

"A kid named Lowell?"

"You follow me perfectly. To do this job right, I had to smear the Society's idol. I had to lay Jimmie's finest moment on the line, and show it's a colossal fraud."

"Wasn't he a hero after all?"

"It was a case of mistaken identity. Jimmie won't mind, of course. He's been dead for quite a while. It's going to be another story with his mother."

"The papers say she was guest of honor at last night's powwow."

"She's a fine woman. I hope she'll get over the shock when she reads the truth in Carleton's column. Now do you understand why I had to call him in?"

"I won't until you tell me."

"Hal Reardon's the answer. Last midnight, I decided to cut him down to size—with the help of a gossip columnist who'll print anything. Unfortunately, I had to destroy Sergeant Lowell's image in the process. There was no other way."

"Then this is a move to stymie Reardon—at the UN Conference."

Bruce raised his glass. "Your brain is functioning at last,

Eric. Today, Hal claims to have ten million Lowellites behind him. This time tomorrow, the Lowellites will cave in—because their idol no longer exists. With his voters gone and his sponsors backing out, Senator Reardon will be just another isolationist in a get-together world."

"I still don't see how the smear will be applied."

"Look at your Society *Bulletin*—with the hero on the cover. The first man to be wounded on Pearl Harbor Sunday. The first casualty of World War II."

"It's part of their folklore."

"Their folklore stinks—like the mess they've made of Jimmie's credo. Sergeant Lowell did *not* die of wounds. He died from an amoebic abscess of the liver—caused by off-limits chow in the Philippines, long before a shot was fired."

The man from Wisconsin whistled softly. "That's a black mark on any hero's record. Where did the rumor start?"

"It isn't a rumor. It's a fact. Jimmie was my patient at Scranton General. The diagnosis is part of his hospital record, and it was confirmed by surgery. I signed the death certificate."

"Did you give Carleton a copy?"

"His investigator in Washington tracked it down. A photostat of that certificate will be part of his column tomorrow. Lowell Society members will see it on the front page of all the big-city dailies, including the San Francisco *Chronicle*. The headline will read HERO BY ACCIDENT."

"Are you sure you can stop Reardon with a headline?"

"I'll stop him cold at the UN Conference. That's all I care about."

"Reardon's never admitted a formal connection with the Lowellites. He'll duck out from under."

"Let him. Without his propaganda machine, he can't stand in the spotlight alone, making noises like an America Firster. I'd call that a good day's work, in any language."

"So would I, Bruce. Congratulations."

"Do you think I'm *happy* about it?"

"In your place, I wouldn't be too downcast," said Badger. "If I'd known sooner, I'd have pitched in and helped."

"This is a one-man job. I'll take the blame tomorrow."

"Why should you be blamed?"

"Idol-smashers are never thanked for their pains. Now you know the worst, will you let me drink in peace?"

After his deputy had left the cabin, Bruce discovered he had lost the need for another bourbon. The attempt to push reality aside had been a failure now that he had confessed his infamy. At midafternoon, when he could endure self-enforced solitude no longer, he wrapped himself in an Army raincoat and left the ship to walk the city's streets.

He had no clear memory of his wanderings. For a while he circled Nob Hill and stared up at the windows of Shane's hotel, wondering which room was hers. He would have given a great deal to ask her forgiveness in advance—but prudence dictated that he keep his distance. . . . In the end, he contented himself with a glimpse of the cobbled courtyard, where diplomatic limousines from all corners of the world awaited their owners. As dusk was falling, he drew back out of sight when he saw Janet Reardon emerge from the lobby, between a turbaned Hindu and a sari-clad beauty.

Still later, aware that he was faint with hunger yet unwilling to seek food, he climbed Telegraph Hill, to stand at the parapet and look down at the steep-pitched streets below. Even now, he could feel nothing—beyond a blank self-loathing at the trick he was using to topple Hal from his pedestal.

Later still, he descended to the foot of Market Street and entered the ferryhouse for the first of several crossings to Oakland. Standing on the top deck among circling gulls, letting the salt wind clear his brain, he had found composure of a sort before he returned to the *Helen S Peters*. Hunger was now a tangible thing, but he ignored it. A double bourbon would guarantee hours of unbroken sleep: he knew it would be far more potent on an empty stomach. . . . Tomorrow, after he had seen the front page of the *Chronicle,* he would recognize the demands of the body.

His last shock of the evening came when he paused at his cabin mirror, to laugh aloud at the haggard stranger he faced there. It was good to know that oblivion was already creeping in from the corners, thanks to the six ounces of whiskey he had downed: he could not have endured the intruder's company an instant longer.

Next morning, he was finishing a second coffee—and fighting the need to go topside—when the cabin door swung open. Expecting an orderly to collect his breakfast tray, he faced Phil Owen. The folded newspaper the medical chief carried was advertisement of his errand.

"Eric's gone for the day, Bruce. He asked me to show you this."

"Have you read it?"

"Every word. I've got to check a case of hives in the crew's sick bay, or I'd enjoy it with you."

Carleton's column, as Bruce had expected, was a front-page feature. Written in the rainbow prose the former press agent favored, it displayed his talents at their finest. Two illustrations were crowning touches. One was a photostat from Sergeant James Lowell's hospital record, signed by Bruce himself and complete with diagnosis: the question *Line of Duty?* was answered with a heavily circled NO. Below the column itself was a reproduction of the photograph featured in the *Bulletin,* and the now-damning caption: *America's First Sacrifice at Pearl Harbor?*

The question mark had been Carleton's inspired afterthought: the column itself was a blow-by-blow exposé of the Sergeant Lowell myth, counterpointed by Carleton's waspish analysis of the aims of the Lowell Society itself—which, he suggested, were as infection-ridden as its ex-hero's liver. Capsule interviews had been solicited from the Society's more conservative sponsors—who had learned, for the first time, that the sergeant's death had resulted not from wounds at a crossroads of history, but from amoebic dysentery. The columnist had also explained just how Jimmie had contracted the disease, stressing the fact that the offense—save for the clemency of his superiors—could have resulted in his court-martial.

Two of the Lowell Society's sponsors, both food magnates from the Midwest, had already sent in their resignations. Others stated that they would petition the Society's board of governors, suggesting that the organization disband, rather than march under so tarnished a standard. . . . Carleton had done his work well. Bruce looked up from his perusal as Phil Owen returned to the cabin.

"It's always a pleasure to watch a killer in action," said Owen. "Providing, of course, the quarry's worth bagging. Today, Lethal Lew has surpassed himself."

"What's the reaction on the ship?"

"You've been voted a valuable public servant, ten to one. You won't find many Lowell *Bulletins* aboard today."

"Do you think the Society will disband?"

"My guess is the members will simply go back to the woodwork. The moneybags are already closed, now that Reardon's lost his claque."

"In that case, I've accomplished my purpose."

"Reardon himself hasn't been hurt too badly. After all, he was bright enough to keep clear of the Lowellites. Wouldn't it be fun to make *him* bleed a little too?"

"I'm not in this deal for fun, Phil."

"Eric thought otherwise."

"I've already told Eric to stay out of my affairs."

"He couldn't stay out of this one, Bruce. Nor could I. The reason's on your desk. We put it there, while you were asleep. Shall we have a playback?"

"A playback of what?"

"Of a special recording we made at Salerno. One we decided to keep for posterity."

Bruce did not stir while the medical officer tuned the volume of the recorder to its lowest level, then touched the starting button. The effect was shattering—a backflash to this same ship, when Hal's tale of self-mutilation behind enemy lines had poured from an identical microphone. . . . Owen made no attempt to play the entire spool. Noting Bruce's flint-faced anger, he cut the voice in mid-passage.

"I agree with your reaction," he said. "It was a shocker at Salerno. It's a shocker today."

"I gave Eric specific orders to destroy that spool."

"He disobeyed you, Bruce—for excellent motives. At Salerno, you were reluctant to smear a brilliant staff officer, and endanger our careers in the process. Now that the colonel's a civilian, this evidence could be useful in another quarter."

"What did you have in mind—a playback for *Senator* Reardon? Or his wife?"

"I'm sure the senator has long since erased that black night from his mind. I can hardly advise you to spoil the best-run marriage in Washington. Another one-woman audience would profit greatly from a playback."

"If you mean Shane McLendon—"

"Judging by her recent columns, she could do with a stiff dose of truth. How else can she learn that her idol has a self-inflicted limp?"

"Is it fair to brand a man for life, because he yielded to a moment of panic?"

"In this case, it's only common justice," said Owen. "Reardon parlayed his limp into a Silver Star. It won him a full term in the Senate—and a build-up in your girl friend's column that's losing her readers every day. If you want to save her career, *make* her listen."

Bruce looked up quickly. "What's this about Shane losing readers?"

"She's been so busy singing Reardon's praises lately, she's

almost forgotten how to be a reporter. Right here on this ship, her public's been cut in half."

"Carleton's stopped Hal at the UN Conference. That's all I mean to do."

"If you still love Shane McLendon, it's your duty to rescue her from the biggest phony since the Cardiff Giant." The medical officer picked up the recorder and set it on the foot of Bruce's bunk. "She thinks Reardon's a world statesman. This spool proves he's a liar *and* a coward. Take my advice, Bruce. Use that proof where it will really help."

"I doubt if Shane will see me, now she's read Carleton's column."

"She'll see you, all right—if only to give you a piece of her mind. Go to the Mark Hopkins now. And take the evidence with you. If you don't, you'll be sorry all your life."

"Maybe I've given up on Shane. Had you thought of that?"

Phil Owen shrugged, and turned to the cabin door. "Go to hell in your own wheelbarrow if you insist. But if *I* knew a girl like Shane McLendon, I'd go all out to save her from herself. After all, she isn't the first woman in history to back the wrong horse—or a portion thereof."

When the medical officer had departed, Bruce stared for a long time at the cowhide-covered box while he pondered his friend's advice. The memory of Shane's thin, intense face, of the tears he had seen on her cheeks, was still vivid. So was the rage he had felt when he had turned to leave the Mark Hopkins—when he had faced Jimmie Lowell's portrait in the foyer, and found, in the eleventh hour of his desperation, a way to inflict the first defeat Hal had ever known.

Phil had said the evidence on his bunk could save Shane McLendon from herself: he knew that Phil had logic on his side. Ten minutes later, dressed for the fog-wet day, he wrapped the recorder in his Army raincoat and left the ship.

It was still concealed when he stepped from the elevator at the Mark Hopkins and knocked on Shane's door.

The sound of typing inside suggested his presence had gone unheeded. About to repeat the knock, he tried the knob, found the door was open, and stepped quickly inside. Expecting a hotel bedroom, he saw that Shane's suite was not much smaller than the Reardons' quarters; moving through the vestibule, he entered the living room, to find her at a table beside the window. . . . The slacks and open-neck shirt she wore were familiar touches, like the haze of cigarette smoke surrounding her. They steadied him a little while he put the recorder, still covered by his coat, on a chair by the door.

Shane had just ripped a sheet from her machine. She had taken no note of his arrival—but he had expected that. When he saw her hands were trembling, and realized she was using the tools of her trade to disguise her agitation, a great rush of tenderness engulfed him.

"Well, Bruce?" Her voice was far steadier than her hands. "Did you *have* to use a toad to do your dirty work?"

"There was no choice," he said slowly. "My time was short—so I borrowed Hal's own weapon. Publicity, where it really counted."

"Why Lew Carleton, of all people?"

"You would never have used my story. He was second choice."

"Why give it to anyone?"

"Because I had to put a small-time politician in his place."

"Do you hate Hal enough to destroy him?"

"Not destroy—*stop*. No one's been destroyed but Jimmy Lowell. Hal and Derwent had already started that demolition job. This morning, with Carleton's help, I presided at the burial."

"You must see what that column has done to Hal's career."

"Hal's career be damned. Hal's indestructible, as we both know. He's lost nothing, except a voting bloc. And a chance to flex his muscles—at a peace conference where he's waded beyond his depth."

"Even if all you say is true, what right had you to interfere?"

"Being in love with you, I had every right. I couldn't stand by and watch you go to pieces."

"What do you mean?"

"I'll grant you my methods were beyond contempt, Shane. When I gave the facts to Carleton, I was behaving like a boor and a scoundrel. Generations of Grahams are probably whirling in their graves at the way I've betrayed the family name. I can survive their censure—and my own—if my real purpose is accomplished."

"And what, may I ask, is that?"

"To help you to see Hal Reardon plain. To persuade you to give up supporting him, once and for all."

"Did you think a column by a third-rate press agent could make me desert Hal?"

"Will you at least admit he's finished at the UN Conference?"

"Of course he is, thanks to you," said Shane. "So is the Lowell Society, since you're adding up your victories. Are you proud of that hatchet job?"

"I just told you I'm anything but proud."

"Have you thought how much this exposé will hurt Jimmie's mother?"

"I've thought of it constantly. Perhaps she'll realize Jimmie would have done the same—if he'd lived to see his dream perverted."

Shane sat at her worktable and ran a fresh sheet in the typewriter. "Very well, Bruce. I appreciate your motives—but they fail to impress me. Take your excuses elsewhere. I've work to do."

"I'm not here to make excuses for myself—or to feel sorry for Jimmie's mother. I'm here because of you. What are you going to do now?"

"Finish my column, of course."

"Still supporting Hal?"

"He needs support today, more than ever. Would you like to read what I've said, before I take my copy upstairs?"

"In the old days, you never showed your copy to outsiders. Since when has Hal told you what to write?" He had been purposely blunt, hoping to shock her: her sudden flush told him how well he had succeeded. "No wonder you've been losing readers lately."

"Will you please get out?"

"You tell me you're about to clear your copy with Hal. Haven't you been in touch since Carleton's column appeared?"

"Hal's been too busy to see me."

"Don't tell me you've been sitting here alone—and writing in a vacuum."

"I talked with him this morning, on the phone."

"Aren't you worth more to Senator Reardon than a phone call?"

"Mike Derwent flew in early. They've been in conference ever since."

"If Derwent's in town, Hal must be really desperate. Isn't the President arriving today, to address the UN Conference?"

"He's speaking at eight tonight. What of it?"

"How much will you bet Hal hasn't decided to switch? Or that he'll announce that switch, to the head of his party?"

When Shane turned aside, Bruce knew that he had reached her at last. He pressed on without pity: it was too late for compassion.

"Phone his suite. Ask if he has an appointment with the President *before* he speaks tonight. I'll give odds he's ready to jump on the bandwagon, now he's lost in San Francisco."

"You've said your piece, Bruce. You've rubbed my nose in the dirt. Why don't you go back to your ship and stop tormenting me?"

"Because I'm waiting for you to admit I'm right."

"Haven't we both said enough?"

"More than enough. But I won't leave this room until I know you're free."

While he spoke, Bruce had turned to pick up the recorder. Shane's eyes widened when he put it on her table and zipped open the case.

"Is that mine?"

"Actually, it's a twin of the machine you left aboard at Gela. Eric Badger would call it my clincher. The proof Hal Reardon can turn anything to his advantage."

"How can *this* concern Hal?"

"It's a recording my staff made on shipboard during an operation. While their patient was under an anesthesia called sodium pentothal. I don't have to tell you the patient's name."

"Did this happen after Hal was wounded?"

"After he 'jumped to nowhere,' to quote your most famous column. Don't say another word. Just listen."

He had already touched the playback button: Hal's high-pitched wail filled the room before he could step back. In another moment, Hal's taut voice, so unlike his usual orator's tone, was pouring out the story of his drop at Salerno.

Standing with his back to the machine, Bruce kept his eyes lowered. There was no way to escape Shane's tension while the two-way microphone echoed the self-wounded man's last curse, seconds before the pentothal took over. . . .

Bruce did not budge when the wire spun to its close. It was Shane who moved to cut the switch.

"Believe one thing more, and I'm done," he said. "At Salerno, I ordered that spool destroyed. Captain Badger kept it, without my knowledge. I brought it here today as a last resort."

"It's the most horrible thing I've ever heard." Shane had steadied herself against the desk: he saw that she was shivering—as though she, too, had just emerged from a night-

mare she could not shake off. Moving by instinct to put an
arm around her, he stopped himself in time.

"No one else need hear this," he said. "I'll dispose of the
spool at once. Shall I leave the recorder?"

"I don't want to see that evil thing again."

"Try not to judge him too harshly, Shane. All of us have
been afraid—and yielded to our fears. Anyone can crack, if the
stress is great enough. What you *can't* forgive, I hope, is the
way he's cashed in on that act of cowardice. The way he's
made himself an ersatz hero—and sold you a bill of goods in
the bargain."

He had added the final cruelty, on the chance she would
break at last. When she buried her face in her arms, and burst
into a flood of tears, he knew his visit had served its purpose,
though it had used the last weapon in his arsenal.

"It isn't easy, watching an idol fall apart," he said. "It can
be even harder for the man who does the breaking."

When she gave no sign that she had heard, he picked up
the recorder and left the room.

At the pier, Bruce dropped recorder and spool into San
Francisco Bay, and watched them swirl in the tide before
they sank from view. The whine of the winches told him that
the last supplies were going aboard his ship. The sound was a
welcome one. After the hurt he had inflicted on Shane
McLendon, he was glad to be putting an ocean between them.

Exchanging salutes with the officer on watch as he came
up the gangway, he noted a package on the sign-in desk. His
name was scrawled across the wrapping, in a spidery hand.

"When was this delivered?"

"A half hour ago, sir. The lady brought it herself. Said her
name was Lowell."

Bruce felt a sudden constriction of his heart. He had hoped
that Jimmie's mother was on her way to Concord.

"Did she ask for me?"

"No, Colonel. She said this would explain itself."

In the companionway, he paused to break the string on the package. For a stunned moment, he stared down at the medal in the velvet box, and the folded note below it. When he reached his cabin, he sat for a while on his bunk before he read the message that Sergeant James Lowell's mother had delivered in person.

Colonel Graham:

This is Jimmie's Congressional Medal of Honor. I am sure he wouldn't want me to keep something of his he had not earned.

Perhaps you would like to put it among your own trophies from this war.

CONSTANCE LOWELL
(Mrs. James Lowell, Sr.)

Washington

The speaker's voice had reached Bruce clearly before he could climb the last steps: it seemed resonant as ever, and just as sincere. Unbuttoning his Army greatcoat, he took the last empty seat at the rear of the Senate gallery. . . . It was three full months since the conclusion of the Pacific war: he had entered the Capitol on impulse, after he had finished the business that had brought him to Washington this chill November day. Listening to Senator Harold Reardon begin his peroration, he could not regret the detour.

Every Solon was at his desk in the Romanesque chamber below. On his way to the Hill, Bruce had picked up an early edition of the *Star*, announcing that Hal would speak at the afternoon session, in support of a bill that would pay his country's entrance fee at the first plenary meeting of the United Nations. That autumn, Senator Reardon's name had appeared often on the front page, as a tireless worker on the Administration team. In the new year, he would be one of the members of the Upper House assigned to observe the UN in action.

Bruce needed a moment more to separate the theme of Hal's discourse from the organ notes of his delivery. The Senator was describing the ceremonies that had marked the UN's formal launching—an event staged six months ago, at the San Francisco Opera House. Hal—converted overnight, as dramatically as any sinner brought into the fold by Billy Sunday—had remained with other American delegates to watch representatives of the fifty-one participating nations march onstage and write their names on the gold-embossed copies of the charter.

Most of the signers, Hal told his audience, had uttered appropriate sentiments. Each man, he felt sure, had spoken from the heart—but brevity had not been the soul of wit that day in San Francisco. Hal's own heart had sunk, at times, in a sea of ennui. Was this fustian eloquence a preview of the UN's own future? Would this new league—like others that had gone their dusty way to oblivion—stifle in truisms, in platitudes celebrating the might-have-been?

His spirits had revived with the appearance of General Romulo, the soldier-journalist from the Philippines. Asked to observe a two-minute deadline when he signed for his country, Romulo had promised to convey his message in seconds: he had made a seven-word speech as he slashed his name across the page:

The Man from Galilee was here today.

Hal paused, to let the import of his anecdote reach his listeners.

The Man from Galilee, he resumed, *had* been present at the San Francisco Opera House that June day: He was present always, at each watershed on man's climb from the primeval ooze. . . . Christ was still the great revolutionary of history in his plea for human brotherhood. Surely, He would have blessed this latest attempt by Homo sapiens to join hands and seek a better tomorrow.

World peace, said Hal, had been a misty ideal. Today, with the horrors of Hiroshima and Nagasaki fresh in memory, world peace was, quite simply, the *sine qua non* for human survival. Grave though its faults might be, perplexed though it was by unfulfilled pledges, the United Nations Charter had vastly expanded the working space of other covenants. Until its dedication proved in vain, until the hopes that had inspired it were dead beyond recall, the charter deserved all that its members could bring to it in money, dedication and patience.

The House, Hal added, had brought in the President's first bill for America's share of UN expenses, with few subtractions. He, for one, meant to support the bill as it stood. And he would pray that those funds—large though they might seem to bookkeeper minds—would prove the best investment Washington could make in the future. . . .

There was more, but Bruce had ceased to listen. He rose from his seat after Hal returned to his desk on the floor below and the gallery burst into a roar of applause. At the rail, in the section reserved for relatives of the members, he saw that Senator Reardon's wife was applauding as vigorously as the others.

Bruce had come to Washington after a reunion with Dr. Abram Schoenfeld at Lakewood. He had agreed to return to the campus for the new term—as an instructor, as well as a researcher in surgery of the heart. During that visit, he had been glad to learn he would not quite be taking up where he had left off, three and a half years before. Dr. Schoenfeld had made considerable progress with his experiments in the war years: his assistant's place in the academic world would be comfortable as well as challenging.

The train trip from Baltimore to Washington had followed a flight from San Pedro—where, only yesterday, he had shaken hands for the last time with each member of the 241st Hospital Ship Complement after its disbanding. He had crossed the continent at the request of General—formerly Colonel—Lawrence Wilson of the SGO, who had stated, in Bruce's last order of movement, that his official separation from the Army would take place at Camp Bruckner. . . . Two hours ago, at a brief ceremony in the general's office, he had received the belated award of the Silver Star. The medal was still pinned to his blouse, above his double row of service ribbons.

The eulogies that had accompanied that award, like the good-byes he had exchanged with shipmates in California, were echoes from another world when he descended the steps of the Capitol and took a cab to Union Station. In a few more weeks, he knew they would be part of a larger mirage. Most of those vignettes of war would soon be as meaningless, and as ironic, as the scene he had just witnessed in the Senate chamber. That memory, too, was fading fast amid the relentless pressures of the present.

At the moment, he was neither glad nor sorry that his Army career was ending—with a bus trip to the camp that had once been his billet, and was now a separation center. It was good to know that his services were urgently needed in Schoenfeld's laboratory, that a rewarding, and perhaps brilliant, future awaited him there. He could take no real satisfaction in this native's return, since he would be making it alone.

If he could judge by what he had just seen on Capitol Hill, Hal and Janet Reardon had fulfilled the predictions he had made six months ago. Hal had emerged from the debacle of the James Lowell Society smelling like a rose—and, since he had never allowed his name to appear on its letterhead, he had shrugged off that debacle without turning a hair. Since his surrender in San Francisco, he had moved into the majority camp without breaking stride. Janet, true to her father's teachings, would do her part to see that the history of the Reardon clan repeated itself, as her husband continued to serve the Administration with eloquence, wit and vigor.

Shane McLendon had gone on from that day of revelations at the Mark Hopkins—to cover the final months of the war with her talents unimpaired. She had been among the first to report on the atom bomb; she had been aboard the *Missouri* in Tokyo Bay when the Japanese had surrendered. Judging by recent datelines of her columns, she was now reporting from Washington.

Deep in his heart, Bruce had dared to hope she might join the other journalists this afternoon—when General Wilson had pinned the Silver Star on his blouse. Common sense had reminded him that the war had made Shane's one of the best-known by-lines in America. . . . He could hardly expect her to waste an afternoon on the decoration of an obscure MC colonel—even if she had forgiven him for the wounds he had inflicted.

The taxi swung into the oval before the depot. Caught in a traffic block, Bruce looked across the plaza at the bus platform where his wartime odyssey had begun; in the same glance, his eye picked out the bar where he had met the first of three people destined to reshape his life. In a sense, he told himself, the reshaping had not been too profound. Compared to the meteoric rise of Senator Reardon, the niche Janet had carved in Washington society, and the honors Shane McLendon had won with her typewriter, his own record was on the modest side.

His two promotions, from major to full colonel, would be of no value to the heart research he would begin next month at Lakewood—though he would take the same rank in the Reserve, if only from a sense of duty. His surgical skills would need burnishing after those last long cruises in the Pacific, where his ship had been little more than a floating ambulance. Though his return to civilian life would be easier than most, he was forced to admit that three and a half years' service in the medical corps, judged in practical terms, had failed to advance his professional competence an iota.

And yet, despite the casual cruelties he had witnessed, despite the stupidity in high and low places and blunders that passed belief, he could not regret his experience. The Army, for all its monolithic structure, for all its calcified thinking and its mumbling over outworn creeds, had done the job assigned it. And he had been part of its achievement.

The conclusion, though it was far from original, seemed worth sharing. He felt his heart beat faster as he stepped into a phone booth to call Shane's number on S Street—only to hang up when there was no answer.

Time was a dream again when he crossed the station plaza and entered the bar. It was natural to find the same bartender on duty, to order the same brand of bourbon, to see in the mirror the same older, but scarcely wiser, officer who had sat on this same barstool and wondered how his great adventure would begin.

A little later, after a long swallow of Jack Daniel's had dulled the edge of his despair, it was even more natural to look into that bar mirror a second time and discover a girl on the next stool—a girl who was still a trifle too thin, whose face was still too finely honed for actual beauty. The eyes that met his in the glass were wary.

"You took long enough to get here," said Shane McLendon.

"Some people insisted on giving me a medal."

"So I heard—from General Wilson. I nearly turned up at the ceremony. At the last minute, I decided to observe you from a distance."

"Don't tell me I was followed here."

"The answer's yes and no. When you entered the Surgeon General's Office, I was parked across the street in my Singer."

"The same car you used to drive me to Janet's show in Annapolis?"

"The thirty-five roadster. Believe it or not, it still runs." Shane nodded a greeting to the barman, who had just put a gin rickey before her unasked. "I saw you were headed for the Hill—and realized you planned to catch Hal's show. After all, you put him where he is today. You had every right to look upon your handiwork."

"Speaking offhand, I'd say Hal Reardon was our joint effort."

"Actually, I suppose neither of us can claim too much credit."

"Some people were born to fall with their noses in the butter. Or should I say the United States Senate?"

"To hell with the United States Senate," said Shane. "What about us?"

"I've devoted some thought to that subject. So far, I've reached no solution."

"I asked the same question six months ago," said Shane. "In the same words. Why didn't you answer?"

"Your question never reached me."

"I sent it to your APO, the day after you left San Francisco."

"A kamikaze sank a mail ship that month, just off Okinawa. Your letter must have been aboard."

"It's an unlikely story, Colonel Graham."

"Such things happen, in every war."

"In any case, I decided not to write again," said Shane. "It seemed much more appropriate to save my question for the Station Bar."

"How did you know I'd end up here?"

"It was a reasonable hope," said Shane. "Just to be certain, I asked a friend in Larry Wilson's office to tell me when you'd be separated—and where."

Their eyes met and held in the mirror. He saw that she was smiling—the off-center, gamine grin that made her almost pretty.

"This time tomorrow, I'll walk out of Camp Bruckner a free man. Can you meet me at the gate?"

"In the Singer?"

"In the Singer—with your bags in back."

"Is this by any chance a proposal?"

"It isn't a proposition. I've got a month's terminal leave before I go back to Lakewood. We might spend it at the Gulfview Inn."

"We might," said Shane. "I'm sure it's been given back to civilians by now."

"If the weather's right, we might even make up for lost opportunities on Bonita Island."

"You'll find the Singer a little the worse for wear. So is the girl."

"So, for that matter, is the man. If we lean on each other, I think we can reach a marrying judge in Maryland."

"I'm sure we can," said Shane. Careless of glances in the crowded bar, she leaned forward to kiss him. "Welcome home, soldier."

This is the story of a war behind World War II, a very private war between two public people. The conflict, as old as time, opposes the man of principle to the man who has none.

War holds surprises for all men. Bruce Graham's greatest surprise, when he volunteered for active duty with the Army, was to find himself in a battle against corruption more killing, in its way, than the bullets he would later encounter at the front lines. Entanglement with a handsome, unscrupulous politician, with a Congressional Committee, where his loyalty is impugned, and with two beautiful women, were only some of his troubles. Entanglement with his conscience was constant, until, in a great victorious surge, his conscience goaded him into inevitable, unavoidable action.

In Surgeon, U.S.A., Frank Slaughter has written a compelling novel of a doctor who, under pressure from politics as well as protocol, stands true to the oath of his profession.